Back to your bottle . . .

"I can't leave, you know. I belong to you. But if you insist, I can go back into my bottle," he said, pointing to the bulbous amber glass that sat on the kitchen counter. "I'd rather not be all cramped up again, but it's your call. Just say the word."

"What word?" I said, not getting it. The bottle was about nine inches high. Gene had to be six feet tall. I didn't believe in genies. I didn't believe in magic; magic was just sleight of hand and trickery. I looked at Gene. I looked back at the bottle. There was no way that big, solid, seemingly flesh-and-blood man was going to fit in there.

"Okay, go back in your bottle," I said as fast as I could get the words out. As soon as I said them, invisible bells tinkled, there was a sound sort of like "poof," and a stream of white smoke whooshed from where Gene had stood and dove into the mouth of the open bottle. I rushed over and jammed the cork into its top. In its bottom, a miniature man sat cross-legged. He blew me a kiss.

Careful What You Wish For

~

Lucy Finn

A SIGNET ECLIPSE BOOK

SIGNET ECLIPSE
Published by New American Library, a division of
Penguin Group (USA) Inc., 375 Hudson Street,
New York, New York 10014, USA
Penguin Group (Canada), 90 Eglinton Avenue East, Suite 700, Toronto,
Ontario M4P 2Y3, Canada (a division of Pearson Penguin Canada Inc.)
Penguin Books Ltd., 80 Strand, London WC2R 0RL, England
Penguin Ireland, 25 St. Stephen's Green, Dublin 2,
Ireland (a division of Penguin Books Ltd.)
Penguin Group (Australia), 250 Camberwell Road, Camberwell, Victoria 3124,
Australia (a division of Pearson Australia Group Pty. Ltd.)
Penguin Books India Pvt. Ltd., 11 Community Centre, Panchsheel Park,
New Delhi - 110 017, India
Penguin Group (NZ), 67 Apollo Drive, Rosedale, North Shore,
Auckland 1311, New Zealand (a division of Pearson New Zealand Ltd.)
Penguin Books (South Africa) (Pty.) Ltd., 24 Sturdee Avenue,
Rosebank, Johannesburg 2196, South Africa

Penguin Books Ltd., Registered Offices:
80 Strand, London WC2R 0RL, England

First published by Signet Eclipse, an imprint of New American Library,
a division of Penguin Group (USA) Inc.

First Printing, June 2007
10 9 8 7 6 5 4 3 2 1

PUBLISHER'S NOTE
This is a work of fiction. Names, characters, places, and incidents either are
the product of the author's imagination or are used fictitiously, and any resem-
blance to actual persons, living or dead, business establishments, events, or
locales is entirely coincidental.

The publisher does not have any control over and does not assume any
responsibility for author or third-party Web sites or their content.

In memory of my mother

Chapter 1

I first heard Noxen called "Hicksville" by a red-haired second-grader who carried a designer handbag to school. She also called tomatoes "tahmahtoes," so that tells you something. By high school I agreed with her. I vowed that as soon as I could, I'd get out of rural Pennsylvania and live where there was a Starbucks on the next corner instead of an hour away at the nearest mall.

By the time I was twenty-one, I had done what I promised myself. So how did I end up back in Noxen at twenty-seven, a single mother with her career on the rocks? A crazy one-time-only fling had started the chain of events that yanked me back to my birthplace, maybe for good. I don't know whether the chance meeting with a guy called Jake really had been love at first sight or lust, but if ever a woman had stooped to folly, it was me, Ravine Patton, unemployed attorney-at-law.

I was thinking about my "folly" for about the millionth time as I stood looking out a frosty windowpane at the sleet covering everything, including my Five Series BMW, the last vestige of my former existence as a Philadelphia lawyer. It was a beautiful vehicle in metallic Oxford green with a beige leather interior. The car was wonderful, but if I was honest with myself, I would admit my former career hadn't been so great.

By the end of my first year of practice, I was bored with business law and secretly making fun of the soft-bellied, dark-suited partners in my law firm, which specialized in real estate investment trusts—REITs. Despite that vague feeling of discontent, a bad case of acid reflux, and a sour expression that put vertical lines around my mouth, I was making heaps of money and seemed to be doing well as far as the world, and my mother, were concerned.

However, anybody who took a close look at my life would have seen I was stressed out of my mind, eating junk food at my desk, and buying frivolous designer clothes that hung in my closet with the sales tags still attached. I used my credit cards too much and saved too little. When I finally stumbled into my studio apartment off Rittenhouse Square after a sixteen-hour day to be greeted solely by Baby Kitty, my yellow tabby, I was depressed as hell. By any accounting, my success back then was a sham. But my present situation could get a four-star rating as a genuine failure from any independent appraiser.

This morning my hair needed a good wash. I had an ache that started in my shoulders and traveled in pinched nerves all the way down my back. I hadn't gotten any restful sleep for weeks, the baby had to be at the pediatrician's in an hour, and as I noted, the landscape was glistening with a layer of ice. The temperature had dipped to fourteen degrees during the night even though it was only the week before Thanksgiving, not even officially winter.

I sighed and put down my coffee mug, donned an old down jacket over my Wal-Mart jeans, tugged on snow boots, jammed an orange wool cap on my head, and grabbed my car keys. Then I checked to see that Brady was cooing safely in his infant carrier, which sat on the floor, hopefully out of any drafts.

No drafts, that was rich. This old house boasted a constant stream of fresh air that whistled in through the ancient windows which rattled constantly in their panes. Yep, I needed replacement windows. I would put them on my to-do list right after a new roof, new floors, and new plumbing. I did get new wiring put in. I figured without it, Brady and I might soon be toast, but the cost pretty much used up all my disposable income. I looked and felt like Grumpy in *Snow White and the Seven Dwarfs.*

I pulled open the creaky front door and was hit by a blast of frigid air which came roaring down the mountain to greet me. I started slipping and sliding across the huge flat stone which makes up my front walk. Ice to the north of me, slippery ice to the south of me, and no end in sight. I struggled to keep my balance. Adrenaline raced through my bloodstream. My heart thudded in my chest. Why hadn't I grabbed my cell phone, just in case I fell and couldn't get up?

Of course if I were knocked unconscious, the cell phone wouldn't help anyway, I reasoned. I soldiered on.

Considering that the whole wide world of nature had been covered in sleet, I shouldn't have been surprised that when I finally reached my car, I discovered that my car doors were frozen shut.

Oh great, I thought, *now what*? I didn't have an extension cord long enough to get my hair dryer out here. I needed another bright idea. I gingerly made my way back inside the house, wrinkled my nose at Brady, crossed my eyes to make him laugh, and filled up a saucepan with warm water. Then I half skated, half walked back to my car, trying not to spill all the water, and poured it around the doorframe.

Snap, crackle, pop, and open sesame, the door responded when I pulled on it. I was brilliant. I started the engine, figuring I'd let the car warm up while I got Brady ready to go out.

Best-laid plans "gang aft a-gley," as Robert Burns put it. In other words, they end up in the crapper. I threw some Quik Joe on the walk, wrestled Brady into his bright red snowsuit, then remembered to grab my baby bag and wallet before heading back into the refrigerator that is a typical November day in Pennsylvania's Endless Mountains. The car was purring along merrily as I attempted to enter the driver's side door.

I didn't succeed. The door had frozen shut again, this time with the keys in the ignition and the car running. Brady blissfully stuck his thumb in his mouth. I bit off the obscenity about to issue from my chapped lips. I didn't want my kid's first words to be *Oh shit!* instead of *Mama*.

Back in the house, I ran into the kitchen with Brady in my arms for another pan of water and headed out for the third time. I poured the water around the doorframe, got the door open, ducked into the back, strapped my son into his car seat, threw the diaper bag onto the passenger seat, and figured I was good to go. A smile spread across my face. I, a woman down-and-out and totally alone, had triumphed over the wild.

I kept smiling until I was halfway down the country road that leads from my house to the highway. It was at that point that the car door flew open.

Criminy dickens! I almost had a heart attack as the door swung crazily back and forth and I could see the black asphalt rushing by beneath me. I gripped the steering wheel and hit the brakes; I was totally shook up even though I was held safely in place by my seat belt. When I had slowed the Beemer down to a crawl, I reached out, grabbed the door handle, and slammed the door shut—only it didn't shut. It simply bounced open again. I stopped the car completely and kept trying—*bam, bam, bam!* Finally it dawned on me that the latch had frozen in the open position.

Time was running out; I had maybe twenty minutes

to get Brady to the doctor's, and I had to get the damned door to stay shut. Although a little voice was whispering in my mind that I was making a terrible mistake, I held the door closed and hit the door lock. I heard it click. The door stayed in place. Smiling to myself, I pressed the accelerator toward the floor and headed for the highway, flipping the radio tuner to Rocky and Sue on "WKRZ-FM in the Morning." Feeling good again, I sang loudly along with Pearl Jam and Nirvana. Brady babbled almost in tune too, all the way to the pediatrician. Okay, I should have been playing Mozart. Brady was developing a taste for grunge rock, and I was going to regret that someday. But I needed a good beat to keep me going this morning.

I pulled into the parking lot outside of the doctor's office in Dallas. That's Dallas, Pennsylvania, population about two thousand souls, not Dallas, Texas. Then I tried to get out of the car. The driver's side wouldn't budge. I slammed my shoulder against it a few times, while I yelled out stuff like, "Don't worry, Brady, Mommy will get us out of here in a minute." My son, sitting in the backseat wide-eyed and fascinated by my flailing, seemed more amused than concerned. I, on the other hand, was rapidly beginning to panic.

I climbed over the console into the passenger seat, smashing my knee on the shift lever and knocking the baby bag onto the floor, where all its contents spilled out. I lifted the door handle and launched myself like a Scud missile against the side of the car. The door was like a rock, immovable, uncaring, impassive. After a few more tries, which had my shoulder aching but the door no more open than when I started, I briefly considered smashing out the glass to reassert my superiority over the dumb machine—*me Tarzan, you BMW*—but reason prevailed. I finally dug out my cell phone and dialed the pediatrician's number. I—somewhat hysterically, I confess—told the receptionist of my dilemma, and I thought I heard a muffled snicker.

After what seemed like the longest five minutes of my life, a perky redhead came prancing out into the parking lot with a pan of warm water. Brady and I were freed in no time, and I should have been appreciative, but the receptionist couldn't stop laughing, so I glared at her as I mumbled "Thanks."

By the time Brady and I got home again, I was sinking fast with exhaustion. I wanted to lie down and die, or at least cry my eyes out. Don't get me wrong, I was crazy nuts in love with my baby with his big brown eyes and ready smile. I sometimes thought he was born happy. His temperament was certainly much better than mine—blissfully sunny while storm clouds chase across my emotions ten times a day. Like me, however, he had the Pattons' iron will—or what has been more often called pigheadedness. Cross him and his cry was not a whimper, but a roar. And I could testify from firsthand experience that a screaming baby was more effective torture than anything used in the Inquisition.

But I was grateful beyond words that I had such a good, healthy baby. I was even grateful that I had a baby at all, although I never planned on having one as the result of an afternoon of lovemaking in a rural Texas motel somewhere near Route 83 south of Laredo. I was sure the whole thing would never have happened if it hadn't been for the bottles of Dos Equis and the blistering heat—and the fact that I, Miss Always in Control and Reasonable, had fallen smack-dab completely in love at first sight.

Hell, I knew only the first name of my baby's father, a tall, lanky, utterly gorgeous Texan who rode an Indian motorcycle. He'd said his name was Jake, and I'd bet dollars to doughnuts even that much was made up. My car had broken down; he gallantly offered to help. The affair was nuts. Of course it was nuts! I got sunstroke or something riding along behind Jake on that motorcycle, my hands around his hard-muscled chest and my . . . my more sensitive parts . . . right against his backside. Look at the risks I took. The whole episode was so unlike me, I have to think it was fate. You want to know what happened?

About a year and a half ago, my law firm sent me down to Zapata, Texas, which is nearly on the Mexican border, to talk to a millionaire client who was a hang glider fanatic. The guy turned out to be a jerk and the deal I was supposed to close never happened. I had wasted hours standing around while the client sailed off into the wild blue yonder—and ended up breaking his leg. I was in a foul mood when I started back to the airport. Then the damned Honda Civic I rented crapped out on me and stopped dead.

It was late August and the summer sun was out in full force. The car was getting so hot inside that I couldn't breathe. My blond hair was sticking to my face with sweat. I climbed out, pulled off my suit jacket, and heaved it into the backseat. I felt a lot cooler in the sleeveless cotton T-shirt I had been wearing underneath it. Then I tried to make the cell phone work. No service. No luck.

Maybe I should have been scared when this tough-looking biker came careening off the highway, his wheels spitting stones, and stopped in front of me, but I wasn't. The guy rode what looked like a vintage motorcycle even to me, who knows nothing about bikes. He put his long, denim-covered legs down on either side of the bike, his cowboy boots biting into the dust. He leaned back, and then he took off his helmet. I sort of gasped when I saw his face, and I felt as if someone had sprinkled me with fairy dust. I couldn't move a muscle; I could only stare at him. He was the handsomest man I had ever seen.

"Need some help?" he asked.

I hesitated.

"I won't bite. Honest," he said with a lopsided grin. He dismounted, and stuck out his hand. "My name is Jake." He smiled again, and his face seemed to catch the sun, lighting up and dazzling me.

I stared. I couldn't seem to find my voice. Heat waves shimmered all around him, making everything seem like a dream, while he stared right back at me. This humming started in my blood and I felt inexplicably happy. Finally, after we stood unmoving for God knows how long, he smiled and asked again if he could help. His eyes didn't let go of mine. I said something witty like, "Yeah, sure," while my heart did somersaults in my chest and I irrationally felt like throwing myself into his arms.

He said he'd take me into Laredo to the rental car place to get another vehicle, and I said sure. After I climbed on the back of his bike, he asked me if I was hungry, and I said sure yet again. We ended up at this biker bar—Jake called it an "icehouse"—in the middle of nowhere. When we walked in, we were already holding hands, only I'm not quite sure how that happened. Pretty soon we were laughing together, talking nonstop, eating fajitas, and drinking Dos Equis out of frosty glass bottles.

Jake showed me how to push a wedge of lime into the bottle and turn it upside down with your thumb over the top of the neck. We had quite a few beers like that, and I was laughing even more while the jukebox played Willie Nelson's "On the Road Again" and "Fallin', Fallin', Fallin'" by Ray Price and the Cherokee Cowboys, over and over again.

I stared into his eyes, which were the color of root beer and unfathomably deep. His hair was reddish brown, sun-streaked and pulled back in a ponytail. I memorized the angles of his cheekbones, his nose, his mouth. I liked the way his skin felt under my fingertips. I drank him in as if I was dying of thirst, and I surely was.

I also ended up telling Jake that I was a lawyer in Philadelphia but that I hated it and wanted to quit— a thought I had never put into words before. He said he understood that because he used to have a job he didn't like too, and he used to be somebody else, but now he was Jake and he rode with an outlaw motorcycle gang called the Bandidos. He also told me an awful lot about his motorcycle, which he seemed to love as much as a cowboy in the Old West would have loved his horse.

Then he kissed me, his lips a little salty with sweat and his mouth tasting of beer and lime. My head started spinning and didn't stop. I said I couldn't believe I was sitting there kissing him in a roadside bar outside of Laredo. He said he couldn't either and that he had a better idea, and that's how we ended up at the motel for the best sex I ever had in my entire life.

Wait a minute, that's not the whole story. The total experience was much more than lust in the Texas heat. Jake and I fit together in a way that I had never experienced before. The way I felt reminded me of a couple I knew who realized they were soul mates on the first date. They started living together that same night. By the time I was introduced to them, it was ten years later, and they were still crazy about each other. That's how it was with Jake and me—

Or it would have been, if this voice in my head hadn't kept whispering: *This can't work. He's a biker, an outlaw. I'm a lawyer. This is just sexual infatuation. This is crazy. This can't work,* over and over like a mantra. The whole time my heart kept telling me it felt so right. And Jake was telling me that too, saying stuff like, "This is so amazing. I can't believe I met you."

"Me too," I said, "me too."

But it was I who pulled away, not Jake. It was I

who sat up in bed sometime around nine that night and wrapped my arms around my knees. I didn't want to leave and I wanted to tell Jake that I loved him, but that was too nuts—or so the little voice in my head warned. So instead, I shut my eyes and whispered, "Um, Jake, this has been great. You've been great. Unbelievable, really. But I've got to be leaving now. I have a red-eye flight back to Philly." I opened my eyes and looked over at him.

Jake was propped up on the pillows, his hands behind his head. A wave of sadness seemed to pass over him like a shadow. He started to say, "I wish—" and I thought he was going to tell me not to go, but he didn't. He stopped midsentence. Then what he said was, "Yeah, sure. You're right. You have to go. I'm not in a place you can be right now." He reached out and gently turned my face toward his. "Maybe someday things will be different, but now, yeah, you got to go."

Jake dropped me off at the car rental office, and I was going to give him my business card at the last minute, but I didn't. I stood there in the humid Texas night, my heart breaking in two, telling me not to leave, while he kissed me one last time. The touch of his lips made me want him all over again. Then he took my hand, looked into my eyes, and said, "This sounds sort of dumb . . . anyways, I'm going to say it, Ravine." He said my name right and he said it slow, *Rah-vine,* not *Rah-veen,* which is how it looks. "In another time, another place, I'd ask you to stay. To marry me. But it's here and now, so I wanted to say I'll never forget you. And somehow, I promise you, if you need me, I'll be there. If fate is kind and it's supposed to happen, I'll find you, and be the kind of man you would want me to be, because right now— for a lot of reasons—I'm not."

Then he winked at me and rode off into the night on that bike, leaving me sort of dazed in front of the rental car place. And no, I didn't try to find him after I discovered I was pregnant, but I did think about seeing him again almost every single night.

Now look at me. I was living in a "fixer" of a Pennsylvania farmhouse, with a six-and-a-half-month-old baby, no job, and less than a thousand dollars in savings. I had exchanged the urban diversity of Philadelphia for a rural slice of northeast Pennsylvania where many people lived and died without ever venturing farther than the creaky old coal towns of Wilkes-Barre or Scranton. The teenagers had little to do here besides raise hell and explore the joys of sex in the backseats of Chevys. Sometimes the girls got pregnant and found themselves stuck here with little hope. But most of the young people left to find better-paying jobs and a different life.

I had been one of them. I had changed from a gawky, earnest college student who packed a Samsonite and went off to Penn State into a high-powered attorney who ordered lattes and was on her way to making a million dollars a year. But the joke was on me. What I had found wasn't what I had been looking for at all. Now here I was back in the place I had started. I had gone full circle. I was starting over. Maybe this time I could get it right. Yeah, sure I could—maybe with the help of a miracle or two.

Mostly I worry about raising a little boy without a father. It's not that I'm a bad mother, because I really think I am a doggone good one, but I worry that if I meet somebody one day and get married, will he really love Brady like his birth father would? I believe in my heart that a boy needs a man around, so I worry about that too. My own father died a long time ago, and my mother didn't remarry. And speaking of my mother, I wasn't home five minutes when I heard her pickup truck pull into my driveway.

Chapter 2

My mother means well, I know that. A farm girl with a no-nonsense outlook on life, Clara Bishop Patton hid an eccentric streak behind her practical exterior. After all, she did name me after a town—the tiny Pennsylvania hamlet of Ravine where she and my father had pulled off the interstate to get lunch the day I was conceived. My mother was "no spring chicken," as she put it, and hadn't gotten pregnant in nearly twenty years of marriage. She attributed her unexpected fertility to the homemade "piggies" and perogies she'd ordered at a little Polish place.

My mother was a rock in any crisis, and I had moved back to my hometown to be near her and my other relatives—there were dozens of them, mostly all Pattons—right before the baby was born. I wouldn't have made it without her, especially through the dark, seemingly endless days of Brady's colic. Don't ask. I was so sleep-deprived that in another century I would no doubt have thrown myself down a well.

I look a lot like my mother, so I am told. We both have the same pug nose that's too short and tilts up at the end. We both have slate blue eyes, and once upon a time her hair was a light, nearly white blond like mine. Our temperaments, however, are polar opposites. A retired high school teacher, my five-foot-three-inch mother made hulking football halfbacks tremble in their seats with simply a glare. She never got ruffled by anything. In fact, when I phoned her to break the news that I was pregnant, she said without a hint of emotion, "I thought you said you didn't want to have children."

"That's not true," I snapped. "I was on a career track. I said I didn't want children *until after I made partner*. Plans can change, you know," I finished in a tight voice.

"Yes, I know," she answered with a brief hint of unexpected softness. Then she continued as if she were a loan officer and I was applying for a mortgage. "Do you plan on telling the baby's father? Or did you use a sperm bank?"

"No, and no." I felt aggrieved. I hadn't expected my mother to get all starry-eyed and mushy when she found out she was going to be a grandmother—she's not a mushy person—but I had been hoping for some show of enthusiasm on her part.

"Okay then. Your grandfather's house on the old farm is empty. He always wanted you to have it. Why don't you come back to Noxen?"

I hesitated. It was exactly what I'd thought she'd say. I had looked at all my options and decided that was the best one of the bunch. I had no one in Philadelphia except some business friends. I couldn't afford to keep my apartment. I knew nothing about babies or being a mother. I was smart enough to know I needed the best help available—and that was Clara.

But as I have already mentioned more than once, I had deep reservations about the "coming back to Noxen" part. Noxen is an old, small rural town where rusted-out cars sit on cement blocks in the front yards and the inhabitants are so interrelated with cousins marrying cousins that the whole county tells "Noxen jokes" such as:

Question: "Why can't the police solve crimes in Noxen?"

Answer: "Because the DNA is all the same and there are no dental records."

It didn't help that maybe five years ago one of the Krantzes—a family of farmers who live on the flats down near the highway—was caught having an affair with his favorite sheep, and it was all over the newspapers that the SPCA had him arrested. I've had to put up with snickers my whole life when I tell anybody local where I'm from.

It's not fair. If you overlook the junk in some of the front yards, you will see that Noxen is nestled in a beautiful valley with a wide bubbling creek running through it. A quaint hundred-year-old post office still operates on Main Street, and the postcard-perfect Methodist church with its white wooden steeple perches on a green lawn along Route 29. On the worn mossy stones of the church's graveyard are the names of my ancestors who died fighting for liberty in the Revolutionary War. Life's not fair, as they say, so I finally responded to my mother's offer of my grandfather's house by whispering softly, "I'd like that."

Right now, however, I balanced Brady on my hip while I peeked out the window and watched my mother wrestle a big box out of the back of her ten-year-old Ford pickup. Fiercely independent and proud of her self-sufficiency, she doesn't take kindly to offers of help, so I let go of the curtain and went over to open the front door while she marched determinedly up the front walk with her package.

"What's that, Ma?" I asked.

She shot me a smile. "Just what you need. A Diaper Genie."

Now I need a lot of things, but a Diaper Genie wasn't even on my list. "A what?" I asked.

Noticing that I hadn't closed the front door, she did, muttering something like, "You'd think the girl was brought up in a barn," under her breath, then saying louder, "It's a device to help you dispose of the diapers without the stink. I mean, with your 'poopaphobia' and all, it's perfect." She chuckled as she reached out and took Brady from my arms and gave him a face full of kisses.

My mother thinks it's hysterically funny that I can't handle strong smells. I never could. I'd be gagging for days when the farmers around here spread manure on the fields in the spring. I have used every deodorizing additive on the market in my cat's box, which is one of those litter pans with the odor-shield hoods. Even so, pooper-scooping was a daily challenge. And nothing, but nothing, had prepared me for dirty diapers.

When Brady was a newborn and being breast-fed, I managed to change his diapers by holding my breath. In those first blissful weeks, I even thought, *Hey, this isn't so bad.* But once Brady started on solid foods I found myself hanging my head out of the bathroom door trying not to retch. Recently I've taken to using swimmers' nose plugs, which really help. That's supposed to be a deep dark secret, although I'm pretty sure my mother is spreading it all over town.

The big problem is that garbage pickup out here in the boondocks happens only once a week. A seven-day buildup of dirty diapers was making me act like a lunatic. I had a green garbage bag which I privately referred to as *the old bag of shit* stashed in the ramshackle chicken coop out back, but dragging the bag down to the road for the Monday morning pickup was almost more than I could bear.

Suddenly I was very interested in this device called a Diaper Genie. "Really? No smell?"

"Yes, really," my mother answered. "Your Aunt Loretta told me all about it. You put the used diaper in the top, where it's then deodorized and stored until you empty the container. You never have to touch it again—and you never have to smell it again," she assured me. "But look, I have to run. Cal Metz and I are running the Thursday Bingo Bonanza at the Kunkle Fire Hall, and I still need to get to the Weis Market. Let me know how this thing works for you," she added and handed Brady back.

Cal Metz and I? My mother had mentioned the retired landscaper a few times this past month. Cal, a poetry-writing ex-hippie of the sixties, used to own the Mums & Roses Garden Center. Now he devoted his time to saving the planet and had started a side business selling compost toilets. She even asked me if I minded his coming to Thanksgiving dinner this year. It crossed my mind that after umpteen years of widowhood, my mother had a boyfriend. But I didn't say what I was thinking. I said, "Thanks, Ma," and leaned over to give her cool, wind-reddened cheek a kiss. As she turned to go I added, "I really appreciate this. The Diaper Genie might change my life." I laughed. I didn't know how true those words were about to become.

I waited until I gave Brady his lunch and put him down for his nap before I took another look at the Diaper Genie. The first thing that I noticed—and it really annoyed me—was that the box had already been opened. Right away I realized that my frugal mother had picked up "a bargain" that somebody else didn't want. Since she had mentioned Aunt Loretta, I guessed this had been a duplicate baby shower present from when my cousin Margie was pregnant last year. With some relief I noticed that the Diaper Genie looked new and unused when I pulled it out of the box.

The Diaper Genie was a white plastic cylindrical device that stood about twenty inches high. I couldn't wait to get it set up, even though fatigue was making my movements clumsy. I needed a nap as much as Brady did, and perhaps more. I'm not a happy camper when I'm sleep-deprived, so when the directions said the lid was easy to open, and it wasn't, I felt really and truly out of sorts.

I gripped it as hard as I could and turned. It wouldn't budge. I tried getting my fingernails under the edge. I twisted and pushed. I couldn't see any reason why the lid was stuck, and I was beginning to swear and see red. Finally I straddled the thing, held it with my knees, and found some leverage as I gave a mighty heave on the rim—and I fell arse over tea-kettle as the top sprang open. I landed with a thump on the carpet right on my behind.

I put my hands over my face and thought that this was turning out to be a really bad day. As tears leaked between my fingers, I felt sorry for myself for a minute, then realized crying wasn't going to help. I sniffed, blinked, and pushed my hair back behind my ears. I glanced toward the ceiling and took a deep breath. That's when I noticed, up there above me, a white tendril of smoke curling from the open Diaper Genie.

Holy shit! I thought. *The frigging thing's on fire!*

With my heart beating at least a thousand times a minute, I scrambled to my feet ready to call 911. But as I reached for my cell phone, I noticed that the white "smoke" was more like a thick mist and it was curling up from a dark brown bottle that had rolled out of the Diaper Genie and it's cork had fallen out. As I watched, it began to form into a human shape. *What the hell?* I thought. I must be even more tired than I'd realized. Then I heard a sound, something like *Poof!* followed by the tinkling of little brass bells.

Suddenly a cocky-looking young guy in ragged khaki shorts, dusty combat boots, and a faded khaki shirt, unbuttoned to expose his bare muscular chest, stood in front of me. I could see that the unruly hair beneath the upturned brim of his slouch hat was a sandy blond. He had a tattoo of a kangaroo on his right forearm. He wasn't conventionally good-looking—his nose was too hawklike and his face a bit too long—but he had bright blue eyes in a deeply tanned face and a wide, sensual mouth. He was leaning back against my living room wall, his arms folded, a lazy smile on his face.

As I stared at him, he winked at me, and said, "Thanks, lady," with a strong Australian accent.

I pinched myself hard, figuring I was either dreaming or had hit my head when I fell. *That's it, I'm hallucinating,* I thought. The pinch accomplished nothing but to give me the beginnings of a bruise. I squeezed my eyes shut and opened them again. The stranger was still standing in my living room grinning at me.

As fear cascaded over me like a bucket of cold water, I looked around the room for something to use as a weapon. All I could spot was the TV remote, so I snatched it up and held it out in front of me. "Don't you dare come a step closer or I'll let you have it!" I yelled.

The guy raised one eyebrow at me and didn't move.

"Who the hell are you?" I yelled. "And what are you doing in my living room?"

"Well, now, lady"—it sounded like "li-dee" when he pronounced it—"I'm Gene. At your service," he said with exaggerated formality. With that he pushed off the wall to stand up straight, and I noticed he had to be six foot two or better. He swept his hat off with a flourish and bowed, although he didn't act in the least bit servile. He seemed to be enjoying himself. He slapped the hat back onto his head and said, "As to 'who the hell I am'—I'm a genie, of course. I've been trapped in that there bottle, and because you popped my cork, so to speak"—he winked at me again—"I now must grant you three wishes before I'm free. That's the tradition, y'know."

"You have got to be kidding! Do you really expect me to buy that?" I screamed at him. "What are you, some kind of pervert? How did you get in the Diaper Genie? How did you get in my house?"

"Hey, lady, let's set the record straight," he said matter-of-factly. "I didn't get here under my own steam. Somebody brought my bottle here, and *you* let me out. Until you make three wishes, I can't leave. I have to serve you. Believe me, after sixty years in a bottle, I have other things I'd rather be doing. So why don't you cool off, *master,*" he said in a mocking tone. "Or should I call you *mistress*?" he added irreverently.

"Don't call me anything!" *Oh hell,* I thought, *I have to be dreaming. I fainted or something. I must have hit my head. This can't be real.* "What do you want? What are you doing here?"

Gene rolled his eyes at me and said sotto voce, "Me, I had to get a hysterical one." He took a deep breath. He stood tall. He seemed to take over the room. I could even smell him: He had a sort of salty, sweaty odor that reminded me of being at the beach on a hot day. He caught me staring at him. He stared back. "Look, lady. Why don't you sit down. I'll explain, but from what I've seen of you so far, you aren't going to believe me." I swear he was trying not to smile.

I felt behind me for the couch and settled onto it without taking my eyes from this Gene guy. "All right, but don't you come one step closer or—"

"Or you'll attack me with that thing you're holding?" Gene coughed to cover what I was sure was a laugh. "Really, lady, don't get your knickers in a twist. I'm not going to hurt you. I have to *obey* you. That's the deal."

This guy, whoever or whatever he was, obviously didn't take me seriously. Since he wasn't threatening at all, I was beginning to feel more annoyed than scared. "I don't know who you think you are," I huffed, and sat up very straight, "but I am a member of the bar in the state of Pennsylvania."

"I'm trying to tell you who I am. And you might try to keep an open mind, Miss Hoity-Toity Member of the Bar—"

"Excuse me!" I broke in, instantly taking offense. *I never had anybody in my dreams insult me before. This is getting weirder and weirder.* "You are a trespasser," I said sternly. "In fact, your being here uninvited might even be called a home invasion. You are in big trouble, buddy, or Gene, or whoever you are. So start explaining, and make it quick or I'm going to call nine-one-one," I growled.

"Lady," he said, holding up his hands in a placating way. "Before you go calling anybody, hold on a minute. Listen to me. I am a genie. I am *your* genie. I'm not a trespasser."

"Yeah, sure. You're a genie. And I'm Santa Claus. You know what," I said mostly to myself, "you have to be a figment of my imagination." Anxiety washed over me. Maybe I wasn't dreaming. Maybe I was having a breakdown. The abrupt loss of my career, the return to Noxen, the baby and all those weeks of fatigue—they evidently had affected me more profoundly than I thought. I looked around for my cell phone, wondering who to call for a reality check.

The genie had been watching me. "You know, your eyes are sort of twitching. Try not to get upset," he said with a hint of concern.

"What do you mean 'try not to get upset'? I *am* upset. I don't understand this—you—" Tears threatened to stop my words.

"Bloody hell. Now she's going to cry," the man said under his breath. He stooped down in front of me, offering me a handkerchief that seemed to appear out of nowhere like a magician's trick. I took it and blew my nose.

His eyes were level with mine and I looked into their blue depths. I got a funny feeling in my stomach. I squeezed my eyes shut. "Go away."

"I can't," he said. "Look at me."

I opened one eye. "Why?"

Even with one eye, looking at him looking at me made my stomach dance.

"Let me explain," he said.

"What possible explanation is there? I've lost my mind," I wailed and turned my head away.

The genie muttered, " 'Hope not for mind in woman,' as John Donne once said." To me he said, "Don't you think you're overreacting?"

"Overreacting! I am not! And for your information I have a mind. A good one!"

The genie started to laugh. "I'm sorry. I just said that for fun. I couldn't help myself. You look cute when you get mad, even if your nose is all red," he said and winked, then stood back up before I could respond. "Look, let me talk a minute before you jump to any more conclusions. To start off, I'm a jinni, or as you might say, a genie."

"Yeah, right," I interjected, folding my arms across my chest. "A genie is a mythical creature."

"Ah, lady, I only wish they *were* mythical creatures. Then I couldn't have been turned into one."

"What do you mean you were 'turned into one'?"

"I had the bad luck to get on the wrong side of some desert caliph. He had me put under a spell and stuck me in a bottle. No, don't look like that. It's the truth. It was in the middle of W-W-Two—that's World War Two, you know—"

"I know!" I broke in. "Get on with this ridiculous story!"

"Righto. Here's the whole tale, short as I can make it." He came over and sat down next to me on the couch. I felt the sofa cushions shift under his weight. He was big, male, and undeniably attractive. I inched away from him and hugged the arm of the sofa.

Gene stretched out his long legs. His eyes were wide open, yet he didn't seem to be looking at anything, except maybe his memories. He had joined the RAF in 1940, he told me, and by 1942, his squadron was chasing Rommel through North Africa, first in Algiers, then in Morocco. Wherever the Desert Fox ran, Gene and his men followed. One night he was flying a P-38 Lightning fighter and went out on a sortie along with ten other planes. They flew deep into the Sahara before they spotted a line of German tanks and started a strafing run. The Nazis fired back. Ack-ack fire hit Gene's plane, tearing through the right wing. It must have hit the fuel line, because all of a sudden the plane was on fire and started diving to earth in a death spiral. Gene yelled to his crew to bail out. He watched their parachutes clear the plane before he ejected.

"I never saw any of those chaps again," he said. He glanced over at me, then his eyes went to that far-off place again. He said he'd come down hard and the chute dragged him through the sand, banging him up "bloody good." His leg broke, and a couple of ribs too. He managed to cut loose the chute and bury it. All that night he hid from "the Krauts," thinking that any minute they'd spot him and he'd "cark it." But when dawn broke, they were gone. Gene was alone out there in the sand, the sun frying him "like a shrimp on the barbie." After a day in the desert with no water, he was out of his head and dying of thirst. That's when he got picked up by a tribe of Bedouins.

"On camels." The genie laughed. "I thought I was dreaming, but they saved me life."

"Okay," I broke in. "It's a good story—"

His voice got hard. "It's not a bloody story. It's what happened. It's the truth."

"If it did," I said, "if what you say is true, this happened over sixty years ago. That makes you, what, pushing ninety?"

"Lady, look at me. I ain't seen thirty yet. Do you think you can stop interrupting?" he snapped.

"Sorry," I said and pretended to lock my lips.

Gene glared at me for a moment, then continued. After a couple of months, when he was feeling good again, he wanted to get back to his squadron. When he asked the headman, the tall robed chieftain shook his head. But Gene wouldn't quit badgering him. Finally the chieftain took him to a palace in an oasis somewhere.

"I think it was along some river . . ." he said, lost in thought and falling silent. Then he turned his head toward me and looked at me with smoky eyes, his voice turning lazy again.

"Before I go yabbering on with a geography lesson, let's say I was still stranded, but having a fine old time until I got caught boffing one of the wives of the chap who ruled the place. Naturally, he was mad as a cut snake. Before I knew it, I was stuck in a bottle. Since then I've tossed around the Seven Seas and pretty much been knocked all over the world in my prison here. Nobody ever set me free until you did."

"You have got to think I'm gullible," I interrupted. "But go on, you have quite an imagination. You'd make a great defense lawyer. How did you end up in that Diaper Genie?"

"Oh, that. It would be more fun to tell you about the time my bottle got picked up by a polar bear—"

"Spare me the tall stories. Say something I can believe." But in truth I didn't believe any of this. I squeezed my eyes shut again. I mentally counted to ten and told myself to please, please wake up. But when I opened my eyes, the genie was still there, staring at me with an insolent smile. I raised my chin and composed myself. "Please continue," I instructed. "Tell me how you ended up in a Diaper Genie."

Gene rubbed his face with his hand and hunched over in thought. "Let me see, now. That kink in the unraveling thread of fate happened maybe a year ago." Gene had been reclining in his bottle in the dark of a hall closet, tossed in there among a bunch of old boots and forgotten for ages. He was bored, and the days marched past without light or hope. Then one afternoon a little girl opened the closet door. In the room beyond the closet, Gene could see a bunch of women sitting around. One of them was squealing in a piercing voice while she opened presents. Before he saw much more, the "ankle biter," that is, the little girl, sat right down on top of the bottle and hid behind some coats. Then he heard somebody calling, "Paulina, where are you? Paulina!"

The girl refused to answer. She sat there giggling.

That was Margie's firstborn, the very spoiled Paulina, I thought to myself as Gene went on with his tale.

Then the closet door opened again, a lady's arm reached in, and the child was pulled out, none too gently. The little girl grabbed Gene's bottle and whacked the woman, likely her mother, in the shins. After getting a scolding, the child waited until nobody was watching and stuffed the bottle into this white plastic device. That's where it had remained for the past year until my mother brought over the Diaper Genie and I unstoppered the bottle.

The genie sat there and waited for me to say something. He was only a few feet away from me. I could see the sun-bleached hair on his legs above khaki socks that peeked out above his combat boots. The boots were white with dust, and sand was packed around the laces. I raised my eyes and looked into his. His eyelashes were bleached nearly white. He cocked his head and winked at me again. My stomach did this stupid little flip. I felt very strange indeed.

"I don't believe this," I said.

"Crikey, lady, I told you—"

"Hold on a minute. It's not that I don't believe you. I don't believe *this*. I think I hit my head and I'm unconscious. This is merely a dream."

"Lady, you're not dreaming. I'm real. Look, I'll prove it to you." He stood up and reached out, taking my hand. He pulled me upright until we were standing together very close. He put his fingers under my chin, tilting it up so our eyes locked again. My skin tingled where he touched me. Suddenly I wanted nothing more than to kiss him. Blood rushed into my cheeks. I smacked his hand away. It was flesh and blood, all right.

"Keep your hands to yourself. Look, if you aren't a dream I don't know who or what you are. I think you better leave." I stepped aside to put more distance between us.

The genie looked exasperated. "I explained to you, I can't leave until I grant you three wishes. Then *poof,* I'll be gone. Go ahead, try it out. Make a wish, and I'll grant it," he said, his arms crossed defiantly, his combat boots planted firmly on the rug.

"Sure you will," I said, suddenly feeling exhausted, as if I hadn't slept well in weeks—and I hadn't. That must be why I was hallucinating. "All right, buddy, I mean Gene." I let out a deep sigh. "Here's my wish. I wish I could sleep without interruption and wake up in my own bed on clean, freshly ironed, fine Egyptian cotton sheets—"

"Any color preference?" Gene interrupted.

"Make them robin's-egg blue with a satin stripe." I tossed off the first thing that came into my head. "And they have to match an expensive down comforter from Bloomingdale's that's keeping me warm. And when I wake up, I will feel happy, refreshed, and not the least bit tired."

"That's it?" Gene asked.

"That's it," I answered.

"Your wish is my command," Gene said, without a trace of sarcasm, and winked. Immediately I heard the tinkling sound of brass bells. The air around me began to fade to white; then it slid into a rosy, misty light. The next thing I knew I was snug in my bed and that rosy light was streaming through my bedroom window.

Baby Kitty was snoozing comfortably against my leg, and I felt so good, I found myself smiling. I glanced over at the bedside alarm clock. *Oh wow! It's four thirty,* I thought. *I've been out for hours.* Then I noticed the sheets. The material was fine cotton that caressed my body like silk. The sheets were gorgeous, the kind you find at those thousand-dollar-a-night hotels, and they were robin's-egg blue shot through with a satin stripe. Atop the sheets was a lush matching down comforter. I sat up and heard Brady through the baby monitor, burbling and contentedly making nonsense sounds.

I jumped out of bed and realized I had been sleeping in a nightgown instead of my usual old T-shirt. It was a beautiful garment in robin's-egg blue made out of a fabric that resembled the satin stripe of the sheets. And I felt happy, ridiculously happy and totally rested. I remembered dreaming about a genie. Or at least I thought it was a dream. But if it was, how did I explain the luxurious bedding and my nightgown? I couldn't.

I quickly put on my jeans and a sweater and went to get Brady out of his crib, unable to shake the glow of sunny optimism which made my step light and energetic, even though I should have been a wee bit worried that there really might be a World War II Aussie flyer who said he was a genie in my living room.

Chapter 3

With Brady in my arms I headed down the stairs and immediately smelled food. Chicken soup? Chocolate chip cookies? Maybe my mother had stopped by, or . . . It couldn't be. It was impossible. I got to the bottom stair, made a sharp left, and there he was— Gene, the Aussie genie, standing at my kitchen counter, a spatula in his hand, putting fresh-baked cookies on a pretty blue plate. A pot of soup simmered on the stove. Brady stretched out a chubby hand and pointed his index finger.

I stood there staring, trying to make sense of what my eyes beheld. The man wasn't transparent. He didn't look like a ghost. He looked like an ordinary young guy—dressed inappropriately for November, sure, but other than that, he looked real. Really *real*. I was starting to freak out again.

"Want one?" Gene said lightly, extending the spatula holding a cookie in my direction. He was grinning at me.

"This situation isn't funny," I said, trying to hold on to my squirming son until I decided to put him into his high chair.

"Ba ba ba ba," Brady chanted. I knew he wanted a bottle, but I didn't have one ready. I grabbed a banana, peeled it quickly, and put a piece on the tray in front of him while I kept my eyes on Gene.

My thoughts were racing. Gene looked real. The
food looked real. Nothing made sense. Since I knew
I wasn't dreaming now, I thought frantically that I
must be having a breakdown or that I was the victim
of an elaborate joke. My hands were shaking, my
breath was coming fast, my words spilled out in a rush:
"What are you doing here?"

Gene gave me a careful look, then said in a kind,
even voice, "I'm cooking for you, but obviously I'm
upsetting you. I gave the whole situation a good think.
I suppose that having a genie pop out of a bottle is a
shock. Do you want to talk about your feelings?"

I shook my head. "I don't know who you are. I
don't understand this at all, but you can't stay here."

"I explained that. I can't leave. I belong to you. But
I can go back into my bottle," he said, pointing at the
bulbous amber glass that sat on the kitchen counter.
"I'd rather not be all cramped up again, but it's your
call. Just say the word."

"What word?" I said, not getting it. The bottle was
about nine inches high. Gene was over six feet tall. I
didn't believe in genies. I didn't believe in magic,
which was sleight of hand and trickery. I looked at
Gene. I looked back at the bottle. There was no way
that big, solid, flesh-and-blood man was going to fit
in there.

"Lady, I don't know what word," Gene said and
sighed. "You can say 'Go back in your bottle,' or
something like that."

"Okay, go back in your bottle," I said as fast as I
could get the words out, then held my breath. As soon
as I said them, invisible bells tinkled, there was a
sound sort of like *poof,* and a stream of white smoke
whooshed from where Gene had been standing and
dove into the mouth of the open bottle. I rushed over
and jammed the cork into its top. I let out my breath
in a deep sigh of relief. Then I held the bottle up to
the light. In the bottom of it a miniature man sat

cross-legged. He blew me a kiss. I flinched. I opened a kitchen cupboard and put the bottle in next to the cereal boxes and slammed the door closed.

Ohmygod, ohmygod, ohmygod, was all I could say over and over. Irrationally, I looked over at Brady to make sure he was all right. He was mashing down the piece of banana with his little fist, totally content. I looked around. Nothing in the room seemed out of the ordinary, except perhaps Gene's homemade goodies. I picked up a chocolate chip cookie and bit into it. It was still warm and melted in my mouth. It was yummy, a classic Toll House cookie, made with the recipe right off the Nestlé wrapper.

I didn't know what else to do, so I fixed a bottle of formula for Brady and poured myself a glass of milk. I stood there enjoying milk and cookies while I tried to make sense of the last few hours. I couldn't. Nothing in my legal education prepared me for acquiring and/or using a genie. My rational, sensible life, which had started to become unglued when I met Jake, had collapsed entirely, and I didn't know what to do.

I took a deep breath and decided to focus on getting Brady his dinner—from glass jars containing strained lamb and strained peas. It wasn't my idea of a gourmet meal, and Brady seemed to hate commercial baby food. Along with his bottle of formula, he preferred regular table food that I smooshed up or put in the blender. So I wasn't surprised when he determinedly pushed the spoon of strained peas away and closed his lips tightly. When I tried the "here comes the truck, open up the garage" game, he clamped his mouth shut harder, squeezed his eyes shut and started to cry. The Patton will was asserting itself. I felt like bawling myself.

Finally I threw the baby food in the garbage and put some Cheerios on his tray. This white high chair made out of some space-age plastic was a new addition to Brady's world, and any food that went on the tray immediately became something to play with. Brady is never one to stay mad; his tears quickly stopped. Within seconds he was having a good time pushing the Cheerios off the tray edge, and Baby Kitty was knocking them around the floor. Brady thought that was hilarious.

I wasn't laughing. I was worried out of my mind about that bottle in the cupboard, but I did what I had to do. I pulled out the blender and, using the goodies sealed up in Tupperware that my mother had brought over—I chose creamy mashed potatoes and baked chicken—I made some homemade baby food. A few minutes later, as I sat there feeding my happy little guy, my brain wouldn't quit thinking, going over the same subjects again and again.

I had so much on my plate lately—no pun intended—that the last thing I needed was a genie in my kitchen cupboard. Coming back to my grandfather's house and having a baby had changed my life irrevocably. And while I thought I'd miss the city, in fact I rarely thought about it. Until the recent cold snap, every day I had put Brady on my back and we walked through the fields. My legs had gotten hard and lean from our hikes. I had worn a path through the grass and up toward the old apple orchard. I realized one day that I felt like the maples and oaks that lined the stone walls. This land is where I had my roots. I was profoundly connected to this place whether I chose to be or not. The rolling hills that stretched in every direction, the clouds that dropped so low I could almost reach up and touch them, and the solitude that embraced my baby and me as we walked where there was no other house or human in sight brought me a kind of peace I had never felt in Philadelphia.

Yet lately I had been waking up at night with recurring worries. Did I really have a future here? I needed to start making money, for one thing. But I didn't want to leave Brady all day, even though my mother would gladly take care of him. I definitely didn't want to join another large law firm. I could practice law at home, but did I want to? Putting out my shingle might not earn me much, and my savings were running close to empty. I could always ask the diaper genie for a million dollars. *Let's not even go there,* I thought. I still hadn't figured out if I had imagined the whole thing or if I was truly losing my mind, but that bottle in the cupboard was scaring the bejeezus out of me.

Brady had long since finished his bottle. I took him out of the high chair to cuddle in my arms, the sun went down, and the weak light of the gray November day turned into the murky shadows of dusk. The same thoughts kept running through my mind like a toy train around a track. Finally I stood up and turned on the kitchen lights. Brady had fallen asleep. I gently put him into his baby seat and carefully strapped him in. I kissed him and told him I loved him. He was the sweetness in my life.

I let out a deep sigh and straightened up. I was hungry. I remembered the pot of chicken soup on the stove and I ladled out some into a bowl. It was delicious; the broth was rich with just the right amount of pepper. Light green celery and vivid orange carrots floated in it. Little bits of chicken lay on the bottom of the bowl. My mother couldn't have made it; she makes plain, hearty foods, nothing gourmet. I took another spoonful and realized I was starved, hungrier than I had felt in months. I ate the entire bowlful quickly, and I admit I felt better with a full stomach. My usual evening meal was a Healthy Choice frozen dinner which—on nights that I was feeling stressed, depressed, or tired (check all of the above most nights)—I followed up with a dish of Ben & Jerry's Cherry Garcia ice cream.

Tonight I skipped the ice cream and sat there at the kitchen table not knowing what to do next, besides the dishes, so I picked up my bowl and headed for the sink. I was saved from having to make any serious decisions by the sound of my cousin Frederika Ann's voice calling, "Ravine? You home? Hello!" from the sunporch. I leave my front door unlocked except at night; my relatives walk right on in. As crime creeps out into the boondocks from the nearest city, Wilkes-Barre, I should be locking up all the time, but we never had out here, and I still wasn't in the habit of doing it. A locked door wasn't neighborly, somehow.

"Freddi! I'm in the kitchen! Come on back," I answered.

My cousin, as short as a fireplug, came bursting into the kitchen, her nose red with cold and snow clinging to her boots. "Wow, your house looks great. You must have spent all day cleaning," she said as she peeled off her coat and put it on the back of a chair.

"What are you talking about?" I said.

"Your house. It's spotless. I mean, I'm not criticizing how it usually is, but the dust bunnies are the size of grown-up rabbits, no offense."

I got up without answering her and walked into the dining room, then the living room, then the sunporch. I could smell Lemon Pledge. The rugs were vacuumed. The furniture was dusted. The normal clutter of magazines and books was neatly piled on the coffee table. I shook my head in amazement.

"Great chocolate chip cookies," Freddi was saying when I came back to the kitchen. "I hope you didn't mind me taking one."

"No, take as many as you want. Would you like a glass of milk? Cup of tea?"

"Tea would be great. I didn't know you baked," she added, as she polished off a cookie.

"I don't," I said as I put the teakettle on the burner, leaned back, and put my butt against the counter as I mulled over what I wanted to do. My cousin Freddi, sole proprietor of Freddi's Beauty Shop, is a little younger than I am, but she and I are close. She had married her high school sweetheart, and she always thought she'd have a half-dozen kids. It didn't happen. Three months ago she had made the decision to start taking fertility drugs. If she thought it unfair that I ended up pregnant without trying, she didn't say so.

That was Freddi's nature. She doesn't have a mean bone in her body. A sweetheart, a softie, a friend through thick and thin, that's my cousin Freddi. I made my decision as I poured her tea and set the mug in front of her.

"Freddi, can I show you something? It's a little weird," I asked as I opened my kitchen cupboard and pulled out the brown bottle. "Tell me if you see anything inside this? *But don't pull out the cork!*" I added as I handed it to her.

"Sure," she said, and held the bottle up to the light. "Euccch. There's something moving in there!" She nearly dropped the bottle. I grabbed it out of her open fingers before it fell, my heart racing.

"What is it? Did a mouse crawl in there? That's gross! Why don't you let it out?"

"It's not a mouse. Now hang on to the damned thing and look again, please." I handed the bottle back. "I mean it now, get a grip and tell me what you see."

Freddi took the bottle in both hands and held it up to the light again. "Wow! Oh wow!" she said. "What is this, a trick bottle? It looks like there's a little man in there. And he's waving at me. He's so cute!"

I snatched the bottle out of her hands. *"No!"*

"Yes! Honest, he's in there," she insisted.

"Yes, I know. I meant no, he's not cute. Okay, he's sort of cute. You really do see a guy in there, right?"

She looked at me with a question in her eyes and answered in a puzzled voice. "Yes, there's definitely a little guy in there. He's got shorts on and a bush hat. What is it? A projection game? A hologram?"

"No, it's a genie. At least he says he's a genie," I said, watching her face for a reaction.

She pressed her lips together and wrinkled up her nose. "Get out of here. Genies aren't real. What is it? A little computer thingie?"

"No, Freddi, I'm serious. He says he's a genie. His name is Gene. He's Australian—at least that's where he told me he was from."

Freddi's eyes were getting round like saucers. "He talks? He's spoken to you? In the bottle?"

"No, not in the bottle. He was here, in the house. I let him out. He did the cleaning—and the baking."

"Shut up. This is a joke, right? Ravine, what's going on?"

"It's not a joke. And I don't know what's going on. I need you to help me figure it out."

"Serious?"

"Dead serious."

"I swear, Ravine. This could only happen to you. Hey, he's rapping on the glass." She reached over and pulled on my hands to put the bottle up close to her face. "He's pointing at the cork. You know he is really cute. I think he's saying he wants to get out."

"No! Don't—" I started to say, but it was too late. Freddi had yanked the cork out. To the accompaniment of those damned tinkling bells and a puff of white smoke, Gene appeared, all six feet two inches of apparently hale and hearty Aussie man, standing with his sandy combat boots on my clean kitchen counter and stooping to avoid hitting his head on the ceiling.

"Get down off of there!" I said testily.

"Right, lady," he said, and suddenly he was standing on the floor near Freddi and me.

Freddi's eyes were almost popping out of her head and her mouth was a little O.

"My name's Ravine, not 'lady.' " I bit off the words.

I don't know why having Gene in my kitchen made me feel more irritated than frightened, but it did. Now that I knew I wasn't crazy—unless Freddi was bonkers too—I wasn't scared. I felt out of sorts. Gene rubbed me the wrong way. He had cooked me dinner, cleaned my house, and I felt pissed. I wasn't sure why. I mean, I could *feel* his body heat even though he was positioned maybe two feet away from me. I was acutely aware that his shirt was unbuttoned and I could see his chest with its well-defined pecs and light sprinkling of bleached blond hair.

I hadn't been this close to a young male since, well, since Jake. My body was reacting in a traitorous way even though my mind was saying, *This guy isn't even real. He's a genie, a spirit. And he's, what, if he was chasing Rommel in the Sahara? Ninety years old? Okay, he looks twenty-eight or something, but he was in World War II!* My body, however, wasn't listening to a word. Gene was staring at me with those big blue eyes of his. A blush was creeping up my neck into my face and I felt hot all over.

"G'day, Ravine," Gene drawled in his Aussie way. "Who's the pretty lady with you?"

"This is my cousin Freddi," I snapped, feeling even more annoyed as his eyes left me and looked Freddi over from head to toe. Then he stretched out his hand and said, "Please to meet ya, Freddi gal."

Freddi giggled and shook his hand. I gave her a dirty look. "So you're a genie?" Her voice became girlish and shy. "A real genie?"

"As real as they come," Gene answered. "Kept by magic in a bottle, and now a slave to your cousin here. Raah Vine. It's sort of a strange name, ain't it? Is she always this grumpy, by the way?" he asked, his voice teasing.

"Grumpy—why you, you—" I sputtered.

"Oh no," Freddi jumped in. "Ravine's not grumpy.

She can have a temper, but she's an up person, really. You surprised us, that's all. Isn't that right, cousin?" Freddi looked at me.

Before I got a chance to answer, I heard the front door open. Freddi and I froze as my mother's voice called, *"Hello! Anybody home?"*

Panic overwhelmed me. "Get back into the bottle!" I hissed at Gene and he vanished in a puff of smoke. I grabbed the bottle and held it with one hand behind my back. "Not a word!" I said to Freddi, who was nodding yes as my mother walked into the kitchen.

"Hello, Aunt Clara," Freddi said.

"What's going on?" my mother asked. I was afraid she'd see my guilt written all over my face.

"Nothing!" I said quickly. "Freddi stopped by, that's all. You look nice. How come you're wearing lipstick? You wouldn't want a cookie, would you?" I asked, picking up the blue plate and shoving it toward her, hoping to change the subject.

My mother shook her head and said, "Don't tell me you baked," her voice filled with suspicion.

"No! Of course not," I said. "Freddi brought them, didn't you, Freddi?"

"Oh yes, Aunt Clara. I stopped by to drop them off." She looked at me. "Look, I have to run. I'll call you . . . uh, later."

"Wait. Why don't you hang out a while," I pleaded, not wanting to be left alone with my mother and that damned bottle. I managed to set it down on the counter and was trying to shove it behind a loaf of bread.

Freddi was shaking her head in a definite no. She grabbed her coat and ran for the door.

Coward! I mouthed at Freddi from behind my mother's head.

"You're in an awful big hurry, Frederika Ann," my mother said. "How's your mother?"

"She's fine, Aunt Clara. Really, I've got to go. See

you, Ravine. And . . . and good luck!" she said as she beat it like a bat out of hell from the kitchen.

"What do you need good luck for?" my mother asked while she turned her attention to Brady. "How's my little prince tonight?" she cooed. "Did you have a good din-din?"

Brady had woken up and was babbling something that sounded like "Ga ga ga."

"It's din*ner,* not din-din, Ma," I said.

"Whatever," she said, straightening up and looking me right in the eye. "I asked, what do you need good luck for?"

"Nothing. Really. We were talking about me getting back to work, trying to figure out how to do it, you know, that's all," I said while I leaned my elbows back on the counter, trying to keep my body in front of the bread and the bottle. "I thought you were going to bingo tonight."

"I am," she said. "I'm on my way. But it's funny you should bring up your going back to work, because that's why I'm here."

"What do you mean?" I asked.

"I have a case for you."

"A legal case? What do you need a lawyer for?"

"For heaven's sake, Ravine. I don't need a lawyer. That sweet young couple who bought the B and B up on the hill need legal advice. They're Buddhists, you know."

I had heard that the Yeager farm had been bought and turned into a yoga meditation retreat. The sale happened about the time I moved back to Noxen. The whole town had talked about it for weeks. Most people were worried about some cult moving into the neighborhood and the rumors got pretty crazy for a while. The "cult" turned out to be a married couple from Japan who renamed the B and B Jade Meadow Farm. After a few months people seemed to accept them better than I'd expected.

This summer the Katos had opened a small roadside stand where they sold organic produce and free-range eggs. Whenever they sponsored a Buddhist retreat, the guests kept to themselves, never even coming into town to the post office. Every now and then somebody would mention meeting a monk in a red robe walking on the road, but the locals had gotten pretty used to the new neighbors.

"Yes, I know they're Buddhists," I said, hoping that I completely blocked the bottle from my mother's view. "What happened? Somebody bothering them?"

"Not exactly," my mother said. "It was a murder attempt on one of their hens, and they're all upset."

"Murder attempt?" I said, thinking this sounded totally wacky.

"Maybe not really murder. The hen was almost hit by a pickup truck. Mihoko and her husband—his name is Ken—felt the driver was intentionally trying to hit it. I told them you'd stop by and talk with them."

"Me? Why? Chickens get hit by cars all the time if they're wandering in the road. What can I do?"

"I'm not sure, but they'd like to know who did it and then, well, they have something in mind, I guess. I told them you were a lawyer, and they asked if they could discuss it with you. I said you'd be happy to see them."

"I would? Ma, I don't know if I'm going to go into private practice, and this isn't really a legal issue anyway. If the hen had been killed, maybe we could get the driver to pay for the dead chicken—"

"Ravine, before you jump to any conclusions, go talk to them. Tomorrow morning, around ten. I'll come by to watch Brady. Now look at the time. I'll be late for bingo if I don't get going." She turned away, then stopped and looked back at me, her eyes soft and kind. "You know, I think it's a really good thing that you cleaned up the house so nice. It's time you got back to living again," she said, and before I could protest that I *was* living, that I had a son who took up all my time, before I could say anything at all, she had gone, and a few seconds later the scent of Lemon Pledge came wafting back on the cool draft from her opening and closing of the front door.

Chapter 4

That night in bed I tossed and turned except for the hours between three thirty and six a.m. when I lay on the mattress flat on my back, wide awake, staring into the darkness toward the ceiling. I didn't know what to do about the genie in the bottle, and throughout the slowly passing hours, no wisdom descended upon me, just more worries: *Was Gene dangerous? Was he telling me the truth? Was he real? Could he really grant three wishes? Make that two wishes. I had already used up one wish on getting new sheets and a few hours' sleep. If Gene's magic was genuine, what should I wish for? Would he leave after he granted the wishes? He was really a good-looking guy. I wonder what it would be like to kiss him . . .*

As soon as the last thought crossed my mind, I sat up as fast as if someone had thrown cold water on me. Whoa! What was I thinking? No! I definitely did not want to make out with Gene. This guy, this genie or Aussie or whatever he was, could complicate my life in so many ways. And the complication I definitely didn't want to deal with was that he was sexy and he made me feel . . . what? Desire. He made me feel like making love with a man and losing myself in the feeling. And *that* was something I never wanted to feel again, not for anyone—and definitely not for a guy who said he had been living in a bottle for over sixty years.

I angrily turned over and punched my pillow into a mound, then buried my face in it. I told myself there was no such thing as a genie, and Gene couldn't possibly be real. I would wake up in the morning and find out it was all a dream. Right?

Wrong. The first thing I did the next morning before Brady woke up was to slip as quietly as possible into the kitchen and carefully open the cabinet door. *Crap!* The amber bottle sat right where I had left it. I could see Gene inside waving at me and pointing at the cork. I shook my head no and slammed the door shut.

Even after two cups of strong black coffee and a shower, I was out of sorts when my mother showed up to take care of Brady. Before she arrived I hid the genie's bottle behind the cereal boxes in the cupboard, ignoring Gene's tapping on the side of the glass while I was doing it. I refused to look at him at all. I shoved the bottle behind the Cheerios. But from the moment I shut the door on him, I began suffering from pangs of guilt for keeping him imprisoned in there, in the dark. And I had no reason to feel guilty, did I?

"You're looking nice today," my mother said.

This morning I had put on a fawn-colored suede skirt with a matching jacket, one I used to wear at my law office. It was the first time in about a year that I hadn't worn maternity clothes or a pair of comfortable jeans. My hair was clean, and I had used the curling iron to give it some body. I made myself a mental note to call Freddi to make an appointment for a good cut. I needed to call Freddi anyway—to impress on her the importance of keeping the genie secret, even from her husband, Bobby.

Despite the weirdness of the last twenty-four hours, I felt pretty doggone good. I was looking forward to the day ahead for a change, not daydreaming and looking backward to a past I could never recapture.

I pulled my Beemer out of the driveway and began the three-mile drive to Jade Meadow Farm. The sun

was out, the sky was blue, the air was cold. As I drove,
I wondered what had made a young Japanese couple
come so far from their home to settle in this rural
community. Perhaps they saw the beauty of the region
the same way I did: the dark green pines that lined
the winding roads; the narrow valleys tucked between
low rounded hills; and the ever-present sound of shal-
low, icy water murmuring over the rocks of the area's
myriad creeks. But as I passed pastures and woods
without seeing a single house, a wave of sadness
washed over me. I wondered how long this beautiful
landscape would be here. Would Brady ever see it or
would the pastures be replaced by ticky-tacky town
houses and condos?

My fears were very real, based on the changes I
had seen in this rural valley. Fast, cheap housing had
transformed the nearby town of Harveys Lake from a
lazy summer boating resort into a crowded, busy sub-
urb. The transformation had started a couple of years
back when a developer bought the Picnic Grounds,
an old amusement park. Now row after row of new
apartments stood where we had once ridden the roller
coaster and merry-go-round.

Around the lake itself, the cottages had disappeared
one by one to be replaced by McMansions. Condos
had gone up next to Grotto's Pizza at the end of the
lake called Sunset Beach. The wealthy newcomers
took over the city council, and soon the original home-
owners could no longer afford the taxes and were
forced to sell out. Long-time residents shook their
heads about it, but nobody had been able to stop it.

On the other hand, Noxen, the object of so many
sneers and snickers, had remained unchanged for the
past hundred years. There was something special and
rare to be treasured in that stability. I looked around
me as I drove. At that moment I was passing a true,
original Noxen institution, Torchy's Bar. Torchy's occupied a decrepit one-story wooden building in the

middle of town, its neon signs for Rolling Rock and Budweiser glowing red behind grimy widows. A hand-written sign saying SUNDAYS WE ARE CLOSED GO AROUND THE BACK was nailed crookedly on the weathered clapboard.

I personally had never set foot in Torchy's. My aunts always spoke of it in voices laden with disapproval: *Did you hear about Percy, Ray's boy? He left Torchy's staggering and the next thing we knew a report came over the police scanner that his car was down the bank with its front end in Bowman's Creek. And do you remember Durlyn Rayce? He spent the whole weekend at Torchy's and drank up his disability check. His poor wife didn't even have money for milk for the children on Monday.*

Without any other kind of recreation available in Noxen—unless you count church suppers—Torchy's had provided beer and a place to drink it for as far back as anyone could remember. Legendary throughout the region for downright seediness, Torchy's was familiar and authentic, and so far had not been bull-dozed and replaced by an Olive Garden restaurant or Outback Steakhouse.

Those were my thoughts that morning before I pulled into the gravel-covered parking area behind the neatly kept, two-story B and B called Jade Meadow Farm. A brisk wind blew through withered cornstalks in the fields surrounding the house. A lone crow appeared as an inky silhouette against the azure sky. When I opened my car door, a flock of fifteen or twenty Rhode Island Reds came running over to greet me, clucking and crowding close to my feet when I got out. I guessed that the chickens were treated more like pets than farm animals. Three nanny goats stood up in their corral on the edge of the parking area and called out with their disturbingly humanlike cry of *maaa maaaa maaa,* vying for my attention.

A slightly built Asian man opened the front door

before I reached it. Dressed in jeans and a sweater, he greeted me with a respectful bow as I entered. Then he indicated where I could take off my shoes. "I am Ken Kato. This is my wife, Mihoko," he said, turning toward a delicate, pretty woman who was coming toward me with small steps and a shy smile. I introduced myself, and we all walked into the great room beyond the entrance hall and sat upon cushions on the floor. Ken and Mihoko kept smiling and nodding at me expectantly.

"Ah, hmmm." I cleared my throat to break the ice. "My mother said you wanted to talk to me?"

Both Ken and Mihoko nodded vigorously. "We would like to hire you," Ken said. "As our lawyer."

"Why? I mean, why do you feel you need a lawyer?"

"We told your mother about our hen. She said we should call you," Ken replied, looking at me hopefully. "We have this for you." He leaned over and put a pale blue rice-paper envelope in my hand. I opened it. Inside was a check made out to me for a hundred dollars. "It is a retainer. For your services," Ken explained. "Okay?"

"Yes, it's fine, but I'm not sure what you are hiring me to do."

Mihoko turned her eyes away from me and I thought I saw tears on her lashes. "Our hen was attacked."

"My mother told me that. She said it was nearly struck by a pickup truck. I'm not sure why you need a lawyer, though," I said.

"I need to explain better, I think," Ken began.

In her light, high voice Mihoko broke in, her words coming fast. "Mishi wasn't even in the road. She was on the lawn. The man in the truck swerved off the asphalt to run her down. We were working outside and saw it. If she hadn't screeched and jumped into the air, he would have killed her deliberately. He left tire marks in the grass and he drove away very fast."

"When did this happen?" I asked.

"Last Saturday," Ken answered.

"Did you get a good look at the man? Can you describe him?"

"Oh yes," Mihoko said, clasping her hands so tightly together that her fingertips had turned pink. "We saw him most clearly. He had a cap on his head and wore a long beard."

"And a dog was riding in the passenger seat. We couldn't see the dog very well, but we could hear him barking," Ken added.

I sighed. At least half the men in Noxen wore long beards, drove pickup trucks, and had dogs riding around with them. "What about the truck? What color was it? Do you know the make or model?"

"It was brown and old," Ken said.

"And very noisy," Mihoko added.

"Was the back of the truck open or did it have a cap on it?"

"It was open."

"Did you get the license number?"

"Oh, we wanted to. We thought of it right away, but the license plate was covered with mud. We couldn't see the number. But we would know the truck because of the picture," Ken said, brightening.

"Picture?"

"Yes. These were tombstones painted on it. They had writing on them, but I couldn't see what they said. They were on the tailgate of the truck," he added.

"That should make the truck easy to find if it's local. But what do you want me to do?"

"We want to find the man," Mihoko said, her voice so low I had to strain to hear her. "To talk to him. What he did was wrong, but maybe he doesn't understand, you know. That animals have feelings too. They have souls. And we want to know why he tried to kill her."

I could only shake my head. These two were total innocents. They didn't realize that hunting was the statewide pastime in Pennsylvania. People who worried about animals' feelings were few and far between. I had no doubt the driver was drunk and trying to hit the hen on purpose—for the fun of killing it. But I didn't say that. I said, "I understand your feelings, but I think the best we can do is to find the driver and ask him to pay to repair the damage to the lawn. That might more effectively deter him from hitting another animal than trying to appeal to his conscience, because he probably doesn't have one. I'm not trying to discourage you, but I still don't see why you need a lawyer."

"We do not explain well, I know." Ken sighed and glanced down at his hands. He looked up at me then, his face earnest. "We do not want to sell our B and B. It is a beautiful house, a beautiful farm. Very good energy. We think trying to hit the hen was to scare us. To make us want to leave."

"Have there been other threats? If there have been, you should call the police, the state police," I said sternly. Noxen was too small to have a police force of its own, and the staties handled crimes and complaints.

A look passed between Mihoko and Ken as if one was warning the other to keep silent. Finally Ken said, "It is hard to say what is a threat and what isn't a threat. It depends on what makes one feel afraid, you understand? Someone complained to the board of health about our inn. We got a notice that they will come for an inspection. It is second time. Last month, same thing. A chicken had wandered into the kitchen when he was there. The inspector threatened to close us down. Then we could not have our retreats. We would have no income. We think . . . we are afraid there will be more complaints. We want you to help us stop it. To find out who is doing this. To stop them.

The negative energy, being afraid, it isn't good for the spirit. You understand?"

I said I did and asked Ken to let me take the notice from the health department with me. I didn't know if the hen incident and the complaints to the health department were connected, but I could see that Ken and Mihoko thought they were. And I knew there was something they weren't telling me. I retrieved my shoes and after we all bowed, I told them I'd be in touch with them soon. The flock of happy hens rushed over and accompanied me back to my car.

As I drove toward home, I had to admit I was taking the attempted hen murder more seriously than I expected. In fact, I had the gut feeling that real trouble was headed Ken and Mihoko's way unless I found out what was going on.

Just then an elusive thought battered like a moth against a window in my mind. I couldn't quite grasp it. I had seen a truck with tombstones painted on it, but I couldn't remember where.

When I arrived in "downtown" Noxen, which consists of a stop sign where the only two roads through town intersect, I pulled into the Pump 'n' Pantry, the twenty-four-hour gas station/convenience store next to the Lutheran church's social hall. When I went in, I brushed by one of the Dallas police officers walking out with a coffee. He nodded and smiled.

Peggy Sue Osterhaupt sat behind the counter watching soap operas on a portable television. Her long, colorless hair hung down lankly, and her face was haggard with fatigue or troubles. Although she wasn't much older than I was, Peggy Sue, a second cousin once removed, seemed to be falling fast without a parachute into middle age. She also didn't have any upper teeth. I never asked what happened to them or why she didn't get implants or wear false teeth. It was none of my business and I figured she'd tell me if she wanted me to know.

"Hey, Peggy Sue," I said while I grabbed a local paper from a rack and brought it to the register.

"Hiya, Ravine," she answered. "Cold out today?"

"Not too bad," I said as we began the ritualized weather conversation everybody in town holds to be polite. "At least it's not snowing."

"Vince on Channel 28 says we got a monster storm coming in this weekend. Din't ya hear? Better get your bread and milk, Ravine. We'll be all sold out by tomorrey."

"Okay, thanks," I answered and grabbed some two-percent milk from the cooler and a loaf of white bread from the shelves. I brought them up to the register, and while she rang up my items, I asked, "Peggy Sue, who-all around here has a brown pickup with tombstones painted on the tailgate?"

"Shoot, Ravine, everybody knows who that is. Your total is four seventy-nine," she said as she put my things in a plastic bag.

I pulled out a five and handed it to her, keeping my voice light as I responded, "I guess I'm not everybody, Peggy Sue, 'cause I don't know. Who is it?"

"It's Scabby Hoyt, a-course."

My hand raking in my change froze. Scabby Hoyt. That wasn't good news at all.

Chapter 5

The best word to describe Alvin, aka "Scabby," Hoyt was *mean*. Scrawny of build, his face pockmarked from adolescent acne and a rampant case of childhood impetigo, Scabby was a binge drinker and a schemer. He was the kind of guy who sat on his front porch with a .22 rifle on his lap hoping a neighbor's dog would wander onto his property so he had an excuse to shoot it. Worse, Scabby had a running feud with the Pattons. It started decades ago when his grandfather Perry Traver had a falling-out with my grandfather Tom Patton, and although they lived within a stone's throw of each other, they never exchanged a word for forty years.

When the cow incident occurred last year, Scabby's inherited dislike of my extended family blossomed into open hostility.

As I had heard it told—several times—the cow incident went something like this. Last summer, Scabby had planted half his fields in sweet corn and the other half in field corn. Come August, his sweet corn started disappearing before he could pick it. He blamed the missing corn on my Aunt Milldred's cows. He swaggered onto her front porch "a-yelling," as they'd say in these parts, threatening that if he ever caught her cows in his field, he'd shoot them.

Aunt Mill came flying out of her front door with a

broom in her hand and whacked him with it four or five times while she told him to get the hell off her porch. In their younger days the Patton girls—there were eight of them in my father's immediate family—had a reputation of being able to "hit like mules," meaning they could use their fists as hard as a mule could kick. Faced with a superior fighting force, Scabby hightailed it out of there. Aunt Mill knew—and so did everybody but Scabby—that his own nephews were stealing the corn after the sun went down and selling it the next day, but Pattons didn't tattle.

A few weeks later, one Saturday around dinnertime, Scabby was driving home from an afternoon of beer drinking at Torchy's when he saw that a herd of cows had broken through a pasture fence. The sweet Jersey cows with their big brown eyes stood placidly in the road in front of my Aunt Mill's farmhouse. Being a mean man, Scabby decided to get his revenge on "those goshdarn cows." He pressed the accelerator to the floor and was going to ram his pickup right into the herd.

Fortunately for the cows, the truck fishtailed, Scabby lost control, and he missed every single cow as he ran off the asphalt road onto the berm. What he did hit was a whole row of roadside mailboxes—about twelve of them altogether, which included his own.

By nightfall, the whole town was laughing and talking about Scabby trying to ram the cows, not because he missed them but because they were actually Scabby's own cows that had gotten out, not Aunt Mill's! Not only did Scabby have to cough up some big bucks to pay for the mailboxes and his DUI citation, but he was also the object of ridicule for weeks. He couldn't step foot out of his pickup without somebody yelling, "Hey Scabby, kill any mailboxes today?" Or, "Hey Scabby, you want me to turn your cows loose so you can play demolition derby?"

Scabby's pockmarked face got redder and redder as the anger built up inside him. He started frequenting the Dew Drop Inn over at Harveys Lake and stayed away from Torchy's for a few weeks until the talk died down. He blamed Aunt Mill and everybody related to her for his own stupidity. I had no doubt Scabby Hoyt would have wanted to run down the Buddhists' hen just for fun, but he was also somebody who'd do anything for a fast dollar. I figured it was time to go talk to him, and I didn't look forward to the encounter.

Having made up my mind to pay Scabby a visit, a plan formed in my mind. Instead of going straight home, I drove out to the Wal-Mart in the nearby town of Tunkhannock and bought a few things.

The big digital clock in front of the bank at Bowman's Creek was flashing 12:00 before I got back to Noxen. When I walked into the kitchen, a wave of warmth greeted me. My mother had started a fire in the old coal stove that sits in the corner and was finishing giving Brady his lunch. I picked my son up in my arms, gave him a kiss and a hug, and asked him if he had missed me. Being a wriggle worm, he was squirming and wanting to get down, so I put him into his ExerSaucer, the new play station that he loves. That got me a big smile. He'd be ready for a nap soon, but meanwhile he was occupied and happy.

I thanked my mother for babysitting and much to her disappointment, I'm sure, I didn't tell her anything except that I had met with the Katos and would try to help them out. Fortunately, considering what I had in mind to do, she said she had a lunch date and quickly gathered up her things.

"A lunch *date*?" I asked.

Her lips pressed together and her cheeks turned a little pink. "Oh, for heaven's sake, Ravine. It's not a date date. Cal and I need to talk . . . to talk about getting a better turnout for bingo nights."

"Ma, you know, if you are dating Cal, I think that's okay," I said. I noticed she was wearing lipstick again and had on a pretty sweater that showed off her curves.

"Whatever gave you such an idea? Me dating Calvin Metz? At my age? Don't be silly." The color in her cheeks deepened. "I'll give you a call tonight," she added and hurried out.

I waited until I heard her pickup back down the driveway before I grabbed my cell phone and called Freddi. She answered on the first ring, and I asked her if she had a minute to talk. She said she had just put Mrs. Boland under the dryer, so to fire away.

"You didn't tell anybody about Gene?" I asked.

"You told me not to," Freddi said, sounding annoyed.

"You're evading the question. Did you say anything, like to Bobby?"

There was a pause—not a good sign. "Ah, not exactly."

"Not exactly? Freddi, what did you say?" I was almost wailing.

"Calm down. I didn't say anything about you finding a genie in a bottle. Bobby would have called nine-one-one and had me hauled away. He already thinks I'm acting nuts because of the hormones I'm taking. I merely said I met a guy at your house, that's all. And ah, hmmm, that I thought you might be seeing somebody."

Oh terrific, I thought. *Bobby will be telling everybody at the Charmin plant.* "Well, do me a favor. Don't say anything else. Chances are Gene will be gone before anybody runs into him."

"Don't count on it. Aunt Clara will find out. You know she will."

"She will not. Not if you don't blab."

"I won't say a word, but remember, I told you so."

"Listen, Freddi, I called up for a reason. You hear anything about Scabby Hoyt lately?"

"Funny you should ask. Zelma Sickler was in for a perm. You know her hair is so thin now, it helps to have some curls. Anyways, she was talking about Scabby."

"What did she say?"

"He's been flashing around some hundred-dollar bills. In fact, he put a down payment on a four-wheeler over at Caddy LaBarr's. Why?"

"I have a hunch about something, that's all."

"Well, watch yourself around him. He's a snake."

"I will. Look, I gotta go. I'm going to let Gene out again." I hesitated. "Do you think I should—let him out, I mean—or what?"

"You know it don't matter what I say you should do. You'll do what you want to anyways. But yeah, let him out. He's the best-looking guy I've seen around here . . . well, in just about ever. Since Bobby got out of the service, anyway. Gene seems sort of military too. I don't know, but whoo-ee, he's sexy."

"He's a genie, Freddi. He's some sort of spirit. Anyway, he's not really a guy."

"If it looks like a duck and walks like a duck. . . . Go for it, Ravine."

"Shut up, Freddi."

"Back at you," she said and we both hung up.

Okay, the moment of truth had arrived. I opened the cupboard doors and pulled out the genie's bottle. I had begun perspiring from the heat in the kitchen and my rapidly escalating nervousness. The amber bottle was cool beneath my hands, and I could hear a steady, insistent tapping coming from inside it.

I hesitated a minute; then I strengthened my resolve and pulled out the cork. White smoke slithered out of the mouth of the bottle, invisible bells made a joyful jingling in the air, and with a *poof,* Gene stood in front of me in the kitchen. Even though this was the third time I had witnessed his materializing from the smoke, the sight still left me amazed. I had no explanation for the phenomenon, but my rational mind couldn't accept that it was actually magic.

What wasn't magical was the scowl on Gene's face. He didn't seem happy to see me. Since I needed to ask him for a favor—not a wish—I decided to turn on whatever charm I could muster.

"And how are you today, Gene?" I said brightly.

"How am I? How would you be? I get a taste of fresh air after sixty-some years, then I end up back in that musty bottle in the pitch-dark for nearly twenty-four hours. I'm getting ready to spit the dummy, to tell the truth." Gene turned away from me then and walked over to stare out the window at the sunlit fields. His back was broad, his waist was narrow, and his posture was straight, but his shoulders sagged a little. I heard him let out a deep sigh. He kept his face toward the window while he said, "I thought a lady like you would have more compassion, that's all."

He definitely had an attitude, and maybe he had a point. I chose my words carefully, using those "I" statements I remembered from psychology class. "Look, Gene, I am really sorry about locking you up. I panicked, that's all. My mother was coming over. I don't know how to explain you. Stashing you behind the cereal boxes was all I could think of on the spur of the moment. I don't blame you for being mad about it. I hear what you're saying to me. You're right. I should have been more . . . more sensitive to your feelings. Let's try to work things out between us about what to do in the future in emergencies—okay?"

Gene turned around. He looked very young. For a moment, lines of sorrow etched his face, but they vanished so quickly that I wondered if they had ever been there. Now a smile played around his lips. He folded his arms across his chest and in a voice as cocky as ever said, "Technically I am your slave, Ravine. You can do *whatever* you want with me."

I thought I detected a suggestive undertone to his statement, but I ignored it. "This is America, Gene. Lincoln freed the slaves. How about a partnership between you and me? As long as you're here," I suggested.

"That would be beaut. As long as I'm here anyway. You still have two wishes to make. Any idea how long you're going to take?"

"Not really. I was hoping I could ask you some questions first." I pulled out a kitchen chair and sat down. "Why don't you come over and sit with me. We can have a cup of coffee and talk it over."

I never saw Gene move, but suddenly he was seated at the table. A mug holding steaming hot coffee sat in front of me; a small plate holding the chocolate chip cookies was next to it. The table in front of him was empty, however. He sat sideways in his chair, draping his arm over its back and stretching his long legs out into the room.

"Nothing for you?" I asked. "Aren't you hungry after living for over sixty years in a bottle?"

"Can't right say I am," he answered and looked at me, his blue eyes twinkling. "I don't have an appetite yet. For food, anyway."

I ignored the hint of lewdness. "I guess I am thinking about your appetite or appetites, Gene. I don't know what a genie needs to exist or what you can and can't do—as far as your magic goes. And I'm wondering if there is any fine print that goes along with the wishes. I mean, are there any strings attached to them?"

"What do you want me to answer first, Ravine? About what I am capable of doing or about the wishes?" he answered me as a shadow of sadness chased across his face again for an instant.

I may not have liked practicing business law very

much, but I had killer instincts when it came to questioning a witness. "Let's start with you, Gene," I began in a serious, remember-you-are-under-oath tone of voice. "First off, are you really alive or are you actually dead, like a ghost?"

Gene shifted in his chair, leaned his elbow on the table, and rested his chin in his hand. "Lady, take a good look. Do I look dead to you?" he said.

He and I were closer together than we had ever been. His eyes were bright and alive, and to prove it, Gene winked at me in that insolent way he had. His lips were full and pink, smooth and inviting. I could smell his breath as he exhaled; its light odor was clean and minty. A stubble of reddish brown beard, a darker shade than his long, sun-bleached hair, covered his chin and his upper lip. His unshaven state was extremely sexy. I was feeling unexpected hungers building deep inside me, but I did my best to ignore them.

"You're going to need a shave soon," I commented.

He rubbed his cheeks with his hands. "You're spot on. I could do with a shower too." Then he reached out his hand toward mine. "May I?" he asked and picked up my fingers with his. A shock of electricity raced up my arm. His hand was big and strong, his grip was warm, and I had no doubt he was very much alive.

"Do I feel dead?" he asked, giving my fingers a gentle squeeze.

"Nooo." My voice had turned into a breathy whisper. I eased my hand out of his. "You feel pretty normal, I guess." Getting hold of my emotions, I hardened my tone and returned to the business at hand.

"All right, part two of my question. What's a genie anyway? A spirit? A demon? I read *Aladdin and the Magic Lamp* when I was a kid, but I figured genies were a myth. You already said you weren't a myth. So what are you?"

Gene was studying me closely. If I could read his

mind, I'd say he was thinking, *Where is she going with this?* After a long pause during which I didn't blink, he answered me: "I guess the best word for what I am is *enchanted*. The caliph, you know, the big boss of the oasis I was in, figured death was too easy for me. He had his magus—that's the magician fellow who worked for him—put a spell on me instead. The magus made me a genie and stuck me in the bottle. I'm not meaning to rush you, but once you finish up your two wishes, the spell will be broken and I'll be free."

"Free? To do what, Gene? Will you be an ordinary man again? And if so, will you be like Dorian Gray and start getting all decrepit and old within minutes? You've been in the bottle for decades, obviously without aging. What's going to happen when the spell is lifted?"

He looked off behind me somewhere after I said that, and his eyes took on that faraway look again. "I don't know. I only know it has to be better than being three inches high and stuck in a bottle for eternity. But after your third wish, I hope I can go back home."

"Back to 1942?" I asked.

He turned his face back to me, pinning me with eyes that for a fleeting moment held both hope and fear. Then he threw his head back and laughed. "Oh bloody hell, I don't know. Maybe I'll be dust I cheated death once out there in the sand. I'll take my bloody chances." Then he stopped and looked at me. "Why do you care? Do you think you'll miss me?"

"No, I won't miss you. Why would I? I simply need to know what I'm dealing with here so I have a sound basis to make some decisions."

"Spoken like a barrister. But you know, little lady, the law is the law and life is life. Yours seems a bit empty, don't you know. I can be good company. I'm handy too—in all sorts of ways. Your house and your life can use some fixing. Maybe what you need is a man."

"Need a *man*. You arrogant, chauvinist p—" I began.

He held up his hands. "Whoa. Lighten up. I was trying to be funny. I like to see that fire come into your eyes."

I wanted to take Brady's bottle and bop him with it. I restrained my urge for violence. "You are not funny. I'm trying to be serious here."

"Okay, Miss Member of the Bar. What's your next question? Would you like to know if I can eat? Drink? Function like a man—in every way?"

Like most red-blooded young guys, Gene seemed to think with his little head as much as with the one on his shoulders. I let out an exasperated sigh. "You are something else. Since you are thinking about sex, evidently a lot, I can safely assume you have retained all your, shall we say, *faculties*. Believe me, I couldn't care less. What I do care about is the issue of the wishes. First off, can I wish for anything at all, or are there restrictions?"

"Restrictions? Not from my end. I'll grant whatever you request. My magic is apparently limitless, or almost. I can't use it to help myself. And of course, I can't resurrect the dead. That's in the hands of a higher power."

I looked at him hard. I had a nagging sensation there was something he wasn't telling me. He kept a poker face and stared right back at me. Being this close to Gene made me tingle. The very air had an electric charge.

I steeled myself not to react and kept my voice steady while I hammered out the words. "But there is a trick to the wishes, isn't there? I remember from old fairy tales that wishes have to be worded exactly or the person wishing can end up with something unintended or suffer from some unexpected consequences, such as . . . Now I'd like to give an example, I'm not wishing for this—all right?"

"Right." He nodded. "This is hypothetical." He blew me a kiss when he thought I wasn't looking.

"I saw that. Stop it."

"Yes, mistress." He didn't sound contrite.

"All right, hypothetically. If I wished never to die, you could grant me immortality, but I'd keep getting older and older until I'd be better off dead. Right?"

"I'm not supposed to give you any hints. But you have the idea."

"And if I wished for a hundred million dollars, *for example,* I'd get the money, but I couldn't spend much of it without having the cops or the Internal Revenue Service swoop down demanding to know where it came from. I could even end up in jail or something, now couldn't I?"

"It's a possibility. Been known to happen. You're smart, Ravine. I think you've caught on. Wishing for money or gold or jewelry never works out. Too many tax problems," Gene said lazily. While I was talking, he had put his hand close to the coffee mug I was holding. Now his fingers were lightly brushing across my knuckles, sending tingles of pleasure up my arm. I gave him a dirty look and pulled my hand away.

"What do you think you're doing? Keep your hands to yourself." My words were as frosty as the November air.

"Aye, aye, mistress. Sorry 'bout that. It's been a long time since I've been this close to a beautiful woman. And as we've discussed, I'm not *dead,* Ravine."

"That's just great. You're not merely a genie, you're a horny genie. So, do you think you are going to be living in my house *and* making passes at me? I don't think so! I think if you want to stay out of that brown bottle, we'd better set some ground rules."

"I have to obey you. That's what genies do . . . obey. Whatever you say goes." Gene smiled and leaned his chin in his hand. "So. What are the Ravine house rules?"

"For starters, don't touch me."

Gene rolled his eyes. "Not only a hysterical mistress, but she's a prude too," he said under his breath.

"I heard that." By now my voice had turned to ice even though I was quickly melting inside. "I'm not looking for a sexual adventure with a genie, so get that straight. I don't even know you, and if I did know you, I don't know if I'd like you, so *back off*!"

"I read you loud and clear," he responded with a sigh. "What are the other rules and regs?"

"Stay out of my bedroom."

His eyebrows rose. His forehead wrinkled. He looked insulted. "I haven't even been *in* your bedroom."

"I want to make it clear, it's off-limits."

"Okay, your bedroom is off-limits. Anything else?"

"About the cleaning and cooking—"

"You want me to stop that too?"

"No! Not at all. I want you to carry on with *that*, Gene," I said and smiled. "Don't forget to do the laundry. And right now I have something else I need your help with. I'm not making a wish, but it's a job— a legal case actually—where I might need some assistance. As my partner, not my slave, okay?"

"An unequal partner, obviously," he answered, "but yes, we agreed on it. What do I have to do?"

"I bought you some clothes. You might want to wear them. It's your decision, not a wish. Do you have any problem with that?"

"No, no problem. These duds from the desert are definitely tatty and getting a bit *ripe,* if you know what I mean." He lifted his arm and sniffed under his armpit. "I don't know if I'm going to like your taste in clothes though," he added.

I handed him the Wal-Mart bag. "This isn't for a fashion show, Gene. Your desert fatigues aren't suited for a Pennsylvania winter. I got you some clean under-wear too. Are you wearing underwear? Wait a minute, don't bother to answer that. You'll also find a pair of blue jeans, a few shirts, a six-pack of socks, and a winter jacket. I guessed at the size; they're all large. I think they'll fit. You could use some new boots too, but I decided it would be better if you tried them on, so I didn't get them this trip."

"I take it we're going out?"

"You're quick, Gene. We are." I explained to him where we were going and what I needed him to do.

Chapter 6

If an ancient RV, sun-faded with rust creeping up the seams, could be called a house, then Scabby had one. The decaying trailer was a step up from a tar-paper shack, but not by much. My Beemer jolted down a dirt driveway filled with ruts. I pulled over onto a patch of weeds and parked out of reach of a frantic Labrador retriever tied to a coop. The dog was barking madly and throwing himself in the air until his chain pulled him cruelly back to earth.

Scabby's pickup wasn't anywhere to be seen, but an old John Deere tractor stood next to an aluminum-sided barn, about fifty yards behind the RV. Some skinny cows had gathered around a pile of hay thrown at the end of an enclosure surrounded by an electric fence.

Gene and I climbed out of my car. The weak November sun slipped behind a distant cloud and gloom descended on Scabby's place. I shivered and hesitated, thinking I should drop this whole crazy idea. Gene looked at me, his eyebrows raised in an unasked question. Suddenly, as if the time were deliberately chosen, the sun broke through, and I watched the light chase toward us across the drab fields, turning them gold. When the world was bright again, I stole another glance at Gene, my stomach churning both with anticipation and excitement.

"I don't think he's home, but let's see," I said.

"It's your party, lady. I'm here for backup," Gene said, but I noticed he was taking a careful look around. When he turned toward the barking dog, he whispered something I couldn't hear, and the dog lay down and put his head on his paws, his body no longer quivering. Gene walked over and talked to him again. The dog wagged his tail and finally Gene scratched his chest. I noticed that a cat was sitting calmly on top of the dog's coop so, true to his breed, the yellow Lab wasn't a vicious dog, simply a vigilant one.

With some difficulty, I took a huge step up onto a "front porch," which was some boards lying across cinder blocks, and opened a storm door that had the top piece of Plexiglas missing. Gene waited on the ground below me. I knocked. No answer. I tried the door handle and it turned. I pushed the door open a foot or so and called out, "Scabby, yoo-hoo! Anybody home?"

Silence greeted me, followed by the acrid smell of stale beer. "He's out," I called over to Gene.

"Brilliant deduction, Sherlock," Gene replied. "Now what?"

"Geez, I don't know. The door isn't locked. Maybe Scabby's lying on the floor unconscious inside and needs help."

Gene's eyes rolled. "You're not thinking of going in?"

"I'm way past thinking about it," I said. "Yell if you see anybody coming." I opened the door wider and stepped into the RV. I didn't know what I was looking for, but I figured I might as well poke around.

The interior of the RV was one room with a waist-high partition between the living area and a double bed. I noted the pile of dirty clothes sitting on the bed's bare sheets and decided to concentrate on the small space that held a recliner, a TV, and a kitchen table between two bench seats. A two-burner stove, a washbasin-sized sink filled with dirty dishes, and an under-the-counter refrigerator took up one wall. I wrinkled my nose at an old pail filled with discarded beer cans. But what quickly drew my attention was a locked gun cabinet. Behind the glass I could see a well-worn .22 caliber rifle and a brand-new Winchester Super Shadow with a fancy scope. That big-game gun was way beyond the means of most country hunters around here. Deer season started the Monday after Thanksgiving, and it looked as if Scabby was ready for it. He must have come into some serious cash to buy this gun.

The only other item of interest was the notepad beside the pink 1970s vintage Princess phone that sat on the kitchen table. On the top sheet I read "Call Joe" above a phone number with a Scranton exchange. It might mean nothing, but I scribbled down the numbers on the back of a grocery receipt I pulled out of my purse. At that moment I heard the dog starting to bark again and Gene's voice calling, "Mayday! Mayday!"

I rushed through the storm door in time to see a brown pickup barreling down the driveway spitting stones. The truck skidded to a stop at the back end of the RV, the tailgate about even with my BMW. Scabby Hoyt came tumbling out of the driver's door and tore ass around the rear of the truck, a baseball bat in his hand.

"Whatcha doin' in my house!" he was screaming. His eyes were wild and fixed on me as he ran toward the front door brandishing the Louisville Slugger. My heart thudded so loud I could hear it. I was thinking about jumping off the porch and making a dash for the Beemer, when Scabby suddenly stumbled, his feet kicking behind him up into the air. He came down hard, flat on his face, a green John Deere cap flying off his head and tumbling into the weeds. I didn't see Gene make a move, but suddenly the genie was standing between me and Scabby. What's more, he was now holding Scabby's baseball bat.

Scabby tried to scramble to his feet, but Gene planted a dusty combat boot right between Scabby's bony shoulder blades and pushed him back down. I hurried over and stood behind Gene.

"Scabby," I said standing on tiptoe and peeking my head over Gene's shoulder. "It's me, Ravine Patton. I have something for you and was bringing it over."

Scabby said something that sounded like, "All you Pattons can go to hell," but since his face was pressed into the dirt I couldn't be sure.

Gene pushed his foot down harder on Scabby's back. "Listen, bud. I don't like your attitude toward my girlfriend here—"

"Girlfriend?" I squeaked.

"We came by to be neighborly. Now you need a little attitude adjustment. You are going to be nice and polite when I let you up, aren't you. What? Louder, I can't hear you." With that Gene gave Scabby a light tap on the head with the bat. "What? Did you say yes? Maybe you better nod your head. Be careful you don't smack into this bat again."

Scabby managed to nod his head a little.

"Good enough," Gene said and removed his foot. "Now let's see your manners."

Scabby pulled himself upright. A streak of dirt crossed his forehead, his little pig-eyes were flashing hate, and his pockmarked face above his scraggly beard had turned crimson. "Whatcha want, Ravine?" he snarled. "Whatcha doin' snooping in my trailer?"

"I wasn't snooping, Scabby, I stepped in to see if you were home. I wanted to give you this." Holding a white envelope, my hand snaked out from behind Gene.

"Whaz this?"

"Your door prize. You won it at bingo last night."

"I weren't at no bingo last night," he said sullenly but took the envelope. He tore it open. A twenty-dollar bill was tucked inside. He looked at it. "Well, maybe I was." Scabby stuffed the twenty into the breast pocket of his buffalo plaid jacket and pulled out a can of chew. He opened the can and stuffed a wad of chewing tobacco behind his lower lip. "Hey-yah," he said, reverting to the way old farmers still talk around Noxen. He spat tobacco juice into the weeds. "Hey-yah." He rocked back on his heels. "Whatcha really want?"

I looked over at Scabby's pickup. Painted on the tailgate were three tombstones, each about a foot high. One tombstone was marked TOM B. 1967 D. 1992. A second read JIMMY B. 1975 D. 2005. The third tombstone was labeled ALVIN B. 1977. D.? Having a tombstone for himself was real creepy, but that's Scabby for you. "I have a question I want to ask you," I said.

He spat another stream of tobacco juice into the dirt. "Yeah?"

"What do those tombstones mean on your truck?"

"Huh? You know. My brother Tom, he went first. A truck tire exploded and hit him in the head. Jim, that damned fool, hung hisself. Doncha remember? The staties pulled him outta the woods. Had to use helicopters to find him."

"I was in Philly then, Scabby. Sorry for your loss. But look, about your truck. You know those Buddhists at the B and B over near the old school?"

"You mean those Japs that moved in?"

"They are Japanese, Scabby. Yes. So you know who I mean. Have you been bothering them?"

"Whatcha mean, bothering them?"

"I mean like running your pickup onto their lawn and trying to hit one of their chickens?" I stepped out from behind Gene, who was watching every move Scabby made.

Scabby spat again. "Weren't me. You want anything

else?" Scabby reached down and picked up his John Deere cap. As he jammed it back on his head, he said, "I got cows to tend."

"Scabby, listen to me," I said in a quiet voice. "If you go near that B and B again, I'll have you arrested. You understand?"

Scabby shot me a look filled with loathing. Then, so quick I saw only a blur, Gene's hand landed on Scabby's shoulder and squeezed it hard. Scabby yelped.

"Do you understand the lady, mate?" Gene's voice sent shivers through me. Scabby's hat flew off his head again, although I didn't feel any wind. The busted storm door on the RV started swinging back and smacking loudly against the siding. The sun disappeared behind another cloud, and the air turned very cold. A look of stark terror crossed Scabby's skinny face, which went from candy apple red to paper white.

"I said, do you understand the lady?" Gene repeated.

"Ye-yes," Scabby said.

"Good. Now, sweetheart, let's go," he said to me.

"Sweetheart?" I squeaked again as Gene took my arm and led me to the Beemer. He opened the car door and practically shoved me inside. Then he appeared in the passenger seat.

"How did you do that?" I asked.

"Just get out of here, Ravine," he said through clenched teeth.

I started the engine and didn't bother turning around. I hightailed it in reverse all the way down the driveway. When I finally screeched out onto the state road, I turned my head for one last look at the old RV. Scabby was standing on the makeshift stoop. His new Winchester Super Shadow was in his hands.

"I'm not your girlfriend," I said to Gene as we drove toward home.

"What was I supposed to call you? My mistress?"

"No! But maybe you could have said *my friend* or something."

"I said what would work with a guy like Scabby. Why knock me when *you* made a mess of things."

"What do you mean? I handled it pretty damned good."

"Oh yeah, you were terrific. You almost got hit with a baseball bat. In another minute Scabby would have shot your car full of holes. If I hadn't been there, you might have got yourself killed."

"I can take care of myself," I huffed.

"Right. I can see that. You're no Sam Spade, that's for sure."

"Who?" I asked.

"The detective in *The Maltese Falcon.*. Don't you go to the films?"

"Maybe I saw it on Turner Classic Movies, I don't remember. It's an old Humphrey Bogart movie, I think."

Gene didn't say anything for a minute. When he finally spoke, I could barely hear him. "*The Maltese Falcon* came out the year before I crashed."

I stole a look at him. It was hard to believe he was last out in the world in 1942; he looked my age. "What year were you born?"

"Nineteen thirteen," he said and looked out the window at the empty fields. "I'll be twenty-nine on my birthday."

"When's that?" I asked lightly, trying to keep the sadness I suddenly felt out of my voice.

"December twenty-fourth. I was born on Christmas Eve. In Melbourne. My da called me his best Christmas present. I bet he's dead by now. I wonder what happened to him . . ." Gene's voice trailed off.

"Do you mind talking about yourself, I mean about your life before—before the enchantment?" I asked.

"No. Yes. I don't know. Better leave it," he answered. I could only see the back of his head. I couldn't tell for sure what he was feeling.

"Can I ask you one more thing?" I said, reaching out and touching his sleeve.

"Go ahead," he answered, still not looking at me.

"Is your name really Gene?"

His head whipped around, and he glared at me with surprise. "Of course it is. Technically it's Eugene, but everybody calls me Gene. My full name is Eugene Hugh O'Neill."

"Eugene O'Neill? That's a famous playwright. You sure you're not making it up?"

"For Pete's sake! O'Neill is a common name. So's Eugene. Why the hell would I lie to you?" he snapped.

"You have to admit that Gene the genie is a little much. And your whole story sounds like fiction, you know."

"Damn it all to hell! I can't show you a driver's license. But you know what? You can write somebody and get my service record. Captain Eugene Hugh O'Neill. I trained in Canada. In the RAF. Go ahead." I swear I could almost see steam coming out of Gene's ears.

"Keep your shirt on," I said. "You can't blame me for being skeptical. Put yourself in my shoes."

Gene stared at me for a minute. Then he did something unexpected. He reached out and pushed a stray strand of hair out of my eyes and gently tucked it behind my ear. I held my breath. It felt so good when his fingers stroked my forehead and trailed across my cheek. "No, I can't blame you," he said. "And you were brave back there, for a girl, that is."

"For a *girl*— I'm not a girl!"

"What did I say? You look like a girl."

"I'm not a *girl*. I'm a mother. I'm a lawyer. I'm a *woman*."

Gene appeared perplexed by my outburst. "I know

you're a woman. But you're young. You're pretty. What's your point?"

I took a deep breath. We were from different generations and different times. "Never mind," I sighed. "Never mind."

Gene's lack of political correctness was soon the least of my problems. After I pulled into my driveway, Gene and I were getting out of the car when I noticed my mother's red pickup inching around the turn from the main road.

Crap, I thought. It was too late to get Gene back in his bottle. I steeled myself. Gene looked at me. I could already hear Freddi's *I told you so.*

I whispered, "Play along."

"Righto," he said, but I felt uneasy about the grin he gave me along with his answer.

My sixty-five-year-old mother, clad in blue jeans, work boots, and a barn coat, exited from her pickup, a large Tupperware bowl in her hands. She took in the scene in front of her: me and a young guy. I could almost see the possible-husband-for-Ravine radar unfolding above her head. Gene and I stood next to each other as she approached. He put his arm around my waist. I'm sure a look of horror crossed my face. Now I knew I was really in for a third degree. I exhaled a deep, long sigh.

"Hi, Ma. I didn't expect to see you again today," I said and stepped away from Gene.

"Obviously," she answered. "I'm Ravine's mother," she said to Gene as she put out her hand. "Clara Patton. You can call me Clara. And you?"

"Gene. Gene O'Neill. Pleased to meet you," he said and stuck out one of his big hands to clasp hers. "Can I carry that for you?" he offered as she struggled to balance the Tupperware. I could see his eyes twinkling. He was really turning on the charm, or the magic. My mother was starting to glow.

"No, but thank you for offering, *Gene,*" she replied, her voice sounding younger all of a sudden.

"Gene is a friend of mine, Ma. A friend. Just a friend."

"A friend from where?" she said, ignoring me and smiling up at Gene.

"Melbourne, ma'am," he said. "Australia."

"Really? All that way, imagine. Do you have a job there?" she asked.

"Ma!" I said, my cheeks starting to burn from embarrassment.

"I'm in the military, ma'am. A pilot in the RAF," Gene said easily.

"You're an officer then?"

"A captain, ma'am."

"You're a career military man?"

"No, ma'am. I'm doing my duty during the war, that's all. I hope to get work for a commercial airline when it's over."

"Hmmmph. With all of them going bankrupt, good luck to you. You'd be better off sticking with the military."

"Really?" Gene said. "I will seriously consider your advice."

My mother beamed. "Thank you very much. It's refreshing that *some* younger people realize that they don't know everything."

My mother was annoying me in the way only my mother can annoy me. I decided to break up this little chat. "Can we go inside? Freddi needs to get home. She's watching Brady."

"Are you staying with Ravine?" My mother ignored me as she went fishing for information like a prosecutor seeing which bait might catch a confession.

"No, he's not," I answered as I strode briskly toward the front door. "He only stopped by on his way to . . . to . . ."

"Actually, I am staying in the area for a while,"

Gene said as we began to walk to the door. "I wanted to spend some time with Ravine before I got called back."

"Really?" my mother said while I shot Gene the dirtiest look I could muster. "Now isn't that nice. You two should come over to dinner."

"That's very kind of you. We'd love to," Gene said. I nearly choked. As we went through the front door, I grabbed his arm and pinched him as hard as I could without my mother seeing it. He didn't flinch.

"Well, how about tomorrow? At six?" She smiled broadly as we all got inside.

"I don't think—" I began to say.

"I'd like that," Gene said. "I haven't had a home-cooked meal in . . . in a very long time."

"Ravine doesn't cook, you know," my mother apologized.

"A pretty woman doesn't need to," he said as I began to sputter, "You . . . you . . ."

"A *mother* needs to," my own mother said, her mouth set in a hard line.

"I can cook!" I said. Gene and my mother looked at each other, suddenly allies.

At that moment, Freddi walked into the living room from the kitchen carrying Brady. She looked at Gene. She looked at my mother. Her head swiveled back and forth. With her mop of red curls she looked like Little Orphan Annie. She looked at me with *I told you so* written all over her face.

"I just introduced my *friend* Gene to my mother," I said quickly.

"Oh. Oh, okay," Freddi said. "Your friend, Gene. Hi, Gene."

"Hi, Freddi," Gene said.

"Brady's ready for his dinner, I think," she said, handing him over, whispering in my ear, "What are you doing!"

"Shhh," I whispered back.

"Freddi Ann, whatever is the matter with you," my mother said. "You seem to have the heebie-jeebies every time I see you. You act as nervous as a turkey at Thanksgiving. Which reminds me, Ravine. Are you still a vegetarian? I had to get that tofu turkey for you last year when you were pregnant."

"No. I mean sort of. Can we discuss this some other time? Freddi, you said you had to go?"

"Huh? Oh yeah. I have to go. Bobby will be home soon." She grabbed her handbag and coat. "Call me later, okay?" she said to me.

"Sure," I said. "Thanks for watching Brady."

"No problem. Bye, Aunt Clara and . . . um, Gene." She backed out of the room staring at him all the way.

"I have to be going too," my mother said and shoved the Tupperware in my direction. "Here. It's piggies. I made them for the church dinner. These were extras. They do have a little meat in them, but you used to love them."

"Thanks. Is that why you stopped by? To give me piggies?" I asked.

"Yes. But also I wanted to tell you to call Peggy Sue Osterhaupt. The number is taped on the Tupperware top."

"Why?"

"She needs your help. Legal help."

"Ma, I'm not practicing law right now. I told you that. She should call somebody local." Brady started squirming in my arms. He looked at Gene and started chanting, "Ba ba ba," and clapped his hands. "Ba ba! Ba ba!" Then he leaned out over my arm.

"May I?" Gene said and took Brady, tucking him under one arm as if he were a football. "Let me get this little bloke a bottle," Gene said. "Is that okay?" he asked me.

"Ah, sure," I said as Gene and Brady headed for the kitchen.

"Such a nice young man," my mother said. "He

could use a shave, but that's the style these days, isn't it? Brady seems to have taken right to him." Then she held me with her eyes like a butterfly stuck with a pin. "About Peggy Sue. She is poor. You know that. She works hard but she can't afford a good lawyer. And she's your cousin."

"She's a distant cousin. I hardly know her." My voice faltered. I could feel the guilt machine springing to life inside me.

"She's my cousin Eunice's child. She is your blood kin. Talk with her. She's desperate. She doesn't know where else to go."

"And you told her to come to me?"

"Not exactly. She said you had stopped in at the Pump 'n' Pantry, and she wanted to know if you were still a lawyer. I said you were, of course. That you had moved back home and that you had quit your job in Philly."

"And?"

"And that you might be taking on some cases here."

"Ma! How could you say that! I'm not!"

"Yes, you are. You're representing Ken and Mihoko. And Peggy Sue needs somebody in her corner. She really does."

"To do what?"

"Let her tell you. Her husband ran off and she has all those kids—"

"Not a domestic case! Ma, you know my field is real estate law." I could feel sweat popping out on my forehead. I hated divorce cases because of the anger and pain that accompanied them. And there were kids involved in this one. If this was a custody dispute—oh, I didn't want to do this. "Ma, I can't—"

"Of course you can. Hear her out, that's all. And it's not really a domestic case. I think it has to do with an accident she had. Or her husband had. Or something like that. Anyway, there's big money involved. I'm asking you to call her. As a favor to me," she said.

What could I say? "Okay. All right, I'll call her," I conceded.

"That's my girl. So I'll see you *and Gene* tomorrow night. Now don't you all forget."

"Not likely," I muttered.

I marched into the kitchen. I pulled the number off the top of the Tupperware lid and stuck it on the counter. Then I put the Tupperware bowl inside the microwave, slammed the door, and stabbed at the number pad. I knew Gene was watching me as he stood behind my son's high chair. Brady looked up and watched me too.

"Why did you do that?" I said.

"Do what?"

"What you did with my mother. Don't play innocent." I turned and stared at him. My heart fluttered. His blue eyes were vivid against his tanned face. He was big. He was gorgeous. He was . . . a frigging genie, for Chrissake. "Why did you make her think we were going out? That we had a relationship? Why did you say we would go there for dinner?"

"Which question do you want me to answer, Counselor? You asked three of them."

"Gene! Stop playing with me. What are you up to? Answer that one."

"You said to play along. I played along. That's all."

I looked at him hard. He returned my stare with a level gaze. I felt my whole body react to him. What was going on? Was he using magic on me? I thought about his putting his arm around my waist. I thought about how I secretly liked it. But I didn't like this, the way I was feeling. It didn't make sense. His being here didn't make sense.

The microwave starting dinging. I turned away and

opened the door. I gingerly took the bowl by the top rim so I didn't burn my fingers. At microwaving I'm an expert.

Without looking at Gene, I said, "Don't."

"Don't? Don't what?"

"Don't play with me. Don't pretend there is something between us that there isn't. What are you trying to do, get me to hurry up and make my wishes, so you can get out of here?"

I turned around then. My son was in Gene's arms, falling asleep on his shoulder. My heart lurched.

"Is that what you think I'm doing? Pushing you to make a wish?" he said.

"Well, isn't it?" I said.

Gene walked over, or rather he moved over somehow, having instantly crossed the room so that he was standing in front of me. He was so close I could smell him, a scent like salt and sunshine, desert sand and a sexy musk odor that was affecting me in a visceral way.

"Let me put Brady to bed, then we'll deal with this, okay?" he said, his voice low.

Suddenly I felt confused. Was Gene trying to seduce me? I didn't understand him, and I certainly didn't understand why my hands were trembling and goose bumps were running up and down my arms. In a flash, Gene and my son were gone, but I could hear him talking to Brady through the baby monitor as he put him down in his crib. I stood there listening. There was so much gentleness in his voice and it sounded as if he sincerely cared. My heart squeezed and tears started in the back of my eyes. Then I heard Gene's voice talking to me.

"Sit down at the table, Ravine. I'll be right there."

I turned around and gasped. My mother's special piggies—a hamburger and rice mixture wrapped in cabbage leaves and cooked in tomato sauce—were artfully laid out on a plate. A fresh salad made of baby romaine lettuce and grape tomatoes sat next to a small carafe of some kind of vinaigrette. A glass of red wine had been poured for me. A glass of water with a slice of lemon stood next to it. Two candles burned in silver candleholders.

A chill washed over me. One thing I shouldn't and couldn't forget. Gene wasn't a man. I didn't know what he was, but he couldn't possibly be real.

Chapter 7

I sat down. A few seconds later the air directly across from me started to sparkle like dust caught in sunlight. With the sound of bells, Gene materialized in the chair on the other side of the table, a grin on his face, the blue work shirt I bought him electrifying the color of his eyes. He looked confident, self-satisfied, and very sexy.

Me, I looked pissed off, an angry cat with her back up about to hiss and spit.

"What did I do?" Gene said.

"I don't know. What did you do? Or more specifically, what are you doing?"

"I think I'm being an excellent genie and by the way, a nice guy," Gene said, leaning back in his chair and folding his arms across his chest.

"Look, this won't do. You can't pretend to be my boyfriend," I said.

"Why not? It provides an explanation for my being here. It's logical. If you were expecting me, your beau from Australia, to visit, it even explains why 'you' suddenly cleaned the house—"

"I don't need any cracks about my housekeeping. It was a little cluttered, that's all. I clean. I don't need you as an excuse."

"Sure, you clean all the time," Gene said. "That's

why there was an unopened electric bill from two months ago behind the refrigerator."

"Who cleans behind the refrigerator?" I said.

"I rest my case," Gene said.

"Let's not get off the subject here. You and I can't be dating, and that's that." I felt funny, sort of weak all over. My mouth was dry. I reached for the wine. Before I could chug it down, its wonderful scents made me stop. I realized this wine definitely wasn't from a box. I held the glass up to the light to appreciate its deep ruby color. I swirled it around. Then I put my nose into the glass and sniffed, detecting bittersweet chocolate and smoke notes. I closed my eyes. I took a sip and noticed a tart acidity that balanced layers of black cherry, boysenberry, and black plum flavors. "A Shiraz," I murmured, and there was no doubt about that. It was a very good Shiraz indeed. For a moment I was back in Philadelphia, reliving the best parts of my old life.

"Australian." Gene nodded, seeing my pleasure. "It's from Greenock, a prime growing area in the Barossa. They've developed some excellent wines Down Under in the last sixty years. I was really surprised by that. Maybe when I get back, I should buy some vineyards and get in on the ground floor."

I set the glass down hard, causing some of that divine elixir to splash up the inside of the glass and drip down the outside, staining the tablecloth a deep purple. "That's the point I was trying to make," I said through clenched teeth.

"I don't follow you," Gene said.

"You are temporary. You aren't staying here. You can't insinuate yourself into my life, into my son's life, when you are going to disappear in the near future. It's wrong."

Gene looked at me for a minute before he responded. "You like me, don't you? You're feeling something for me—and it's scaring you, isn't it? I bet you've kept men at arm's length for a long time. I don't know what happened between you and Brady's father—"

"Nothing happened," I spat out.

Gene's eyes widened. "Well, obviously *something* did."

"I mean we didn't have a relationship. Look, I don't want to talk about it. My past with men has nothing to do with your being here. And Brady's father is not the topic. You are. Look, I'm not stupid—"

"I never implied you were."

"Oh yes you did. You are a total male chauvinist. It's ingrained in you that women can't possibly be as smart as you are. It's what you were taught. Sixty years ago most men thought that. But you can't fool me. I can see that what you have been doing for the last few hours is trying to push me to make my last two wishes, so you can get out of here. That's why you're flirting with me, embarrassing me in front of my mother, trying to push my buttons so I want to hurry up and get you out of my life. So get one thing straight, Mr. Gene the genie. I have two wishes left. They can change my life. They can change Brady's life. And until I make up my mind exactly what they should be, I'm not making them. No matter what you do. Got it?"

"That's what you think I'm doing?" Gene's voice was almost a growl.

"That's what I *know* you're doing," I shot back. Before I knew what was happening Gene was standing next to my chair and pulling me up into his arms. His mouth came down on mine, kissing me with hungry lips that were soft and warm, sending flames shooting through my body.

Involuntarily my lips parted and his arms tightened around me, pressing his body into mine. His tongue darted into my mouth, kissing me deeply. I began to moan, and my eyes flew open. My hand came up and slapped Gene hard. I had never hit a man before. Gene looked at me with a shocked expression.

"Oh!" I said. "I'm sorry. I didn't mean that. I mean I did mean it, but I shouldn't have hit you." I stopped babbling and pulled myself up straight. "You had no right to kiss me."

"You kissed me back," Gene said. He didn't seem mad.

"I did not."

"You have a talent for self-deception, or maybe twisting the facts to suit your case, Miss Barrister Lady. You kissed me. You liked it. It's time you stopped fooling yourself."

I looked at Gene hard. "Maybe I did kiss you. But it's not going to happen again. And in case you think you can convince me otherwise, get back in your bottle." I saw disappointment cross Gene's face before he vanished in a puff of smoke, and I jammed the cork back on his amber glass prison. Then, feeling angry with myself as well as with Gene, I went to bed and realized how empty and lonely it felt being there alone.

I didn't sleep well; I was chased through the night by worries and regret. I woke up with the morning's first light when yellow sunbeams poured like butterscotch through the window next to the bed. Despite the sunshine, I shivered when I climbed out from under the warm covers and my bare feet hit the cold floor. The old-fashioned radiator in this room never got hotter than lukewarm, and the cold leaked through the loose windows on three walls of the generous-sized, L-shaped room. I put on an old bathrobe whose wool was scratchy and smelled faintly of cat. I slipped my feet into well-worn fleece clogs. My hair fell in tangled waves around my shoulders. My eyes were puffy as if I had been crying during the night, and maybe I had.

I caught a glimpse of myself in the mirror. I was no beauty. I looked like a frump most mornings. I never cared about my appearance because nobody ever saw me before noon except Brady. In fact, most days the only visitor I had was my kindly mailman, Tom, whose car with the noisy muffler pulled up to the mailbox around two p.m. Prone to gout and bad knees, he was reaching retirement age, but he was a treasure. He always called out, "How's my girl Ravine today?" and brought a smile to my face.

Now that I thought about it, loneliness had been my constant companion over the past months. I had gone from seeing dozens of people at the office and fighting battles in court to waving at the mailman as the high point of my day. Maybe I had to rethink a lot of things about my life.

I took a quick glance at the genie's conjured-up robe of robin's-egg blue silk that hung in the back of my closet. It was pretty but impractical. During a Pennsylvania November, its silk would feel like cold water on my skin. I made a mental note to remember that some things looked attractive but didn't fit my needs—*some things like Gene,* I added with a mental grimace.

I started for the stairs, and halted. The problem was me, not Gene. I had to stop blaming the genie for my conflicted feelings. I had misused my power by sending him into the bottle last night. It was a Draconian punishment considering the "crime." Now I felt terrible about the whole episode. I had behaved like a teenager and reacted without thinking.

Determined to make amends, I headed downstairs, all the while having a stern talk with myself. I needed to acknowledge that I had a powerful physical attraction to Gene, and I needed to accept that it had nothing to do with him. No doubt my self-imposed celibacy had left me vulnerable to any attractive man—even one who was a genie. I was starved for affection and—okay, I admit it—I was horny. I hadn't been with a man since Jake, and before Jake I had been too busy with my career for a relationship. That meant, to be honest, that I had had one intimate encounter in over two years.

No wonder Gene only had to smile at me to make my heart beat faster. But I bet he wouldn't be smiling this morning. I hurried into the kitchen and grabbed the squat amber bottle off the counter. I could see him inside, sitting with his back to me. I tapped. He refused to turn around. I pulled out the cork. No smoke issued from the bottle's mouth. I tapped the bottle again. Gene still refused to budge.

"Genie, I order you to come out of your bottle. I need to speak with you," I said.

White smoke slowly dribbled out of the bottle's mouth. The once merry tinkle of brass bells now rang in a lower tone, sounding melancholy. The smoke coalesced into Gene's form, and he stood there, his face tight and sullen.

"Your wish is my command," he said flatly, his eyes looking somewhere above my head.

"Look, Gene, I apologize. I was out of line. I was dead wrong to slap you, and it was unconscionable of me to order you into the bottle. I'm asking you to please forgive me." I hoped I sounded contrite, because I was. Gene didn't respond. His rejection of me shot through my heart with a sharp, searing pain.

"Please. I can't take back what I did, but I deeply regret it. I promise never to do it again," I said.

His face softened ever so slightly, but he still didn't look at me as he answered. "It was a paltry, puny, cowardly thing you did. You were a right drongo. I didn't hurt you. I kissed you."

"There are many ways to hurt someone," I whispered. "Playing with my feelings, and my son's feelings, can hurt very much."

Gene looked at me with wounded eyes. "I wasn't playing."

"So why did you kiss me?"

"Are you blind and deaf, woman? You are a beauty. Any man would want to kiss you. I haven't been with a girl in sixty years. I'm a young, healthy bloke. And I'm not dead—not dead in any way, as you well know."

"So that's why?" I said, feeling aggrieved. "You needed a woman and I happened to be handy?"

"By all that's holy and all the saints, Ravine! You are the most impossible woman I have ever met. You twist everything one hundred and eighty degrees opposite to what I mean. Give a bloke a fair go, won't you? I sat in my bottle all night thinking of one thing—you. I mooned about like a lovesick teenager, thinking how headstrong, willful, and brave you are. Thinking how good it felt to have you in my arms . . . how much I wanted to kiss you . . . how much I'll miss you when I go—"

"Do you mean that, really?" I asked.

Suddenly, without my seeing him move, Gene was standing so close in front of me we nearly touched. He lifted my chin so that my eyes and his met. I could see deep within him, into a well of desire that needed to be filled and wanted to be filled by me. His lips came down slowly and took mine softly, as light as a butterfly. Then Gene broke the kiss, leaving me hungry for more.

Something broke open within me. I couldn't keep denying my sexuality. I needed a man, and this man surpassed all my expectations. This man was virile, strong, and kind. This man was gorgeous. My arms went around his neck and I stood on tiptoe. I kissed his cheeks, I kissed his nose. When he closed his eyes and sighed, I kissed each eyelid. Then my lips found his, and I kissed him hard, letting all my yearnings and pent-up hungers loose as I devoured him with a fierce passion that leapt out like a tiger released from its cage.

Gene moaned and held me tight, kissing me back with a ferocity that matched my own. Putting his hands under my armpits, he lifted me up as if I were no heavier than a doll. My arms tightened around his neck. My legs encircled his waist while his hands moved down to cup my ass through my scratchy wool bathrobe. Without my understanding how we moved, we were in the living room, and Gene was putting me down on the sofa, untying the belt of my robe. I had nothing on beneath.

He smiled as he looked at me, running his hand gently from my neck to my breasts as he knelt above me, straddling my hips with his strong legs still clad in his jeans. "You are the most beautiful woman I have ever seen," he whispered. "Your skin is the color of pale peaches and soft as eiderdown. Your breasts," he said as he stroked them with his hands, "take my breath away. You are robbing me of my will, Ravine. I am your servant, not by the rules of enchantment, but by the rules of the heart."

I reveled in the shivery sensations his fingers made as they roamed across my breasts and teased my nipples. Part of me was warning that this was the second-most foolish thing I had ever done. Another part of me was demanding that I continue, telling me that I was a grown woman and I had no other commitments, telling me that I had needs that had gone unmet too long, telling me that this wasn't even real and I should enjoy the dream or whatever it was that was going on. At that point my rational mind broke in again to insist that this was no dream; Gene was by all external evidence a corporeal, living, breathing person, and the act I was about to commit was irrevocable. Nothing could be the same afterward. Was I completely sure I wanted to be intimate with this person about whom I knew so little and understood not at all?

Then, as if by magic, I stopped thinking completely and lost myself in feeling as Gene lay full length, fully clothed, atop me. He kissed me while he took both my hands in his and pressed them against the cushions above my head. He was staring into my eyes, and I watched his face which shone with a radiant light. "I want you," he said. "I want you more than I have ever wanted anything."

"If you want me so much, my genie," I whispered, "you are going to have to take off your clothes."

He grinned, a cocky, happy grin because even as I said the words, he was naked atop me. His body was warm and hard-muscled. His scent was light and musky, still tinged with desert breezes. I raised my head and licked his shoulder. It was salty. My body became warm then, as hot as if the Sahara's sun beat down on us. Gene used his legs to part mine. He was breathing hard. "Do you want me to do this?" Gene asked. "I will stop right now if you tell me to. But I confess, I do have a condom on."

"I guess genies think of everything," I groaned. "Please. Don't. Stop," I said, quivering beneath him, and in one quick, fluid motion he entered me. Gene groaned, the sound coming out low and aching, as he laced his fingers tighter in mine. When he pushed upward into me, I made a sound, somewhere between a scream and a moan. Then we rocked together in a mad, fast coupling, rushing toward release, mindful of nothing but the wild, spiraling ride upward toward fulfillment that I suddenly wanted more than I had realized. I began panting then, faster and faster. Gene covered my mouth with his and kissed me hard as he took one, two, then three long hard thrusts into me before the stars in my mind exploded in a shower of white sparks. I trembled, tightening around him, wanting the pleasure to continue and never end.

Afterward my body was slick and drenched in sweat. Gene let go of my hands and leaned his weight on one elbow. With his free hand, he pushed the damp strands of hair from my face. He lay there and stared into my eyes. We didn't talk; we stayed joined, in the flesh and in the spirit. He stroked my forehead and cheeks.

"You're smiling," he said.

"I am," I said. "So are you."

"We have something to smile about," he said.

"Do we?" I asked.

"Ah, we surely do," he said and kissed me. And I kissed him, and soon we were kissing each other for a long time until I felt him growing hard inside me.

"Should I give you something else to smile about?" he whispered.

"Yes, yes, yes," I murmured. And he did.

I dozed off afterward, falling into a deep and peaceful sleep as if to make up for my troubled night. When my eyes opened again, I smelled food. I also heard no sounds coming from the baby monitor. I bolted off the sofa and went running wild-eyed into the kitchen. My son was sitting in his high chair and Gene was spooning scrambled eggs into his mouth. Brady looked up at me, waving a chubby fist in my direction. It was wrapped around a spoon. "Ma ma ma!" he chanted happily and beat the spoon against the chair's tray. "Gee gee gee gee," he added.

"Gee nah," Gene said to him as he spooned egg into Brady's mouth. "Gene."

Brady shook his head back and forth as egg dribbled out of the corner of his mouth. "Gee gee nah," he crowed happily.

Misgivings flooded over me. When Gene left, what

would my son feel? It wouldn't be good if he became too attached to this genie person. My good mood vanished. For a quick second I felt something like hurt; then I felt mad. Damned mad.

"If you are feeding him what I think you are feeding him, I am going to be really pissed," I growled and reached for the dish in Gene's hand. He pulled it out of reach.

"Whoa! What are you talking about? Babies can eat scrambled eggs."

"Oh yeah, they can eat them. Then they poop them. Do you know how scrambled eggs that turn into poop smell? Do you have any frigging idea? I can't even think about it without retching, you—you—dummy!"

"Hey, keep your britches on. I'll change Brady when the poop hits the fan, so to speak. It's nothing to get upset about."

"That's what you say now," I muttered darkly. "You'll find out."

"Honest, I can handle it. Why don't you eat your breakfast? I made you an omelet with whole wheat toast."

The sound of tiny bells rang merrily. A crystal vase holding a long-stemmed red rose materialized on the table next to a plate holding a perfectly made omelet accompanied by a side order of bacon. Completing the setting was a crystal goblet holding orange juice next to a sturdy mug filled with coffee, black, steaming, and so freshly poured its aroma came floating toward me. My stomach growled. I was starved. I was tempted. "All right," I groused. I sat down and devoured the omelet, saying to Gene between bites, "We need to talk."

"Is *that* what we need to do?" he said and wriggled his eyebrows as he wiped Brady's face with a washcloth. "I have a better idea."

A flash of desire jolted me, but I said evenly, "Yes. We need to *talk*. We have some business to cover." I put down my fork, took a long swig of the coffee, daintily wiped my lips on the damask napkin by my plate, and stood. "But right now I am taking my son upstairs." I lifted Brady out of his high chair. "When I'm done getting him cleaned up and dressed, I will be back—to talk. In the meantime, perhaps you can scrub the kitchen floor and create a few casseroles that I can keep in the freezer."

"Sir, yes, sir," he said and saluted. He was the genie; I was the mistress; somehow we both seemed to be forgetting that. I needed to get busy making up my mind about my remaining two wishes. Keeping Gene around was getting far too complicated. The sooner he was gone the better.

I took my time before coming downstairs again. I played with my son and intentionally dawdled until I was sure I could face Gene with a composed mind and emotions in check. I also needed time to think. An idea was buzzing around in my head. I might have a solution to my unemployment dilemma—and with a little help from a genie, I could make it happen. Finally, around ten, I came downstairs to find my kitchen spotless and enough casseroles packed and labeled to completely fill my freezer.

I put Brady down on the clean floor and opened the bottom cupboard where I kept my cooking pots, which were still in like-new condition. I pulled out a few saucepans and their lids. Brady loved to smack them together and push them around the floor. He also liked to play with Tupperware. He kept himself occupied for ever so long with them. Any toys I bought held his attention for maybe fifteen seconds.

While Brady banged away with a pot lid, Gene was lazily leaning against the counter. The jeans I had bought him rode low on his hips, and he had paired them with a green Henley shirt, open just enough so the golden hairs on his chest peeked out of the top.

My stomach squeezed. Looking at him, even from a distance, did something I did not want to my libido. I shifted my eyes toward the floor and noticed he still wore his desert combat boots.

"I think a trip to the mall is needed to get you some footwear," I said, "unless you can conjure them up and save some time."

"Sorry, lady, my magical powers cannot enrich or enhance my own poor self in any way. I don't know why it works like that, but I suppose if I could fulfill my own wishes, I would have gone home a long time ago."

There it was again. The six-hundred-pound gorilla in the living room. Gene was temporary. He wanted to get out of here. He wanted to go home, and I couldn't blame him. I had to remember that we didn't have a relationship and it wasn't possible for us to have a relationship. As for our lovemaking, we had been two adults enjoying each other, nothing more. We were ships that had passed in the night—well, technically it had happened in the morning, but you get the idea. I could not care about him—I simply couldn't, unless I wanted to end up with a broken heart.

I looked away, pretending I had gotten something caught in my eye as I surreptitiously wiped away a tear. "Of course you would wish to go home." The words stuck in my throat. I coughed. "However, we are going to the mall. Besides the matter of getting you some shoes, I need to enlist your help while I do something about Scabby."

"What about Scabby?" Gene asked.

"I need to find out who he has been working for. Then I might be able to figure out why the Katos are being harassed. I have the phone number I copied down from his notepad, so first off, I'll do a reverse search on the computer."

"On the what?" Gene asked.

"Never mind. I'll show you later; it will be easier than trying to explain it. I also need to make a phone call to my distant cousin Peggy Sue. In other words, I need to put in some time at the office, only I don't have an office and I don't have a babysitter. That's where you come in."

"You want me to take care of Brady while you work?"

"For today. Just this once. Then I'll set up a regular child-care schedule with my mother and Freddi."

"Okay, I don't mind babysitting Brady. I'll watch him anytime you need me to. I used to watch my brother, Mickey. He was a little kid when the war started and I left home. Brady reminds me of him a lot. I wonder . . . Maybe Mickey will still be a kid when I get back. If I get back . . ."

"As a matter of fact, I might be of some help to you with that," I announced. "I am ready, or almost ready, to make my second wish. But I have a question first."

"I'd be surprised if you didn't," Gene said under his breath.

"Can I be very specific about the contents of the wish? I mean, like, if I show you a catalog can you create the things I show you?"

"Absolutely."

"It might be easier if I put it all in writing. Is that allowed?"

"I imagine so. As far as I know, it's not required that you speak the wish. I guess you can write it out."

"Okay, give me a half hour to get it together."

Using the computer, I searched for supplies, reference books, furniture, phones, a new computer, and anything else I could possibly need to set up a fully functioning legal office in the downstairs back bedroom of my farmhouse. I printed out pictures and descriptions and soon had a thick file folder filled with the items. I even remembered curtains for the windows, a sturdy rug, an ergonomic desk chair, and a sign saying RAVINE PATTON, ATTORNEY-AT-LAW to hang on a post in the front yard.

I could use a legal secretary, but I figured if I was successful in attracting clients, I'd hire one. In the meantime I'd handle my own paperwork. Having Gene conjure up an employee would be far too risky. I might end up with a troll or something.

Before I headed back downstairs, I printed out a photo that approximated what I wanted my home office to look like. I was determined to get this wish right.

I went back to the kitchen, my nerves dancing and my heart speeding up. I mentally rehearsed exactly what I had to say in order to make the wish come true exactly the way it should. I got to the door and took a deep breath. Gene was on the floor with Brady; they were playing with some toy trucks that Gene must have produced, because I had never seen them before.

"I'm ready to wish," I announced.

"Wish away," Gene encouraged.

"Not so fast. I need you to hear me out and hear the *entire* wish. Agreed?"

"I live to please you," Gene said and winked. "I thought you'd have figured that out by now. I'll please you when you wish, and I'll please you without having to wish, if you catch my drift."

"I'm being serious here."

"So am I. Believe me, so am I."

"Gene, come on. I need to get this done perfectly. Listen. I put together this folder which contains all the components of a complete home office where I can practice law. These items need to be installed in the back bedroom which is located behind what used to be called the parlor in old farmhouses built like this one. That room even has its own exterior door.

There needs to be a walkway from the driveway to that door and clear signage for clients. May I give you the folder?"

"Hand it over."

"All right, using the information I have provided to you in that folder and the parameters I set forth, I wish for a home office."

"Spoken like a true lawyer," Gene said as he took his hands, showed me they were empty, then like a magician said, "Abracadabra." He made a tossing motion and from his empty hands sparkling confetti flew up into the air. Shards of light spun around the room. Baby Kitty hissed and ran. Brady clapped and laughed. Bells rang gleefully, long and loud. Gene looked at me. "All that didn't have anything to do with granting your wish. I wanted to make it dramatic. Go look at your office, Ravine." A grin stretched wide across his face. I scooped up Brady, sat him on my hip, and went out the kitchen door, across the living room, and stopped at the doorway to my back bedroom. I gasped. The room contained every item in my folder, but it looked nothing like the picture I had included. It was far nicer.

The walls now had white wainscoting. Two beautiful Mary Cassatt reproductions in lovely gold frames hung on the walls. At least I hoped they were reproductions, but a voice in my head suggested they were real. The chairs were upholstered in sky blue; my desk, which was beautiful carved and exactly the right size, appeared to be made of real mahogany. It matched the floor-to-ceiling bookcase behind it. Atop it stood a brand-new computer. Stained glass had replaced the casement windows. Beneath the windows a printer stood on a long counter next to an espresso machine. A small refrigerator with a wooden door was tucked under the counter along with storage units. The floor had been limewashed white, and an oriental rug added bright colors. A blue vase filled with white peonies stood on a side table. The entire effect was bright and impressive. It reflected my taste exactly. Tears sprang to my eyes. I kissed Brady's forehead. His mother had an office.

Then I felt Gene's arms encircling us both from behind. His face was in my hair. "Do you like it?" he murmured.

I nodded, not trusting myself to speak without crying. My knees were growing weak. Gene's arms tightened around me. "You made a good wish," he said. "It will help you build your future, I promise you that. Have I made you happy?"

I nodded again. I managed to say, "You didn't have to do all this."

"Yes, I did," Gene said. "I had to. I'm crazy about you. You are the queen of my heart and I live to please you." He nuzzled my ear. "So have I pleased you?"

"Very much," I sighed. Having his arms around me pleased me too, and it would be so perilous to my emotions to like being held by him too much. I straightened up and pulled away.

"I need you to take Brady again while I work—in my office. I should only be an hour or so." I handed my son to Gene and Brady nestled into his arms. "Gee gee nah," he muttered, his eyelids starting to slide downward. I reached out and took his baby hand and pressed it to my lips. "Love you, Brady boy," I said and as I did, my genie watched me with shining eyes.

Chapter 8

I don't know what I expected when I searched the reverse directory for the source of the phone number I had found in Scabby's trailer. I figured at best it was a long shot, but there was a small chance it would lead me to whoever hired him. When the number turned out to be for London's Salvage and Junkyard, I felt as if I had struck out. Scabby was likely trying to find a part for his truck. I called the number anyway and found out Joe was Jo, a woman with a whiskey-and-cigarettes voice who answered by saying, "Junkyard. This is Joann. What do you want?"

"I'm calling for Alvin Hoyt," I said, improvising. "Did you find what he was looking for?"

"What are you talking about? Who the hell is this?"

"Me? I'm—I'm—you know, a friend of Alvin's."

"Well, 'friend' of Alvin's, you go tell that damned fool that I sure as hell didn't find what he was looking for."

I'm not sure what I said but it had pushed her buttons. I could hear her take a deep draw on her cigarette before she started talking again and when she did, her voice was loud and angry. "Now you listen good. Tell 'Alvin' that he better learn to shut up and be satisfied with what he got already and not go blabbing to his old lady who is no doubt as dumb and greedy as he is. Now don't call here again or you'll get something you sure as shit don't want."

The phone went dead in my hand. Maybe I didn't strike out after all. I took out a file and labeled it "Kato." I put the scrap of paper with the junkyard's number inside it; then I wrote down the conversation with Joann as close as I could remember it. I made a note to take a look at any public records and news articles on London's Salvage and Junkyard. Located right off the interstate, the huge, sprawling junkyard was one of the biggest eyesores in the county. I didn't know what link it could possibly have with Jade Meadow Farm, but there was a connection to Scabby. I figured it was worth taking a closer look.

I took out another file and labeled it "Peggy Sue." I was about to get up to retrieve her number from where I had stuck it on the kitchen counter when my phone rang. I made a mental note to get a second line installed for my law practice, but I answered my home number by saying, "Patton law office, Ravine Patton speaking."

A soft voice said, "Ms. Patton? This is Mihoko. May I talk to you at this moment?"

"Yes, go ahead. How can I help you?"

"We had a—a something happen. Very upsetting."

"What happened?"

"Somebody wrote on our cows."

I paused, squeezed my eyes shut, and pinched the bridge of my nose, trying to get a handle on what Mihoko was actually telling me. I finally asked, "Do you mean like graffiti? Somebody painted graffiti on your cows?"

"Yes, graffiti. Words in spray paint. We are very upset."

"What did they write?"

"Three words, one on each cow. On Miss Milky it said *Out*. On Lulu was *Get*. But the third word on Hilda I don't know."

"Spell it for me."

"H-E-T-H-U-N. Ken looked it up in the dictionary. We can't find *het-hun*."

"Yeah, well, the graffiti artist couldn't spell. I think he was trying for *heathen*. When did this happen?"

"Sometime this morning. The cows stay in the barn all night. Ken lets them out right after daybreak."

"Did Ken see anyone? Did either of you hear anything?"

"The cows were grazing up by the woods. We didn't know anything until they came down for water at the fence. Then Ken saw the words."

"Did you call the police?"

"We don't want trouble, Ms. Patton. Ken is washing the cows. But I am afraid."

"Look, Mihoko. I think you should call the police."

"No, please, you handle it."

"I'll do what I can. I may want to talk with you and Ken tomorrow, but in the meantime, you need to take some precautions. Do you have a pen to write down what I want you to do?"

"Yes, Ms. Patton."

"Okay, first, keep your doors locked." I spoke slowly and paused often so Mihoko could record what I was telling her. "Next, buy and set up a driveway alarm so that you know if anyone pulls in. Third, install security lights, the kind that go on when they detect any motion. Put them by the driveway, in the front and back of the house, and at the barn. Do you understand?"

"Yes. We'll go to the Home Depot and get them right away."

"And one more thing—do you have a dog?"

"No, just the kitty cats."

"Think about getting one. A big one with a loud bark. They're better than cats when you're dealing with rats."

"Rats?"

"Yeah, I'm beginning to think there's a big one involved here."

I put off making the call to Peggy Sue. I needed some time to mull over the situation with Scabby and the Katos, so I decided to take a break and get out of the office. I figured it was the perfect opportunity to run up to the mall with Gene and Brady. If Brady wasn't already asleep, he would be as soon as I put him in the car seat. He always dozed off the minute the car started moving.

Since I did my best thinking on the road, the ride up to JCPenney's at the mall and maybe a drive past London's Junkyard might help me formulate a plan. The fly in the ointment to my drive-to-think scenario might be that I was used to driving solo or with Brady. Traveling with Gene meant I was no longer alone with my thoughts.

Now, with Gene in the passenger seat, Brady in the backseat, and Brady's stroller and baby bag in the trunk, I pulled out of the driveway and headed toward Wilkes-Barre. I hadn't gone more than a few hundred feet when I passed my neighbor Jerry walking his King Charles spaniel. He waved. I waved. Gene waved. Then I spotted Mrs. Henny out getting her mail from the box. She waved. I waved. Gene waved. By the time I had driven the mile from my house to the highway, no fewer than six of my neighbors had seen Gene and me together.

I couldn't have made a more public announcement that I was "seeing someone" if I had put an ad in the *Citizen's Voice* newspaper. The whole town would know about it by nightfall. When Gene left, they'd all be whispering and sending me pitying looks. They'd also be staring at my waistline to see if I had gotten myself "in trouble" before I got dumped . . . again.

This was not how I had ever envisioned my life

turning out. I had seen a future for myself in which I would be rich, urbane, happily married to an equally rich and urbane lawyer, and— That was as far as my vision had ever gotten. My barely articulated goals would have led to an empty, meaningless life. I saw that now. But fate stepped in and put the kibosh on it all. I had been completely and utterly blindsided by events: my sudden passion for Jake, my pregnancy and resignation from the law firm, my return to a backwater town in the boondocks of Pennsylvania, and then single motherhood.

That last situation was the part that haunted me. I had a baby and I didn't have a husband, and it was something that I had always vowed would never happen *to me.* My mother never criticized me about it. She never said a word. She didn't have to. I had heard often enough her despair about her girl students, so bright with promise, who ended up pregnant and trapped in a dead-end life instead of going on to college. For years, my mother had fought with the school board about including birth control and family planning in what we used to call "hygiene classes." Now they were euphemistically called "life skills." But the Bible thumpers of the community protested, said the school was encouraging teens to be sexually active instead of saying no. So teaching about birth control was forbidden. The girls with so much promise ended up on public assistance, and I heard my mother crying more than once, late at night, over the waste of it all.

I know she must have cried for me. Maybe she felt as if she had failed. I hoped that she could see my pregnancy as a kind of divine intervention. It had put an abrupt halt to the direction of my life, which had been leading to nowhere. Getting pregnant smacked me hard with a reality I couldn't ignore. I needed to build a life that mattered. I had to make my life count. I knew that now. In the back of my mind an idea had started to grow, that maybe I was supposed to come back here to Noxen. Maybe this was the place I could make a difference.

But aside from this seedling of an idea, I was still looking through a glass darkly. And now a genie had shown up in my house, again challenging my basic assumptions about life, time, reality, even my spiritual beliefs. I couldn't explain his existence by any kind of reason; I had to accept that Gene existed through magic, mystery, or, perhaps, a miracle. I had had no control over Gene's appearance. I did have total control over his disappearance. In fact, I did not want Brady to grow up with a string of different men in his life. As soon as I decided on my third wish, Gene would be gone and there would be no other man riding around in a car with me unless I found somebody I wanted to marry. With my track record of recent intimate encounters—one with a biker and one with a genie—my chance at finding an acceptable partner seemed highly unlikely. I was better off with no man at all; I was better off single and independent. I sighed and got very quiet as I tried to focus on the traffic.

"Penny for your thoughts," Gene said as I turned off the back road onto the highway.

"Nothing much," I responded disingenuously. "I'm a little worried about the Katos, that's all. Somebody wrote on their cows."

"What are you talking about?"

"Graffiti. It was a threat telling them to get out of town. I'm pretty sure Scabby did it, but who told him to do it? He called them 'heathens.' Scabby hasn't stepped foot in a church since he was a kid. I'd bet he hasn't a clue what a Buddhist is, let alone care whether any moved into town. No, he's too lazy to go buy spray paint and sneak up on some cows unless he was getting something out of it, you know?"

Gene thought for a moment. "You're probably

right. But isn't this something the local constable should handle? You're a lawyer, Ravine, not a detective."

"First off, we don't have constables. The only form of law enforcement we have in this area is the state police. I don't think they'd take an attempt to run over a hen or spraying paint on cows very seriously. They're stretched pretty thin with manpower and this is what we call 'criminal mischief.' They'd pay more attention to kids breaking windows—unless something worse happens."

"Which it could."

"Yeah, I think so, unless I figure out what's really going on. Who wants the Katos to leave and why?"

Somehow, while we were talking, Gene's hand had ended up behind my head. "You're very tense, you know," he said as he began to massage my neck.

"Don't," I said. "I can't concentrate."

"That's good to know," he said and smiled as he moved his hand back to the headrest. "Anyway, about the Katos, somebody could be after their land."

"I don't know about that. There's a lot of farmland around here, so why would anybody go to all this trouble to get theirs?"

"So find out."

"Yeah, I'm going to try. I should talk to them again and see if anybody has made an offer to buy them out. There's a missing piece to this puzzle, and it's one I don't have good feelings about."

Gene was quiet for a minute. "Promise me that you won't do anything risky, like going to talk to Scabby alone."

"Don't worry, I won't. Whatever I do, you can come with me."

"I can't if I'm gone," he said, staring straight ahead out the car window.

A stab of pain shot through me. "Well then, I can't promise you, can I? I'm used to being on my own,

Gene. But yes, I'll be careful. I've got Brady to consider. Don't worry about me."

Gene didn't answer and we didn't talk the rest of the way to the mall.

It was early afternoon on a Friday. The sky was gray and the wind was raw. The parking lot was more empty than full, and the generic buildings of the mall looked forlorn. The Christmas madness hadn't yet gripped otherwise sane people who in a few weeks wouldn't be able to control the desperate feeling that they had to possess the toy du jour or a flat-screen TV.

Today I didn't see another human being as I turned the Beemer into the area by JCPenney's and parked toward the far end of one row. Gene hopped out and retrieved the stroller from the "boot," as he called it. Brady stirred a little when I lowered him into it and made sure he was securely strapped in, but he was more asleep than awake. I went behind the stroller to start pushing just as Gene did the same thing. Our hands touched on the handlebar. A rush of sensation flashed up my arm from the place where Gene's fingers brushed over mine.

"Oh." The sound escaped from my lips before I could stop it.

Then Gene's lips were brushing across mine and I was saying "Oh" again. He kissed me, right there in the mall parking lot. I backed up until I was pressed against the Beemer, but I was kissing him back. I didn't seem to be able to help myself. I turned my head away only with difficulty. "Don't," I said.

"You're not driving now," Gene said into my hair.

"We're in public. In broad daylight. With Brady."

"We're only kissing. There's nobody around. And Brady's asleep."

"But still," I said, ducking my head so I could only see my feet and pushing him back away from me with my hands. "I can't. Not here anyway."

"I can conjure us up a private place. In a blink of an eye. Just say the word."

I looked up into Gene's face. "No. It's not really about the place. We shouldn't, that's all. You're being too forward."

Gene took my face in his hands. "I'm sorry. I can't stop myself when I'm around you. I want to kiss you all the time. Breathe the air you're breathing. Ever since this morning, all I want to do is make love with you. I'm a man being driven mad."

I'd be lying if I said I didn't feel the same way. But that's what I did when I answered Gene. "Sorry to disappoint you, but I'm not being driven mad. I'm perfectly sane and this morning was—well, it was nice. And it was a mistake. Now let's go in the mall." I couldn't look at Gene when I said it. I had moved away from him as I pushed the stroller.

"I don't believe you," he said, walking up behind me. "The air vibrates around you, you are trembling so much. I want you. I can't help that."

I turned an anguished face to Gene. "Don't, please don't. Don't want me, because I can't want you. Can't you see that?"

Gene grabbed my arm and stopped me in my tracks. He turned me to face him and said, "We don't choose our fates, Ravine. We're together. We've been brought together, maybe for a reason. I don't know. But I know what I feel. If you need me to go slower, okay, I'll go slower. If you don't want me to kiss you in public, okay, I won't. But don't ask me to not desire you. I do. I did from the minute I first saw you sitting on the floor after you pulled the cork out of the bottle."

The words made me warm and excited, but I couldn't forget they were only words. I didn't want to get hurt, and caring about a genie who was going to disappear like a puff of smoke brought with it a one hundred percent guarantee that I would end up with a broken heart.

I made my face as blank as I could and looked at him. "You hadn't been with a woman in sixty years. You said so yourself. I could have been an old hag and you would have wanted me. It didn't have anything to do with me. Your desire doesn't have anything to do with me. It's all about you, Gene. Your needs. Not mine. I get your hormones going, that's all. It's practically an insult. Now as I told you before, don't. Don't touch me. Don't kiss me." I disengaged my arm and started walking toward the mall.

Gene didn't move. He stood there in the parking lot.

I turned around to look back at him. "Gene, come on. We need to get going here. You need boots. Let's get them and get this over with. Don't make this harder than it needs to be."

"Don't," he said, mocking. "I do desire you, Ravine. And it has *everything* to do with you."

"You're an impossible man. Can we drop the subject for now? The clock is ticking." And it was, and I knew that only too well.

Despite my resolve to act angry with him, or at least disinterested, Gene's sense of wonder as we went into the mall tickled me.

"Now this is really something," he said, looking around, his head leaning back to see the second level and his eyes staring at the glass elevator that all the kids loved to ride. "Why, there's a waterfall right here inside. And all these stores. Like a town, only all inside a building."

"That's the idea. The sad thing is, what used to be towns are now mostly abandoned buildings. It was the lack of parking mostly that led to malls. Everybody drives." I don't think Gene was listening to me at all. He was headed toward the food court. I pushed Brady faster to keep up. "Don't tell me you're finally hungry," I said.

"I'm right peckish, don't you know. How's this stuff called pizza taste?"

"I can't believe you never had pizza."

"How could I? Nothing like it in the outback. Then I was locked up in that bottle. I never heard of it, but it smells great."

I bought a whole pie—half sausage, half pepperoni—along with a couple of Cokes. Brady must have smelled the food too, because he woke up. I had bought some french fries for him. We sat on white plastic chairs at a little table. I handed Brady a fry. He enjoyed trying to get it into his mouth and mushing it up in his little fist at the same time. Gene devoured most of the pizza as if he hadn't eaten in, well, years.

"That's the best stuff I ever had," he said with a small belch. He didn't bother to apologize about his lack of decorum. He finished off his soda and belched again like a typical guy. "I don't think I can eat another bite. Maybe we can take some home for later?"

"You're a cheap date." I laughed. "Sure, we'll pick up a pie on the way home, or better yet, we'll get one tomorrow night. We're supposed to go to my mother's tonight for dinner, remember." Suddenly I felt uncomfortable. Being with Gene in the mall, having pizza, going to my mother's—it seemed as if we were . . . as if we were . . . a family. I liked the feeling, too much. We *weren't* a family, and pretty soon Gene would be gone.

"You look sad all of a sudden. What's the matter?" Gene asked.

"Nothing. Really. Let's get your boots and get out of here, okay?"

"Okay." Gene shot sideways glances at me as we walked. We didn't do much more talking, but somehow Gene ended up pushing Brady's stroller with one hand. With the other he reached out and took mine and put it on the bar, keeping it covered with his. We walked through the mall to Penney's. Nobody gave us a second glance. We appeared to be a normal couple. I felt inexplicably happy and sad at the same time. I had never done this before. It was a first for me as much as it was for Gene. Since it might never happen again, I didn't want the experience to stop. I didn't say *don't* to Gene again.

We were in the middle of picking out a pair of Red Wing work boots, size eleven, when what I feared might happen, happened.

Gene looked at me with a puzzled expression. "Do you smell sulfur? Wow, it's really strong." He glanced around trying to find the source of the truly noxious odor.

I didn't look around. I stood up and walked directly over to the stroller. I cautiously peeked down the waistband of Brady's pants. I gagged and nearly retched.

Then I shot Gene an angry look. "What you smell is what happens to scrambled eggs when it turns to poop," I said. "Brady needs to be changed, and he needs to be changed right now."

"Don't act so annoyed. I said I'd take care of it."

"You can't. The baby changing station is in the ladies' room, not the men's. I'm stuck with the job."

"No, you're not."

"Yes, I am."

"You're forgetting something," Gene insisted.

"I'm not forgetting anything. Brady's diaper is so stinky that everybody in the store is staring at us. I've got to go change him right now." My voice had taken on a shrill sound.

Gene kissed me on the nose. Then he winked.

"You are not funny," I announced and turned away to push Brady's stroller to the nearest bathroom. My eyes had been nearly tearing from the stench of sulfur-laden air rising from Brady's poopy pants. I was attempting to hold my breath, and I was afraid to look around me. I felt people's accusing eyes on me and Brady. My cheeks burned red with embarrassment. With my lungs starving for air I had to take a breath, and when I gasped, expecting the worst, I smelled not poop, but roses.

I stopped in my tracks. I took a cautious sniff. The air smelled delicious. I checked Brady's diaper. It looked completely clean and unused. Gene, on the other hand, looked smug and self-satisfied. "There are advantages to going out with a genie," he said. "It would serve you well to remember that."

"I'll make a mental note," I answered.

Within a half hour, Gene had his new boots and we were driving back to Noxen. I made a short detour in order to take the interstate instead of the most direct route home. After we drove for a few minutes on that busy highway, the first of acres and acres of decaying cars came into view: London's Salvage and Junkyard. Cars were stacked five high, one on top of another in shaky pillars of crumpled fenders and smashed windshields. In a cleared area, a big crane with a huge hanging magnet on the end picked up a car and dropped it into the crusher, which smashed it into a steel pancake. I couldn't hear the terrible noise it made except in my imagination, but I got chills watching this mechanized destruction.

Throughout the junkyard, rivulets of rusty water made reddish streams across the bare dirt. A squat white building sat near an eight-foot-high wire mesh fence. I figured that was the office where Joann puffed away on her cancer sticks. Shadows crisscrossed the landscape, exaggerating the size of the jagged pieces of metal that had gouged out a permanent scar in the hills. I shuddered. It was an ugly place with an ugly feel. I couldn't even begin to guess what it had to do with the gentle fields and happy animals of Jade Meadow Farm.

Once we got back home, Gene took over the care of Brady again. Before I went into my office, I watched him playing a bouncy game with Brady on his knee and holding his hands.

> Ride a horse to Melbourne,
> Ride a horse to Katherine,
> Watch out, Brady,
> Don't fall in!

Then Gene spread his legs to let Brady fall just the slightest little bit before lifting him by his hands and putting the "horses" back under him. Brady squealed and laughed. They were doing it over and over again while I went into the kitchen to get the adhesive tape with Peggy Sue's phone number and then slipped into my office, shutting the door behind me. I punched in the numbers to call Peggy Sue. The phone rang, but nobody answered, not even one of her kids. Finally a machine picked up and I left a message for her to stop by here around eight a.m. tomorrow before she went to work if that hour was early enough. If not, I asked her to call me and set another time.

I put down the phone receiver and gazed outside the window at the gathering dark. I saw that a fine, light snow had begun to fall. A feathery line of white fanned across the glass before the wind swept it away. I realized that I had forgotten to listen to the weather report. I wondered if the big storm that Peggy Sue had mentioned was due in tonight. My car was not good in the snow even though it had something called "traction control." I generally avoided using my BMW when the weather got bad. I should trade it in for a vehicle with four-wheel drive.

A wave of uneasiness swept through me. I stood up, suddenly agitated and on edge. I hurried into the living room, where I picked up the remote control.

Without thinking about it, I clicked on the TV to get the news.

"Whoa! What is that? Your own cinema?" Gene asked.

"Oh, it's television. You missed the years when it developed and became popular all over the world. It's like radio, only with pictures. But we can play movies on it too, with the DVD player." Gene gave me a totally blank look. He didn't know what the hell I was talking about. "Never mind," I said. "I'll show you the DVD later. Right now I need to get the weather report."

Gene stared mesmerized at the screen as the news team sat behind the storm desk on channel 28, our NBC affiliate. They were big at having "desks" on this station. They had a war desk, a flood desk, a bird flu desk. It cracked me up. Now, sitting proudly at the storm desk, Andy Mehalchik, who looked like Alfalfa of the Little Rascals all grown up, was doing a voice-over of clips showing giant salt trucks out after the big blizzard that hit us last March. In a serious tone he warned that we should all be ready because there was a chance tomorrow's storm, a true nor'easter, could be worse.

I wriggled my way next to Gene on the sofa, and we sat there together, Brady still on Gene's knees as we watched the rest of the local news. In our valley there is so little crime that a holdup of a convenience store is breaking news. Nothing much ever happens here. As a result, two of the stations actually "shared" their news broadcast, so that it didn't matter which you watched in the mornings. NBC and CBS had the same news team and show. When they first started doing that, some lady who had bought a new TV took it back to the store because she thought it wouldn't change the channels. I always thought the arrangement was truly bizarre.

Almost as strange was that they broadcast virtually

the same lineup of stories every night. The news always started out with a spectacular car wreck or a heartbreaking fire. A microphone was shoved into the face of a cop or fireman at the scene. Then the reporter found some bereft family wailing and standing in the street, crying that they had lost everything. After that came an in-depth story on the daily cultural event which always had to do with eating, whether it was St. Kashmir's church bazaar or the Pittston Tomato Festival. The reporter stared into the camera holding food in one hand and took a big bite at the end of the story. At that point, one member of the anchor team asked the reporter to be sure to bring some of the food back to the studio. And at least once a week somebody's beloved pet was lost, or found, or rescued. I don't know why anybody bothered to tune in unless it was to see somebody they knew making a fool of himself, staring into the camera like a deer caught in the headlights.

But Gene thought the entire show was great, even the commercials. In fact, he like the commercials best. Finally it was time for the weather, and I learned that although we were going to get the big storm eventually, tonight's snow should be a light dusting. The heavy snowfall would start tomorrow afternoon and we could get up to a foot or more. The live cam at Wegman's Supermarket zoomed in on mobs of people grabbing at loaves of bread and other staples. Did people really think they wouldn't get out of their homes for days? Around this area, citizens panicked every time snow was predicted. I didn't understand it, but they did.

After the weather I was going to switch off the set, but then I had another idea and got up to put in a DVD of *Walk the Line*. It was Brady's favorite movie. As soon as the action started, he started to keep time to the music, pumping his little fists up and down. My mother said he could keep the beat because when I was pregnant I used that listening program that played Mozart and Gregorian chants. Supposedly a fetus could hear music in the womb. But Brady doesn't react much to the classics. His taste in music runs more to Nirvana and Pearl Jam, Emmylou Harris and the Red Hot Chili Peppers. He occasionally listened to Enya, but he absolutely loved the opening of this movie, where Johnny Cash is going into Folsom Prison to put on that famous concert.

"Looks like a good film," Gene said as he watched.

"It is. I can strap Brady into his chair, and he'll be happy to stare at the screen right to the end. If you'll sit down here with him, I'll go get changed for dinner."

I went to leave the room. Gene caught my hand. "Wait."

"Why?" I said.

He pulled me down onto his lap. "We have an hour before we have to go," he said, putting his arms around me.

"We do. And if you're thinking what I think you're thinking, no. For one thing, Brady is awake."

"I'm a genie, remember? Watch." Gene winked and a shimmering wall or some kind of curtain fell between where Brady was sitting watching the movie and us. "Brady can't see us or hear us, but he won't look for us anyway. If he makes a sudden move or if he needs you, I promise you we'll know at once." He burrowed his face between my breasts. "Brady won't hear us, he'll be safe, and he'll be content."

Suddenly the curtain became opaque and I couldn't see Brady or the TV. Gene and I seemed totally alone in the room.

I put my hands on Gene's shoulders to push him away. Touching him was the worst thing I could have done. I could feel the solidity of him beneath my hands. "Gene, I told you before. I don't want you the way you want me," I said.

"Don't lie, Ravine," he said, inching my sweater up with his hands and undoing my bra. I was weakening fast. My pupils were dilating as I watched what Gene was doing as if hypnotized by him. And indeed I was.

He was speaking in a low, coaxing voice. "I want you. I want *you,* not just any woman. And you want me. Look how your skin is getting all goose bumps. Your nipples are hard. I want to make love to you. I'm begging you. Please, Ravine," he coaxed and lifted my sweater far enough to take my nipple into his mouth.

I inhaled quickly, my breath making a sharp sound. The feeling of his lips shot sparks right down through my belly. But I gathered all my will and pushed his lips away and lowered my sweater.

"Look, you," I said, getting off his lap. "I said *don't* before, and I say *don't* now. Plus, you promised, or at least suggested, that you would slow down. I don't know if I want *any* relationship with you besides that of mistress and genie. Do you understand that?"

Gene sat there studying my face. "Your words are saying one thing and your body is telling me something else," he said softly. "I hear what both parts of you are saying, though. Let me try to make your mind and heart say the same thing."

My legs were a bit shaky as I stood there in proximity to Gene, and we were both much too close to the spot where this morning's lovemaking had happened. "You're not going to accomplish that by coming on to me like a clumsy adolescent," I told him as I refastened my bra and made sure my clothing was in order.

"I have a suggestion," he said.

"What?"

"Let's talk for a while."

"About what?"

"About you. About me. Get to know each other. After all, your mother thinks we have been dating. It would seem funny if I knew nothing about you."

"You have a point," I said and cautiously sat down on the sofa not too close to Gene. The light was dim with the magic curtain closing out the rest of the room. We were enveloped in shadows. "So tell me about yourself."

Gene reached over and took my hand in his. "What do you want to know?"

"I don't know, stuff like where you grew up, how many brothers and sisters you had, what your father did, if you had a girlfriend, or a fiancée, or even a wife—"

"No wife," Gene said.

"But you had a girlfriend?"

"Yes, I did."

"Oh, that's terrific, Gene. So you had a girlfried, yet you were 'boffing' a caliph's wife in the oasis." I didn't mean to get mad, but I surprised myself by sounding angry.

"Aha. You think I'm a dog of a man. That's it, isn't it? Because I was caught in a—shall we say, a compromising position by the caliph, you conclude that I am a Don Juan. Right?"

"What else can I think? You didn't waste any time trying to get into bed with me."

"I didn't get into bed with you. We were on this sofa, and to get technical, I did more than try," he said, grinning.

"That's what I mean! It's 'gather ye rosebuds while ye may' with you. Obviously I made a mistake this morning and I'm not about to repeat it." My face was very flushed and my heart was beating fast. I had been a fool. Why couldn't I have seen that before breakfast? Gene had used me to satisfy his sexual needs. I didn't blame him, exactly. Maybe I had used him too. I jumped up.

"Hold your horses," Gene said and didn't let go of my hand. "Let me tell you my side of the story."

"I think I've heard enough."

"Now, Counselor, you've only listened to the prosecution. The defense gets a turn, isn't that right?"

"I guess," I said. "But I have to shower and change my clothes. Make it fast."

"Come on, sit down. Hear me out." He gently pulled me back down on the sofa. "First of all, when I was caught in flagrante delicto I was very far away from home."

"As you are right now."

"Yes, that's true. Only in the desert—that desert—things were very different."

Gene had been a stranger in a strange land, in a green desert oasis. Within it sat a gleaming white palace made of alabaster decorated with green jasper, yellow topaz, and blue lapis. He said he found it a far stranger land than even this one, in America sixty years in the future. The caliph who ruled the oasis had a troupe of midgets and circus acts who performed for his amusement. Wild tigers roamed the grounds. A favorite pet was a white elephant that had a golden bridle and a silken saddle. And a magus was called upon every day to dazzle the caliph with magic tricks for which Gene could find no explanation.

In that oasis he had met Haidee, who wasn't exactly a wife. She was a young concubine. Haidee lived in the seraglio, the posh part of the caliph's palace where the ladies of the harem lounged about a pool and spent their lives, not really prisoners but not free either. One day as Gene sat thoroughly bored on a bench in a central courtyard, staring off into space and thinking about how he could get back to his squadron, a small door opened. A beautiful young woman dressed in silky pants and wearing a veil stepped through it. She looked around to see if anyone else was nearby. Reassured that Gene was alone, she hurried over and fell on her knees in front of him. She was a tiny creature, maybe standing as high as his chest. The smell of jasmine enveloped him as she took his hands in hers. She unhooked her veil to reveal a face of breathtaking beauty. Her trembling lips were pink and moist. Tears glistened in eyes as soft and brown as a fawn's.

Gene said hello. Haidee said hello back. She could speak a little English, although Gene couldn't say anything in her language.

I felt irrationally jealous as Gene described the young concubine, but I sat silently as he continued.

Despite the language barrier, Gene came to understand that Haidee had been sold to the caliph, who had to be at least fifty years old, when she was thirteen. Although the separation from her parents was difficult, she felt it a great honor to have been chosen to be in the caliph's harem. She lived in luxury and she had only "been with" the caliph a few times since she had arrived two years earlier. This infrequency, however, did not please her at all. She felt slighted by him and unhappy not to be his favorite.

By the time Haidee met Gene she was fifteen, a spoiled, bored, and lonely teenager looking for excitement. She wanted to run away to Bombay to become a movie star. Before she slipped away to return to the seraglio that first afternoon, she convinced Gene to come back and meet her the next day. He did, and every day after that. Their assignations became a routine. Mostly they played cards and backgammon. Mostly. Gene left the details vague, but he admitted they had been intimate and that he enjoyed her "company."

Foremost in Gene's thoughts, however, was to find a way out of the oasis and make it back to his unit. He asked Haidee if she could help. At first she hesitated, saying she didn't dare because the caliph would kill them both if they were caught escaping.

Gene told her he wasn't asking her to escape with him. He wanted to leave, and after all, he wasn't a prisoner. He was a guest, so he wasn't escaping, just leaving. Haidee didn't understand that he was an Australian. Aussies have a can-do attitude and they figure they "can-do" anything. For example, a bomber crew that had crashed near Java decided to build a boat and row back to Australia instead of getting captured by the Japanese. They crossed hundreds of miles of open ocean before they rowed right into the Timor Sea and landed in Darwin.

Even though Gene's squadron had flown out of Malta and there was no way he could return to that island, his plan was to reach the British troops up near Oran, Algeria. He managed to win a camel at cards from the stable guy and some food supplies by playing dice with the cook.

I broke into his story at this point. It was hard enough to hear about his dalliance with Haidee; now I was expected to admire his talent at gambling.

Gene looked at me hard and told me that his war experience had taught him that being a good gambler came in handy. He wanted to know why I was such a prude.

"I was raised a Methodist," I said sourly.

"That explains it," Gene said and unexpectedly kissed me on the cheek. Then he turned my face toward his and kissed me lightly on the mouth.

"We're supposed to be talking," I murmured with his lips still pressed to mine. They felt so soft and enticing. I had to really force myself to break away. "You're presenting your case and trying to convince me you're not a man without morals or scruples. So far you've failed. You've only convinced me that you routinely take advantage of women and like to gamble."

"You're twisting my words again, Ravine," Gene chided.

"Well, go on and talk. It's getting late."

He returned to his tale, talking more quickly and cutting down on his meandering narrative. After winning the camel, Gene stole enough provisions to ride off into the desert during the next moonless night. The sun had slipped down behind the sand dunes, and the sky had turned purple on its way to black. The sand was still warm beneath his feet, but the air was cool. He planned to ride all night and rest during the day. He had just finished tying a goat's bladder filled with water next to his saddlebags when Haidee appeared.

She begged Gene to take her along. He tried to refuse but she cried. Moved by her tears and feeling protective, or maybe guilty because they had been lovers, he put her on the camel and then got on himself. Haidee rode behind him as they began their trek into the endless waste of the Sahara. She put her arms around his waist and snuggled herself as tight next to him as she could get. Gene confessed that they hadn't gotten far when she was doing things with her fingers that distracted him from thinking about where they were heading. He ordered her to stop. She giggled.

Finally Gene pulled the camel to a halt and threatened to take Haidee back to the oasis if she didn't behave. He jumped down and decided to lead the camel for a while, letting her ride and keeping a distance between them at least until he—and she—cooled off. Instead, she slid down the side of the camel and threw herself at Gene. She started kissing him and tearing at his clothes like a little wildcat. Gene wasn't interested in a quick poke and tickle; his priority was to get back to the war. He overpowered her and he was trying to control what had now become a full-blown temper tantrum at his rejection of her when the caliph rode up with a bunch of his men.

"So why didn't the caliph kill you? Kill both of you?" I asked.

Gene explained that the caliph was indeed furious, mostly because he felt Gene had disrespected his hospitality. His men grabbed Gene, yanking his hands behind his back. He was shoved facedown in the sand.

He closed his eyes and began to pray, sure that the sharp edge of a scimitar would be the last thing he felt before the blade chopped off his head. Instead he felt Haidee throw herself on top of him, crying and pleading with the caliph to spare his life. She had plenty of spunk, because she was arguing with the caliph that the entire escapade was all *his* fault for neglecting her. It no doubt helped that she was also immensely beautiful and even as she pleaded with the caliph she was describing to him how she, and she alone, could please him.

The caliph, despite his age and absolute power, was also a man. He forgave Haidee and took her up onto his horse. She wrapped her slender arms around his neck and covered his face with kisses. She really was a very convincing actress. Before they rode off, the caliph ordered his men to have the magus enchant Gene instead of killing him. The wily old man laughed and said that it would be a far worse punishment than a beheading.

As Gene wrapped up his story, he turned to me. "So what am I, Counselor? Guilty as charged? Guilty with an explanation?"

"I think this is a case of nolo contendere."

"Whatever that is."

"It means you neither admit nor deny your guilt. The case is complicated. You're not as bad as the charge makes you seem. You're basically throwing yourself on the mercy of the court."

"And will the court be merciful?" he whispered and took his fingers to turn my face toward his again.

In the dim light, I looked into Gene's eyes, which seemed large and dark. I found no deception there. They were looking at me with tenderness as well as desire. He kissed me then, without urgency, a sweet undemanding kiss.

" 'The quality of mercy is not strain'd,' " I quoted. " 'It droppeth as the gentle rain from heaven upon the place beneath: it is twice bless'd; it blesseth him that gives and him that takes.' "

"Portia's speech from *The Merchant of Venice*. And you are as fair a maiden," Gene murmured as he slipped his tongue into my mouth. I moaned.

"And you have a silver tongue," I managed to say, but only barely, before my voice became another moan.

Gene drew back and looked into my eyes. "My silver tongue is at your beck and call. I want to use it for other things than talking." He kissed me again, his silver tongue doing lovely things in my mouth.

I enjoyed his kissing immensely but finally I sighed and pulled away. "It's late and we have to go soon. I still don't know anything more about your life."

Gene gave me a final kiss on the lips. "Okay," he said. "To be quick. I have a brother, Mickey. I told you about him. I have a sister, Cecilia, two years older than I am. My father is a sheep rancher. My mother teaches school. I grew up on a farm outside of Melbourne—*way* outside of Melbourne. I liked to read and believe it or not, I planned to be a schoolteacher like my ma. I was at graduate school in Canada when the war broke out. I joined the RAF. Once I got a taste of flying, I changed my mind about sitting in a classroom all day. I wanted to fly, and that's pretty much it."

"And what about your girlfriend?"

Gene didn't answer quickly. He turned his head away. After a long moment, he finally said, "She was back in Melbourne. We were supposed to be married when I got back from the war. Her name was Laura."

"And I suppose when you go back home, you still intend to marry her. What are you doing kissing me, Gene Hugh O'Neill, when you have a girlfriend." My voice was quavery and I decided it was time to leave. I had heard enough to realize getting intimate with Gene had been a worse idea than I even guessed. Pain seemed to crawl up into my throat, making it feel tight. I had started to walk away when Gene jumped up and grabbed me, pulling me to him. He looked at me with anguished eyes.

"I *had* a girlfriend. That was sixty years ago. I'm sure she thinks I'm dead. I have no doubt she's married and a grandmother, assuming *she's* still alive."

"But what if you go back, Gene? As soon as I make my third wish, you may be able to pick up the pieces of your life. If you can do that, you're cheating on her. Have you thought about that?"

Gene looked out over my shoulder into the dark of the room. "When I think about Laura, I start to believe that I can't go back. If I did, it would change history. Laura wouldn't marry someone else. She wouldn't have the children and grandchildren she most likely has. And to tell the truth, being with Laura seems like it happened in another lifetime. I miss my family very much. But I honestly don't know if I'll ever see them again. I know they've already mourned me and given me up for dead long ago."

I put my arms around him. "I'm sorry. I really am. You must miss them terribly."

"I do." He moved so that his cheek rested against mine. "Let's not talk about it. Whatever happens is going to happen. And you know, what I care about right now is what is happening between me and you."

A shiver went up my spine. I told myself I didn't care what he was going to say, but I asked, "What is happening between us, Gene?"

"Magic. It has to be magic."

It was then, after Gene confessed he didn't know if he could ever get back home, that I first considered the possibility that my third wish could be to keep Gene with me. Of course, that meant I had to make up my mind that I wanted him to stay, and I wasn't sure I did. Except for the explosive chemistry between us, I didn't know if we had enough in common to be a couple. So as soon as the idea popped into my brain, I pushed it out of my mind. After all, that third wish should be to make life better for Brady and me. Besides, Gene was determined to go back to his family. I had no right to stop him, and he would resent me if I did. I felt ashamed of myself for even thinking it, yet I had thought it. After all, I had the power to make the wish, and I was human enough to want to.

Chapter 9

Snow as fine as sand danced across the windshield as we drove to my mother's later that night. Ribbons of white were snaking across the surface of the road. A light coating of powder was fast covering the grassy berm. The digital thermometer glowing green on the dashboard showed that the temperature had dropped, dipping into the teens and gripping the landscape with an icy fist. I would have rather been curled up in front of the TV eating that pizza that Gene had wanted than out driving in this blustery night. I felt cold inside and out. Gene looked over at me, then started fiddling with the heater control. A weak stream of lukewarm air reached my toes, and I had thawed out a bit by the time we pulled into my mother's driveway.

Appearing through the flakes which were now coming down from the low clouds like flour being sifted, my mother's home was brightly lit, every window glowing with a warm yellow. When we opened the front door and stepped inside, four dogs ran barking to greet us across bare wood floors. Long ago my mother gave up on rugs, saying dog piddle and wool were an unfortunate combination of smells. She also had virtually no upholstered furniture because the cushions became flytraps for animal hair and the arms turned into cat scratching posts.

Instead the house was furnished in the blond wood

and clean lines of the Danish Modern decor which had been popular in the late fifties and early sixties. Today my mother's retro taste was very much in fashion, but that was accidental. Clara Patton, rescuer of strays of both the two- and four-legged variety, was being practical.

Against one wall, tanks filled with tropical fish flashed neon colors and made bubbling sounds. A greenish gray iguana peeked out from under the wood-lathed sofa. Two cats, one white, one black— I'm sure there were many more and I never asked just how many—sat atop a perch near the ceiling and stared with big yellow eyes down upon us. Even though the room was spotlessly clean, the smell of dog-cat-fish-reptile life couldn't be completely erased. It asserted itself boldly along with the pleasant smell of the Yankee "Sugar Cookie" Candle burning on the dining room table.

My mother didn't care what anyone thought. If visitors weren't "animal people," she didn't have much use for them. If they were, they didn't notice—or didn't care—that the house had a zoolike aroma.

I had grown up in this house and to me it was simply home. While I put down a shopping bag filled with empty Tupperware containers and handed over Brady to my mother's open arms, I glanced at Gene to see his reaction. He was talking to the dogs and before I knew it, he was down on the floor letting them sniff his hair as he scratched one fellow's chest. Another went belly-up, waiting his turn for a rub, as a red tongue lolled goofily out of his mouth. Gene was scoring big points with my mother. She nodded at me approvingly and handed Brady back.

"Dinner's ready. I just have to put it on the table," she said. "How was the driving?"

I told her the roads were clear and she told me to be sure to watch the evening news because the big storm scheduled to hit tomorrow had turned into a "weather event," bigger than expected and nearly a blizzard.

I sat Brady on the counter, holding him with one hand while I dipped a piece of celery in some dip. I crunched into it and said between chews, "You know, I think I'm going to see if I can get a practice going. I did specialize in real estate and with all the housing going up, I think a good real estate lawyer might be needed around here. It's worth a try, anyway."

My mother turned off the gas on the range and turned to face me. "Good. We're going to need a lawyer."

"We? Who? Why?"

"Cal Metz and I. We're starting a charter school. The old Dallas middle school hasn't been used for years. We want to buy it."

"I thought you had retired from teaching," I said.

"Actually, I pretty much quit. First the school board eliminated the music department, and you know the band had won national awards. It was one of the best programs in the state. They took the money and built a new football field. When they started talking about teaching 'intelligent design' along with evolution, I knew it was time I left. The whole political climate was driving up my blood pressure."

"And Cal Metz fits into this how?" I said as I handed Brady a Triscuit from a nearby plate. "I think he's teething," I said. "He seems a little feverish."

My mother stopped what she was doing and put her hand on his forehead. "You might be right." She put her finger in his mouth and ran it over his gums. "Some top teeth, I think," she announced. "His gums are hard as rocks." She took a clean washcloth out of the drawer and ran it under the tap water which came from a deep well and didn't ever need refrigerating. Then she handed the cloth to Brady. He immediately stuck it in his mouth and started biting on its coldness.

"That might help. Rub some of that stuff the doctor gave you on his gums before you put him to bed."

"About Cal Metz," I reminded her.

"I've known Cal for twenty years. He's not a talker. He's a doer. We came up with the idea together. We intend to offer young people an alternative, especially kids that the system has already lost."

"Like teenage mothers," I said.

"Of course. But we want more than those girls. We want the students who aren't into sports. Who feel left out and excluded. The charter school will offer the music program the school abandoned. Theater arts. Graphic design. Maybe even culinary arts. A quality writing program. That's for starters. Other 'retired' teachers just like me are already on board. But the legal obstacles are huge, and even getting our hands on the building will be a struggle. Are you with us?"

A fire burned in my mother's eyes. She loved a good fight with a passion nearly equal to her belief in the transformational powers of education. I couldn't say no to her request, and I didn't want to. The school had the potential to change lives and hearts. Maybe this was why fate brought me back here. I told her to count me in.

"We're calling the school Warrior's Path High School. It's named after the famous path used by the Iroquois down near the town of Saxon. Plenty of Native Americans lived here in our valley and the name is symbolic. To embrace art and learning takes courage. The reward is power, the power of the mind. It's the warrior's path, see. We figured the kids would relate to it."

I agreed. As I held Brady on my hip rocking him a little, my mother found some pot holders before she pulled a roasting pan out of the oven. She gave me another long look that I felt was evaluating something inside me. "And I think you're making the right decision by starting a practice out here. A lot of folks in this region need somebody to stand up for them. Too many have already gotten cheated out of their land."

"What do you mean?" I asked, noticing that my shirt was getting wet from Brady's dripping washcloth.

My mother plated a roast chicken and started filling serving bowls with some buttered carrots and her nightly special, mashed potatoes. "Take the Sikorskys over in Buttermilk Hollow; they're pretty close to the Katos," she said while she worked. "Their well got tainted; nobody knows how. They didn't have the money to drill another, so they put their farm up for sale. They didn't get a quarter of what they should have because the EPA said PCBs had even contaminated the creek. What could they do? Half a loaf is better than none, so they sold out and moved down to Florida to live with their daughter. Then the guy who bought their farm had the water tested again. Nothing wrong with it. He turns around and sells the land to a big developer for close to a million dollars. Now there's two hundred condos being built up there. And the Sikorskys aren't the only ones with a story like that."

"Who was the guy that bought their farm?"

"I don't know. I never heard of him. Nobody ever saw him around before or after. Maybe you can find out?"

"Yeah, maybe I can," I said as I walked over to the table and secured Brady in his chair. My shirt was drenched, clearly outlining one breast. I pulled it away from my body and saw that Gene was staring at me as I did it. I flapped the shirt back and forth for a few seconds trying to dry it out. I ignored him, opened the silverware drawer, and started to set the table.

Gene immediately got up off the floor, washed his hands, and helped me. Then we all sat down and wouldn't you know it, Gene said grace. My mother was beaming at him. I wasn't. My heart felt heavy.

She was getting the wrong impression, thinking Gene and I were together in any kind of normal way. This was such a sham.

We talked all through dinner, sticking mostly to discussing classic movies, but even that was dicey because Gene had no references for any films made in the last half of the twentieth century. We managed to get into a rip-roaring argument over which movie director did a better job, Orson Welles with *Citizen Kane* or Alfred Hitchcock with *Rebecca*. I thought Hitchcock was far superior and the only thing Orson Welles could top him in was his waist size. Then we got on the topic of farming and Gene's family in Australia. Crop management had changed since the 1940s, but fortunately my mother belonged to an organic gardening club so the methods Gene's father used seemed right up-to-date.

As for the war, my mother assumed Gene had been flying his plane in the Middle East. He answered her few questions without elaborating and she sensed he didn't want to talk about it.

Gene and Brady had seconds of the mashed potatoes. When everybody's plate was clean, my mother served us all lemon meringue pie. Gene raved about it and then asked if he could do the dishes. Score two more points.

My mother said no, that she and I would do them. She suggested that Gene and Brady could watch television in the living room. Gene's face lit up. I knew he was dying to spend more time exploring what he considered an astonishing invention and seeing what it could do. The four dogs, and I think the iguana, went with them into the living room. My mother and I ended up at the sink.

"So?" my mother asked. "Is it serious?"

I rolled my eyes. "No. Gene is visiting, that's all. He won't be around very long."

"I wouldn't count on that," she said.

"Really, Ma. Gene's only going to be here a few days. He wants to get home to Australia. We're old friends, that's all."

Her eyebrows shot up. "Is that what he thinks you are? A friend?"

"Of course."

"I don't think so. He's in love with you."

My heart stopped. "What? No. Absolutely not. He's not. Why would you even say that?" I sputtered.

"He doesn't take his eyes off you, Ravine. He watches every move you make. He looks at you the way your father looked at me, like you are the most fascinating creature to ever walk the face of the earth. I know that look well. He laughs at your jokes, and Ravine, you're not funny."

"I'm very witty."

"*He* thinks you are. And he wants me to like him. He cares about whether I like him or not. He is crazy about Brady. He's still quite a young man, but I think he's going to ask you to marry him."

"He is not. I can guarantee it. He is not going to ask me to marry him."

"How can you be so sure? If ever I saw a man ready to settle down and have a family, it's that one. I know what I'm talking about. I know when I'm right," she said and began to vigorously scrub the roaster pan. She didn't believe in no-stick cookware so it took a major effort. I could tell from the way she was doing it that she was getting agitated.

So was I. Once again she was pushing my buttons. I snapped at her. "You might know when you're right, but this time you've got it all wrong. Gene's not in love with me. And he is never going to settle down with me and Brady. Gene's family lives in Australia. He misses them terribly. I can say with complete certainty, he is not going to stay in the US."

She looked over at me, her hands in sudsy water,

and said in an unexpectedly soft voice, "So would you go with him to Australia if he asked you to?"

I felt as if a dagger were stuck in my heart. "That's impossible. Trust me, it's completely impossible for me to go with Gene. He is a nice guy, Ma. He's just not the right guy for me."

"Are you sure? How do you feel about him?" she demanded.

I was shocked by my mother's question. She has never asked me about my feelings, ever. I didn't know what to say. I stared at her.

"You care about him, don't you. You were looking at him the same way he was looking at you. Ravine, don't fool yourself. If being with him means moving to Australia, you should consider it. I think he's the one."

The blood drained from my face, I'm sure. It would be my luck if "the one" for me was a ninety-year-old genie. I knew how to mess up my life, I guess. I was getting really good at it. "I can't go with Gene to Australia, Ma. I really can't. And he's not able to stay here. It's not going to work out."

My mother got very busy scrubbing the sink with cleanser. Finally she rinsed it out and put down the sponge. She turned her body so she was facing me. "Ravine, I have never interfered in your life. Maybe I should have, but it's not my way. Now I think I better speak my mind. You can't always run away from your feelings. I guess you are scared of love or afraid of being hurt. Maybe because your father died. I don't know. If that hadn't happened, maybe Brady's father would be around instead of being a ghost you don't talk about. No, don't interrupt. I'm not asking about him. But Gene is a good man. And Ravine, it's pretty obvious you two are sleeping together—"

"Ma! I mean—"

"For heaven's sake, don't look so shocked. I've

worked with high school students for thirty years. They don't hide what's going on any better than you two do. I'm not judging you. I'm merely saying, try not to mess this up. Things can't always be all your way. You have to compromise when you really love somebody. You have to work things out together. I think that man would try to move mountains for you. Give him a chance. That's all I'm saying."

Tears sprang into my eyes. "Oh Ma, you are so wrong about Gene. He's not simply a pilot. He's—"

Just then the phone shrilled. My mother reached out and answered it before I could blurt out the truth.

"Yes," she said into the receiver. "Yes, she's here. I'll tell her. How bad is it? Okay, she'll get there right away." She hung up. Her voice was brisk but calm when she spoke to me. "Now don't get all upset, Ravine. But you have to go right home."

"Why?" I asked, my heart racing. "What's wrong?"

"There's a fire at your house."

"A fire! Oh my God. Gene!" I screamed and went running toward the living room, and he suddenly appeared at the door with Brady in his arms.

"Gene! We have to get home. There's a fire." I was grabbing Brady's coat and getting him into it.

Gene looked over at my mother. "How bad is it?"

"I don't know," she said. "That was Jerry, her neighbor. He said the Kunkle fire department's there, and that's all he knew."

"It must be that coal stove. I knew it. I knew it," I was saying. "I should have had the chimney cleaned."

"You didn't have the stove lit today," Gene reminded me.

"Yes, you're right. So I don't know. What else can it be? Let's go," I urged frantically as we dashed into the night.

"Drive safely!" my mother called out the door after us. "It won't help if you crack up the car!"

I was backing down the driveway when Gene said in a calm, even voice, "Get out of sight of the house and stop the car."

"Why?" I said, my voice trembling. I didn't want to stop. I wanted to get home.

"I'll get us home."

"Maybe you should drive. My hands are shaking," I said as I pulled off the side of the road and stopped the car. I took the keys out of the ignition and handed them to him.

He wasn't smiling, but he did wink at me. I heard the merry sound of bells and suddenly we weren't four miles away at my mother's; we were on the side of the road in front of my house. I looked at Gene quickly and whispered thanks before I opened the door and went running up the lawn. I slipped and skidded on the snow-covered grass beneath my feet. As I got closer, I could see that my house was still standing and I didn't see any flames. I let out a sigh of relief. Maybe it wasn't as bad as I had feared.

I hurried over to the fire chief. "What happened?" I cried. "Is my house on fire?"

"Calm down there, Ms. Patton. Your house is okay, but somebody sure as shooting tried to burn it down."

"What do you mean? What do you mean?" I was practically shrieking. Gene walked up behind me, holding Brady. He put his arm around my shoulders.

"Somebody poured gasoline all around the outside of your house, lit it, and tore out of here. Your neighbor Jerry Moore and his friend David saw a pickup truck racing down the road. It almost hit one of those peacocks of his. Good thing too, because Jerry looked over and saw flames. He called it in."

"But my house is okay?"

"Yeah, it never caught fire. You were lucky it's snowing. The heat melted the snow and made the grass wet. The house didn't catch, and besides that the guy didn't bring enough gas to do much more than dribble a thin stream. He didn't get it close enough to the siding either. You had a really dumb arsonist or you wouldn't have a house. The gasoline fire had pretty much burned itself out by the time we got here. The fire marshal will want to talk with you tomorrow though. You got any enemies, Ravine?"

I nodded. All I could think was, *Scabby Hoyt.*

Gene said he'd stay downstairs and keep watch during the night. I asked him if he needed a pillow and some sheets for the couch. He said no, he'd duck into his bottle if he wanted some rest. I wasn't going to put the cork back in it if he did, now was I?

I gave him a dirty look. I still felt guilty about doing that the other night. I tucked Brady into his crib, taking the time to read to him for a couple of minutes and sing him his favorite lullaby. He usually liked to listen to a CD while he fell asleep, so I held out a couple of jewel cases and let him grab one. I don't think he really picked any particular album on purpose; it was more a random choice, but tonight he latched on to Cowboy Junkies' *Lay It Down.* I put it in the player and as I kissed him good night the first track began to play. It was "Something More Besides You." My throat got tight; I couldn't bear to listen to it.

When I slipped into my own bed, sleep wouldn't come although tiredness had seeped into my bones. I tossed and turned thinking the same thoughts in a Möbius strip of repetition: *My mother thinks Gene loves me. Gene had a girlfriend back in Australia. He's going to marry her if he gets back there. He made love to me. He's going to leave me. I'm so dumb. No, I'm not dumb, I'm easy. Yes, I am dumb. I really care about him. He's not even a real guy. He's a genie. He lives in a bottle. Genies aren't real. Gene is real.*

I didn't understand it. And he was going to leave me. I couldn't get past that. Even if he did love me—

and I only had my mother's word for that—he was going to leave.

I punched my pillow. I felt mad and sad at the same time. Plus I kept berating myself for underestimating Scabby. I knew he hated the Pattons, but I hadn't believed he'd go as far as setting my house on fire. My stupidity could have endangered my son and cost me my home. I was finished with it. I'd tell the fire marshal what I knew and maybe he'd get Scabby arrested on an arson charge. Scabby was so dumb he probably still had the gasoline cans in the back of his truck.

Having made a decision, I felt a little better and finally dozed off around four a.m. For the next few hours, I slept the sleep of the innocent—and the ignorant, because I was dead wrong.

When I finally managed to pry my eyes open the next morning, I felt like a steamroller had run me over in the night. I ached everywhere. My face was puffy. I felt fat. I figured I was getting the worst case of PMS in the history of the entire universe. I made my way downstairs with my eyes barely open. I was operating on three hours' sleep. Along with the adrenaline jolt of last night, I suspected that my surging hormones were the reason there was a hammer beating on my skull from the inside out.

I entered the kitchen and made a beeline for the Mr. Coffee machine. The contents of the carafe were fresh-brewed, strong, and hot. I couldn't find anything to complain about. I stared at the wall as I gulped down half a cup of Morning Blend. Then I took a deep breath and turned around.

Of course, I had noticed that Gene was feeding Brady before I reached the coffee machine. I just hadn't acknowledged him. Some mornings I didn't want to talk to anyone. This was one of them. I made no excuses for my grouchiness. Among other things, I was an owl, not a lark.

"Hello, Miss Merry Sunshine," Gene said, saluting me with a spoon filled with rice cereal.

"Why are you feeding my son?" I grumped.

"Because he was hungry. Because I thought you'd get to sleep another half hour if I did. Because I'm really a nice guy."

"He's getting too attached to you. I don't want him grieving when you disappear. I'll feed him from now on. Got it?"

Gene looked taken aback. "Got it," he said. "Anything else you want to blame on me this morning? Your bad hair day?"

"What's wrong with my hair?" I put a hand up to find it felt like a bird's nest stuck to the side of my head.

"Or maybe it's my fault it's snowing."

"It's snowing? It didn't stop? The monster storm wasn't supposed to hit until this afternoon. Oh crap. Double crap. Triple crap." I made my way to the kitchen window. The world outside was white. The sky was white, the ground was white, the air was white. "We don't usually get our first big snowfall until after Christmas. It looks as if there's a couple of inches out there already," I said more to myself than to Gene.

"Maybe three inches. Or at least there was when I cleaned off the walk and shoveled the driveway. The snowplow already went by. The road doesn't look too bad. Your appointment should be able to get here."

I squeezed my eyes shut. "Oh sweet Lord. Peggy Sue." My eyes popped open as I glanced over at the clock on the microwave. "What time is it? Geez, it's already seven thirty. I need to take a shower. I have to get dressed. I need to get Brady dressed. I'll never have time—" I stopped talking and looked at Gene.

"Uh, do you think you can change Brady's diaper and give him a bath?"

"What happened to 'He's getting too attached to you'?"

"Oh shut up, Gene. Genie. Whoever the hell you are. I've got a lot on my mind. Scabby Hoyt tried to burn down my house. I have to figure out a way to support myself and my son. And—and—I had sex with you! Then I found out you have a girlfriend!" I stomped out of the kitchen but I could hear Gene say to Brady as I started up the stairs, "Women! I can't understand them, do you?"

Brady sang out at the top of his lungs, "Ma ma ma!"

Chapter 10

Despite the dreadful weather, Peggy Sue rapped at the side door that led to my new office precisely at eight a.m. She had on an old down jacket and plastic boots. Her hair and her eyes appeared equally lifeless, her upper lip sank back because of her missing uppers, and her stooping shoulders conveyed an overall impression of a woman who was close to giving up.

"You fixed this room up real nice," she said, looking around.

"Thanks. Take off your coat, Peggy Sue. You're all wet. Let me hang it up for you. Sit right there on that blue chair. Can I get you some coffee?"

"Don't go to no trouble for me. I can get a cup when I get to the Pump 'n' Pantry."

Once I took Peggy Sue's coat, I could see that her collarbones jutted out above a "Made in America" T-shirt. Her arms were skinny and her jeans hung on her hips. Maybe she hadn't been eating. I didn't remember her being this thin.

"It's no trouble, Peggy Sue. I have a refrigerator and coffeemaker right in here under this side counter. I need a cup myself. I won't feel right if you don't have one."

I poured out two cups. I kept mine black, but I put extra cream and sugar in Peggy Sue's, which is how most farm people drink it around here. I didn't ask; I handed her a big mug. She took a sip.

"Good coffee, Ravine. I 'preciate it. And I 'preciate you seeing me."

I usually don't like having a desk between me and the person coming to see me, so I sat down in the chair next to hers. I leaned toward Peggy Sue. "Okay, tell me how I can help you."

"I sure hope you can, because I don't know how much longer I can go on like this," she said and a tear slipped out of her eye and ran down her hollow cheek. Unhappiness was rolling over her like the tide coming in. "I'm working two jobs and there still ain't enough money to take care of my kids. I'm afraid I may lose my house. I thought my troubles were over when that insurance company settled, but things got a passel worser."

"Start at the beginning, Peggy Sue," I urged. "What was the insurance company settling about?"

"The accident, the one where my teeth got knocked out two years ago. A tractor trailer hit my car. I was on my way to my job at Offset—I work the night shift—when this guy plowed into me nearly head-on. He fell asleep at the wheel and crossed right over into my lane. Don't know why I wasn't killed, but I guess the good Lord don't want me yet. I got a big scar where my head split open." Peggy Sue turned her head and parted her lank hair with her fingers. An ugly scar ran from the top of her head right down the back of her neck. "I get fearsome headaches all the time."

"So how much did the company settle for?"

"Eighty-eight thousand two hundred dollars and twenty-nine cents. Do you believe how much? I kept thinking I could quit my job at Offset and open a day care right at my house. I'm real good with kids. My husband, John, don't work. He can, but he don't. He's collecting unemployment and soon as his check comes he's over at Torchy's. I wanted to use that insurance money to put an addition on the house for the day care. It would have a bathroom and kitchenette. Everything. I'd still have plenty left to put away for my kids. I had it all figured out."

"So what happened?"

"I signed the check and deposited it in our account over there at the bank in Bowman's Creek. Afterwards John, me and the kids went to Vic-Mar's Seafood House down in Plymouth, you know, and celebrated. I never suspected a thing, no I didn't. That lying polecat no-good sonabitch went back to the bank the next day and withdrew the money. He's up in New York State with some young tramp."

"When did this happen?" I said, thinking there was a good chance that the money had already been spent.

"Two weeks ago. Mary Ann, the teller from the bank, she's a neighbor. She called me as soon as John walked out that door. Yes she did. But it was too late. I didn't know where he went. Finally his mother told me he called her and where I could find him. Even she knows he's no damned good." Anger gave her eyes some life.

"Do you have an address for him?"

"I sure do." She opened up a plastic handbag and took out a sheet of paper. She handed it to me. Her husband was at Happy Trails RV Park up near Binghamton, New York.

"Can you get me the money back, Ravine? It's mine, hain'a or no?"

I started to explain without getting too technical that Pennsylvania was a community property state, where a husband and wife held assets jointly. But that didn't apply to all assets, and in this case the insurance money was Peggy Sue's. Could I get it back? I didn't know. I asked Peggy Sue if she wanted John back.

She practically jumped out of her chair. "Hell no!

I want me a divorce. But I need that money for my kids."

I told her I'd draw up a divorce petition and file it on Monday. I also explained that since her husband had fled the area, I could file an injunction to stop him from spending the money, but I'm not sure if Peggy Sue was following me. She didn't look reassured.

"I guess them's good ideas. But it sounds to me like getting my money back is gonna take a long time."

"It might. The money might have to go into escrow."

Again Peggy Sue looked at me without understanding.

"You're right," I said. "It takes a while for things to happen in the legal system."

Peggy Sue was staring at me with haunted eyes. "What am I going to do? I don't even have the money to pay you, Ravine, until I get that money back. I don't have a red cent. I'm real sorry. Will you still help me?"

I let out a deep sigh. I didn't have much more in the bank than Peggy Sue did. "Yes, sure. I'll help you." Then I had an idea. "Look, maybe I can find some other way to get the money back from John. It would help us both."

"Your mother said you'd come up with something. She said you're real smart, Ravine."

I looked at Peggy Sue again, sitting there fragile in body and spirit, beaten down by life. She had been one of the girls my mother lost, one who had gotten pregnant and never had a chance. Sometimes you don't know what you've got until you see somebody who has a whole lot less. I replied to Peggy Sue from my heart. "Thanks for the compliment, but I need you to be real smart too. If you get sick—and it looks like the next stiff wind is going to blow you over—you're not going to be able to work or take care of your kids. You have to stop working at Pump 'n' Pantry."

"I know that," she said, reaching for a Kleenex from the box on the edge of my desk. "I'm so tired I can't see straight. But I can't make it without the extra money." She blew her nose. Her shoulders sagged even more.

"Let's compromise then. The weather's getting so bad that the convenience store isn't going to have much business today anyway. I want you to go home and call in. Tell them you can't make it to work. Do the same thing tomorrow. Stay home this weekend and get some rest. Will you do that for me? Give me your word on it."

I could see Peggy Sue arguing with herself mentally about her pay, which, if I guessed right, couldn't be more than forty dollars. "Peggy Sue," I broke in, "trust me. It will be all right. Trust in the good Lord to provide, will you?" I'm not a religious person but I'll bring in the big guns when I need to.

I could tell she wasn't convinced, but she said, "All right, I promise."

I spent another half hour with her filling out information so I could file her divorce papers first thing on Monday. Then, after I glanced out the window and saw that the weather had worsened, I told her to get herself home. I promised to call her on Monday and give her an update. If things worked out as I planned, I might have something more tangible for her than just news. I told her to keep thinking good thoughts.

Peggy Sue looked at me and nodded. Hope had crept into her eyes and a new spark of life had put the palest of pinks into her wan cheeks.

"Women rule!" I said and high-fived her. It was an act of bravado. I couldn't let her down.

As soon as she was out the door, I hurried into the living room where Brady and Gene were sitting on the carpet watching Barney on television. Evidently even Barney was fascinating to someone who had recently discovered the boob tube.

"Done already?" Gene said.

"I'm taking a break. I still have a couple of hours of work to do on the computer, but I need to ask a favor. It's not a wish, mind you. Whether you do it or not is strictly your choice."

Gene propped himself up on one elbow and gave me a warm smile. "I'm trying to get on your good side. It makes me a sucker for doing favors. What is it?"

"You remember those casseroles you made up for me the other day, the ones in the freezer?"

"Sure. You want me to fix some lunch?"

"No," I said, my words spilling out trying to catch up to my racing mind. "I need you to get them over to Peggy Sue's. Maybe you can put them in a box or something. Sneak up to her front door and leave it on the stoop. She's having a hard time of it right now. I suspect she's not eating, using the money to feed her kids. I know she won't take charity. She's proud. Would you do that for me?" Even as I spoke the words, the holes in my plan became clear to me.

"But maybe that won't work. My car's not good in the snow, and you don't have a driver's license, do you? I guess I could drive—" My nerves were getting all worked up. I glanced over at the window. The snow looked like sheets of white, and the wind was blowing it sideways. I wondered if this "snow event" had reached blizzard force. I couldn't take Brady out in that, so Gene would have to stay here. If I left right now maybe I could beat the worst of the storm.

Gene sat watching me. "Ravine," he called softly.

"What?" I said, shaken out of my thoughts.

"Look at me."

"Okay, I'm looking. What?"

Gene winked. I heard bells again. Today, their clear, high sound made me think of prayer bells in Tibet. I concluded that their pitch varied with Gene's mood.

"Your wish is my command." He smiled.

My heart skidded. "I didn't wish!"

"Sorry, it was a turn of phrase. I know you didn't. I wanted you to stop worrying. You don't have to go out. A box of groceries with everything Peggy Sue and her kids could possibly need for the next week is sitting in front of her door. I was glad to do it."

I exhaled with relief. "Thank you. Thank you a million times over. You don't know how much I appreciate what you did."

"I can think of a way to show me how much," he said, his eyes full of mischief.

"Okay, I'll call for a pizza. Maybe Joe's Grotto at the lake is still delivering."

"That wasn't what I had in mind."

"You have a one-track mind. I need to get back to work," I equivocated.

"I can take a rain check," he offered.

I didn't answer, but started back to my office.

"Okay, order the pizza. Order a couple," he called after me.

I had just gotten back to my desk when the phone rang. I figured it had to be my mother, so I simply said, "Hello?"

"Is this the lawyer?"

"Yes, this is Ravine Patton. Who is this?" I glanced up at the clock. It was barely nine o'clock on a Saturday.

"You don't know me. I got your number from a friend. My name's Tawnya Jones. I wanted to hire you for . . . uh . . . a legal matter."

"What kind of legal matter?"

"Queen Nefertitty went and stole Ron."

"Queen Nefertiti? The Egyptian?"

"No, not that Queen Nefertitty. This one's an exotic dancer. Her real name is Sandy."

"Who is Ron?"

"My husband."

I put my forehead down on the desk and stifled a groan. Then I sat up and said, "Ms. Jones, if you want to file for divorce, I can do that. But if you want to reconcile with Ron, that's between you and him."

"Hell, I can't do that. Ron's dead."

"Huh? Are we talking about a body snatching?"

"No, course not. Don't be crazy. She took his urn. You know, with his ashes in it. She has it in her backpack and she's going around saying that Ron was going to leave me for her, and now he is sleeping in her bed every night. It ain't right."

"Did she break into your house to get the urn?" I asked.

"No, she didn't have to. A bunch of his buddies took it down to the Shadyside Inn for one last drink. She stole Ron off the bar. It's still stealing, ain't it? I paid for the cremation and all. The ashes belong to me."

"Absolutely. But this is a police matter. You need to file a complaint."

"I knows that, but they wouldn't listen. They said it was a domestic matter."

"I could understand how they might get the wrong idea. I think you have to explain the whole story."

"To tell the truth, I don't want this to get on TV. If they go arrest her, it will, won't it? I'll look like a fool. I can't even hold on to a dead husband. You go talk to Queen Nefertitty. Tell her she's going to be in real trouble with the cops if she don't give you Ron."

"I don't think I can do that. You need to let the police handle it."

"Ms. Patton, it's real hard for me to beg, but I'm begging you. I miss Ron something terrible. Those ashes are all I have. Can I send you—what do you call it? A reminder?"

"A reminder?"

"You know, like a deposit. I can put a hundred dollars in the mail right now. I make good money. Queen Nefertitty talks big, but I don't think she wants Ron bad enough to get into trouble over him."

I thought for a moment. She would be my second paying client and beggars can't be choosers. "Okay. Please include your phone number on the check. Do you know where I can find Queen Nefertitty?"

"Sure. She dances down at the Ring Ding."

The Ring Ding was a topless bar in Wilkes-Barre. I knew that much, and I knew I had no intention of going there. "Look, I need her home address. Whatever else you can find out, write it down for me. Can you do that?"

"Sure will. Thanks. I mean that."

"Thank me after I get the urn back. I can't promise anything."

"Sure, I understand. And one more thing—"

"Yes?"

"Be careful, hear? The guys down at the Shadyside say Queen Nefertitty has a gun in that backpack with Ron."

Before I could tell her I was changing my mind, Ms. Jones had broken the connection. Now what had I gotten myself into? I was supposed to be a lawyer, not a private investigator. Gene could be my backup for now. But what was I going to do when he was gone?

Around noon, I did make the call to order pizza. The girl on the other end of the phone line said it would be at least an hour. The roads were still open, but they could only use their four-wheel-drive delivery van. I figured by the time the pizza arrived, I would have finished up all the work I could get done at home. The records on who bought and sold the Sikorsky farm would have to wait until I got to the courthouse, and I'd combine the trip with filing for Peggy Sue's divorce on Monday. But I intended to do a computer search now to try to dig up some news articles on London's Junkyard and its owners. My gut told me that some thread wove everything together. I had to find it.

What didn't fit into the picture was the escalating violence. Contaminating a well and running over a chicken were dirty tricks. Nobody got hurt. No felonies committed. No cops very interested. Trying to burn down my house landed in an entirely different category. It was arson. Of course that act might have been strictly a personal vendetta for Scabby and have nothing to do with the Katos.

I tapped my pen for a minute on a yellow legal pad. Outside of that small sound and the barely audible noise of Barney's "My Family's Just Right for Me" leaking in from the living room, the house had the distinctive hush it gets during a heavy snowfall: the silence of snow. As the day progressed the house would be wrapped in a cocoon of white. The roads would start to close down one by one, the ever-present background rumbling of traffic getting fainter until it ceased altogether. Across the valley filling with snow, logs would be piled in fireplaces; smoke would curl from chimneys; the sharp smell of burning wood would travel for miles from house to house.

Until the storm was over, there was nothing to do in the country except to stay inside. Some people made popcorn and watched movies. Others found a good book and curled up in a soft chair. Scrabble and Monopoly boards appeared. For me, I'd love to climb into bed this afternoon with Brady and take a nap together. It was one of our favorite things.

But I didn't want to think about naps, bed, and spending the weekend isolated here with Gene. I needed to avoid another intimate encounter, and proximity to him weakened my resolve. I too easily remembered the salt-tinged smell of his skin, the hard muscles of his arms, the taut, smooth flesh of his belly. I kept pushing away the niggling thought that I should be getting that third wish over with. Gene could get back to his life, and I could go on with mine. I was prolonging the agony by procrastinating.

That thought slipped in and I let it go, leaving a gray, achy feeling behind. Then I had an idea that was part genius, part scheming. I would need Gene's help when I went looking for Peggy Sue's John and Tawnya's Ron. It made sense to put off the whole business of the third wish until those two cases were over. I walked over to the coffeemaker and poured another cup. Again I felt much better having made a decision.

I stood there looking out the window. The wind had bent back the dark green branches of the big hemlock tree at the edge of the yard. Snow drifted into mounds around fence posts and stumps. Every few seconds, a gust of wind threw snowflakes against the windowpane with such force that they sounded like handfuls of dry rice smacking the glass. I loved watching the familiar landscape disappear and become a mysterious geography, as dangerous as it was beautiful. I couldn't deny that the energy of the storm gave me a thrill—its invisible force made manifest in the whirling snow and windblown trees.

Tomorrow, after the storm had passed, it would be fun for Gene and me to take Brady outside. Maybe we could build a snowman, and I couldn't deny that I was thinking that maybe my family—me, my son, my cat, and my genie—was just right for me.

Although my Internet search turned up a few facts that went into my Kato folder, I quickly became frustrated by the maddeningly little that I uncovered about the salvage yard's owner. I did find a report that George London had bought up a large tract of land several years ago that turned out to be dab-smack in the middle of a highway expansion. Had it been a lucky guess? I doubted it. London turned a very quick multimillion dollar profit. But George London, on paper, looked simply like an astute businessman and pillar of the community. The owner or joint owner of dozens of companies, he was unusually generous to only one big "charity"—political contributions. Officeholders from Scranton to Harrisburg had accepted hefty sums for their campaigns, and if I counted in the monies given through London's companies, the amount literally climbed into the millions. I'm sure London saw every dollar as a wise investment.

Oddly, though, few people actually knew what George London looked like. Not one single picture of him appeared in the archives of any local media. One news story described him as "reclusive," rarely appearing in public and never attending charity functions or social events. And tucked away in an old news story, which I had found only by following a series of links, was a heart-stopping find: a felony conviction from a quarter century ago and rumors about London's ties to a Philadelphia crime family. Back after the devastating Wilkes-Barre flood of '72—the disaster during the Nixon administration that gave birth to FEMA—London had gotten a suspended sentence for running a scam to obtain flood relief money. Considering the huge sums involved, a suspended sentence, for a felony no less, smelled rotten. I was surprised it hadn't given birth to a major scandal. I could use the LexisNexis search engine to get the details, but reading through the material might take me days, and I didn't know if it would have any bearing whatsoever on the Katos' problems. I made a note of the date of the trial and stuck it in the folder.

As to the alleged mob ties, I found no hard evidence that Citizen London was "connected" to the

Scarfos, Testas, Bufalinos, D'Elias or any other Pennsylvania mafia family. Nothing of substance had ever surfaced. Recently London had tried to get state approval to turn one of his Pocono properties into a gambling casino. He had been turned down in favor of granting a license to a Seneca tribe who promised to turn an antiquated city racetrack into a major gambling emporium. This huge project was supposed to boost the area's sagging economy.

Even so, the ruling caused a community uproar: The Valley remained an old-time Methodist and Assembly of God stronghold where gambling was a vice, no two ways about it. But no amount of protest stopped the Seneca and work was going forward. For complicated legal reasons, Native Americans enjoyed loopholes in the gambling regulations that allowed them to thumb their noses at the white man's laws. Considering the betrayals and land grabs they had endured three centuries ago—Penn's Walking Purchase and the dispossession of the Delaware people helped create the state of Pennsylvania—I can't say I blamed them.

All in all, I dug up no smoking gun to connect London's enterprises and the efforts to drive the Katos out of their Buddhist B and B. I hoped looking at the records of deeds and land transfers in the courthouse would turn up something. I had done as much as I could. I turned off the computer and called it a day. I stretched and yawned, then stood up when the doorbell sounded. The pizza had arrived.

"Perfect timing," I said aloud. After I settled up with the delivery guy, I marched triumphantly into the living room holding not one, not two, but four pizzas, two boxes of CinnaStix, and an order of buffalo wings with sides of blue cheese and celery. I figured Gene needed an introduction to some of the great junk foods developed in the late twentieth century. All we needed was a pro football game on television, and he'd have the entire cultural experience. When the thought struck me that Gene would probably be gone by Super Bowl Sunday, a frisson of sadness coursed through me.

Live in the moment, I reminded myself as I set down the goodies, and Gene immediately conjured up plates, napkins, and tall glasses of soda complete with ice. The bells that announced this little bit of magic were loud and triumphant. Obviously Gene was a genie with the potential for a pizza addiction. Within seconds, two slices were gone—no magic involved—and strings of melted mozzarella decorated his chin.

I suggested we watch a DVD, hoping to help Gene get up-to-date on the films of the last fifty years. I chose *RV,* starring Robin Williams, partly to continue Gene's cultural education and partly because it made me laugh a lot.

Gene was soon glued to the screen and inhaling the pizza. "Try the wings." I nudged the box toward him even though I might be paving the way for clogged arteries in his future.

Keeping a slice of pizza in one hand, Gene started in on a wing. "Spicy," he said with his mouth full. "Sort of like chicken on the barbie." Pretty soon he didn't know which to eat first and alternated between bites of the cheesy pizza and the buffalo wings. Bones piled up quickly on his plate. Brady, who sat in his baby seat gumming a pizza crust, laughed at Gene's performance. I had forgotten how much a young man could eat. I munched daintily on a single piece of pizza and enjoyed watching his gustatory adventure.

"You know, there are definitely some things worth staying in the twenty-first century for," Gene announced as he grabbed a napkin and mopped up the grease and tomato sauce on his face.

"Like pizza?" I said, teasing.

"And buffalo wings and television," he answered in all seriousness.

Mentally I pushed the *Family Feud* WRONG ANSWER

buzzer and my good mood vanished. I pushed my plate away, folded my arms across my chest, and leaned back on the couch.

Gene looked at me, perplexed. "One slice, that's it? Aren't you hungry?"

"Not anymore," I said.

"What did I do?" he asked.

"If you don't know, I'm not about to tell you. Can we end this conversation? I'm trying to watch the movie."

Brady must have felt my tension because he started fussing in his chair. I unstrapped him and picked him up. He held his arms out toward Gene. I felt even more pissed off.

I certainly didn't hand him over. Instead, I positioned him on my hip. "I'm getting Brady a bottle. Hit the PAUSE button, will you?" I said and marched out of the room clearly trailing an attitude. "Why don't you try making love to the pizza while I'm gone," I added. I couldn't help myself.

"Ravine?" Gene asked when Brady and I returned to the living room. "Are you mad because I didn't say *you* were worth staying in this century for?"

"Oh *nooo*. I'd never presume that I could possibly mean more to you than pizza or television. Even though you did have sex with me," I muttered under my breath as I got Brady settled in his seat with his bottle.

Gene came up behind me. "And I'd like to have sex with you again," he whispered in my ear.

"Fat chance," I said and stepped away. "Talk to your pizza about it."

"I didn't mean to hurt your feelings," Gene said. "Can I have another chance?"

"It's called a 'do-over,'" I said, turning around to face him. "And no. In real life, you can't have one.

You only get a do-over when you're playing a kid's game."

"This is no game," Gene said and moved close enough for me to feel his breath on my face before his mouth touched where his breath had brushed my skin. He lightly kissed my cheeks and held my lips with his.

I turned my head away from him. "Then what is it? A diversion? A way to pass the time until I make my wish?"

"You don't really believe that. You know I care about you. You're excitable, and exciting. You're pretty and smart and—"

"And living sixty years too late for us to be together, right?" I bent down to pick up Brady's bottle off the floor where he had thrown it.

"We seem to be going around in circles. Can't we just enjoy each other's company and stop worrying about where this is going?"

I stood up and looked at Gene. "In one word. No."

"Why, if you don't mind me asking?"

"I cannot believe you're asking that. I really can't."

"Humor me. Tell me what you are thinking. I'm a genie, I can do magic, but I can't read minds, especially women's minds."

I squared off my stance in front of him. My hands rested on my hips. "Okay. I'll spell it out. I can't stop worrying where this is going, because where you want it to go is pretty obvious. To bed, or to the couch, or to wherever, as long as we're horizontal. And I can't do that."

"You already did, if I might state the obvious."

"I can't do it again. It's not an option. Not as long as you intend to leave."

"Why does that sound like extortion?" He stepped close to me again.

I took a step backward. "It is absolutely nothing

like extortion. If you wanted a mistress and a no-
strings-attached affair while you were granting her
wishes, you should have popped out of your bottle
with a different woman, that's all." I turned and
looked at the television. It was still on PAUSE. I picked
up the remote and pushed PLAY.

"Let's watch the movie," I said, feeling terribly hurt
but determined not to show it.

"Okay," Gene said, sounding more than a little
grumpy. We didn't talk for the next hour, but I was
aware of every move Gene made. Sitting near him
had the most disturbing effect on me.

By the time the movie ended, it was almost four.

"Teatime! Let me make us a cuppa," Gene announced, and did his wink-bell thing. Petit fours and
little sandwiches with the crusts cut off appeared,
along with a darling chintz-patterned Sadler teapot
that I had never seen before and two matching porce-
lain cups. A silver sugar bowl and creamer sat on a
silver tray. For Brady there was juice, and melba toast
on an Alice in Wonderland plate.

"Oh!" I exclaimed. "It looks 'loverly.' But I'm
going to get fat eating this kind of food. Tomorrow
I'll have to start eating yogurt again."

"You are absolutely daft. You don't eat enough.
Food is for pleasure, not simply sustenance. I'll prove
it to you." He picked up a petit four and fed it to me.
I took the little chocolate-covered cake from his fingers and then licked the chocolate from them. Gene
made sounds of approval before he leaned forward
and gave me a gentle kiss. I kissed him back, and we
held the kiss while we shared the chocolate between
our mouths, which turned out be a wonderful combination of sensual elements.

"If chocolate is the food of love, eat on, till I am
sated," Gene said, changing a line from Shakespeare
to fit the circumstance as he fed me another petit four
and we repeated the whole routine again.

After that, we drank tea and talked about the movie. Time slipped by. Snow fell steadily. I felt unaccountably happy. When Brady started to get restless, I put him in the Bouncy Bounce that hung in one doorway. He giggled and jumped, and Gene and I both got a kick out of watching him. Somehow I ended up inside Gene's encircling arm. My feet were tucked up under me on the sofa. The afternoon faded away until the remaining daylight burned out like a spent candle.

When it was time for Brady's dinner, I told Gene I would like to make it the old-fashioned way, with the contents of the refrigerator, not by genie magic. He countered that he'd fix something for us both. I suggested he stick with a salad; I wasn't very hungry. But of course Gene had to show off. When I finished with Brady and handed him his bottle, I saw that two bowls of clear consommé sat on the table, along with a Caesar salad and fresh fruit. A bouquet of lilacs—lilacs in November!—graced the table. I looked at Gene with sparkling eyes.

"I know exactly what you like," he whispered.

"How?" I breathed.

"I don't know," he said. "It doesn't have anything to do with genie magic. It must be some other kind."

Our gaze locked and held. I don't remember eating; I only remember staring into Gene's eyes.

I stood up to clear the table, but Gene winked and the dishes disappeared. Then suddenly, he moved up behind me. He lifted my hair and started kissing the back of my neck. Shivers were going up and down my spine. I started to tremble. Gene put his arms around me. "I can't help but want you. I apologize for desiring you, but I can't stop what you do to me." His hands crept under my sweater.

"Oh my," I said and leaned back into him. All my firm arguments about why I should keep my distance from Gene started to wobble. My thoughts flew by, telling me I was an adult, I could handle this, and after all Gene couldn't go until I made my wish. I surely had time to figure everything out before then. Then I didn't want to think at all because I was enjoying the contact of our bodies so much. My breath quickened. I thought I heard bells just as I decided to surrender to the desire that was fast turning into a raging flame inside me.

"Gene?" I breathed.

"Yes?" he answered in a barely audible voice.

"Oh," I breathed as his fingers started playing across my skin. "Please—" Gene pressed his lips into my shoulder. "Oh please," I sighed as my head bent back and his hands roamed my body. "Let's not wait, let's—"

And at that minute the lights went out. We were plunged into total darkness.

"Hmmm, what perfect timing," Gene said and worked his way up under my stretch bra. "And I didn't even turn them out."

Brady began to whimper. Cold water couldn't have cooled off my amorous mood any quicker. I pulled out of Gene's embrace. "We've had a power failure. The storm must be getting much worse. I need to get the coal stove going."

Gene pulled me back into his arms. "Not now. Let's do what we were about to do. I'll take care of the lights after we—"

Somehow what he said didn't sit right. I had been aroused. I had been willing, yet all of a sudden, I suspected that maybe I had been not only seduced, but helped along with a genie's powers of enchantment. What had happened to my resolve to keep my distance?

Surrounded by darkness, I straightened my clothes and snapped at Gene, "I'm sure you can take care of the lights 'after,' but you know, I've had enough of you and your magic tonight. I can light the Coleman lanterns. The coal stove will provide plenty of heat. I can function quite nicely without you, Captain O'Neill, thank you very much. Please stay right here with Brady."

I left the room, feeling my way along the wall, and did what I said I would. About then the emergency sirens started to wail, calling the volunteer EMTs and firefighters to the nearest firehouse. The sirens' mournful sound always gave me chills. Everyone who lived in the country knew the sound meant terrible trouble for someone: a person struck ill, a home burning, a creek flooding, or most of the time, a car crashed with dead or injured inside. A feeling of foreboding passed over me. The sirens sounded again and faded away.

After I had found the Coleman lanterns in the storage closet by the basement stairs and started up the coal fire which was soon burning nicely, I started to return to the living room when I passed a window and realized I couldn't see out. Snow had plastered it over with white. I could hear the wind though; it was whistling down the chimney and rattling the panes. Suddenly Gene was beside me, holding Brady. My annoyance of a few moments ago softened a little. We stood there together in the light of the Coleman lantern, the storm raging outside.

"Let's put Brady to bed," Gene said. "He's tired."

"I can do it," I said and took my son into my arms.

"Then can I do it with you? I'd like that very much." His voice was soft.

"As long as you behave yourself," I said, and we went upstairs together.

Gene sat in the rocker in Brady's room while I read some of *Winni-the-Pooh* out loud. Then I sang one of the lullabies Brady especially likes, the old English song "Lavender's Blue." I hadn't thought much about the lyrics until they were coming out of my mouth, but when you come right down to it, they're all about two people in love. Gene watched me closely while I sang.

Brady was fast asleep by the time I finished. Gene and I slipped quietly from the dark room. When we were in the hall, only a few steps from my bedroom, Gene put his hand on my shoulder. "Can I ask you something?"

"It depends," I said.

"I told you about Laura. Will you tell me about Brady's father?"

"No," I answered.

"Why? Did he leave you? Didn't he want Brady? Is that why you're so hurt?"

"I am not hurt at all. I told you that Brady's father and I didn't have a relationship. It was merely something that happened one afternoon. He doesn't even know about Brady."

I felt Gene's body stiffen. "What? You never told him you were pregnant?"

"I didn't know where to find him, and quite frankly, I can't imagine that he'd want to know."

"A man would want to know he had a son," Gene insisted. "What are you going to tell Brady someday? That you never told his father he existed?"

"I don't know what I will tell him. I haven't made up my mind. Can we change the subject?"

I was holding a lantern in my hand, and we stood in a circle of yellow light, with darkness all around us. Gene took hold of my other arm and faced me. "No changing the subject. Not before I say what I think. I think—in fact I know—that you need to contact Brady's father. I 'get it' that you don't want a relationship with him. I assume he 'got it' too, and that's why he's not here."

"I don't think you'd better *assume* anything, Gene," I said, agitated. "Brady's father is none, I repeat, *none* of your business."

"Do you still care about him?" Gene's voice now had a hard edge to it.

"I don't know that I ever did, not in the way you mean. There was an attraction between us. I never stuck around to see if there could be anything more. We lived in different worlds. Physical attraction is simply not enough to maintain a relationship," I said and started to move away.

Gene's hands held me fast. "I think you underestimate physical attraction."

"It's chemistry. It's not love, Gene."

"Who says? What's love? Isn't it chemistry? It sure isn't about living in the same worlds. I saw it all the time during the war. A guy and girl fall in love—he's Aussie, she's Javanese or Malaysian or Chinese. But all the differences in social class, religion, even skin color doesn't stop them from wanting to get married. I saw guys fight all kinds of red tape and defy their families to get hitched. And you know what? The ones who didn't fight—the guys who walked away—they got bitter. They never stopped regretting that they didn't at least try."

"That's a different situation. It doesn't apply to Brady's father and me."

"Okay, maybe it didn't. Maybe you were afraid you could love Brady's father, and he didn't fit in the lawyer's world you inhabited. Wasn't he up to your standards? Wasn't he good enough?" Gene's hands had tightened on my arms.

I tried to move, but he held me fast as I replied. "No. Yes. I don't know. Whatever happened, it's finished."

"But we're not, Ravine. Not by a long shot." Gene's mouth descended and took possession of mine. He wasn't gentle now. There was something like anger mixed with his passion and it made him more aggressive. Caught between his body and the wall, I could feel the length of him pressing against me. We fit together in every curve and angle. His harsh, grinding kisses soon took my breath away.

I felt my resolve weakening once more. I was swept away with passion. Had he carried me off right then, to the sofa, the floor, or my bed, I don't think I could have resisted, but to my surprise Gene suddenly stopped and stepped away from me.

"Don't go," I whispered, and tried to pull him back.

"It's time you looked at yourself, Ravine. And it's time we both went to bed," he said in a voice that was hard and sad at the same time. "As you made it clear, your bedroom is off-limits to me. We're from different worlds too, remember? See you in the morning. Sweet dreams," he said and vanished.

Chapter 11

I lay in bed, writhing in frustration. I had been left in a state of acute passion interruptus. There was nothing to stop me from getting up and going downstairs to find Gene—except my pride. My good sense might be exerting pressure on me as well. What was I doing? What did I really want? Ambivalence tormented me. Plus, Gene's speech about my finding Jake had opened up, as the saying goes, a whole new can of worms.

I had spent many hours during my pregnancy thinking about Jake and analyzing every minute of our time together. I had come up with some conclusions. First off, we'd talked nonstop from the minute I climbed on the back of his motorcycle. During those conversations, Jake had referred to Freud, Jung, Camus, and Jack Kerouac, among others. He'd talked in philosophical terms about whether existence had meaning and if it did, how could we know what that meaning was? He extolled the virtues of life on the road and rebelling against society. We threw Shakespearean lines back and forth; both of us knew several sonnets by heart.

I never doubted for a moment that Jake was highly educated or had a family who had raised him with care. He was neat and clean. He had manners. He used the king's English. He didn't exhibit sociopathic behavior at any time. In the bar where we had gone for a drink, Jake was well-known and well-liked. In fact, some of the people who spoke with him that day treated him with deference. One of them had called him "Doc." I had spun many scenarios in my imagination about why he had become a Bandido and whether or not I could "save him" from himself.

After Brady was born, my sense of responsibility as a parent stopped any fantasies about riding off into the sunset with Jake on his Indian motorcycle. I had seen something very good in him, but as he readily admitted, his life as a member of a outlaw biker gang put him in a place I could never go.

Practicing as an attorney, even one sitting most of the time on the upper floor of a Philadelphia law firm, I had firsthand knowledge of the weak, deranged, criminal, and greedy side of the human race. After the first few years in the profession, I became more forgiving of human weakness and tried not to judge my clients, taking a page from psychiatrist Carl Rogers's philosophy that his patients should have "unconditional positive regard." I didn't go quite that far, opting instead for unconditional neutral regard. But over time I became adamant that I didn't want to deal with a life of problems, desperation, or criminality anywhere but in the office.

Jake lived that kind of dark and lawless existence. My gut instincts as well as my experience on the streets told me that, at heart, he was no criminal, but he chose to be part of a dangerous and violent world. I didn't. I became convinced that was why he didn't ask me to stay when I said I had to leave. I also held an unshakable conviction that he was running away from something—maybe himself—and that his choices were self-destructive.

My rational mind saw all that very clearly, and hindsight is always twenty-twenty. If I had regrets, I pushed them away. I had never reached out to Jake or tried to locate him, but I knew Gene had a point.

On one level, Jake had a right to know about Brady. My son was his flesh and blood, and in fact Brady looked so much like him, I would never, as long as I lived, forget Jake's face. On another level, did I want Brady to have an ongoing relationship of any kind with Jake the biker?

No way.

I sighed. I sat up. I stared into the empty room. I saw, without needing a scintilla of light, the flaw in my well-thought-out, logical view of things: Life isn't logical, predictable, or controllable. The dilemma over whether or not to tell Jake about Brady boiled down to one very simple reality. The alternative to disclosure was to lie to Brady about his father.

Another truism I learned from my time practicing law: Lies never turn out well. Never. No exceptions. The truth is a funny thing. It surfaces no matter how deeply it's buried. If I didn't take the initiative soon and talk with Jake on my terms, one day, whether I liked it or not, the truth would come knocking at my door when I was least prepared to deal with it.

The minutes ticked off one by one on the travel clock by my bed. As I lay there sleepless in the snow-hushed night, I realized another truth. I had to decide on a clear and certain course to take with Gene. I needed to begin by facing and accepting the fact that he was a genie in a bottle. If I truly did—and I couldn't come up with an alternative explanation—I had to rethink my dismissal of all the other beliefs and myths that didn't fit into my legal eagle mind, such as angels, ghosts, fairies, leprechauns—and love. By love I meant a Romeo and Juliet kind of love, the kind of love between flyboys and their war brides that Gene spoke about, the kind of love that needs neither words nor socially acceptable boundaries—not only to exist, but to make men and women move mountains in order to be together.

Obviously something profound and irrevocable had

happened to me from the minute I opened that damned Diaper Genie. The appearance of Gene had shaken the very foundations of my beliefs—and more than that. It had shaken my heart. As Shakespeare asked, "Who ever loved that loved not at first sight?" Was it possible that my wild, crazy desires for a genie in a bottle were really . . . love?

The silence of the snow enveloped me, and with that last, life-altering thought I fell asleep.

Snow crystals are diamonds that fall from heaven. The sun, striking them by the millions, makes a shining path across the fields. The wind tosses them into the pellucid air, where they sparkle with a blinding radiance. Hollows and crevasses glow with icy blue depths, and the very air, filled with reflections, shimmers and dazzles. Into this magical world of glitter and glory I awoke at sunrise on Sunday, the day after the storm.

It was a new world for me. I had made a decision. I was, by this time, rock-sure I had fallen in love with Gene. It was time for my flyboy to lose his heart in return—or to realize he already had, since I trusted that my mother knew love when she saw it. If this was a move-mountains love, then at the right moment, I would talk with Gene about how wish number three could keep him in this century, whole and human once more, with me. In the meantime, I intended to take the risk I hadn't taken last night.

I left my bed with these thoughts running through my mind. Brady was still sleeping when I peeked into his room. I closed the curtains tightly to keep the sunlight from disturbing him. I blew him a silent kiss and tiptoed down the stairs.

Gene had gone to sleep on the living room floor. His eyes were closed, and his relaxed features made him look very young. My heartbeat speeded up. I could barely breathe. I knelt down next to him and kissed him softly on the lips. His eyes fluttered open and stared into mine. We didn't say a word. We didn't need to.

I took off the robe I was wearing and lay naked next to him. He held me in his arms. We kissed for a long time until he finally rolled on top of me. Then Gene found my nipple with his lips. He sucked hard, his teeth teasing and arousing me. My hands slipped into his hair. It was soft beneath my fingers. I lowered my face into it. It smelled clean and good. I pulled his head harder against my breasts. I became lost in my desire and unable to control the feelings that were washing over me.

From somewhere in the corner of the room came a soft ringing of tiny bells, and they sounded muffled to my ears as if I were wrapped in a fog. And in that second Gene's clothes vanished and he was naked. I closed my eyes, but I knew once again, he had protected himself and me with a condom.

My breath caught in my throat when Gene's fingers stroked the inside of my thighs. "Let me show you some magic that has nothing to do with being a genie."

"Yes," I said.

And he did. I sighed and began to relax. Gene pushed rhythmically in and out of me, and as he did, I put my hands over my eyes and smiled. It was a sweet, smooth ride that I wanted to last and last. I burrowed my face into Gene's shoulder until our movements together felt so good it almost scared me. The room tilted and spun. At last, I let go of any last vestige of self-control.

"Gene!" I cried. I held on to him with all my strength, gripping his back and biting his shoulder. My entire body tensed as I felt the most intense pleasure imaginable spread from my core outward, making me dizzy. I gave myself without holding anything back. I couldn't tell where his flesh stopped and mine began, and we climaxed together in an act that fulfilled and sated me as none had ever done before.

Afterward, Gene lay next to me and gathered me in his arms. He looked at me with great tenderness and kissed me hard. He didn't say anything; he didn't make the promises I longed to hear. For me, it had been a union of two who became one. I hoped he felt that too, because I wanted him forever with all my heart and to lose him now would be more than I could bear.

I am a fool for love.

After our lovemaking, I went upstairs to bathe and dress myself, then do the same for Brady. Gene ventured outside to clean the walks and driveway. Whether he did it with a shovel or by magic, I never knew. The electric power still hadn't been restored, but that didn't deter Gene from fixing a breakfast of Belgian waffles with fresh strawberries and whipped cream for me and a mushy version of pancakes and peaches for Brady. Black coffee steamed in a carafe. We tarried over breakfast, our fingers touching across the table, my feet against his leg beneath it. I gazed at him with eyes aglow. We fed each other. We kissed a dozen times.

All was going splendidly until I said, "Gene, we need to make a road trip tomorrow. I'll drop Brady off at my mother's because I need to borrow her truck. The highways should be cleared by then."

"Where are we going?"

"Up toward Binghamton, New York, to get Peggy Sue's money back from her no-good husband John."

Gene looked at me with an unreadable expression before he said, "Break that down for me, will you?"

I briefly explained Peggy Sue's dilemma and how I proposed to handle it. Gene didn't react to my ideas with much enthusiasm. Instead, he looked skeptical.

"Do you think this wanker John is going to hand over the money, assuming any is left?" he asked.

"I'm sure he wouldn't under normal circumstances, but I have a secret weapon that is sure to convince him."

"Tell me, but I think I can guess." Gene's mouth had become a tight line and his eyes went from open and friendly to narrowed and guarded.

"The secret weapon is you. I have this plan." I proceeded to lay it out. Gene listened carefully.

Then he remained silent for a long, uncomfortable moment before he said in a voice loaded with disapproval, "You know I don't have any choice when it comes to this crazy scheme of yours. As your genie, I have to obey your orders. However, you did suggest we behave as if we were in a partnership rather than in a master-slave relationship. Correct me if I'm wrong, but don't partners consult with each other *before* making decisions?"

"Yes, you're right. Consider what I just said as if I'm consulting you. What do you think?"

"I think you've got a few kangaroos loose in the top paddock. You're a barrister, not Nancy Drew, girl detective. This whole escapade could blow up in your face. Maybe this guy has a rifle same as Scabby did—only maybe this guy will be quicker to use it."

"I think the chances of that happening are quite slim," I said, straightening my shoulders and sitting up very tall in my chair.

"Slim? It's a dead cert."

"I don't agree. However, I hear you. Even with the element of danger, a rather minor danger in my opinion, will you do what I asked you to?"

"This is a real dog's breakfast. What are my alternatives, to let you do this alone? You're a girl. You'll end up getting the bejeezus kicked out of you—if you're lucky and nothing worse happens."

"I really can't handle your male chauvinism," I said, getting huffy.

"My what? I don't bloody know what you're talking about. But you better get your head straight. If you mean that you aren't a man and this guy is—that he will be double your size and weight—that you don't know how to fight, and he has probably been in dozens of brawls—that you don't know how to fire a weapon, and he without a doubt can and will, then hell yes, *girl,* I am a male chauvinist and what's more, I'm right!"

After he had finished, Gene jumped up and pushed his chair back so hard that it banged against the wall. His face was red, his jaw was tight, and he stomped out of the kitchen.

I watched this male hissy fit from my place at the table, making sure I appeared unmoved and calm. I regally raised my chin and turned my head to look out the window. The man was being totally irrational. And what was with the chair banging? A woman wouldn't do something like that. And what's wrong with Nancy Drew? She was a positive role model for two generations of young women.

Once Gene had disappeared from sight, I got up and carried the breakfast dishes over to the sink. As I rinsed them off and stacked them in the drainer to dry, I kept thinking. *So that's how he is. I'm glad I got to see another side of Gene before I said anything about his staying around. The man has a temper. And he is definitely a chauvinist.*

And I hadn't even told him yet about going to see Queen Nefertitty the exotic dancer.

As disappointed as I was with Gene's behavior, I felt it would be a waste to let him stew in anger all day. Brady had never seen snow before, and although he was too young to throw snowballs or build a fort, I wanted to take him outside for the experience. I wanted Gene to go too. In the daydreams I spun while getting dressed, I had envisioned that we would have a wonderful day together, and that Gene would immediately see how we fit as a family.

For that to happen I first had to coax him out of what was by now probably an exceptionally bad mood. I picked up Brady, and we went into the living room where Gene was watching Brady's DVD of *A Charlie Brown Thanksgiving*.

"Gene?" I said in as sweet a voice as I could.

"What?" he said gruffly.

"I'm sorry if I upset you. I automatically assume you'll be able to help me out, you know? After all, you can do anything. I didn't mean to take you for granted. And I didn't consider the danger because I don't feel afraid in situations when I know you'll be there." I was watching his face carefully to see if my flattery was getting me anywhere. I hoped I wasn't overacting.

"Yeah, I guess," he said. "But you don't think things through. You leap before you look. I'm afraid you're going to get hurt sometime, after I'm gone."

So he's still planning on going, I thought. *So much for mountain-moving love. Maybe he doesn't realize how deeply I care about him. Should I say something? No, this is not a good time. I need to pick my moment carefully.*

"And you are so right," I practically simpered. I walked over and sat down next to him with Brady on my lap. I kissed Gene's cheek. He turned his head and kissed me lightly on the lips. "Let's not fight anymore," I suggested.

He looked at me in surprise. "We weren't fighting."

"All right. I guess we were having a difference of opinion. Can I ask you something?"

"Go ahead, shoot."

"This is Brady's very first snow. Would you go outside with him and me? I have an old toboggan in the shed, and it might be fun for the three of us to go sledding."

"Let me see if I understand what you're really asking," he answered with a straight face. "Since Brady is far too young to be going downhill at thirty miles an hour, I bet you and Brady are going to ride on the toboggan, and I'm going to pull you around."

"Would you mind?"

"No, I'd like to. Let's go." He stood up, took Brady from me and tucked him into one arm, then, taking my hand, pulled me upright. Putting my arm behind my back, he pressed our bodies together. He kissed me. I kissed him back. For a chauvinist, he was a great kisser.

I sank into the snow past my knees. I had to wear sunglasses, the glare was so blinding. Gene immediately made snowballs and fired them off at trees. We all laughed a lot. Brady's cheeks got very red, and he was so bundled up he couldn't bend his legs very easily, but he was wonderstruck by the changes in the world he knew. He worked his hand out of one mitten, which hung by a string from his sleeve. He stuck his baby hand into the snow to touch it, splash it as if it were water, and squish it to make it melt in his fingers. I let him put snow in his mouth and taste it too, before I warmed up his cold hand and got his mitten back on.

After a few minutes, Gene went around the house and got the toboggan out of the shed. As I sat on it with Brady between my knees, Gene dragged us down the driveway and pulled us along where the snow had been packed hard by the snowplows. It had been pushed into piles as high as Gene's head along both sides of the road, and we seemed to be in a roofless tunnel of white. I noticed Gene kept looking around with a big smile; he appeared to be as fascinated as Brady.

"What's the matter? Never seen snow before?" I called out.

"Matter of fact, no, I haven't. We didn't have snow in Melbourne, mate," he explained. "In the worst of our winter, it's around sixty degrees. This stuff is dead amazing. I'm knocked out by it, I really am." His face looked like a kid's; his eyes shone. He pulled us a good half mile, and we didn't see any traffic at all because the highway had closed during the night and hadn't reopened yet.

When we got to the next farm, my neighbor Jerry had hitched one of his ponies to an old-fashioned sleigh and was out on the road. The dun-colored coat of the Welsh pony contrasted with her bright red halter, and the hardy animal shook her head up and down as we approached.

Jerry, a man past his youth but not quite middle-aged, had hair cut so short he looked nearly bald and a redness of skin that told of days toiling outside. He always wore bib overalls even though he held down a day job at a paper box factory for a salary and farmed for the love of it. Since the 1960s, few farmers could earn a living wage; those who did more than break even had turned to the exotic crops of artisan farms and organic produce. Jerry raised sheep, selling the wool to local craftspeople. His twenty acres of pasture and white Victorian house with green shutters had belonged to his parents, and his mother still lived with him. The barn had long ago fallen into ruin, and Jerry made do with sheds for the sheep, chickens, and a couple of noisy peacocks.

Mucking out sheep sheds and hauling feed in frigid weather might not sound like fun, but Jerry loved every minute of it. He was like most of his generation of farmers: He couldn't make money at farming, but he couldn't give it up. And there's nothing he wouldn't do to hang on to his land.

I'd seen farmers forced to sell out. They looked around them with haunted eyes, and an air of sadness hung over them like a miasma. They had lost their land; the very soil under their feet had been taken from them. A person's land was more than dirt and rocks, more than a livelihood. It was an anchor to the earth, and ripped away from it, most families grieved that loss for the rest of their lives. Knowing this and believing that somebody was out there scheming to force local folks off their land, I felt anger surge up from somewhere deep within me. Stealing a farm killed part of the owner's soul; it wasn't a far step from murder. I felt a new determination to dig out the truth about who chased out the Sikorskys, who wanted the Katos gone, and why.

As I waved to Jerry, Gene pulled the toboggan toward the sleigh. The pony whinnied and stamped her feet, shaking the rump strap of her brass sleigh bells and filling the air with music. Brady laughed, his eyes wide with wonder.

"Hiya!" Jerry yelled from atop the sleigh.

"How you doing, Jerry?" I called out from where I sat, and when the toboggan glided to a stop, I stood up with Brady. "Can he pet the pony?"

"Sure. Buttercup's a gentle mare. She don't bite."

Brady leaned over and put his tiny hand on the pony's neck.

"You can set him on Buttercup's back long as you hang on to him," Jerry suggested.

I did and Brady laughed in delight. "Oh!" I cried. "It's too bad we don't have a camera."

"We do." Gene winked, and bells that sounded remarkably similar to Buttercup's made a merry sound. "And it's a digital one," he announced as he pulled a camera from his pocket.

Gene took pictures from every possible angle of Brady, Buttercup, and me. He ordered me to remove my sunglasses, and I argued I'd be squinting in every picture. We squabbled for a minute, and finally Jerry said, "Let me take one of you three."

He jumped down from the sleigh. Gene handed over the camera and came to stand with us. Gene put his arm around me, we all grinned, and Jerry snapped away.

"You sure look like a happy family," Jerry said as he took the photos.

If I had my way, we would soon be one.

The sun had disappeared behind a bank of clouds, and the wind had started blowing as the morning waned. We were chilled but still in high spirits when we tromped into the warm house and stamped the snow off our feet. Boots went onto newspaper to dry, and Brady's snowsuit was hung in the kitchen to catch the heat from the coal stove. I shoveled nuggets of anthracite into it from the bucket on the floor.

Gene quickly conjured up hot chocolate with marshmallows and sandwiches of thick ham on homemade bread for him and me and warmed up a bottle of formula for Brady. Lately Brady had insisted on holding his bottle for himself, but this afternoon he was so sleepy it slipped from his hands. Then his head nodded onto his chest, and his eyes closed. I took him to his room and tucked him in for a nap.

When I came back downstairs, Gene and I lingered over lunch, not saying much. Before we were finished, the refrigerator sprang to life with a whirring sound, and a few lights clicked on. The power had been restored. A lightbulb clicked on in my mind too. Peggy Sue and her defeated, hangdog look kept reappearing in my memory. I excused myself from the table to go and telephone Freddi from my office. Gene said he'd clean up the kitchen while I was gone.

"Freddi," I said after she picked up the call, "I need you to spin a clever lie for a good cause."

"Not another of your schemes." Freddi no doubt

was remembering the trouble I had gotten her into while we were growing up. One time I convinced her to help me steal a salt lick from way back in our aunt's cow pasture; I don't remember why I even wanted it. We got caught after she fell on the slippery rocks of the creek and gashed her leg so badly, she had to go to the emergency room to get it stitched. She still has the scar. Another time I egged her on to climb up Noxen Mountain farther than we had ever been allowed to go. We kept hearing this funny noise, sort of a buzzing but not quite. When we clambered up on some rocks, we saw hundreds of rattlesnakes sunning themselves not twenty feet from us. As Freddi tells it, "We liked to have died of fright." She says she should know better than to ever listen to me again.

"You know Peggy Sue's going through a hard time," I said.

"Yeah, we all heard about her no-good husband running off with her money."

"Right. She's working two jobs, she's exhausted, and I really think she's depressed to the point it could injure her health. She looks ten years older than she is too. It might give her a mental lift if she got fixed up a little. If you can, would you do Peggy Sue's hair? The works: dye, cut and style it. But you know she won't let me pay for her. You have to think up something so she feels as if she's helping you."

"Hell's bells, that's an easy one. I'll tell her I need to practice for a big wedding party, that I have a new hair product, and I'm afraid to try it out on the bride—whose hair is the same color as Peggy Sue's. I'll even get one of the girls to come up from the beauty school and do her makeup."

I was a little surprised she thought up a lie so easily. Still waters run deep. "That's good. That's really good. I'll pay for everything, don't worry."

"Shut up, Ravine. You aren't going to take credit for my good deed."

I laughed. I asked her how "things" were going, meaning what was happening with the fertility drugs. Having a cousin for a best friend is a twofer. We shared the same family, and we shared secrets. I could hear the sadness and frustration in her voice when she answered. She hadn't gotten pregnant but she felt lousy because of the medication. She and Bobby were fighting over dumb things. Their sex life had lost its joy, it was so purpose-driven. Bobby had begun avoiding coming to bed at night. At that point Freddi broke down and started crying.

Freddi didn't cry easily. In my mother's family, feelings were private, and farm life didn't produce what my mother quaintly called "pantywaists." We were expected to be tough and stoic. No whining, no crying, no complaining. Buck up and bear it. To hear Freddi break down put a hole in my heart.

"Can I do anything?" I asked gently. "Anything. Tell me."

"I know you would," Freddi said, sniffing back her tears. "But this is between me and God. If I get pregnant, it will be a miracle. I'll keep praying and taking these awful pills."

"Okay, I'll pray for you too," I said. But after we hung up, I got to thinking again. I had that one wish left. I was scheming to use it on Gene. Maybe that was wrong. Maybe I should start thinking about using that wish for something more than my own needs. Would it be right or wise to wish for Freddi to get pregnant? My lawyer mind immediately raised a host of objections, but I tucked the thought away to take out later and ponder.

After Freddi and I hung up, I called my mother. I needed to borrow her truck tomorrow and have her take care of Brady while Gene and I went to find Peggy Sue's husband. After quickly agreeing to both favors my mother asked in a funny voice if I had seen the news that morning.

"Our power was out until lunchtime, so I haven't seen anything today. Why?" I asked.

"Seems Scabby Hoyt froze to death."

My hand tightened on the phone. "Huh? What happened? What killed him?" An uneasy feeling washed over me. "Did they say?"

"Beer killed him, that's what. He was drunk as a skunk. He must have gone out to feed the cows during the storm and sat down in the snow. They found his body a few feet from the barn door."

I let out a deep sigh. "He was a miserable man, and he squandered his life hating. I wanted him locked up, but I wouldn't wish him dead. I really wanted to find out if he tried to burn down my house. Now we may never know."

"I guess we know near enough," my mother answered in a hard voice. "Calvin Metz, he's the one who found the body. He went over to Scabby's trailer after he heard Scabby's dog just a-howling and a-howling. The cows were making a terrible racket too because they hadn't been milked. After the cops and ambulance came, Cal said the cops looked around for gas cans. They didn't find any, and that was suspicious because everybody has at least one. But the cops told Cal—one of them is his nephew, you know—that they had photographed the tire tracks in the snow at your house the night of the fire. The right front tire was worn right down to the steel belt. They're sure it's going to match up with Scabby's truck."

"That's a relief," I confessed. "But I was hoping if Scabby got arrested, I might have a shot at getting him to say who hired him to scare the Katos."

"You think somebody did?" my mother asked.

"I have a gut feeling. No evidence. Scabby drank all the time, Ma. He couldn't function without alcohol in his system. I don't see him stopping to rest or even passing out so close to the barn. If he were out hunting in the woods, yes, it would make sense. But while he didn't have much use for people, Scabby loved those cows, and he wouldn't have stopped anywhere until after he fed them. Something about this doesn't sit right with me."

I went back to the kitchen and told Gene about Scabby. He didn't comment at first, simply drummed his fingers on the table for a minute. Then he said, "When people start dying, you better think again about what you're doing."

"The cops say Scabby's death was an accident." I felt defensive and wasn't sure why.

"Is that what you think?" He looked at me steadily.

"I don't know what to think. It's possible that somebody got nervous he had attracted too much attention with the arson attempt and decided to remove him from the picture. It wouldn't be hard to get him drunk enough to pass out, then sit him out in the snow. But what about a second set of footprints?" I sat down and put my head in my hands.

"If it was snowing hard enough, there wouldn't be any by morning," Gene answered while he looked out the window at the acres of white beyond it.

"Then I guess we'll never know," I said.

"Ravine?"

"What?"

"Let it be a warning, okay? Somebody out there may be ruthless enough to commit murder. We don't know what really is at stake here." Gene got up and began pacing back and forth. "I've seen guys try to kill each other over nothing more than a dice game. It's no doubt useless to ask you to drop the case—"

"It is." My mouth became a tight line.

"You're unreasonably stubborn," he said.

"I'm a Patton," I responded. "We didn't survive out here in the middle of nowhere for two hundred years by walking away from trouble. And we're used to it. My great-great-great-grandfather was an Indian."

Gene looked interested. "What kind of Indian?"

"I don't know. He could have been local. This area was populated by Eastern Woodlands Indians, and several different nations settled in Wyoming Valley— Delaware, Iroquois, even some Shawnee. But family lore holds that our Indian came from Canada, up by Fort Niagara, and moved here to fight during the French and Indian War. My Aunt Pauline used to say she didn't know what kind of Indian he was, but judging by the Pattons, one thing was for sure: He was a wild one."

While Brady napped, I decided to download the pictures Gene and Jerry had taken by the sleigh. Gene wanted to watch me do it. As the snapshots came up on the screen, they took my breath away. The ones of Brady on the pony were classic, and the last few with the three of us together reflected so much happiness that I knew I'd always cherish them.

Gene was amazed by the technology. He immediately asked if I'd teach him how to get online and search the Web. I did and left him alone for the next couple of hours. I went into the living room and picked up the Tony Hillerman Navajo mystery I had been reading. I dozed off on the couch and woke up around four when I heard Brady through the baby monitor.

Before I started up the stairs to get him, I paused at a window that looked out toward the back pasture. The clouds had broken up, but the light was dying fast. The trees were a long black line at the edge of the yard, and angry red streaks crisscrossed the deep blue sky. I thought I saw the dark silhouette of a person standing upright between the house and the trees, like somebody watching. But the sun ducked behind a cloud for a moment, shadows moved over the landscape, and when the light returned, dimmer than before, the form was gone. A shiver shook me from head to toe.

Chapter 12

I didn't say anything to Gene about the figure in the field. It might have been my imagination playing tricks on me or a cross-country skier passing through. It might have been anyone or no one; it didn't have to be someone who wished me harm. Besides, if I did tell Gene, I could envision another speech about the weak and the strong.

After a light supper and a quiet evening, during which Gene spent more time on the computer, I retired alone to my bed. As strong as the physical attraction was between us, I decided that which is too easily won is too little prized. I smiled and said I'd see him in the morning before giving him a warm good-night kiss and leaving him wanting more. A few hours earlier Gene had once again said, "When I'm gone." Doubts about our future overcame me again. I also decided that changing his mind about leaving meant I needed to listen to my brain more and my hormones less.

As I lay in bed that night going over my plans for the next day, I also did some hard thinking about what would make a man like Gene stay here in the twenty-first century rather than trying to return, with no guarantees that he would get there, to the past he knew. I pondered the kind of man he was. In September of 1939 he had been a bookish grad student who volunteered to go to war because his country needed him. Three years later he had become a rakish RAF pilot who made sure his crew reached safety before he bailed out of his burning plane. It became obvious to me that love, even a great love with exciting sex, would never keep Gene here with me and Brady. After all, he had loved his sweetheart, Laura, but left her because a greater duty called.

As I drifted, tired and troubled, toward slumber, the words of a long-dead poet came to me in a misty dream: "I could not love thee, dear, so much, loved I not honor more." It described the kind of man Gene was. Even as I spiraled down into darkness and the oblivion of sleep, I realized with a rock-hard certainty that if I wanted Gene for a life partner, he had to feel needed. In fact, I had to convince him that he was indispensable and irreplaceable in my own and my child's life. That was a blatant manipulation of Gene's emotions. Could it backfire?

I rose with first light on Monday morning. I could hear the dull roar of traffic on the highway a mile below at the base of the mountain. The roads had obviously returned to normal, and the early weathercast on the local NPR station reported that the temperature would climb above freezing and stay there over the next few days. The snow would soon be gone.

I wanted to get on the road to Binghamton early enough to get home before dark. Located where the Susquehanna and Chenango rivers meet, Binghamton lies about sixty-five miles due north of Noxen and a world away. In its heyday Noxen had hosted a tannery and a few lumber mills; Binghamton had given birth to IBM. Noxen, a one-street town, sported a yearly Rattlesnake Roundup and a restored train depot; Binghamton, a jewel of a small city, was graced by a university and at least four bridges, and called itself "the carousel capital of the world" because six antique wooden carousels still operated in the city and surrounding towns. The largest of these had seventy-two figures, four abreast, and was considered a national treasure. But now, in the grip of winter, the merry-go-rounds were silent, and I had more serious business to attend to there, and a different kind of gold ring to snag if I could.

In the back of my closet I found a severe navy blue wool suit that I used to wear to court and put it on. I pulled my hair back into a chignon. I threw a pair of low-heeled pumps into an oversized purse, but wore chunky snow boots and thick ski socks. I wanted to project an image of authority, but I didn't need to freeze my feet any longer than necessary. By the time I got Brady dressed and his baby bag stuffed with everything he'd need for a day at Grandma's, Gene had a hearty breakfast of scones and oatmeal, which he called "porridge," waiting in the kitchen.

As I stood at the counter, hastily downing a bowl of the hot cereal, Gene asked, "Why are you eating standing up?"

"Force of habit." I bit into a scone and washed it down with black coffee. "We're in a bit of a rush today. When I was working, I'd grab something at Starbucks and eat at my desk. Even now, I'd skip breakfast if you hadn't made it. Brady gets his bottle, but I don't bother making anything for me."

"You don't take very good care of yourself. You'll end up with indigestion."

"Agreed. I used to take Prilosec, my heartburn was so bad. Hope I don't end up on it again now that I'm getting a private practice going. I guess I need somebody to watch over me." I tossed off the comment carelessly, but I did so deliberately.

Gene did his wink and bell-ringing trick to clean the kitchen while I hurried into my office to pick up the last of my things. I put all the papers I thought I'd need into the briefcase I hadn't used in over a year. I admit it felt good to be working again, even on quirky cases that weren't going to pay much. The three of us managed to get out the front door before eight, and Gene and I had dropped Brady off and switched vehicles with my mother minutes later.

I filed Peggy Sue's divorce papers in Tunkhannock at the county court, which occupies a large white wooden building that looks like a Puritan meeting-house. Gene waited in the truck, and because I wanted to get to Binghamton and return home as quickly as possible, I didn't take the time to look at the deeds for either the Sikorsky farm or the Katos' B and B. They went on my "to do" list, and I'd figured I would have to return tomorrow.

Back on the road, I continued following Route 29, a narrow two-lane secondary highway, instead of the interstate, because it was the most direct route to the New York State border. Melting snow made the pave-ment wet and slick. I had to concentrate on my driv-ing, so Gene and I didn't talk much. I wouldn't say he was a white-knuckled passenger, but I could see his hand gripping the armrest and the muscle in his jaw twitching.

I did ask him at one point if he understood what I needed him to do when we found Peggy Sue's hus-band. He answered with a terse yes. He then asked me if I wanted him to get us to Happy Trails Camping and RV Park "his way" instead of going through what he characterized as this "torturous ordeal."

I replied that a Ford F-150 pickup truck suddenly materializing from out of thin air in the middle of an RV park might attract attention, didn't he think?

He muttered under his breath, "She didn't mind me using magic when *she* found it convenient."

I shot him a dirty look and decided to turn up the sound on the radio. I put on a Golden Oldies station. It would help Gene fill in the gaps of what had hap-pened during the sixty years he was imprisoned in his bottle. He seemed underwhelmed with the Beatles even though I explained they were British and had changed music forever. He liked Neil Diamond's "Sweet Caroline," which should have sent up a red flag about his tastes. When Led Zeppelin's "Black Dog" started playing, he gave me a pained look and suggested that I lower the volume.

I did. "What music was popular before you became a genie, when you went to war."

His eyes looked inward when he answered. "Vera Lynn singing 'White Cliffs of Dover' and 'There'll Always Be an England.' We also listened to a lot of American songs by Glenn Miller and Kay Kyser. I don't know, I guess 'Chattanooga Choo-Choo' was big with the Yanks right about the time I crashed." As he spoke, his face got so sad that I was sorry I asked.

"I don't get most of this stuff you call music," he added. "It gives me a headache if you want to know the truth."

If Led Zeppelin provoked a migraine, I could only imagine his pain at Bush, Green Day, or, God help us, Metallica. I wondered how important it was for a couple to like the same music. Come to think of it, I had once dated a guy who was a huge Bee Gees fan, and his incessant playing of "Stayin' Alive" definitely factored into our breakup.

I had to remember that Gene might have many of the likes and dislikes of someone my grandfather's age. It gave me a weird feeling. Of course, if I thought about who Gene was, *weird feeling* didn't begin to describe my emotions. Here I was, a woman of the twenty-first century, seriously trying to build a relationship with a genie—who came out of a bottle in a Diaper Genie in my living room. And I was worried we didn't like the same music? *Get real,* I mentally screamed at myself. *That's the least of your problems.*

About an hour later I pulled the pickup in front of the office at Happy Trails. A balding guy with a Styrofoam cup of coffee in front of him and a cigarette hanging from his lips glanced up over a newspaper when I asked where to find John Osterhaupt.

"Spot six, over by the lake. Not many RVs here this time of year. You can't miss it. Brand-new Jay Feather."

I wasn't surprised by John's possession of a brand-new Jay Feather. I figured that's where part of Peggy Sue's insurance settlement had gone, and it was why I brought my mother's truck complete with trailer hitch. I intended to pull that sucker right back to Peggy Sue's driveway—without John in it. I guessed that it contained a plasma TV and a hefty supply of Yuengling lager, but I hoped not much more of the money had gone into conspicuous consumption. With a little luck and a lot of Gene's help, I was determined to retrieve whatever money remained unspent.

The Jay Feather sat in an isolated RV spot, surrounded by a few inches of snow amid the barren trees. Binghamton had missed the brunt of the storm that had clobbered us, and I was grateful. I would be able to tow the Jay Feather away without a lot of digging or Gene's magic. John Osterhaupt's blue pickup was parked on the access road, and I had to swing around it onto the snow-covered RV lot. I assumed he was home; I didn't know if his girlfriend was too.

It was 11:10 AM when I climbed up the metal steps and banged my fist on the door. I had a clipboard with me. I wore a blue suit. I looked unmistakably official. Gene stood behind me to cover my back, or more likely, to catch me if I got shoved. His face looked hard, and I knew without asking that he didn't like my going out in front.

A paunchy middle-aged man in a green T-shirt and jeans pulled the door open. He had broken veins on his nose and watery eyes that squinted in the daylight. An untrimmed beard covered his lower face, and his lips were chapped. "You here about the dump station? What's it, still froze up?"

"No, I'm here about a different kind of crap." My voice was low and nasty. Surprise and suspicion raced across John's face. He started to slam the door, and I shoved my boot-clad foot in the way, bracing myself for the pain of using it as a wedge. I never felt anything. Gene, quicker than the eye could see, disappeared from his position behind me and reappeared between John and me, his body stopping the door. He pushed the startled man back into the RV.

"Hey! What's going on? I don't want no trouble!" John yelled.

Gene ordered him to sit down and shut up. There were two chintz-covered easy chairs in the sitting area of the RV. John sat.

"Your girlfriend here?" I asked.

His frightened eyes darted back and forth between Gene and me. "She's working the breakfast shift at a restaurant downtown. You cops?"

"No. I'm a lawyer, but if we don't get some legal issues straightened out in private, you'll be seeing the cops before the hour is out. Do you understand what I'm talking about?"

"I don't know nothing. I didn't do nothing," John replied with mulish stubbornness.

"Now, John, that's not quite true, is it? You took Peggy Sue's money." I stood directly in front of him, acting like a prosecutor with a witness on the stand.

"It's my money as much as hers." He put his chin down like a bulldog's. "It was in our joint account. I had a right to take it." He tried to stand up to get in my face. He couldn't. An invisible hand held him down. He struggled to stand, thrashing and striking out with his hands but finding nothing holding him down. "What? What are you doing to me?" he choked out.

"Nothing," I said. "I'm doing nothing." Gene stood silently at my shoulder, his face like stone. "Let's get back to the money. You ran out on your wife and kids and cleaned out the bank account. That money was her insurance settlement, not yours. You know it, I know it. That's the bottom line. I'm here to get it back."

"I ain't giving you nothing," John said as he sat, flattened against the back of the chair. For all his bravado his face was ashen and filled with fear.

"I think you are, because you know it's not yours."

"You can't make me give it back," he said and struggled to get up again, getting nowhere.

"If you think that, you've got a second think coming," I said with a cold smile. It was time to put my plan into action. I hoped Gene would carry out his end of it. "And John, you know you did a bad thing. Your kids are hungry. Your wife is working two jobs. You're no good, you know that? Have you had any bad dreams yet?" I leaned my face down close to his ear, my voice dropping to a whisper.

"I don't dream. Why should I? My kids will be okay. They'll get welfare." His voice was a whine.

"No, John," I hissed into his ear. "Your wife is a good woman. Too good for you. She doesn't need welfare. You owe her eighty-eight thousand two hundred dollars and twenty-nine cents."

"No," he insisted. "The money's mine." He tried to lift his hand off the chair arm. It seemed glued down. He pulled, making the chair move beneath him, but his hand wouldn't come free.

"John, it's a sin to tell a lie. You're going to get a guilty conscience. You know that? And do you know what happens when your conscience starts working at you, John?"

"You're crazy. Get out of here!" he yelled, panic creeping into his voice.

"Nope. We can't go until we get what we came for. By the way, John, why can't you get up?"

"I don't know. I don't know." He struggled to get to his feet again. The veins on his neck bulged from the effort. The more he tried to get up, the more his back rounded with the invisible weight pressing him down.

My voice was quiet and almost cruel. "I'll tell you why you can't get up. It's guilt, John. Guilt is weighing you down. And do you notice something else? The room's getting dim. Do you see that, John?"

As we stood there, the light inside the trailer seemed to coalesce into a silver stream and pour out the window of the RV like water going down the drain. Pretty soon it was pitch-black inside. "Are you blind yet, John?" I asked.

"My eyes! What happened to my eyes? What did you do? I'm blind!" he shrieked. "I'm blind!"

Suddenly the lights went back on in a blinding flash. "No, you're not. Not yet. But guilt can make you blind, John. Shut your optic nerve right down. Didn't you know that?"

"Who are you? What are you? Let me out of here!" he screamed, still unable to get up and becoming hysterical. The leg of his pants became wet as he lost control of his bladder.

"Well, John," I said in the terrible calm voice I had been using, "I can see you're getting scared. You should be. It's not us that's doing anything. It's your mind, John. Guilt is working on your mind. It's going to keep working on you. It's going to crawl down your throat like a giant worm and twist around in your belly. Can you feel it doing that?"

John's hands went to his throat and his eyes starting bugging out of his head. The only sound he could make was a choked "aaaaggghhh."

"Choking on guilt, John?" I asked sweetly. "It's only

going to get worse. Unless you do the right thing. Are
you ready to do the right thing, John? If you are, you
can show it by signing over the owner's papers for the
RV to Peggy Sue." He was gagging, but he didn't seem
to be asking for a pen. I looked at Gene. He nodded.

"And if the guilt in your gut doesn't kill you, then
the night shadows will," I said and gestured toward
the area at the front of the RV that held the queen-
sized bed. The gray shapes of two muscular monsters
who resembled the Incredible Hulk drifted toward us.
Gene and I moved aside, and they began encircling
John's chair. The shadows made a low groaning noise
and had a loathsome smell—exactly like Brady's sulfur
poop. I tried not to gag and snuck a desperate look
at Gene, who winked at me.

Our captive began coughing and retching and crying
for help.

Then Gene took over, talking to John Osterhaupt
in a hard, deep voice. He put his face close enough
to John's to spray him with spit with almost every
word. John closed his eyes tight and grimaced. Gene
told John that the smell was the least of his problems.
He described how the night shadows would return
every evening. They would stop him from sleeping.
Every time his eyes closed, their hideous moans would
jar him awake. At that point the sound of moaning
filled the trailer, surrounding us with a horrible wailing. Then the clinking metal sound of rattling chains
added to the noise.

John began to scream. Gene ordered him to shut
up. John fell silent, and as soon as he did, all the
noise ceased.

"Those were the night shadows," I said. "You'll
hear them and you'll smell them. You'll know they're
there. And one night, John, when you are so tired you
can't bear it, your heart will stop—and explode. Just
like that, John. Boom! Unless you get rid of the guilt.
Are you ready?"

John was perspiring heavily now. His eyes were rolling with fear. He managed to say yes. I asked him where I could find the title for the RV, and he directed me to the kitchen utility drawer, where I found a brown envelope and a number of Bic pens. I removed the RV's title, put it on my clipboard, and showed John where to sign. He did it with a trembling hand.

"Now I want the money, John. Where is it?" I demanded.

John fell silent. I had pushed him as far as he was willing to go. He balked. I had to up the ante. "Won't answer, John?" I asked. "Then your guilt is going to get you," I promised.

The shadows reappeared in the room. They grew larger and denser. Their hideous laughter echoed around the RV. John went dead white.

"Is your heart okay, John?" Gene asked. "Can you hear it beating? Remember, it's going to stop—and boom! Exploded by guilt. You know I think it's beating awful loud. I can hear it all the way over here."

The sound of John's heart became amplified, sounding like a fast-beating drum. The guilt shadows laughed louder.

"Before it's too late," I coaxed, "give Peggy Sue back her money. With all that guilt hanging over you, you'd go straight to hell, you know?" The sulfur smell grew stronger and the RV started to get warm. The reflection of red flames seemed to dance around the walls. Sweat beaded up on John's forehead and then ran in rivulets down his temples.

"You want the guilt to go away?" I asked. "Do the right thing. Give back the money. Now, quick, tell me where it is."

Gene winked and the flames grew more intense. If I didn't know they were an illusion I'd think we were about to burn to death, but Gene and I stood cool and comfortable in the middle of a ring of fire. John, on the other hand, was perspiring heavily, and I was beginning to worry he might really have a heart attack. I could see the whites of his terror-stricken eyes.

"John! The money!" I insisted. "You still have time to save yourself. Where is it?"

"Under the mattress!" he shrieked. "Get it! I can't take any more. Let me out of here!"

I ran over and found an envelope under the mattress. I pulled out a wad of hundreds and a cashier's check for fifty thousand dollars. I figured the Jay Feather cost around twenty-five thousand, so give or take a couple of thousand, Peggy Sue would get most of her money back. I nodded at Gene.

"On the count of three you'll be able to get up," Gene said. He threw a denim jacket in John's lap. "Your truck key is in the pocket. Run to your truck and drive out of the park. Don't look back, and don't come back. If you stop the truck within the park or try to return, the truck will explode. Nod your head if you understand."

John nodded vigorously.

"Okay. One—" John bolted from the chair, yanked the door open, and ran.

"Two—" Gene went to the open door and yelled after him. I heard the truck motor start and tires spinning in the wet snow, then the sound of the truck racing down the access road.

Gene and I grinned at each other. I went to give him a high five. He didn't know what to do. "Smack your hand against mine," I instructed. He did. "High five! Justice has been served," I said, crumpling into the second easy chair and laughing with relief.

We were both in good spirits, for a while. But after trying to back the truck up exactly right to get the truck hitch above the ball of the RV's, I was frustrated almost to the point of tears. Gene finally ordered me out of the driver's seat and said he'd do it.

Vehicles had changed since 1942. Both the mirrors

and seat controls were motorized. I walked him
through using them. He asked about the clutch. I told
him about automatic transmissions. He mumbled
something about vehicles being idiot-proof. He told
me he was going to drive out onto the access road to
get used to the accelerator. He didn't have any problems. Then he stuck his head out of the window as he
put the truck in reverse. I waved him on back. He
lined up the hitch and the ball on the first try. He
obviously had a healthy dose of the male truck gene.

Despite that, it still took us the good part of an
hour to figure out how to get the RV unhooked from
the camp's electric and water lines and ready to roll.
It was after noon before I got behind the steering
wheel. We were about to pull out when I put the truck
in neutral instead. My head sank down and in a small
voice I confessed that under no circumstances could I
back up with the trailer on the truck. I wasn't trying
to make Gene feel indispensable. I knew my limita-
tions, and I didn't want to deliver the brand-new Jay
Feather to Peggy Sue with a big dent in it where I hit
a tree. It wasn't a helpless female act. Even a lot of
guys can't back up trailers.

Gene and I switched seats. His muscular hands took
a firm grip on the steering wheel. He had no trouble
whatsoever with moving the trailer in reverse, and he
didn't resort to magic. In fact, his face lit up, and he
appeared to be thoroughly enjoying himself as he deftly
maneuvered the RV between two huge oaks. "Reminds me of being back on the farm." He grinned. I
was relieved to see he didn't look forlorn when he
mentioned the past. I guess he was having too good
a time.

With Gene looking as if he had driven a pickup for
years—and maybe he had—we headed on down the
access road. Gene gave a blast of the horn as we
passed the office. I could see the guy inside through
the window. He was now watching television. He

never even looked in our direction, just raised his Styrofoam cup in response.

"You want to stop and let me take over?" I asked after we had left the RV park and were on the main road.

"Why don't you be the navigator this trip? You don't seem comfortable pulling a twenty-seven-foot trailer."

"I'm not, and I'd rather not attempt it. But you don't have a current driver's license."

"Don't worry about it. I'm a genie," he said and winked. A wallet and a Pennsylvania driver's license appeared on the center console. "Put it away for me, will you?"

I picked the license up. It looked authentic. The year of Gene's birth appeared as 1978 and the address listed was mine. "Nice," I said and tucked the ersatz license back into the wallet.

"Thank you," I added.

"For what?" he said as we passed a sign for the interstate.

"Take the next right, south on eighty-one," I directed. "For doing such a great job back there. I couldn't have gotten Peggy Sue's money without you."

"Damn right you couldn't have," he said.

"I agree, and I appreciate it. I'm also grateful you can drive this rig back to Noxen. I don't know what I'd do without you," I said offhandedly.

Gene grunted and drove on.

Chapter 13

Gene backed into Peggy Sue's driveway around two p.m., expertly putting the RV next to her little Ford Escort. Before the truck had even come to a full stop, she was running out the front door without a coat on. Right away I could see that Freddi had made good on her promise: Peggy Sue's hair was now a warm honey color. Despite her missing teeth, she looked years younger. Getting some sleep over the weekend may have helped her too, and right now her face was alight with hope.

I climbed out of the cab and waved the envelope over my head. She realized right away what it was. "You got it, Ravine! You really did!" she screamed. She reached me, grabbed me in a bear hug, and started to cry.

Gene got out of the truck and unhitched the trailer while I awkwardly patted Peggy Sue on the back. She sobbed for a minute, then regained her composure and let go of me. I thrust the envelope into one of her hands while she fished a tissue out of her jeans pocket with the other. She dabbed at her eyes and blew her nose.

"The money's not all there," I warned and her face got a worried look. I explained that John had bought the RV and spent some more on a television, but I showed her the cashier's check for fifty thousand dollars and told her there was another forty-three hundred in cash.

"Oh dear God, thank you," she said, as tears began running down her cheeks again, clutching the envelope to her chest with all her might. "It's more than I expected. Much more. I thought the money was gone for good."

I put my hand on her skinny shoulder. I could feel her shivering under her sweater. I told her to go over to the bank at Bowman's Creek immediately. She was to open a new account in her own name and put all but a few hundred dollars of the money in it. "Keep what you need to spend for the week, but no more. Understand?" I said. "I don't think John is going to bother you, but I want that money safe. Get a safe-deposit box for the title for the RV and leave it there until you sell it, if that's what you decide to do."

Peggy Sue listened intently and promised to leave immediately for the bank. "I don't know how you made John give up the money, but I am so thankful," she said.

"Thank Gene O'Neill, then. He's the one who convinced John to do the right thing."

Peggy Sue took a long look at the stranger named Gene. "Mister," she said, "I owe you more than I have words to tell. I don't know who you are, but you have got to be a miracle worker. Nobody else could have gotten the money back from that skunk, I know that. I thank you from my heart."

Gene's face glowed red from embarrassment. "No thanks needed," he mumbled.

"He is a miracle worker. You're right about that," I said, looking at him, my heart full of love.

Peggy Sue watched the two of us closely.

Gene said to her, "The trailer's unhitched. Is it going to be okay parked where it is?"

"It's real good there. Thanks."

"Then we'll be going," I said. "You go to the bank, right now, you hear?"

"I am. I'm going to grab my car keys. Ravine?"

"Yes?"

"What do I owe you?"

"I filed your divorce papers this morning. I'll send you a bill, okay? First things first. And now you can quit working at Offset," I said, smiling.

"Oh, I'll quit the Pump 'n' Pantry for sure," she said happily. "But I'm going to work at Offset tonight, and I doubt I'll quit there, at least for now. I need the health insurance. When I get the day care going, I might. But don't you worry about me. Thanks to you and Gene, I'm going to be just fine." She gave me a last smile as she turned and hurried up her front walk, her hair floating around her shoulders. When she looked back and waved, I could get a glimpse of how pretty she had once been.

Fatigue caught up with me after we collected Brady from my mother's house and returned her truck. Without elaborating I told her that Peggy Sue got her money back and I'd give her the details later. I wanted to get back home and collapse.

You don't always get what you want.

A car with FIRE MARSHAL stenciled on the side was sitting in my driveway when we pulled in.

A tall, heavyset man with gray hair and an air of authority stepped out of his vehicle as soon as I unbuckled Brady from his car seat. Gene had grabbed the baby bag and came around the Beemer to stand next to me.

"Ravine Patton?" the man asked.

"Yes," I said.

"My name's Joe Barletta. I'm here about the fire you had Friday night. I have a couple of questions for you."

"This is my friend Gene O'Neill," I said, and Gene put out his hand. They shook. "Why don't you come inside," I said.

Gene offered to get Brady out of his snowsuit, and I led the fire marshal into the living room. I asked if I could take his coat as I removed my own.

"No, thanks. I'll only stay a minute," he answered. "I wanted to ask if you knew a man named Alvin Hoyt."

"Yes," I said.

"Did he have any reason to wish you harm?"

"I don't know if he wished me harm or not. He didn't have positive feelings about me, I can tell you that much. For one thing, he hated anybody who was a Patton. It was an old feud, going back years. And a few days ago, I had reason to believe he harassed some of my clients. I warned him to stay away from them."

"Did you warn him in person?"

"I did."

"When was this?"

"Thursday, the day before the fire."

"And how did he react to your warning?"

"He was agitated, mostly because I was at his place without an invitation, I think. He denied bothering anybody, but he seemed to get the message to stay away from them." I shrugged. "I thought that was the end of it."

"Did he threaten you in any way?"

"He didn't threaten me verbally, but he got his rifle out and stood there on the porch with it as I drove away."

The fire marshal kept his face impassive but a muscle near his eye twitched. "I guess Mr. Hoyt might have been more upset than you thought he was. We're pretty sure he's the one who set your fire. You know he died in that storm?"

"Yes, I heard."

"We're assuming you don't have anything more to worry about. In any event, whoever tried to burn down your house wasn't a professional arsonist. Putting gasoline on the ground around a house is mostly for intimidation, to scare people to death. Sure, it might burn down the house—a spark from burning garbage can burn down a house—but this kind of thing, a ring of fire, is for effect mostly. So you got lucky, if you want to look at it like that. An arsonist who knew what he was doing? We would be standing in a pile of ashes right now."

My face turned white and I felt chilled all over. The fire marshal's voice got softer. "Sorry to have upset you. What I was trying to say is that somebody—whether it was Alvin Hoyt, we don't know for sure—was trying to frighten you. So be on your guard, that's all. When we finish our investigation, I'll get back to you. Actually, with Mr. Hoyt's bad feelings about your family and the arson attempt following so close after your warning to him, I think it's an open-and-shut case. Thank you for your time, Ms. Patton."

I led him back to the front door. I wasn't so sure it was an open-and-shut case, but I kept my reservations to myself.

I called out to Gene that I had to make a phone call and hurried into the office to call the Katos. I asked them if they were doing all right. They said they were and that they hadn't had any other incidents. I told them about Scabby Hoyt's death in the snow. Gentle and compassionate people that they were, they were both upset over his dying.

I added, making my voice as grim as I could to stress my seriousness, that we still didn't know if Scabby's death had been an accident; I believed someone else had sent Scabby to scare them. "Please keep taking the precautions I suggested," I concluded.

They assured me that they would, although they still hadn't gotten a watchdog. They were afraid he would bother the cats, they said. I assured them that some dogs would not harm their cats, but they didn't seem convinced.

Their remark about the dog set me thinking. I dialed my mother. "Ma," I said, "what happened to Scabby's dog? Did anybody take him in?"

"Not that I know of. Why?"

"I think the Katos will take him. They need a good watchdog who's also a gentle sort."

"Cal might know. Let me call him and I'll get back to you."

Calvin Metz again. My mother mentioned him almost every time we spoke. The charter school might be something they were tackling together, but I felt certain a love relationship had developed. I hoped so, and smiled as I thanked my mother and hung up.

When I walked back into the kitchen, Gene had Brady in his high chair and was amusing him with some Cheerios on the tray.

"You look worn out," he said. "Come here."

I did and he wrapped me in his arms. We stood there and kissed. I forgot I was tired, I felt so happy. It didn't last long.

"I went out and got the mail," Gene murmured in my ear. "It's there on the table. Why don't you look through it while I make you a cup of tea? It's almost teatime."

I sat down, and spotted a lilac-colored envelope peeking out from behind the electric bill. The return address told me it was from Tawnya Jones. I opened it, and along with the information I had told her to write down, she had enclosed a retainer check for a hundred dollars. I stuffed the check back in the envelope and shoved it under the bills. I felt uneasy at the prospect of telling Gene about another job I had to do, and that there was an outside chance I could end up at a strip club.

The teakettle whistled and without magic, or with

only a little, Gene soon had the Sadler teapot on the table along with a plate of small sandwiches made with minced ham and watercress and another of lemon curd tarts. I took a hesitant bite of a tart, and discovered that the crust was light and buttery and the lemon curd itself—sweet and sour at the same time, very lemony with a hint of a golden egginess—was almost the best thing I had ever tasted. The sandwiches and tarts were washed down with cup after cup of tea from the pot which mysteriously never got empty.

I told Gene about Scabby's dog and my idea to get him to the Katos.

He looked at me for a long minute. "You're always trying to help somebody. Okay, you're also meddling or rushing in where you shouldn't go, but you have a very good heart."

I didn't know what to say except thanks.

"You remind me of my mother," he said, looking away, his mouth turning up in a funny little smile. "She'd do exactly the same thing."

I forgot about Queen Nefertitty with her stolen urn of ashes. The three of us all went into the living room for a cuddle on the sofa, and we dozed off one by one for a brief nap as the afternoon slid gracefully into evening. My hunger satisfied and Gene's arms around me and Brady, I couldn't have found a better way to finish the day.

The night didn't hold the same delights. Dinner was nice enough. If the way to a woman's heart was through her stomach, Gene had captured mine. Along with a basket filled with crusty garlic bread, he had included a glass of red wine, another highly rated Australian Shiraz. Once again I swirled the ruby liquid around in the glass and inhaled the aroma, but this time I didn't comment on it. I didn't want to chance hearing Gene spin out plans to buy a vineyard. Maybe that's what he had been researching on the Internet: the right land to create the O'Neill Vineyards near Melbourne. For all I knew he was even more serious than ever about getting in on the ground floor of this industry of the future.

After a dinner during which neither he nor I said much, I took Brady up for his bath and tucked him into bed. I told Gene I needed to do a few hours' work in my office. Actually I wanted to think. I had to figure out what my next steps should be on the Kato case as well as how to wrap up Tawyna Jones and her ashes problem as quickly as possible. But I no sooner sat down at my desk than my mind wandered to the situation between Gene and me.

First I wondered if my strategy to make Gene feel indispensable was working. If it was, was it the right thing to do? I had been an independent woman for so long that I didn't do "needy" very well. The day had been, by and large, a great success. But thinking now about my independence raised a host of issues I had been avoiding. In Gene's era, the man ruled the household. In his position as a genie under a spell of enchantment, Gene was obliged to obey orders. He fetched and carried, did housework and cooked. If I made my third wish and he became an ordinary man again, what would he be willing to do? I trailed a pen down a legal pad, doodling circles, then wrote "Gene the genie vs. Gene the man."

Gene the genie was compliant, obedient, and a gentleman. Gene the man was brave, sexy, aggressive, chauvinistic, and possessed of a temper. Did I really know what I was getting myself into?

All my girlfriends talked about the honeymoon phase in a relationship when the guy was a prince: He was attentive and accommodating, picked up his clothes and the tab, maintained an affable disposition and was nice to your mother. But at some point Dr. Jekyll became Mr. Hyde, complete with mood swings, outbursts of temper, and a dogged stubbornness about the TV remote control, which movies he was willing to see, how often he'd visit your relatives, and whether he did any housework at all. Personal hygiene had been known to slip; outright refusals to go shopping at the mall were common. It was a scary scenario.

I already knew that Gene had his limits about going along with what I wanted. How much could or would I compromise? Why couldn't life be like a romance novel where all that mattered was, well, romance? Instead I needed to know if Gene and I were compatible about doing housework (he already thought I was a poor cleaner, and he was right), spending money (I was a grasshopper, not an ant), and staying faithful to each other (24/7 for me, no exceptions).

On the other hand, having Gene here gave me blissful feelings of security and belonging, the joy of companionship, and the thrill of sexual play. How did all the elements balance out? Right now, I wanted to be with Gene every minute, and I didn't want to envision life without him.

At that point of my musings about Gene and me, another plan formed in my mind. It was a week before Thanksgiving. Gene's birthday was on Christmas Eve. Five weeks wasn't a long period of time to test a relationship, but we were living together, not just dating. I should know by Christmas if what my whole being was telling me was true: that despite his being a genie, born in 1913, and coming from a world away in space and time, Gene O'Neill was "the one"—the man I had been waiting for.

So I made up my mind. Christmas Eve would be the deadline. If I was sure it was the right thing, and if Gene had committed to staying in the present, on that night I'd wish for Gene to be released from his enchantment. If not—if either one of us had doubts or a change of heart—I'd make another wish having nothing to do with Gene. I hadn't given more thought to helping Freddi with her pregnancy. But that was a possibility. Or I could wish for the charter school to be deeded over to my mother and Cal. I could even wish for a major client to take me on; that would end my financial worries. All of those things could be worthy things to wish for.

I took a deep breath. I had to face facts. Right now Gene still intended to leave—despite our intimacy. If I did the noble thing, the unselfish thing, and made a wish, he would be freed from the magus's spell and perhaps end up back in the Sahara in 1942. A wave of sadness and fear washed over me when I thought about Gene's vanishing. I realized that I was fooling myself. No matter what fights we were bound to have, how many lifestyle differences loomed ahead, or what habits of his were sure to drive me crazy, I didn't want to let him go. The fact that he still planned on leaving just about tore me apart.

I sighed. I wanted to have control of the future and, in reality, I had virtually none. I would go ahead and make sure Gene knew he was needed here, but I wouldn't pretend to change or try to be someone other than who I was. If he loved me, he had to love me warts and all. If I loved him, the same rules applied. And if he stayed, he had to want to be in this time and place without second thoughts, because there would be no turning back.

I took out a desk calendar and put a big red circle around Christmas Eve, as if I would need the reminder. Even as I did it, negativity overwhelmed me. What were the chances Gene would still be here by then? Why was I prolonging the situation? Maybe I should make my third wish tomorrow and get it over with. But even as I thought that, I knew I couldn't do it. I also made up a schedule for tomorrow: first thing in the morning, go to the courthouse to search deeds; afternoon, try to track down Queen Nefertitty; and late afternoon, stop off to see the Katos before coming back home.

At that point, it occurred to me that I needed to come up with some child care arrangements. I wasn't comfortable leaving Brady at all, and certainly not with dropping him off at some day care center with strangers. My mother might be able to take over a few days a week, but with her new charter school in the works, she might not. I figured I'd better call her.

My mother was at home since Monday wasn't a bingo night, a church committee night, or her line dancing night. First thing she told me was that Calvin Metz had found out that Scabby's dog was down at the police station. His relatives took the cows, but nobody wanted the big yellow Lab called Casey. The cops didn't want to take him to the SPCA if they didn't have to, and they were trying to find somebody local to adopt him. I told her I'd pick the dog up before I went out to see the Katos tomorrow.

My mother was also willing to come over Tuesday afternoon to stay with Brady and agreed to sit down with me to figure out how often she could help out as a babysitter. For the past few months, she had been my right hand as well as my mother; I didn't have to tell her how much I needed her. She knew, and she was always there. I started to feel better. I thought I had all my ducks in a row. That was pure self-deception; what happened would turn out to be in the best-laid-plans-get-f'd department.

To start with, Gene and I had a rip-roaring argument over Queen Nefertitty.

"Gene," I had said, "I'm heading out to the courthouse tomorrow morning to look into land titles and recent deed transfers. I need you to watch Brady."

He was in the kitchen up on a chair with a screwdriver in his hand, tightening the hinges on the cabinets. "Okay. I saw some repairs that need to be done on the house. You have a problem with me fixing some things?"

I stood there looking at him. "Why should I? Do whatever you want. I plan to be back around twelve. My mother's coming over to watch Brady in the afternoon."

"Why does your mother need to watch Brady? Am I going somewhere?" His eyes narrowed. Suspicion seeped into his voice.

"Maybe you'd better get off the chair and we can talk about it. I'd like you to come with me to Wilkes-Barre. I have a case there."

He jumped down. He wasn't smiling. "You don't want me to scare somebody to death again, do you?"

"I don't think it will come to that. I need you along for backup."

"Backup? You're a lawyer, not a police officer. What do you need backup for?" His voice was getting noticeably louder.

"Probably nothing. I have to negotiate a settlement with a young woman. I don't anticipate a problem really," I said.

"I've got the feeling you're not telling me something. Don't expect me to walk into something blind. I learned in the war that going out on a mission without knowing what crap the enemy might throw at you is suicide. I want the whole story, and I want it now."

"I don't like your tone of voice." I could see he was going to be difficult about this.

"And I don't like being dragged into your schemes without any say about them. You tell me I'm an equal partner, but your words don't match your actions."

I swallowed hard. He was right, and I had handled this badly. "I guess I have done that. I'm sorry."

"That's what you said the last time. Now you've done the same thing again. How can I believe you?" His jaw had thrust forward.

I felt rotten. I had really screwed this up. "Gene, really, I'm sorry. I got myself into a mess and need your help in getting out of it. I guess I shouldn't expect you to want to help me."

"What mess?"

"The Queen Nefertitty thing. I didn't know she had a gun."

"A gun? Who the hell is Queen Nefertitty and how does a weapon come into this!"

"You're yelling. I knew that's what you'd do. I can't talk to you. I'm going to have to take care of this on my own, I see that now." I started to march out of the room.

Gene grabbed my arm and turned me around to face him. "Not so fast. Explain, and explain everything."

"Let go of me."

"No. Not until you tell me what you're planning to do and how a gun comes into it. This is not a game to me, Ravine. You can't tell me something like that and then walk away. I'm not going to allow it."

"You're not going to *allow* it!" I was so mad I was starting to see red. "I'm not taking orders from you."

"You expect me to take them from you, don't you? I'm your genie. I have to obey you. Well, if that's how you want it, then what I'll be to you is a genie. And that's all I'll be."

With that Gene let go of my arm. His form grew transparent and turned into a wisp of smoke which floated up into the air and streamed over to the kitchen counter before disappearing into the amber bottle.

"Oh you—you—impossible—man!" I yelled after him. I was furious with his behavior, and with my own. I was messing up everything. I stood there for a minute before I suddenly burst into tears and ran upstairs. I flung myself down on the bed and cried my eyes out. It was totally out of character. True, I was pre-menstrual, but I don't think I had ever felt more miserable in my life.

Five minutes later I heard a rapping on the door-frame leading into my room. I lifted my tearstained face and saw Gene standing in the doorway.

"I can't come in," he said. "My mistress forbade me to step foot in her bedroom. But maybe she'd come out here. Please?"

I got up and walked into the hall. Gene took me in his arms and kissed the tears off my cheeks. "I'm sorry I made you cry," he said.

"You didn't make me cry. I did that all by myself," I said, burying my face in his broad shoulder.

"Either way, I can't stand seeing you unhappy. I'm sorry I lost my temper. It's just that I'm afraid you're going to get hurt. Listen, okay? I need you to talk to me *before* you do something that might get your head blown off, that's all." He was stroking my hair while he talked and I didn't want to let go of him. It felt so good to have my arms around his body and not have him a puff of smoke that I couldn't reach and couldn't touch.

I lifted my head and looked at him. "I didn't mean for it to happen. I really didn't. I didn't know about the gun until I had already agreed to try to get my client's ashes back from the woman who took them."

"Ravine, I hate to say this, but you're not making a lot of sense."

"It's a long story. As I started to explain earlier, I committed myself to doing something I shouldn't have agreed to do. Now I need you to help me; I can't do it without you," I said, being only a little disingenuous and starting to brush my lips against his. Then I kissed him, long and hard.

Gene moaned. "I will never be able to say no to you. Not when you kiss like that. I'll watch your back, of course I will. I'll watch your front. I'll watch every inch of you. But I'm asking you, not ordering you, will you say a few crucial words *before* you agree to do something that involves *both* of us?"

"What words?' I asked, kissing him again and letting my lips trail down his chin to his neck.

His breathing was getting shallower, and he whispered hoarsely in reply: "These: *Let me talk with my partner about it. I'll get back to you.* Can you promise me that?" he said, squeezing his eyes shut because I was pressing my body tightly against his in a sensitive place.

"That sounds like a reasonable request. I promise, *partner,*" I said softly and in all sincerity. And at that moment, I did sincerely mean it. "Now if I could address you as a genie—"

Gene's eyes sprang open. "Why?"

"I need to lift the ban on my genie's coming into my bedroom. Is it okay with you, genie, if I allow you to come in?"

"I am pleased to obey you," he said in a raspy voice and lifted me up into his arms. He carried me over to the bed and put me gently down on the crazy quilt that covered it. "Docs this mean you want me to sleep here tonight?"

"Yes, it does. But I had something else in mind besides sleep, at least right now."

"So do I," he murmured as he started to remove my clothes. It turned out we were both thinking about exactly the same thing.

The second thing that happened that night that upset me—in fact, shook me to my bones—was this. Gene was sleeping soundly, his arm across his muscular chest, a soft snore escaping his lips, when I slipped out of bed about midnight. I put on a warm robe and quietly left the room. I wanted to peek in on Brady and make sure he was okay.

I went into my baby's room that smelled of flowery

baby lotion and faintly of wet diapers, despite the Diaper Genie. Brady didn't stir as I leaned down over his crib and kissed him gently on the cheek. He was such a beautiful baby, and so good it brought tears to my eyes just to look at him. Yet as I looked at him, his night-light illuminating brightly enough for me to see his face, I saw, besides Brady's beloved features, how much he looked like Jake.

My involvement with Gene had made my emotional life complicated very quickly. I didn't want any loose ends from the past. I had to find Jake and tell him about Brady, then work something out with him if he wanted to see his son. I couldn't let the situation go. I knew that.

I stopped by the window and looked out at the night. The moon was nearly full and so bright that only the biggest stars were visible. The snow had started to melt during the day, collapsing in spots and losing its fluffiness. After the sun went down and the temperature dropped, the wet snow had gotten hard and icy. The moonlight reflected off the now shiny surface of the wide fields behind the house. I saw no one standing out there tonight and felt comforted by the emptiness.

But when I turned away and headed back to bed, from the road that ran along the front of the house I heard the sharp, quick sound of a motorcycle starting up and then fading out when it drove away. I listened with my heart beating wildly as the silence of the night returned.

Chapter 14

A little after nine a.m. on Tuesday, the wooden floor-boards of the county courthouse creaked under my feet as I made my way through the metal detector and found the first-floor room holding deeds and land transfer information. The affable clerk, her gray hair tightly permed and her bifocals set in pink plastic frames that appeared to date from the 1970s, quickly retrieved the records from the Sikorsky farm and the Katos' B and B. I showed my driver's license to her, signed a large ledger to acknowledge receipt of two dark brown accordion files, and took them over to a scuffed-up wooden table. I opened the first of the files, identified by a parcel number, not a name, and began to read.

The purchaser of the Sikorsky land and buildings—the farm where the well had mysteriously become tainted—was no lone bachelor farmer. The purchaser of record was a real estate corporation called Running Brook Development Company. I made a note to look up the principal shareholders and track down its origins. The Sikorskys had owned the land since the 1920s when it had been bought from one of the Sicklers, an old family that had settled in this region in the early 1800s. I couldn't find the Sicklers' original deed. Instead, transfer of the property from the Sicklers to the Sikorskys included a notarized affidavit that the land was part of the "Last Purchase" made by the state of Pennsylvania in 1784.

I took the file back up to the counter. "If the original deed isn't in here, where might it be?" I asked the clerk.

"If it's not there, it has been lost somewhere, especially if the deed originated before the Civil War. Of course, it might be in Harrisburg, but I doubt it. Let's see." She looked at the folder. "Oh yes, some of the recipients of Last Purchase land were recorded at the capital. You might find something there. These affidavits were accepted up until 1950."

"Okay, thanks," I said and went back to look at the Katos' land records in the other file. The history of the Katos' B and B told a different tale and one that ultimately made my hair stand on end.

The Katos had purchased their two hundred acres, farmhouse, and barn, now the Jade Meadow Farm, from a Richard and Charlotte Yeager. The Yeagers had bought the property from the Kawatchski family in the 1980s. And that's when things got interesting. The Kawatchskis' deed dated from 1785 and was obtained by a Revolutionary War soldier named John Kawatchski in exchange for a certificate, issued to returning Continental Army veterans, entitling him to land for his military service in lieu of pay. What riveted my attention, however, was the very faded note, easily overlooked, written in sepia ink and lightly penned in at the bottom of the deed:

> *John Kawatchski, or Kakowatchiky, was a full-blooded Shawnee Indian, son of Chief Kakowatchiky formerly of Shawnee Flats in Plymouth. His certificate contained a notation in Gen. G. Washington's own hand that any land redeemed by Kakowatchiky was to be considered Shawnee tribal lands in perpetuity in recognition of his acts of*

courage during the War for Independence. This
original certificate, because of Wash.'s note, has
been given to the Penn. Historical Commission
in Harrisburg.

The handwritten note was signed "Andrew Montour, Wyoming County Register of Deeds, 1876."

I had an *aha!* moment. I knew that the state of Pennsylvania had granted a license to the Seneca to run the local racetrack, but the Seneca had competed for the license with other vendors. It wasn't so in other states. Many Indian-run casinos could be found in New York State and Connecticut because the casinos were built on tribal lands. Under federal law, a recognized tribe has the right to run gaming facilities on its land, and the state cannot stop the tribe from creating the facility or operating it. Pennsylvania had none of these casinos because no federally recognized tribes owned land in Pennsylvania, or at least no one knew they did—until now.

I believed the Kakowatchiky deed meant that the Shawnee, a recognized tribe, could develop the Katos' land as a gaming operation. All they had to do was retrieve the land from the Katos. In fact, I bet that neither the Yeagers nor the Katos had had any right to buy the land in the first place since it had been granted "in perpetuity" to the Shawnee.

If the Shawnee contested the sale, the whole thing could turn into a nasty court battle, but the easiest way to obtain the land for gaming would be for the Shawnee to quietly reimburse the Katos for their purchase price. To the best of my knowledge no tribe member had approached the Katos, which told me that the Shawnee didn't know about the Kakowatchiky tribal lands. But I had a strong hunch that someone else did and was looking to make a quick profit by buying the property cheaply from the frightened

Katos and reselling the land back to the Shawnee for big money.

I returned to the counter and asked the clerk if anyone else had looked at the Katos' deed recently. She said someone had.

"Wait a minute." She nodded and ducked down below the counter. "We can find it right here in the ledger." She pulled out the large book that I had just signed and put it down in front of me. "We still don't have these records on computer, although everything in this office is supposed to be transferred over the next few years," she explained. "Then people can do their research online. I don't know if that's a good thing. Especially when it comes to liens against property. It makes it too easy for people to stick their noses into other people's business. I don't agree with it at all." Meanwhile she opened the ledger, ran her finger down a page, and then turned the book around so I could see the entry where her index finger pointed.

"Two months ago. Right there. It was a Joann Kawatchski. She said she was kin to the original owners and was researching her family tree."

"Thank you. That makes perfect sense," I said and wondered if Joann Kawatchski could possibly be Jo/Joann from the London Junkyard. I glanced at my watch. It was still early. I had plenty of time to stop by there and find out before I had to go back home.

Low gray clouds had made the daylight murky by the time I pulled into London's Salvage and Junkyard. So many state police cars had parked around the building that I wondered if there had been a robbery or something, although what a thief might want to steal here, I couldn't imagine.

I grabbed my briefcase out of the backseat and started walking toward the office door. My snow boots didn't look chic, but as I picked my way through slush and mud to get to the squat cement block building, I was glad that I had taken off my Moschino pumps when I left the courthouse. They were last year's style, but I hadn't worn them after my feet swelled up during my pregnancy. With my tight budget, they were the last Moschino shoes I'd be able to buy for a long, long time.

I knocked on the metal door, and a woman's voice called out, "Come on in."

Cigarette smoke mixing with the noxious fumes of a kerosene heater assailed my lungs the moment I stepped into the office, a sparsely furnished room filled by Joann, a plus-sized woman, and her desk. A flashy purple Siamese fighting fish swam around the roots of a plant in a clear vase; it seemed to be the sole personal touch in the bland room.

Joann stared at me. Since I was carrying a briefcase and dressed in a suit, I think she was trying to figure out if I was "somebody." She must have figured I wasn't. A box of Winston cigarettes lay next to an ashtray already containing a dozen butts smoked down to their filters. Joann reached for the Winston box, tapped out a cigarette, and lit.

"What can I do for you?" she asked and blew a cloud of smoke in my direction.

"Are you Joann Kawatchski?" I asked.

"Yeah, who wants to know?" Her piggy eyes squinted at me without warmth.

"I'm a real estate attorney. My name is Ravine Patton. I was wondering what your interest is in Jade Meadow Farm out in Beaumont."

Behind her heavy makeup her face paled. "What's it to you?"

"Quite a lot. I represent the owners, and it seems somebody has been pressuring them into selling their property." My voice was hard. I straightened my shoulders and slapped my briefcase down on a chair with a bang. "What was your business with Alvin Hoyt?"

Her face turned even paler and sweat beaded on her upper lip above the cigarette.

"I don't have anything to say to you," she said.

"Would you rather talk to the police?" I asked, staring her down.

At that she began to laugh. I didn't get the joke.

"I think you better talk to my boss. Hold on a moment," she said. She punched numbers into her cell phone and a few seconds later, she spoke into it. She told her boss that I was out in her office asking about Jade Meadow Farm. Then Joann heaved herself up from her desk chair, and her body was racked by a phlegmy smoker's cough. When the coughing stopped, she took a last puff on her Winston before crushing it out in the ashtray.

"Follow me," she said. I picked up my briefcase and walked behind her as she lumbered toward a door in the back of the room, her terry cloth bedroom slippers shuffling across the linoleum floor. When she opened the door, her girth filled the entrance. I figured she'd have to turn sideways to get through it, but instead she stepped aside. "Go right in there." She gestured with her head.

As I walked by, I could smell the pungent combination of stale tobacco, Jean Naté cologne, and fear.

Against one wall of the room I entered stood a long narrow table, groaning under its load of food: a huge platter of fresh fruits, another laden with rolls, and a long warming station with stainless chafing dishes over Sterno heaters. In the center of the room, at a table covered with a white linen tablecloth, sat a dozen state police officers in uniform. They were eating and talking, their plates piled high with pancakes, scrambled eggs, and sausages. A waiter with a carafe of coffee was silently filling their cups.

As I took in this unexpected scene, a patrician-looking man with a shock of silver hair and a finely tailored pin-striped suit walked over to me, his hand outstretched. "I'm George London. I don't believe I've had the pleasure."

His handshake was dry and firm, with a politician's polished style.

"Ravine Patton. I apologize for intruding. I had some questions about a local property, and I thought I would be speaking to Ms. Kawatchski."

He asked if he could get me anything to eat. I politely refused, but agreed to a cup of coffee.

"Sal!" Mr. London called out to the white-coated waiter and told him to bring two cups into his office.

"Let's have a word in private, and I'll see if I can answer your questions," George London said with a friendly smile that appeared completely genuine. Light twinkled off a diamond pinky ring as he gestured toward another door off the dining room. Handsome and energetic, he reminded me of Bill Clinton, a man whose charisma hid any character flaws and whose power didn't need a display of authority. He had it, he could use it, and everybody knew it.

London's office, even in the middle of a junkyard, was well-appointed, with a modern chrome and glass desk atop a deep red oriental carpet, and Mies van der Rohe chairs in fawn-colored leather. He asked me to sit, and I did.

The waiter entered with a tray holding two cups, a carafe of coffee, and a silver creamer and sugar bowl. He put the tray down on the coffee table between the chairs.

"Thank you, Sal," London said and closed the door when the waiter left.

I put my briefcase down on the floor next to me as George London sat and passed me a cup of black coffee. "Cream or sugar?"

I shook my head no. London took his black as well. He sat back and asked, "How can I help you?"

I began my hastily rehearsed story. "I represent the owners of Jade Meadow Farm, a small B and B in Wyoming County. I have reason to believe that someone wants to frighten them into selling their property. I was wondering if you might know anything about it."

"Why would you think that I did?"

"Because of Alvin Hoyt. I believe he was the person frightening the owners, and he had been in contact with someone from this salvage yard."

George London listened attentively. He didn't appear hostile or threatening in any way, but I felt somewhat uncomfortable and regretted walking into this situation unprepared. "That's a very disturbing conclusion for you to have made. A lot of people contact this salvage yard for car parts. Why would you think I or someone from my company had any interest in the Wyoming property?"

"Because Alvin Hoyt had been in touch with your employee, Ms. Kawatchski, and Ms. Kawatchski recently researched the deed for Jade Meadow Farm." Something in George London's face changed, just for a microsecond, and my uneasiness deepened. I decided diplomacy was called for. I went on quickly. "Please don't misunderstand me, I'm not accusing anyone of anything. And now, especially since Mr. Hoyt has—has passed on, I am concerned. I wanted to personally convey the information that any inquiries into buying that particular property need to go through me."

George London studied me for a moment, then nodded. "Of course. You would be working for a commission. Now I understand your concerns. Do you have a card?" He seemed to conclude that my visit was all about my slice of the pie and was visibly relieved.

I had printed out a few business cards on my office computer before I left for the courthouse this morning. They looked cheap and unimpressive, but they'd have to do until I had better ones made up at Office Depot. I handed one to Mr. London. "I recently moved back into this area and have gone into private practice here. I was formerly with Withersham, Carlisle, and Katz in Philadelphia." My previous employer was a big gun in Pennsylvania real estate. From the look of surprise that crossed London's face, I suspected he recognized the name.

"I appreciate your stopping by, Ms. Patton. If this is a property my company has any interest in—and I'm not aware that it does—I'll be sure we contact you."

That sounded like a dismissal to me. He stood up. I did also and picked up my briefcase. George London escorted me out. None of the troopers busy with their brunch and conversation paid any attention to me; Joann Kawatchski gave me a smirk as we passed her desk. I stepped out into the damp November air wondering if coming here had been a very big mistake.

I had a short discussion with myself on the way back to the house over whether or not I should tell Gene about my experience at the junkyard. It didn't take me long to decide I wouldn't mention it. Okay, maybe that was a coward's way out, but despite my misgivings after speaking with George London, I soon mentally worked out a way to wrap up the Katos' case without any danger to life or limb. Hammering out the details might take a few hours, but I had every confidence that their problems were essentially over—and the case might bring in a substantial fee that I hadn't foreseen.

I felt good about the Katos, but as I drove, my thoughts turned to Freddi. Meddling in people's lives can backfire. I knew that. Just the same, Freddi was somebody I truly loved. Maybe I should use my third wish to give her what she needed—even if it meant not getting what I wanted. What I wanted was Gene, of course. Only I didn't want him if he didn't want

me. Okay, that was a lie. I did want him even if he
didn't want me, but I was smart enough to know that
in the end, that arrangement wouldn't work. Worst-
case scenario: I'd wish for Gene to stay in this time
and place and he would—and would leave me anyway.
He might never forgive me for taking away his only
chance to go home, or . . . or he'd stay and find somebody else. That bastard! I felt myself getting all
worked up.

Ergo, I was back to Plan B, as in B for baby. Thinking like a lawyer as well as a best friend, I decided a
preliminary investigation was necessary. Also, I could
use a haircut. I called Freddi from my cell phone to
see if she had a customer. She told me she was between appointments, so I made a sharp right off the
highway and arrived at Freddi's Beauty Shop in
minutes.

The only occupant of the beauty shop was Cuddles,
Freddi's aging dog. I noticed that Freddi's favorite flea
market find, a painting of Elvis on velvet, had been
replaced with a poster of American Idol Taylor Hicks.

I had put down my briefcase when Freddi walked
into the shop. Her eyes were puffy. I didn't know if
she had been crying or if the fertility drugs were making her bloat.

"What happened to Elvis?" I asked.

"He's in the bathroom. I put the king closer to the
throne." She laughed and followed my eyes to the
poster. "You watch *American Idol*?"

"No. Never got into it."

"You should. Taylor's really good. 'Soul Patrol.
Soul Patrol,' " she chanted.

I looked at her blankly.

"Oh, never mind," she said and ordered me to sit
down.

I settled myself in the barber's chair, staring at myself in the mirror, a sheet wrapped around my neck.
I told Freddi I needed a trim.

"Trim? You need a good cut. Your ends are split. You still lightening your hair yourself?" she asked.

"I don't lighten my hair. That's my natural shade," I protested.

"Yeah, right. You started using lemon juice on your hair in grade school. Remember the time in high school—"

"Don't remind me." I cringed beneath the sheet.

"You decided to go platinum right before the junior prom. Your hair turned green. My mother had to cut most of it off."

"Okay, so I looked like Sinéad O'Connor. It was pretty trendy."

"Your date was horrified."

"I was horrified. He was wearing a powder blue tuxedo and had gotten new glasses. I thought I was with Elton John."

"And you opted to go Goth at the last minute. You looked like Marilyn Manson in drag."

"How could you tell if Marilyn Manson was in drag?"

"Point. But back to your hair." She lifted some strands in the back and studied them. "You've got three or four different shades going on here. I need to give you a rinse. Even it out, okay?"

I agreed and told her to do whatever she wanted, as long as she didn't scalp me.

I stayed quiet while Freddi shampooed me and picked up her scissors. I hated to get her worked up while she was cutting. Last time she had a fight with Bobby I ended up with Mamie Eisenhower bangs. They were hideous. But it was now or never. I asked her how she was feeling, with the fertility drugs and all.

"I feel like crap. Nervous. Jumpy. Bobby can't do anything right. I'm all over him. Then the waiting and suffering ends up being all for nothing. I get my period, and the whole insanity starts all over again. And no way can we afford in vitro. Even if we mortgaged the house. Besides, the success rates are pretty low."

"You're going to keep trying, right?"

"Maybe. I guess. I'm beginning to think I have to accept that I'm not going to get pregnant. And Bobby would be okay with that. As it is, we're fighting all the time. I'm crying or screaming at him half the day. It's like having PMS on steroids. I think if I keep taking these drugs our marriage is going to go down the crapper."

I let out a deep sigh. Freddi and Bobby had been together since tenth grade. "I can't imagine you split up."

Freddi's scissors paused. She looked at me in the mirror. "Ravine, you know I never went to college, but I see a lot of life doing hair. I really do. Couples split up all the time, and over dumb stuff too. But mostly they just change. Grow apart. I'm not the same person I was in high school. I have interests now, like papermaking. I've even used papyrus. I bet you didn't know I did that. I like libraries too. Every town I drive through, I stop off and look for the public library. Bobby likes NASCAR races and tractor pulls. I don't know if we have anything in common anymore. I'm more than 'Bobby's girl.' I could make it on my own."

"Well, what if you do get pregnant? Would it change anything?"

"It would change a lot. I'd fight like hell to keep my marriage together because I want my baby to have a family. Right now, to tell the truth, sometimes I think God knows best. I'm not pregnant because I'd be better off without Bobby Timko. You know, Ravine, you have to be careful what you wish for." Her eyes welled up with tears. Oh great, she was still cutting and I bet she couldn't see. I told her I thought it was the drugs talking. She put down the scissors, thank God, wiped her eyes, and said she guessed I was right.

After a quick blow-dry, I gave her a hug and left.

My hair had bounce and the color was great, but I thought it was a little shorter on the right side. I'd even it out myself if I had to. That didn't bother me. Freddi's situation did. It wasn't clear-cut—no pun intended—that a baby was what she needed right now. Maybe she needed to move on with her life, without Bobby. Or maybe a baby would save her marriage. No matter which way I looked at it, I didn't get the easy answers I wanted. And behind it all, no matter how I viewed it, I wanted things to work out between Gene and me even though I faced the unpleasantness of taking him with me to find Queen Nefertitty.

Gene noticed my hair. He thought it looked good. He didn't say much more until after my mother showed up to watch Brady and we left the house. Once we were in the Beemer and rolling down the highway, he turned to me and asked, "How do you intend to handle this?"

I hadn't come up with any brilliant plan, so I said as much. "Ummm, I'm going to ask Queen Nefertitty to hand over the urn."

"And why should she?"

"Because she is in possession of stolen property. If she doesn't want to surrender it, my client can log a complaint with the police. She faces arrest. I think she can be made to see reason."

"*I* think you're being naive. And I *don't* think it's going to be that easy," he said, looking out the window and not at me.

"Okay. I hear you. What do you suggest?"

"Turn around and go home. Insist your client call the cops, lodge the complaint, and leave it to them."

"I told my client I'd give this a try first," I said, my hands tightening on the steering wheel.

"That was before she told you that this woman carried a weapon, right?"

"Right."

"But you're still going to do this?"

I let out a deep breath. "Yes, I am. So do you have any *constructive* advice on how to handle this better?"

Gene turned his head and looked at me hard. I had to keep my eyes on the road but I could see him watching me. Out of my peripheral vision I thought I detected the hint of a smile before he said, "I might have a suggestion." He ran it by me and I agreed that we should give it a try.

According to the note which accompanied Tawnya Jones's retainer check, Queen Nefertitty lived on South Franklin Street in downtown Wilkes-Barre, a once-elegant neighborhood gone to seed, hookers, and street crime. I pulled my BMW into the nearest municipal parking lot a little after twelve noon. Since my client told me Queen Nefertitty was an exotic dancer, I assumed that meant she worked nights and slept late. All I knew about strip clubs was what I saw on *The Sopranos,* but I figured the odds were good for catching her at home.

The day had gotten even grayer, and a fine rain started to fall as Gene and I walked a few blocks before we found the nineteenth-century brick home which had been converted into apartments. Gene's presence at my side felt comforting, and with him along, I didn't feel apprehensive about the coming confrontation. Instead, I was spinning fantasies about Gene and me working as a team in the future. I should have been focusing on reality and the business ahead.

Instead, as we climbed onto the porch, my heart began to race. Adrenaline filled me with excitement. I looked at Gene. I gave him a thumbs-up. I should have known better. Woulda, coulda, shoulda, but I didn't. So far this day had been filled with surprises. As I was about to find out, I wasn't ready for this one.

Three apartments occupied the building, one on

each floor. I found a buzzer labeled SANDRA THOMPSON, APT. 3C. There was no Queen Nefertitty listed—no surprise there—and I figured Sandra had to be the person Tawnya Jones had called "Sandy." I pressed the button. A few seconds later, the front door buzzed and clicked open. Gene and I pushed through it, went up a wide staircase, and knocked on 3C, the only apartment on the top level.

The door opened wide enough to reveal a black man so massive he had muscles in his hair. "You not Boomer. Who you?" he yelled, and tried to slam the door shut.

I didn't see Gene move but he must have, because the door sprang open wider, pushing the big man backward. The black giant stood there, his mouth gaping open and his eyes huge. "How you do that? And where you get off coming in here?" He got only Gene's stone face for an answer. "You cops?" Impersonating an officer is a crime, so Gene said only that he was Captain O'Neill, which was the truth. Gene introduced me as Ms. Patton and told the man we were here to see Sandra or Sandy Thompson, aka Queen Nefertitty.

At the mention of Sandy, the big man narrowed his eyes. "You narcs?" The question gave me an idea of why the man looked so worried. About then I glanced around and noticed the glass tanks lining one side of the living room from floor to ceiling. They were filled with snakes, dozens of them. My eyes nearly bulged out of their sockets. I nudged Gene and jerked my head toward the tanks.

I heard him say, "Crikey!" under his breath.

Just then a pretty African-American woman came into the room, her eyes heavy from sleep, her hands with red-painted nails tying her robe, her long dreadlocks bouncing on her back, her mouth in motion. "Ar'zona! What you yelling fo'! I trying to sleep, you fool. Hey, who you? You cops? What you want?"

With the voice of authority, Gene again introduced us, not correcting Queen Nefertitty's or Arizona's assumption that we were with law enforcement. I couldn't stop glancing over at the tanks filled with snakes. My skin was crawling, and my knees were shaking so much, I put my briefcase in front of them to hide my nervousness.

Queen Nefertitty saw where I was looking. "Is this about those damned snakes?" she asked me. Before I answered, her head swiveled in the direction of the big man she called "Arizona," and she ripped into him like a chain saw, saying she told him they couldn't keep snakes in the city and that oh no he never listened to her, now look what happened. Queen Nefertitty's taloned hands were on her hips, and she was working herself into a hissy fit. Suddenly she reached down and grabbed an ashtray off an end table and winged it at the man's head.

He ducked and the ashtray smacked into the wall behind him. He forgot about us and started moving toward his attacker, bellowing that he didn't do anything, that the snakes were for her act.

"Hold it right there!" Gene boomed in a voice worthy of a drill sergeant. He moved fast as a cat and clapped his hand on the big man's shoulder. Arizona stopped in his tracks as if a construction crane had gripped him. Queen Nefertitty let go of the table lamp she had grabbed as her next weapon. Gene pushed Arizona over to the sagging sofa and pointed to a recliner positioned in front of a huge television for Nefertitty. Then Gene ordered them to sit down in a voice so cold it froze one's blood. They did, frightened now, their eyes darting back and forth, exchanging glances

"Listen up! You are both in big trouble." Arizona and Queen Nefertitty both began to protest. Gene cut them off. "Quiet! Keep your mouths shut and don't say a damned word. Got that?" As he spoke, his presence seemed to fill the room. I noticed that he had grown a few inches since we walked in. I swear he looked nearly seven feet tall. Both Arizona and Queen Nefertitty stared at him, eyes wide, mouths hanging open, not making a sound.

Barking out orders in military fashion, Gene told Arizona that he had twenty-four hours to get rid of the snakes. Then he told Sandy, aka Nefertitty, that I had business with her and she should shut up and listen carefully.

My mouth was filled with cotton. I swallowed hard and said to the woman, "You are in possession of stolen property that rightfully belongs to my client, Tawnya Jones. I need you to get it and give it to me. Now."

"I don't have nothing of that ho's," she said sullenly, staring at her bare feet.

"I'm not here to argue. Your choice is between giving me the urn or going to jail." She didn't respond and I was feeling helpless. I looked over at Gene and shrugged. Feminism aside, I had a feeling Sandy would respond to him a lot faster than to me.

Gene walked over in front of her. "Look, do you understand we can settle this here or you can come with us?" She didn't answer, but she finally nodded. "All right," he said. "You have exactly two minutes, Miss Nefertitty, before this is out of Ms. Patton's hands and in mine." He made a show of looking at the watch I had never noticed on his wrist before. "The time starts *now*."

Sandra Thompson, aka Queen Nefertitty, glanced over at Arizona, who was giving her a filthy look. She turned to me. "Shee-it. I'll give Ron to you. What I want him for anyway? He dead. Can't do nothing fo' me now." She got up. "He in the bedroom."

As soon as she hurried out of the living room, misgivings flooded through me. "Stop her!" I yelled at Gene, but it was too late. Queen Nefertitty stood in the bedroom doorway with Ron's urn in one hand and a gun in the other.

Before either Gene or I could react, Arizona was off the sofa and running at her, yelling, calling her names and threatening to kill her for wanting a dead man more than him. He barreled into her. The urn went flying. The gun went off. The glass of one snake tank shattered. A ten-foot-long boa constrictor slithered down the wall onto the floor and crawled right at me.

My heart about stopped. All I could see was that horrible, huge thing coming at me. I was dancing backward and screaming, doing a fast two-step as I tried to push the boa constrictor away with my briefcase. I kept yelling, "Shoo, shoo," but the awful snake kept coming. Then I jumped up on the sofa cushions and starting climbing onto the back of the couch. All the while Queen Nefertitty was screeching obscenities at Arizona while he held her in a bear hug, and she beat him on the head with the gun.

Suddenly somebody else was yelling and pounding on the door. I saw Gene scoop up the urn just before he grabbed my arm. The last thing I remembered was the door flying open and the Channel 28 news crew crashing into the room with the cameras rolling.

In an instant I found myself sitting in the driver's seat of the Beemer in the municipal parking lot. My briefcase lay in my lap. Gene sat in the passenger seat, Ron's urn between his knees. Gene's shoulders were jerking back and forth, and I figured he was so mad he was shaking in rage. Then peals of laughter erupted from his lips. He pounded the dashboard. He howled with laughter until tears ran down his cheeks. He tried to stifle himself before he looked over at me sitting there, my face white as chalk. He started to laugh even harder. When he caught his breath, he managed to say, "That sure didn't go the way I planned it. Ha ha ha ha!"

"I don't see anything funny," I huffed.

"You! That snake!" he choked out, and starting laughing again. He didn't stop until I was almost back to Noxen.

Chapter 15

On the way home I called the Katos and told them I would be stopping by within the next half hour. I also told them that I had found a watchdog for them and was bringing him along. As I ended the call, I realized that fatigue was wrapping itself around me like a fog. I suppose my adrenaline rush had worn off. I yawned and took one hand off the steering wheel to rub my eyes. Gene must have noticed because I heard bells, and a cardboard cup of coffee with a lid and a doughnut appeared in the cup holders of the console.

"I'm going to get fat, but thanks, I needed this," I said and smiled at him. I picked up the cup; the coffee was hot and strong.

"You're trying to do too much in one day," he commented.

I knew that, but it irritated me to hear him say it. However, in the interest of building a relationship, I swallowed the barbed wire response I felt like making and said, "I agree with you. I'm learning on the job right now. When I was working before, I didn't have a baby. It changes things."

"So it does," Gene said, his expression unreadable.

I pulled into the Dallas police station parking lot. Cal Metz's nephew, Tom Metz, an old classmate of mine, must have seen me coming because before I even got out of the car, he walked outside with the big yellow Lab on a leash. I swear the dog had a goofy smile on his face. Tom told me he was glad I had found a good home for Casey. He didn't have much of a life at Scabby's at the end of a chain, but despite that, he was friendly and well-behaved. He had found his way into the hearts of all the officers and become a favorite. Tom gave Casey a final pat, and the dog jumped into the backseat of the car without hesitation.

Casey seemed to remember Gene. He stuck his big head between the headrests and covered Gene's face with kisses. I hoped he responded as well to the Katos.

I needn't have worried. Ken and Mihoko waited for us in the yard as I pulled behind their house. When I got out with Casey, the cats all scattered, but he didn't give chase. Instead he made a beeline for the Katos, his tail wagging so hard I thought it would fly off. Both the Katos gave a little bow as the dog greeted them; then Mihoko stooped down and hugged him. She began speaking to him in Japanese, but her tone needed no translation. I would say it was love at first sight.

Gene had exited from the car and was standing next to the BMW. He was staring at the Katos. I should have prepared him for this meeting. He had been fighting the Germans in North Africa, but in 1942 the Allies were also at war with the Japanese. Following the code of Bushido, the Japanese military considered being taken prisoner a cowardly act; a true soldier should fight to the death. Because of that, Japan's treatment of all prisoners of war, particularly captured pilots, was often horrific. In addition, the city of Darwin on the Australia mainland had been attacked a few times, and the country had been threatened with invasion. To Gene, the Japanese were the enemy.

I walked over to him. "Would you rather wait in the car?" I said softly.

He shook his head. "I'm okay. It was a shock, that's all."

"The Allies won the war," I said, realizing he might not know that.

"Yes, I found that out online. I also discovered that Japan is now a strong ally of the West. I know they renounced war and their 1947 constitution is called the Peace Constitution. It's just hard to get my mind around it."

"Things have changed a great deal since 1942. It's a different world," I said.

"It's the future," he replied. "And I wonder if I belong in it." His eyes looked infinitely sad.

We followed the Katos inside and took off our shoes. While Ken got Casey a bowl of water, I stood in the tiny kitchen and told them that the dog had belonged to Scabby Hoyt, who had kept the dog chained outside next to a coop. I added that I wasn't sure if Casey was housebroken or how he'd behave in the house, but that the officers down at the police station were crazy about him. Then I waited to see how they'd respond.

Casey himself sat calmly next to Mihoko, his head cocked as if listening. She looked down at the dog and softly spoke to him in Japanese. He whined and lay down at her feet. "I think he will be fine in the house," she said. "He belonged to the man who tried to kill our hen and now has come to guard us—it is a balance, you see. It is exactly right. And he will have a happier life."

Ken nodded. "Yes, I agree. It is a circle now complete." He looked at the big, lanky yellow dog and pronounced him a fine animal who was destined to take good care of everyone there. Then the couple discussed what they might give him for dinner until they could buy some dog food; then Ken and I went back to Gene, who stood in the great room, where yoga classes were given. Mihoko stayed in the kitchen but soon appeared with a pot of tea and four handleless cups. She put them down on a low wooden table, and we all sat on floor cushions around it. She poured us each a cup of the steaming green liquid, then gracefully knelt on her cushion. Casey lay down next to her, and she kept her hand on his head.

I introduced Gene as an associate from Australia, then told the Katos I believed I now knew why they were being harassed and what we could do about it. I warned them they had to listen carefully to the advice I would give them.

"We are very grateful. We will listen," Ken said solemnly.

"First of all, has anyone offered to buy your property recently?" I asked.

"We had a letter yesterday. We have saved it for you," Ken answered.

Mihoko nodded, stood, and went to a nearby desk. She brought back a letter, handed it to me, and I read it. It was from the Running Brook Development Company. It said they had a buyer for this farm, and if the Katos were interested, they should call the number below. Its content was a soft sell devoid of anything even remotely threatening—but it was from the same outfit that had bought out the Sikorskys, the farm with the tainted well. It was no coincidence for this offer to arrive when the Katos were being terrified by what might be a hostile community.

I asked if I could keep the letter, and put it into my briefcase. "I imagine their next step will be to contact you by phone," I said. "When they call, you are to tell them that you already have a buyer. Don't say anything else except to tell them to contact me and then give them my number."

Alarmed, Ken protested that they didn't want to sell the B and B.

I told him I understood that, but that there was a problem. They might not even legally own the land. I explained about the stipulations in the grant of land to John Kawatchski back in 1785 and how their property was almost certainly Shawnee tribal land. "Tell me, how many acres do you need to run your farm? I notice that you have a great deal of woodland."

"That is true. Thirty acres is what we actually farm. Most of the land is forest. But it is beautiful forest. We would not want it cut down."

I could sense there wasn't going to be a completely happy resolution to this case, but I hoped I could create a compromise that everyone could live with. I proposed that we try to find a middle road. I suggested that I contact the Shawnee and tell them of the deed. I believed that the Shawnee didn't know about the land but that someone both greedy and venal did, someone who wanted to force the Katos to sell out cheaply, and then turn around and sell it to the Shawnee for a great deal of money.

Mihoko said she was getting very confused. If the Katos didn't own the land, how could they sell it to the Running Brook Company or anyone? she asked.

She had a point, but I explained that the land might be sold, just as the Yeagers had sold it to the Katos, as long as the Shawnee didn't know about the property and step in to stop the sale. If they knew, I was certain they would want to claim it. But it would cost the tribe more in a court battle to prove their claim than to offer the Katos a settlement to voluntarily give up the property. That settlement could be for a huge sum, and my job would be to get the Katos as much as possible. If the Katos insisted, I could try to arrange an exemption of thirty acres with the B and B for the Katos to keep. But the peace and quiet would soon disappear. A large, noisy casino would attract thousands of tourists.

Upon hearing this Ken became very upset. It was the peaceful surroundings that had attracted them to the property to start with.

"Then, as sad as it is, you might want to give up all

the land," I advised. "You should think about that. There are many other wonderful farms in this area. I'm sure I can locate another for you. And with the money from the sale you could create a wonderful Buddhist center and not worry about finances." I suddenly realized that I felt happy and excited. We were talking about real estate, and I felt comfortable and confident, brokering a deal here in Noxen as I had brokered dozens of others in Philadelphia. I was thoroughly enjoying myself, and I saw that Gene was watching me with frank admiration.

Getting right to the bottom line, Ken asked what the settlement meant in dollars and cents. He embraced the spiritual side of existence but he grasped the power of money.

I said I thought we were talking a minimum of a million dollars and very possibly more.

Ken and Mihoko exchanged glances. They both looked a little stunned. Ken asked if there was any way to keep the land and not turn it over to the Shawnee.

I took my time before answering. I understood that letting go of a home, or a dream, represented a tremendous emotional loss. I told the Katos that they faced a long, costly court fight that they would almost certainly lose. I strongly advised them to accept the reality that the land rightfully belonged to the Shawnee people and to let it go. I waited a moment, then said, "Ken, Mihoko, this discovery may turn out to be a gift. Perhaps it was meant to happen, to become the path to creating the kind of retreat you could not have afforded otherwise." I asked them to talk things over and consider what I had told them.

Mihoko turned her soft brown eyes to Ken. "We will consider. The Buddha says that attachment to earthly possessions keeps one unhappy and without contentment. We must practice nonattachment."

"Good," I said. "And I must urge you to decide

quickly. I need to tell the Shawnee about this property and make sure their claim to the land becomes public knowledge. That will remove the motive for anyone to frighten you into selling and you will be safe. Do you understand?"

They both nodded yes. I felt very relieved. I wanted to move fast to prevent another incident. Once I contacted the Shawnee, everyone would be out of harm's way, and it would simply be a matter of getting the most money I could for the Katos. And to be frank, my seven percent commission on the sale would buy a lot of financial security for Brady and me.

That night I felt physically worn out but exhilarated. I had taken care of business and I was pleased with the result. When we returned home, I told my mother that I felt the Katos' problems were over. She gave me a hug and a kiss on the cheek, which made a blush start up my neck. My mother is not a frequent kisser.

"First you solved Peggy Sue's problem and now you've helped Mihoko and Ken. Do you see what a difference you can make in people's lives?" Her eyes were shining when she looked at me. "You're smart and you care. This community needs you here," she added. "I'm very proud of you."

"I thought you wanted me to make partner in Philadelphia," I said.

"No, I wanted you to achieve your dreams. But I always felt you could have much bigger dreams." She looked over at Gene. "And now I think you do."

After that brief show of emotion, her manner became as it usually was: unsentimental and practical. She reminded me that we needed to develop a child care schedule, told me she'd call me tomorrow, and hurried out.

Totally beat and barely able to get up the energy to change into a pair of comfortable jeans, I appreciated Gene the genie, as chef and chief bottle washer, more than ever. While I fed Brady, he conjured up a classy arrangement of cocktail shrimp on cracked ice for an appetizer. Then he served grilled wild salmon with dill, spring greens, warm dinner rolls redolent with butter, and a crème brûlée for dessert. I felt my waistline expanding just by looking at it.

"You know," Gene said after the main course was devoured and I had stuck a spoon into my crème brûlée.

"What?" I said, finding his leg under the table with my bare foot.

"Things turned out well today, don't you think?" he asked as he reached down and massaged my instep.

"Hmmm, this dessert is heavenly." I moaned as I licked the spoon and closed my eyes. "And yes, I think the day, overall, was amazing. Thank you, by the way, for your quick thinking in getting us out of that apartment."

"Quick thinking is what I do best. Well, maybe second best." He grinned. "Seriously, when you actually follow my advice, you don't end up A over T."

"I don't know if that's a compliment or an insult." My spoon paused in midair.

"It means arse over tits, and I meant it in the best possible way," Gene said, reaching across the table and taking my free hand. "All I'm asking is that you be open and honest. Include me *before* you commit me to do something. And please—I mean this—please promise me you won't do anything else dangerous."

I squeezed his hand. "Does that mean you care? About me, I mean?"

"You know I care, don't you? I do care, Ravine, very much. I worry about you taking risks. Please answer my question. Will you promise?" He squeezed my fingers.

I looked at Gene intently. I truly meant every word

when I said, "I promise." Then I stood up and leaned
across the table and kissed him. He tasted even
sweeter than the crème brûlée.

After we finished eating, Gene cleaned up in a wink
and joined Brady and me on the sofa in time to watch
the evening news.

The broadcast began, as it always does, with a close-
up of the news team at the Channel 28 news anchor
desk. The anchorwoman, a blond Barbra Streisand
look-alike, smiled into the camera in front of her and
read from the teleprompter: "Good evening. This is
the six o'clock news with Andy Mehalchik and me,
Lendall Stout. Now for our lead story tonight." Then
she turned to face the camera to her left. "What kind
of neighbor would give you nightmares? How about
forty-eight snakes! That's right. The board of health
and the Luzerne County SPCA acted on a tip this
afternoon and entered a home on South Franklin
Street in Wilkes-Barre. Our reporters were there.
What happened, Josh?"

A reporter with a buzz cut, a big smile showing very
white teeth, and a microphone clutched in his hand
appeared on the screen. Some Wilkes-Barre residents
jostled each other as they crowded around the reporter, waving at the camera and trying to get their
faces on the news. "Lendall, around twelve thirty
today our WBRE news van had just pulled up here
in front of the house that you see right behind me.
Neighbors, some of these folks right here, ran over.
They had heard a gunshot coming from the top floor. We
entered the building with our cameras rolling. When
we reached the third-floor apartment, we could not
believe our eyes. First we were met by a mysterious
bright flash—you can see it right here on our video-
tape." The room lit up like a thousand sparklers had
gone off. I thought I caught a glimpse of my foot
though.

Josh continued his report. "We don't know what

that was, maybe a booby trap. Now take a good look right there on the couch." The camera zoomed in. "That's a ten-foot-long boa constrictor!" The camera panned to the wall of glass tanks. "And over here were more! Forty-eight huge snakes in all. How would you like those creepy crawlers living next door, or right above you, like the other families in this building? But don't worry, folks. The SPCA has removed the snakes. And none of them were poisonous. They are safe in the animal shelter in Plains Township—and the people of this neighborhood are now safe too."

The screen switched back to the anchor desk. "We'll have more on that story tonight at eleven. Seeing that snake gives me shivers. Now Andy has a report of a lost family dog in Scranton."

I turned to Gene and high-fived him. This time he knew how to high-five me back. I didn't stop smiling for the rest of the night—not when I sang Brady to sleep and especially not when I went into my own bed where Gene was waiting for me. I was still smiling when I woke up the next day before dawn.

My coffee was good and hot as I sipped it at my desk. It wasn't quite seven a.m., and the whole day was clear of appointments. After I did some paperwork this morning, I planned to suggest to Gene that we take the baby and do something together. Maybe we would ride around in the car, just for fun. In the back of my mind, I had the notion it might be time to talk with Gene about us, about giving our relationship a trial run until Christmas Eve. I saw that he was feeling genuinely conflicted about returning and maybe even wavering on trying to go back to the past. It was true that Gene hadn't said the L word yet. But last night, in his arms, I thought he had come close. Words weren't the only way to express feelings, and our intimacy was increasingly tender and familiar. Without a doubt, I felt loved.

No wonder I started the morning rested and optimistic. And happy. Hell yes, I felt happy. I should have checked my horoscope. It might have warned me to stay in bed and stick my head under the covers. But at the moment, I felt great.

I put a Yeah, Yeah, Yeahs CD on the player. It was a toss-up between them and Garbage. Both groups played music Gene was sure to hate. Tapping my feet to the beat, I created an invoice for Peggy Sue; I kept it under a thousand dollars to cover my hours on Monday, the trip expenses, and the fee for her divorce.

Next, I made a note to call Tawnya Jones during regular business hours. I would tell her I had retrieved Ron's ashes and was shipping them back to her. I got up and packed the urn in a USPS Priority Mail box and included an invoice for 150 dollars along with Ron's remains. Ms. Jones's hundred-dollar retainer barely covered my gas and the postage for the ashes, so I billed her at an hourly rate of 75 dollars, which is 300 dollars less per hour than I used to charge at Withersham, Carlisle. I figured that was about all Ms. Jones could pay. I shook my head when I thought about the slithering boa constrictor and the gun in Queen Nefertitty's hand. I had learned my lesson about making snap decisions to take on a case, or at least I hoped I had.

Next I started drafting a settlement offer for the Katos' property so that I'd be ready to negotiate with the Shawnee the moment the Katos gave the okay. I was making a mental note to call them later if they didn't get back to me this morning, when my phone rang. It was Mihoko Kato. Her voice was frantic as she apologized for calling so early. "Someone came here last night. They had gasoline. We think they were going to burn the barn. Now Ken is in trouble, I think."

"Slow down. Start at the beginning and tell me exactly what happened." My words were deliberately slow and calm.

Mihoko said that late last night the security lights—the ones I told the Katos to install—went on. Casey began barking, so Ken got out of bed. Casey rushed outside ahead of him the moment he opened the door, barking very loudly and running toward the barn. The security lights had gone on there too. Mihoko pleaded with Ken not to go out, but to call the police. Just then they heard a voice yelling and Casey barking with an almost wild sound. Ken rushed out into the driveway as a van drove down from the barn at a high rate of speed with Casey in pursuit. Ken jumped out of the way. He called the dog back and Casey stopped when the truck turned onto the road.

Ken went up to the barn to see what had happened. He found an open gas can. Casey had found something also, retrieving it as he was bred to do. It was a piece of fabric; Mihoko thought it was perhaps the cuff of the intruder's pants.

Ken had come back into the house and almost immediately the phone rang. He answered it. The caller told him that if he didn't want any more trouble, he should sell the farm. Ken repeated what I had told him to say, that the Katos already had a buyer and to call me.

Even though Ken held the receiver, Mihoko could hear the caller shouting and swearing. She clearly heard him say that he was going to burn the house down if Ken didn't meet him right away.

My whole body got tense as I asked what Ken did then.

Mihoko said that Ken became very angry, and when he became angry he became very quiet. He said in his strange and quiet voice that he would go meet the man. He wrote down an address and then hung up. Then he left.

I asked when this had happened. "A few hours ago,

around five in the morning, I think. Ken hasn't come back and I am terribly worried." I was too. I asked if she called the police. Mihoko hesitated, then said she couldn't do that because she was afraid Ken would be arrested.

"Why would you think that?" My assumption all along had been that she feared for Ken's safety. But she said in a small voice that when Ken left he took Casey with him—and his bo stick. I didn't know what a bo stick was, but it sounded ominous.

With soft fast words that I had to strain to hear, Mihoko said that Ken had been an instructor in what Americans called "bo fighting" or "stick fighting." "This was before he became a Buddhist. He accidentally killed a man during a competition in Japan. That was when he put away the bo stick and embraced the peaceful way of the Budda. He promise me he will not hurt the man who called, but when he fights he is not"—she searched for the word—"reasonable. He fights with another mind, the warrior's mind."

I mentally groaned. In one phone call I got put in the middle of an arson threat and now a possible homicide. I asked if she knew where he had gone to meet the man. She said she didn't know.

"I'll be right over. Stay by the phone in case Ken calls. I'll take a look around and try to figure out what to do." I crossed my fingers that Ken would be back before I got there.

"*Arigato*. Thank you," she said and hung up.

Suddenly my good mood had gone all to hell. I stood up, took a deep breath, and squared my shoulders. I had to go talk to Gene.

"I'm thinking about painting the kitchen," Gene said as I walked in. Brady was on the floor banging together the lids of some pots and pans. "Do you want to pick a color?"

"Maybe later. I have to go out," I said.

Gene looked at me with narrowed eyes. "It's not even eight in the morning. Where are you going?"

"There was trouble last night at the Katos. I'm going over there." I saw his body stiffen. The tension was building between us already. "Before you get all worked up," I said, "I'm not going to do anything risky. I plan to calm Mihoko down and try to convince her it's time to call in the police."

"Police? What happened?" His voice took on a hard edge.

"An arson attempt. Maybe Scabby wasn't the one who set our fire. Ken has gone after the guy."

"Ravine, we talked about this. You promised."

"Yes, I did. And I'm keeping that promise. I'm only going over to Jade Meadow Farm. I'd ask you to go, but we can't take Brady. I need you to watch him."

"I don't like this. I feel like we're back to square one. Look, I'm not yelling—"

"It's beginning to sound like yelling. Look, I'm sorry, but I really have to get going."

Gene didn't say anything right away. He gave me a long, hard look before he nodded and asked me to call him before I did *anything*. He promised to answer the house phone. "Don't go off alone and do anything stu—anything risky. Can we agree on that?" he asked.

"I don't see a problem with that," I told him. I put an old barn coat on over my jeans, jammed a cap on my head, and grabbed my purse and cell phone as I headed for the door. Gene walked with me. As I kissed him goodbye, I said, "Of course I'll call you. I told you, I'm going over to talk to Mihoko. Nothing more."

Famous last words.

Chapter 16

When I arrived at Jade Meadow Farm a few minutes later, Ken hadn't returned, and Mihoko still had not heard from him. I honestly didn't know what I could do there, but I asked to see the piece of pant leg that Casey had torn off the intruder. Mihoko pointed to where it lay on the low table. The fabric was a black polyester or cotton blend, cheap-looking. I don't know why I brought it close to my nose, but I did. It smelled of tobacco—and Jean Naté cologne.

I looked over at Mihoko and asked if either of them had gotten a look at the intruder. She shook her head. Ken had jumped out of the way of the truck—maybe he had seen more.

I stood there holding the fabric in my hand. "I wonder if—" I mused. I asked Mihoko where Ken wrote down the address.

She went to the nearby desk and brought me back a small white notepad with a blank page on top. I took it from her. I figured if I was lucky, the old trick of rubbing a pencil over the surface might show us what he wrote.

She quickly found a pencil. I took the side of the point and lightly rubbed it over the surface exactly as I'd seen it done in numerous old movies. To my surprise, the impression of letters did appear. I turned on the desk lamp and canted the pad to see better what was spelled out. Suddenly I could read it clearly: "Interstate Exit 188."

"I have a hunch where Ken went," I said to Mihoko. "What is he driving?"

"A white Toyota Camry," she said.

I mentally groaned. *That's a big help,* I thought. *One of the most common cars on the road.*

"Look. I'm going to take a ride to see if I can spot him. But if I can't, Mihoko, we really have to call the police. I mean that."

She nodded. "Yes, Ms. Ravine. Can I come with you?"

I told her no, that she needed to stay at the B and B in case Ken returned. If he did, I instructed her to call me immediately and had her write down my cell phone number. Then I rushed out into the weak early morning sunlight and cold air of November.

True to my promise, as I started the car I called Gene. I didn't expect him to sound happy. He didn't. I told him I was taking a quick ride out past London's Junkyard on the interstate because I thought that's where Ken might have gone. I promised I wasn't even going to get out of the car. He wanted to know if I had called the police. I responded that I felt that was up to Mihoko. I'm not sure he bought that but he didn't argue with me.

I admit Gene sounded worried, more worried than I was at that point. All in all the call didn't go badly. I thought he would be a lot more upset. In truth, I didn't want to drive out there and search for Ken. All I wanted to do was get this over with and get back home. Maybe part of the day could be salvaged after all. Besides that, waves of anxiety were washing over me, and I was getting cold. The car heater seemed on the fritz. My feet were freezing in my sneakers, and my barn coat wasn't well-insulated.

Even though the sun was up completely by now, the daylight was murky, and low clouds were threatening some kind of precipitation. I started to worry about slick roads, mostly to keep my mind off of whatever might be going on at London's Junkyard. There were plenty of omens telling me to turn around and go home. I ignored them all. As soon as I hit the interstate I found myself in rush hour traffic and by the time I reached exit 188 my nerves were doing a tap dance under my skin.

Finally I pulled off the main road into the junkyard. I slowed to a crawl as the Beemer's tires splashed through the rusty water on the unpaved driveway. I didn't see Ken's Camry in the parking lot by the office, but I was nervous about being spotted by Joann, so I veered left and cautiously steered between rows of derelict cars. I had gotten only about twenty feet when something smacked down on the top of my car with a huge bang. The needles on the dashboard dials started swinging back and forth wildly, and the car stopped, refusing to move forward even though I was giving it gas.

I could clearly see that nobody was near the car. I figured I better get out and see why I wasn't moving. I tried the door. It wouldn't budge. I threw my shoulder against it, figuring the damned lock was jammed again. Nothing moved—at least, the door didn't move. Instead the entire car started to slowly lift off the ground and was soon swinging gently back and forth. I sat there puzzled for a moment; then I realized what was happening.

The huge industrial magnet hanging from the crane in the junkyard had picked up my car and was carrying it to the crusher. My heart started going like a triphammer. I clawed at the window controls. Nothing happened. The windows wouldn't lower. I couldn't get out. I frantically grabbed my cell and called Gene.

"Gene!" I screamed into the phone. "I'm at the junkyard. My car is being sent to the crusher."

"What? There's a lot of static. Say again? A crusher?"

"I'm in my car. I can't get out. The car's being picked up by a magnet. It's going to drop me in the crusher!"

"Get out! Just get out!" he ordered.

"I can't. The doors won't open. I can't get the windows down." Hysteria was making my voice a screech.

"Open the glove box. There's an emergency hammer. Break the window. Hit it hard," he said, his voice unnaturally calm.

I reached over and opened the glove compartment. "Oh, the window breaker thingy! I got it!"

"Ravine! Get off the phone. Get out of the car!" His pretense of calm had slipped and he was screaming.

By that time the car was a good fifteen feet off the ground and swinging even more as the crane holding the magnet turned toward the crusher. *Don't panic,* I told myself, trying to make my fingers work instead of shaking. *Take the hammer and hit the window. That's it. Don't give up. Hit it again harder.*

On my second try, the driver's window cracked crazily into a sheet of square pellets made by the safety glass. I hurriedly pushed them out with my hands and released my seat belt. I stuck my head out of the opening. I pulled myself up by gripping the roof until I was sitting on the window. I looked down. It was a long way to the ground. I was going to get hurt when I dropped, but it was better than being dead.

The crane was nearly to the crusher. I grabbed the driver's side mirror and maneuvered the rest of my body out of the car until I was stretched across the car door. Slowly, I lowered myself as I clung to the mirror, stretching my arms as far as I could and letting my legs dangle. The crusher was nearly beneath me. It was now or never. I started to pray—"The Lord is my shepherd"—and let go of the mirror. The air rushed around me as I dropped.

I didn't hit the ground. I fell into Gene's arms. He pulled me against his chest, holding me to him as tightly as he could. I held on to him for dear life.

"Thank God, thank God," he kept saying into my hair. "I didn't think I'd get here in time. Are you all right? Let me see. Are you hurt?" He stood me up and put his hands on my shoulders to look me over.

"I'm fine. I'm okay, really I am." Suddenly I had a moment of panic. I looked around wildly. "Where's Brady?"

"He's home. He's safe. I put that protective curtain around him, but it took a minute. I was so scared I had taken too long. I thought I had lost you. I love you so much," he said and pulled me to him again.

Time stopped. Everything stopped. My face was pressed into his chest but I felt light and floaty. I lifted my head and gazed into his eyes. "I love you too," I said.

"I know," he said with a smile. "You talk in your sleep."

Just then I heard the terrible roar of the crusher destroying my car.

"My Beemer!" I cried, tearing myself out of Gene's embrace. "Oh no. My car, my poor car!"

"It's only a car, Ravine. You can get another one," Gene said. "Don't cry about it."

"But I'll never be able to afford another BMW," I wailed. "I know I'm being silly, but that was my Beemer!"

Suddenly we heard a woman's piercing screams and a loud staccato of dog barks. Fear stopped my thoughts. "Let's get out of here!" I cried and began to shake from head to toe.

"That sounds like Casey! Wait here," Gene ordered, pushing me behind him and sprinting toward the salvage yard office. I refused to be left standing there alone and ran after him on wobbly legs.

From ten yards behind I watched Gene throw himself at the office door and crash through it. I came breathlessly into the room behind him in time to watch a gun materialize in Gene's hand. He held it in a shooter's stance. "Okay. Everybody freeze!" he ordered.

I saw that Ken had Mr. London backed against the wall, his bo stick across the older man's throat. London's eyes were bulging and his face was turning blue. A few feet away Casey stood stiff-legged, his hackles standing up on his back and his teeth bared. He was barking ferociously at Joann, who was pinned in her desk chair, afraid to move.

"Ken!" I called out. "Stop! Don't hurt him!"

Ken's chest was heaving. He looked at me with wild, unfocused eyes. I called out again. "It's Ravine. It's all okay. Please put the bo stick away." He shook his head and looked at me again. Then slowly, deliberately, he put the bo stick down.

Mr. London rubbed his throat and bent over gasping for air. "Mr. London!" I said loudly above the noise of the barking dog. "I know about the Shawnee. We'll have a deal with them by the end of the week. Your scheme can't work. You cheated the Sikorskys, but it's over. Do you understand? Leave the Katos alone. It's over."

He looked up at me, his eyes red and filled with hate. "I don't know what you're talking about. This madman rushed in here and threatened to kill me."

"No, I don't think so," I said. "You called him to come out here. What were you going to do? Force him to sign a land transfer? It doesn't matter now. The dirty tricks won't work anymore."

Gene spoke in a voice that rolled thunder. "Listen, you no-good sonofabitch. If you or any of your people set foot on Ms. Patton's land again—or on the Katos' land, for that matter—I personally will blow your bloody head off. You got that?"

London didn't answer, but his face turned pasty white.

I walked over and gently touched Ken's arm. "Get Casey. Let's go home," I said.

While Gene kept the gun on Joann and Mr. London, Ken grabbed Casey's collar and pulled him outside. I turned to follow, but before I did, I walked over to Joann. Her face was terrified; her doughy cheeks were trembling. I looked her up and down. Below the purple caftan draped over her immense bosom, she was wearing a pair of black slacks. The right cuff had been ripped away.

"Better get yourself some new pants, Ms. Kawatchski," I said. "Count yourself lucky that the dog didn't tear your leg off."

Ken drove us home in his white Camry, which had been parked on the far side of the office building. I sat in the back; Gene got in the passenger seat. Throughout the trip I was crazy with worry about Brady. Even though Gene assured me he was completely safe, I envisioned him crying and alone with no one to comfort him. I understood that Gene couldn't vanish into thin air without provoking questions with no believable answers, so I fidgeted in my seat and watched the dashboard clock.

As we rode along, Gene asked me if I planned to file charges against George London and his secretary.

I shook my head no. I explained that there was no question in my mind that they were both guilty, but proving anything in a court of law would be tough. After an intensive investigation I might be able to build a case against Ms. Kawatchski, but when you came right down to it, she was just a lackey in all this. Maybe she told London about her family's land belonging to the Shawnee, and maybe she recruited Scabby after meeting him in some bar. I could only guess about those things. I knew she didn't call the shots. She didn't go out to the Katos' to set a fire without orders from London. But could we prove it?

"As far as London goes," I said, "he's a powerful man with powerful friends in politics and law enforcement. I have no hard evidence. I think we'd be wasting our time. But while he may be a criminal, he's also a businessman. There's no longer any profit in harassing the Katos or in trying to get even with me. I may have made a bad enemy, but I doubt he'll risk coming after me."

Gene's jaw got hard and his lips got tight. "It's not fair. Not right."

"It's the way of the world." My shoulders sagged, and my voice was weary. I told him that the best I could do was quietly alert the Pennsylvania gaming control board that they needed to take a closer look at London's land development company. I assumed he was behind the Running Brook people. I would also talk to some old friends in Philadelphia and attempt to put up some roadblocks if he attempted to get a gambling license. There really wasn't much else I could do. Money talked in a louder voice than justice most of the time.

Ken hadn't spoken so far. Now he nodded and said softly, "I understand what you are saying. Mihoko and I want you to get the settlement from the Shawnee, Ms. Ravine. Find us another farm, please, also. Forgive me for my . . . for my fight. I am very sad. I have thinking to do. I thought I had no hate in me. No anger. I learned much today about myself."

Gene turned to him and said brusquely. "Listen, you protected your home. You defended your family. Don't beat yourself up. You're a man. That's what a man does."

Ken, a small smile playing on his lips, glanced away

from the road for a second and looked at Gene. "You make a good samurai, I think."

"You too, my friend," Gene said. "You too."

As Gene said he would be, Brady was fine, napping in his baby seat in front of the TV, which was playing his favorite DVD, *Walk the Line*. I picked him up, careful not to wake him. I cuddled him against my body and smelled his hair, kissing him over and over. Tears squeezed out from beneath my eyelids and ran down my cheeks. I wanted to hold him forever and never let go. I had come very close to losing my life today, and as I held my baby in my arms, the realization crashed down on me like a wall of icy water.

After a while, I carried Brady up to his room and put him down in his crib. While I stood there watching him sleep, I made some decisions. Life is short and unpredictable. It can change or end in a heartbeat. I needed to talk frankly with Gene, and I needed to do it today. If we could build a life together, we had to move ahead with it. If not, I needed to move on. I stayed next to Brady's crib until he stirred. When he woke from his nap, I wanted him to see that I was there.

After I changed his diaper and dressed him again, I brought him with me downstairs to find Gene. My genie was in the kitchen, as usual. A man who couldn't be idle and didn't seem able to relax, he had assembled a stepladder, paint tray, and brushes, obviously ready to start the redo. He also had lunch waiting for me: a thick tuna salad sandwich, some chips, and a cup of hot tea. I put Brady in his high chair and took a seat at the table. I wanted to talk, not eat. I hesitated, not sure how to begin.

I exhaled a long shuddering breath. "Would you sit down? I need to talk to you."

His face held a question but he did as I asked.

"Back in the junkyard, you said you love me, right?"

"Yes. I planned to tell you in a more romantic setting, with some candlelight and wine, but yes, I do." He smiled at me and reached across the table for my hand.

"So what's next?" I said, gripping his fingers.

"Next? As in you and me?"

"Don't be dense. You know what I mean. My third wish. Your disappearing or—not. In other words, do I mean enough to you for you to stay here?"

"My heart tells me yes."

"And your mind? What does it say?"

"It says, I think so. I'd be a liar if I didn't say I have mixed feelings about not trying to go back, about not trying to get home to my family. But—"

"But?"

"I've been using the Internet. I've done a lot of reading about the years between when I was enchanted and now. I found Laura, by the way."

My heart gave a thud.

Gene had discovered that one of Laura's sons went into medicine. He'd founded a cancer research hospital. Another owned one of those vineyards Gene had such an interest in. Finding out that Laura had gone on with her life made him reevaluate what returning home would mean to history—how it would change everything that perhaps should not be changed. I said I understood, but I felt obliged to point out that maybe Gene's son with Laura would have become that doctor. I fought my own selfish desires in order to be fair.

Gene had also found his parents' obituaries. I can't even imagine how painful that must have been. Both his mother and father were well into their nineties when they died, only a few months apart. They had established a scholarship fund in his name, to help children from the outback get a college education. Gene was described as their son who was a World War II war hero.

"I know they mourned me," Gene said. "But they were proud of me. When I 'died,' they didn't fall apart. Life in the outback is harsh; only the strong survive. They were practical people. I didn't come back and their lives went on."

He looked down at our joined hands. "And *I* went on. I'm here, sixty years in the future. That may sound crazy, but I think trying to go back is crazier. I don't know if a genie, or anybody, can stop time." He raised his eyes to my face.

"I don't have any answers," I said softly. "But I do have an idea."

"It seems you usually do," Gene said and grinned at me. "Give me a kiss and tell me what you have been thinking."

I moved from my chair to sit on Gene's lap. I laid out my plan that we take the time from now until Christmas Eve to test the waters—to make absolutely sure our relationship worked and that we were truly in love, not infatuated with each other. It would also give us time to carefully construct my third wish.

For Gene to exist and function in the twenty-first century, we had a myriad of details to consider. He'd need a new birth certificate and other credentials that created a believable past. Would he be Australian or an American citizen? How would we handle his military status? My legal mind saw a maze of obstacles to setting up his new life. It might take me the entire five weeks to figure out exactly what documents he'd need.

With my arms around his neck, kissing him frequently as I talked, I explained that to Gene. He agreed that we needed to dot all the i's and cross all the t's or we faced a potential legal nightmare.

"You know better than I do what documentation I need to get a pilot's license and then to find a job, even to pay taxes," he said. "And what do we need to get a marriage license?" He looked very worried.

"Marriage license? Eugene Hugh O'Neill, are you asking me to marry you?"

"I guess I am," he said, as if it had just occurred to him.

"Then I think you'd better ask me properly," I said and kissed him harder and longer.

When we finally broke the kiss, he gently put me off his lap and I stood up. Then he knelt down in front of me, on bended knee. My hand was cold and trembling when he took it. "Ravine Patton, will you marry me?" he asked.

"Yes," I breathed. "Yes."

Suddenly bells rang and a golden glitter like fireworks' sparks swirled around us, making the air dance with light. An engagement ring, shining blue in the depths of its emerald-cut diamond, appeared in Gene's hand. He slipped it on my finger.

With that act, I had defied all logic, reason, and the laws of physics, and agreed to wed a genie out of a bottle.

Chapter 17

I didn't wear the ring. Gene and I both decided that until I made the third wish, and he was in this century for good, it made better sense to wait to announce our engagement. We hoped to break the news on Christmas Eve when we went over to my mother's for dinner and gift giving. So I slipped the ring off and put it in my vintage jewelry box, the one that had been my grandmother's. I placed it with care on the red velvet where I could see it whenever I opened the cherished box.

That same afternoon, I also called the police and reported my car stolen. I talked to Cal's nephew and said I looked out in the driveway and my car was gone. He took down a description of the car and told me to stop off tomorrow to fill out paperwork. He suggested it might be kids going for a joyride and told me not to get too upset. Few real car thieves ever ventured into the Back Mountain. He thought we had a good chance of getting my Beemer back.

I knew better. My poor car was squashed into scrap metal. It was gone and I had to accept it. The insurance would pay me blue book value, enough to get another car, but it would have to be a much less expensive one than a new Five Series BMW.

Since I believed Gene would end up driving the new vehicle, at least until we earned enough to purchase a second car, he and I carried on long discussions about what to buy. We quickly agreed that we needed four-wheel-drive because of the wicked winters in the Endless Mountains, and we started searching on the Internet together before we went car shopping.

Gene spotted a Subaru Outback and thought it had some nice features. Among other things, he liked the name. I vetoed it as being too small, especially if we started a family and got a dog. Gene and I hadn't discussed children exactly, but he had mentioned he always liked having a brother and a sister, and he bet Brady would too. I figured that meant two more babies pretty much as fast as I could have them.

I had to tell my mother my car was gone, of course. After she clucked her tongue and ranted about crime out here in the country, she urged me to get a Ford F-150 pickup. "You need a truck when you live on a farm, Ravine," she said. "And the Ford truck is a heavy vehicle. Safer than that foreign car you had. With all the big rigs on the road, it used to scare me, you driving around in that little thing."

As it turned out, we didn't get either a Subaru or a Ford pickup. I fell in love with a red Chevy Avalanche. The Avalanche offered a nice compromise between a truck and an SUV: It seated six; it had a comfortable ride; and it still had a truck bed in the back that made it, technically, a pickup truck. It was big enough to make my mother happy, and it was sporty enough for Gene to agree to my choice on the spot. My chic Beemer image took a full 180-degree turn when I got the insurance money and drove off the lot with my new Chevy, but my life had changed at least that much. Boy, it sure had.

In fact, the five weeks between Thanksgiving and Christmas were turning out to be the happiest in my life. Tawnya Jones wrote me a nice note along with her 150-dollar payment; I contacted the Shawnee and they were more than amenable to putting together a

2.5-million-dollar deal. I was pretty much over the moon. The Katos were pleased about the money and, by working with a local realtor, I lined up some beautiful farms to show them, as well as a spectacular riverfront house, a former hotel, where they could run a magnificent B and B and meditation retreat. It came with several outbuildings, including a posh stable which would end up housing their goats and cows.

Aware of their sudden good fortune, they had gotten over the sadness of having to give up the farm, and Casey was being treated like a prince. Every time I spoke with them, they thanked me again for him. It was karma, they said—Scabby's cosmic way of making amends. It was a good thought, even though I wasn't sure I believed it.

But I really did begin to believe in happy endings when we went to Thanksgiving dinner at my mother's.

Cal Metz was there, and my mother looked radiant with happiness. He had even brought over his basset hound, Charlie, to join my mom's crew of canines. Through the dinner, we talked a lot and stuffed ourselves on turkey and dressing, cranberry sauce, mashed potatoes of course, green beans with Campbell's mushroom soup topped with canned fried onions, and succotash—not my personal favorite, but my mother liked it, and so did Cal. It didn't take a rocket scientist to see they were a couple.

"Hmm. So you do have a boyfriend at your age," I whispered to my mother as we cleared the table.

"Hush up," she whispered back and blushed scarlet.

It was both Gene's and Brady's first Thanksgiving, which made it even more fun. Then, right before we got to coffee and pumpkin pie, the doorbell rang. That somebody actually rang the bell meant it wasn't family, so I looked at my mother with a question in my eyes.

"I invited Tom, Cal's nephew, and his fiancée to

join us for dessert," she said and gave Cal a conspiratorial look. I wondered what that was all about.

"I didn't know Cal's nephew got engaged," I said to Gene as my mother opened the door. Gene, who didn't know Cal's nephew from a hole in the wall, just shrugged.

Tom Metz came into the dining room with my mother on one side of him and an absolutely gorgeous blonde on his arm.

"Hiya, Ravine," the woman said and I did a double take. My mouth about hit the floor. The stunningly beautiful woman was Peggy Sue Osterhaupt. I got up and ran over to hug her. She and I jumped up and down like schoolgirls.

"I got me my teeth," she said into my ear and pulled back far enough for me to see her smile, showing her perfect new uppers. "They're dental implants too, not false ones," she confided. "And I had me a little work done on my eyes too, but don't you tell."

"Your secret is safe with me," I answered in a quiet voice. "I'm so happy for you," I added.

"You made this happen." Tears glistened on her eyelashes. "I can never pay you back or thank you enough."

"I only did my job, Peggy Sue." I gave her arm a squeeze. "No thanks needed."

We all sat down for dessert, and in the middle of the second helping of pie, my mother, never one for tact, turned to Gene. "My daughter hasn't said, but when do you have to go back? To the war, I mean."

Gene choked on his pumpkin pie. Then he looked up with a straight face. "Well, ma'am, I'm waiting to hear. My enlistment is up soon. I haven't decided if I'm going to sign up for four more years. I might not have a choice, you know. I may not be able to opt out in the middle of the conflict, but I have reason to want to stick around here, if I can."

My mother gave a smug smile in my direction. "I'm really pleased to hear that. I'm sure Australia is a beautiful place, but this is fine country, a good place to settle down."

My face was burning red by that time. Gene squeezed my hand under the table. "Time will tell, ma'am," he said. "I can't see the future clearly yet, but I'm going to give it a lot of thought."

When Peggy Sue and Tom left, Peggy Sue handed me an envelope. "Here's your money for the lawyer bill," she said, hugging me again. "You deserve every penny. I've never been so happy in my life. And I did quit down at Offset," she added and winked.

"Thank you," I told her, feeling very humble and grateful. "You look very beautiful, you know."

"I know," she said with a blazing smile. "It makes you believe in miracles, don't it?"

"Yes," I said. "Yes, it does."

Later that night, after Gene, Brady, and I were back home and I opened Peggy Sue's envelope, I found a money order made out to me for seven thousand dollars. The note with it said,

> *Don't you dare try to give this back. It's not even ten percent, and folks tell me most lawyers get a lot more than that. It's the least I can do for you getting me back my money—and giving me a brand-new life.*
> ♥*Peggy Sue.*

I could use the money. I still had less than a thousand dollars in the bank and bills were piling up. It might be a few months before the Shawnee settlement went through. That would provide the perfect cushion for Gene and me to start our married life. We'd have the money for him to go back to graduate school or enroll in flight school if he still wanted to be a pilot.

I secretly favored grad school; I didn't relish his being away from home for stretches of time.

I deposited the money order in the bank, and when I did, Mary Ann, the tiny, brown-haired teller who had tried to stop John Osterhaupt, winked at me as I made the transaction sitting in my Chevy at the drive-through. Then the other women who worked at the bank came over to the window to wave and give me a thumbs-up. That's what it's like to live in a small town—everybody knows about your successes, your failures, and most of your secrets.

The days of late November and early December slipped by quietly in a golden haze of happiness. I picked up a few new clients—a couple of divorces and one custody fight over a golden retriever, as well as some real estate cases. I put in a lot of hours on my mother's charter school too.

As for Freddi, I had made up my mind that even if Gene and I didn't work out—and I was so blissfully happy that I couldn't imagine anything stopping my Christmas Eve wish—I shouldn't play God. The decisions I made might ultimately screw up my own life, but the responsibility of screwing up somebody else's was too great a risk. Still and all, I worried about her. She wasn't pregnant, and she had told me during an afternoon of Christmas shopping at the mall that she had stopped taking the fertility drugs.

I asked her if the doctor thought she had given them enough time. She said it was her decision, not the doctor's, and her mind was made up. She had started to look into international adoptions. She said things were a lot better with Bobby since the pressure of trying to conceive was gone.

"So you're staying married?" I asked.

"Ah, Ravine," she said. "You know no matter what, I'm Bobby's girl." Then she said they compromised. He had started making paper with her, and they were doing some gorgeous boutique rice papers right now.

She said she'd go tailgating at the Penn State games next year—if she didn't have to stay home to take care of a baby.

I gave her a big hug and thought about how lucky I was right now. It was a time when things were going so good, it almost scared me. And I saw no more lone figures in the pasture. I heard no more motorcycles in the night. I had begun to think both incidents had been tricks being played by my imagination and nothing more.

I did, however, at Gene's urging, take the first steps in finding Jake. I called a friend of a friend in the district attorney's office in Houston. She checked for me and found no arrest records of any Bandidos in the last fifteen months that fit Jake's description. It was a relief to hear that. She did say a few Bandidos had been busted near Houston for selling crystal meth. At least one of them, a twenty-year-old called Dutch, had been working out a plea bargain with her office.

Dutch, she said, seemed like an intelligent kid, and he didn't have a previous arrest record. He was motorcycle-crazy, but wasn't a hard-ass. She thought he might be willing to talk with her. She took down the slim facts I knew about Jake—his appearance, kind of motorcycle, where he was last seen, and that he might be called Doc—and said she'd call me if she came up with anything. I appreciated that she didn't ask why I wanted to track him down.

I spent most of my days in the office hammering out the details of my third wish. I was worried that I wouldn't get it exactly right, and the slipup could be disastrous. Gene and I talked it over dozens of times. He felt more confident than I did that the wish would work. I started having nightmares that I'd make the wish and Gene would crumble away into dust, leaving me on my hands and knees weeping.

Mostly I spent my time giddy with happiness, grinning all the time. Gene and I rarely fought, and we laughed a lot. On a couple of occasions, he said he needed to go off by himself for a while. I guessed he was grieving for his parents and the past. It never lasted long, and later we'd pack up Brady and take off in the red Avalanche, driving back and forth from Home Depot or Lowe's. We picked out paint and chose replacement windows, decided to install granite countertops, and bought a dishwasher in anticipation that Gene's winking soon would no longer work to make cleanup a snap.

Around the second week of December, Gene sat me down and said he had done a lot of thinking. How did I feel about him becoming an investigator—in other words, a private detective? If I wanted to take on some criminal cases, we could work together, but he had some ideas about starting an agency. For many reasons, including the great gaps in his knowledge of the past, he wanted to be his own boss, and he had thoroughly enjoyed, he confessed, the adventures we had going after John Osterhaupt and Queen Nefertitty. I agreed the idea had merit, but I told him frankly that I was afraid to count on too much, until I saw for myself the third wish had worked. I had never wanted anything more in my life than to be with Gene. The longer we were together, the better life got.

During those halcyon days, we went to the movies at the new Cineplex downtown; we attended a play at the Kirby Theater; we even tried some early-season skiing at Snö Mountain. Every day was a new adventure, and if I hadn't had that dark shadow of fear about the wish hanging over my head, life would be perfect.

When the week before Christmas rolled around, I took a deep breath and decided I had to let myself enjoy the season and the sweetness of anticipating Gene's staying with me forever. Besides, this was Brady's first Christmas, so the three of us went out to a nearby tree farm and picked out a beautiful blue spruce. Gene "baked," or at least he conjured up Christmas cookies and a nut roll. We went overboard buying decorations, and I even starting hoping for snow so we could have a traditional white Christmas.

On the day before Christmas, the day of Christmas Eve, I felt confident that I had all the details of the third wish nailed down. I looked over the wish as I had written it and printed it out. I planned to read it verbatim. I took it into the kitchen where Gene was painting the walls a celery green and the molding a crisp white. We sat down at the table and Gene and I reviewed the wish one last time.

He assured me that it was perfect, and he was the wish expert, so I believed him. We got champagne ready to put on ice in a bucket right before we left for my mother's so we could celebrate privately when we returned home. We packed the Avalanche with food and presents. I went to my jewelry box and brought out my engagement ring. I put it on the table next to the candles we were going to light. And as predicted by the TV's Accuweather forecast, it began to snow.

As the afternoon passed, I was getting increasingly nervous. Gene kept talking to me, telling me he was ready and absolutely sure about his decision. He kept reassuring me that the wording of the wish was without flaw. Finally, to pass the time, we made popcorn and decided to watch the DVD of *The Christmas Story* until it was the hour to make the wish. Brady was in his Bouncy Bounce having a fine time, but I kept glancing at the clock.

"Why wait any longer?" I suggested. "Maybe I should just go ahead and wish."

"If you want to, that's fine," Gene agreed. "It was your idea to make the wish at six ten because that was the time I was born. It would be a symbolic rebirth, but we really don't have to wait."

I got up off the couch and paced. "No, we should

wait. It's only another two hours. I'm being silly. But I have this feeling that something is going to go wrong. Damn, I'm almost hyperventilating." I walked over to the window. The ground outside was covered in a light blanket of snow. The roads must already be slippery, and I was glad I had four-wheel drive instead of the iffy traction of my BMW.

Gene came up behind me and put his arms around me. "It's beautiful," he said. "Merry Christmas. The merriest of Merry Christmases."

"Yes," I agreed and turned around to face him. We kissed and happiness filled me up so full I could have burst for joy.

It was right then that the sirens down at the firehouse began to wail. Their sound made me shiver, and Gene's arms tightened around me. Somewhere out in that snow, someone was in trouble. When the sirens kept going, I knew it wasn't a routine emergency. Something very bad had happened and the Kunkle ambulance crew were calling in all their volunteers. "Oh, that's so sad," I said to Gene. "It's Christmas Eve, and something terrible has happened."

Gene kissed the top of my head. "I know. I'm sorry. Let's count our blessings," he murmured into my hair.

Then the house phone rang. I looked at Gene and my heart started racing. I picked up the receiver. "Hello?" I said in a shaking voice.

It was Tom Metz, Cal's nephew who was the local cop. I heard him tell me that there had been an accident and I needed to get down to Mercy Hospital right away. I tried to get my mind around his words. "Accident? Who was in an accident?"

"Ravine . . . it's your mother."

"My mother? What happened?" My voice sounded like an echo very far away. I heard Tom telling me that her truck was hit by a tractor trailer, and that it was bad, real bad. He said to get to the hospital as fast as I could.

I turned my stricken face to Gene. He had heard enough that he was already grabbing Brady's snowsuit and getting him into it. I found my purse and coat, and we ran out to the Avalanche. "I'll drive," Gene said. "I'll get us there faster."

I nodded at him and got in the passenger side, my body trembling all over.

Gene winked and the bells I heard were sad bells. But in that wink of an eye we went from my driveway to the parking lot of the hospital. "I'll take care of Brady," Gene said. "You get on in there."

I don't remember much. I don't remember going from the car through the emergency room door. I don't remember screaming at the admissions nurse. I do remember Tom walking out to the desk and saying he'd take care of this and looking at me strangely. "How did you get here so fast?" he said.

I looked at him dumbly, but Gene had walked in behind me and explained something about call forwarding to my cell phone and that we were out shopping only a few blocks away.

I hardly heard him. I was pulling at Tom's arm. "Where is my mother? How is my mother?"

Tom shook his head. "I'll take you to her. I have to warn you, Ravine. They have her on life support. They were waiting for you to come."

I couldn't believe it. I just couldn't. He was saying my mother was going to die. I wanted to get to her. And when I did I was shocked. I wasn't shocked so much by the respirator, the beeping machines, or all the IV lines. I was shocked because it looked as if she were sleeping. I couldn't see any injuries. She was unconscious but I didn't see any blood. I went over and took her hand.

"Ma," I cried. "Ma, I love you. Don't die, please don't die."

The doctor came in and I lifted my tearstained face. "What happened? What's wrong with her?"

The doctor said in words that I heard but really couldn't quite believe that her brain had shut down. It had been a freak accident. My mother wasn't injured in the collision itself but the tractor trailer rolled over, spilling its contents onto her pickup. The truck's cargo was bales of down, for comforters. They broke open and feathers cascaded over my mother's truck and through the broken windshield into the cab. She couldn't breathe. By the time the EMTs got to her, five minutes had passed. They found the truck driver thrown clear but badly injured. By the time they found my mother, her heart had stopped and her brain had been deprived of oxygen. They tried to revive her, but it had been too long.

"There's no hope?" I cried. "You can't do anything for her?"

"There's always hope," the doctor said in a kind voice. "But we can't do anything except breathe for her. And at some point, you'll need to decide to let her go. It would take a miracle to bring your mother back. I'm so very sorry. I'll leave you alone with her now."

I wasn't looking at the doctor as he left. As I stood there clutching my mother's hand, I saw that Gene had been behind him, listening to every word the doctor said. He was holding Brady and watching me intently.

My eyes were flowing with tears, and I wanted his arms around me. But I needed a miracle even more, and I mouthed the words to him: *Can you?*

He nodded. "You'll have to take Brady," he said.

"I love you, Gene," I said.

"And I love you, but you need to hurry up and wish, Ravine." He looked down at my mother. "You don't have much time." The machines had started to beep crazily and I saw something change in my mother's colorless face.

Clutching Brady so hard he whimpered and almost

unable to make my mouth form the words, I said, "I wish . . . I wish that my mother wakes up now, as whole and healthy as she was before the accident."

Above the beeping machines I heard the ringing of loud, clear bells, and I watched the color come flooding back into my mother's face. Her eyes opened. She couldn't talk because of the breathing tube, but she squeezed my hand and her eyes told me she loved me.

And when I looked back where Gene had been standing, no one was there. Where he had stood was only emptiness. He was gone.

Chapter 18

Right after I made my wish, doctors and nurses came running into the room thinking my mother had coded. Instead she was trying to sit up. One of the nurses, a former student of my mom's, burst into tears. The doctor looked startled, then hurried over to examine his patient. When he was finished, he shook his head. He looked at me, smiling broadly. "There's no other explanation for it. You got your Christmas miracle."

I had. I had gotten everything I wished for and lost everything at the same time. As John Greenleaf Whittier wrote, "For of all sad words of tongue or pen, the saddest are these: It might have been."

I didn't regret wishing to save my mother's life. She was my mother, and I would have walked through fire for her. When they removed the respirator, I wouldn't leave her side. I hovered next to her bed asking her if she needed anything, or holding her hand. After a few hours, she told me in a croak to go home and stop fussing about her. But I wouldn't. I planned on sleeping in her hospital room.

Freddi arrived shortly after my mother woke up. She had heard about the accident on the scanner, and she and Bobby had driven down here as fast as they could, fearing the worst. She found my mother awake, sitting up, and telling everybody she wanted to go home. Freddi gave me a look filled with her unspoken questions. Finally, in a whisper, she asked me where Gene was.

I shook my head, and said, "He's gone."

Freddi knew all about my engagement ring, and that day in the mall I had even told her about my Christmas Eve plans for making my third wish come true. She understood right away what must have happened. She hugged me and said, "I'm so sorry. But I will thank Gene every day that we didn't lose Aunt Clara."

My throat closed up with tears, and I turned away.

Freddi took Brady home with her. I watched over my mother all night, feeling grateful beyond words for what Gene had done and yet feeling so hurt that the life we had both wanted would never be. I couldn't bear to think about his uncertain fate. I told myself he was fine, and that he'd soon be back in Australia with his family. And Laura. Truly with all my heart I hoped he was.

When I finally stumbled, exhausted, back into my house Christmas night—Cal Metz insisted on staying with my mother after she was discharged and she insisted that was what she wanted—I called Freddi and she said she'd be right over with Brady. I walked into the kitchen. The candles stood in their holders, unlit. The unopened champagne bottle bobbed in a bucket of melted ice. And my ring—was missing.

I hurried into the living room where I had framed the picture of Brady on the pony as Gene and I stood together in the snow. Now, in the photo, Brady was on the pony and only I was squinting into the camera while I steadied him with my hand. Gene wasn't there. I raced around the house. My beautiful legal office, my second wish, was exactly as I had left it yesterday. Nothing had changed. I headed to the second floor, taking the stairs two at a time. The robe from my first wish hung like a silken butterfly wing on the back of the bathroom door.

I barreled into the bedroom and flung open the closet. Gene's clothes, the first few items I had bought him at Wal-Mart and lots of other things we had bought together on our trips to the mall, still hung there. I grabbed a blue chamois shirt he especially liked from its hanger. He had worn it yesterday morning. I buried my face in it. It felt stiff in my hands and smelled brand-new, as if it had just come from the store and Gene had never put it on.

Not only had Gene vanished, but every trace of him had disappeared too. I sat down on the floor with his shirt in my hands and wailed. It was truly over. My genie had really gone.

Life, as it always does, went on. Some days my arms and legs moved like a robot's, coaxed out of inertia by the sheer force of my will. Other days I was okay. I still called my mother every few hours to check on her. She understood and didn't sound too annoyed. At one point she asked me where Gene had gone.

"He got called back to the war. It was very sudden." That was all I said.

"When did he leave?" she asked.

"The day before Christmas."

"Wasn't he with you when I was in the hospital? When I was lying there in the bed, I heard you talking with him. I'm *certain* he was there," she said almost to herself. Then she asked, her voice very kind, "Have you heard from him?"

"No." The word stuck in my throat.

My mother became very quiet. "You know," she said at last, "F. Scott Fitzgerald once remarked, 'Show me a hero and I'll show you a tragedy.'" She didn't ask about Gene again.

I carried the presents I had bought for Gene up to the attic still wrapped in their bright paper and ribbons, and the day after New Year's I took down the Christmas decorations and carried them up there too. And when I finally worked up the courage, I did an Internet search to see if I could find out if Gene had gotten married, or had children, or died. Hard as it would be to find out, at least I'd know he'd survived. When I found nothing, not a trace, my heart became a stone. In the darkest, grimmest part of my mind, I believed Gene had not simply vanished, but that he had died.

By mid-January I had developed a routine of work and caring for Brady. Peggy Sue had gotten her day care center up and running, and although I found it very difficult to leave him even for a few hours, I took Brady over there three mornings a week. I scheduled meetings with clients during that time. When I had a court appearance, my mother or Freddi took over babysitting duties. The rest of the time, Brady stayed with me in my office—with the dog.

Yes, I had a dog now. Tom Metz and Peggy Sue showed up in the middle of that terrible week between Christmas and New Year's when I was wandering around the house like a ghost. They had a puppy with them. She looked like a chocolate Lab, or at least mostly one. Tom said that's what her mother was. I suspected her father was a traveling salesman.

"An officer found her mother in an abandoned house with a litter of nine pups," Tom explained. "This little tyke desperately needed a home." Then he coughed and said in a quiet voice, "And you need a dog, Ravine."

I was certain a dog was not what I needed, but Cocoa did distract me from dwelling on the way my life had gone to hell in a handbasket virtually overnight, and from worrying about Gene. Brady was immediately crazy about Cocoa, and once she arrived, he didn't call out "Gee gee na!" quite so often, but every time he did, it still hurt my heart.

On January twenty-first, I received a phone call from the assistant district attorney in Houston, the woman who said she would ask the young Bandido about Jake.

We exchanged pleasantries. Then she told me that she was calling because she had spoken to Dutch, the young Bandido, when he was taken to court to be sentenced. She'd asked him about Jake.

"Oh," was all I said. Time seemed to stop. Her words became all that existed.

"He said he didn't feel comfortable talking about another Bandido."

"Oh," I said, disappointment coloring my voice.

However, she added, Dutch said "Doc" had gotten him his lawyer. The lawyer was also Jake's, and Dutch gave her the lawyer's name. I could hear clicking— she must have been working on her computer while she talked. After all, I was only a friend of a friend and this was strictly a favor. There was a long pause before she said, "I have to say I was more than a little surprised when I heard who the lawyer was."

"Why is that?" I asked.

She said that most of these bikers had what she called "sleazebag criminal defense attorneys," the kind of guys who will represent anybody as long as he can pay, and they don't care where the money comes from. Bray Bentry, Dutch's lawyer, represented the upper crust in Houston: people like the Bushes and Clayton Williams. He didn't "do bikers." In fact, she added, the judge gave Dutch probation as a first offender. Bentry had pull.

"And you say he's Jake's lawyer?" I asked.

"Evidently. Bray is a good ol' boy. He's always nice to the ladies. I think he'll talk to you. Here's his phone number," she said, and I wrote it down.

*   *   *

I had no reason to put off the call except that my emotions still cut me like broken glass. At the same time, over the past few weeks, my perceptions about life had sharpened too. I understood that the only things humans really controlled in life were their choices. Fate determined everything else. But purposefully making choices—and not letting events or others make them for us—made a tremendous difference in the kind of journey our lives became. To be a villain or saint, activist or recluse—those were all choices. Our mistakes made us human, but our choices kept us from becoming victims.

I firmly believed I needed to act, not react, when it came to Jake. So I dialed Bray Bentry's number. I was surprised when his secretary put the call through instead of saying Bentry would get back to me.

A drawl as quintessentially Texan as the Lone Star flag came on the line. "Ms. Patton, this is Bray Bentry. My secretary says you're calling about Jake Allred."

"I am. I understand you represent Jake."

"That I do," he said. "I must say I'm mighty pleased you made this call."

That was a curve ball. None of this conversation was going the way I thought it would. I paused and asked, "Why would that be, Mr. Bentry? And how do you know who I am?"

I heard Mr. Bentry shift in his seat. The chair creaked. He sounded like a big man, substantial in size as well as in influence. "This conversation would be a mite easier in person, Ms. Patton. Is there any chance you will be coming down here to Houston?"

As I worked hard to keep my professional mask from slipping, I answered, "No, Mr. Bentry. I'm afraid that's not possible. Why would it be easier?"

"Well now, it's a long story, and there's some bad news mixed in with it, the kind of thing I don't like to break to a body over the phone."

I felt a frisson of fear crawl up my spine. In a split

second, I went from Ravine Patton, attorney-at-law, to Ravine Patton, the woman who had met and for a single star-crossed afternoon loved a biker named Jake. "Please continue, Mr. Bentry."

He did. What he said next were words I didn't want to hear—not then, not ever. He told me Jake was dead. "Passed on" was how he put it. Whatever I expected Bentry to say—and frankly I had half expected him to say Jake was in jail—this wasn't it. After giving me a moment to let this sink in, he said he'd answer my questions.

"Some of them Jake might have answered himself," Bentry added, explaining that Jake had left a letter and a package with the lawyer the last time he had seen him. He told Bentry to get them to me if I didn't contact Bentry within six months of when Jake passed.

My head was spinning. I told Bentry that I felt very confused. I asked him how he knew about me. I heard Bentry's chair creak again, and the click of a cigarette lighter. My guess was that he lit a cigar, since I heard him taking a series of little puffs to get it burning, followed by a long exhale.

"I'll come to that in a minute," he said. "Jake's story is a sad one, Ms. Patton. He was a fine boy, that he was. I think I need to tell you a little about him."

Bentry was a man who took his time and I was getting impatient. I told him to go ahead. He told me to hold my horses; then he told me Jake's story in his slow, Southern way. I clutched the phone and listened.

"I've known the Allred family 'bout all my life," Bentry said. "Jake's daddy was—and still is—a surgeon down here at the cancer center. Jake became a doctor too. He wasn't all that sure he wanted to be one, but he did what his family expected. Like I said, he was a fine young man, and he didn't want to hurt his mama, even if medicine wasn't quite what he hankered for.

"I'm not rightly sure what he did hanker for, and I

don't know if he knew either. He had some friends—
I guess they were friends—who raced motorcycles.
Jake had always been wild for those bikes. Once he
told me that if he had his way, he'd build racing bikes.
But I never heard any more about it.

"As it turned out, Jake had just started his residency
down here—this was maybe two years back—when he
got sick. At first he thought it was the flu, but after a
fair amount of time he didn't seem to get any better.
Finally his daddy convinced him to get some tests
done. Turned out Jake had a cancer of the blood, and
not a good kind, if there is such a thing."

There was a long pause, and I heard the chair
creak again.

"His mama was about beside herself, especially
when Jake wouldn't do the chemo or get a bone mar-
row transplant. He said it wouldn't do no good at all,
and his daddy, he agreed. Then Jake started feeling
better again—some kind of remission—but he knew
he didn't have a lot of time. He told his parents he
wanted to live his last months, really live them. He
took off. Nobody knew where he went. Turns out he
was riding with the Bandidos. Jake always was a pistol.
A real wild one. I can't say I was all that surprised."

My mind was reeling, trying to take in what Bentry
was telling me. It was as if I had been riding for a
long time on a straight road, when it suddenly made
a sharp turn and I found myself going in another direction entirely, one where the destination wasn't what
I expected it to be at all.

"Then Jake met you. At least that's part of the story
he told me. He came in to see me—let me see now—
it was last October. He said he was getting sick again.
He needed to make out his will. And he told me that
he had met a woman a while back and he had a
son—"

"He knew about Brady?" I broke in.

"Yes'm, he sure did. He said he had gone looking for you and when he finally found you, you had a little baby. His baby. He knew that. But he felt he had no right to walk back into your life, especially since, well, since he knew his time was running out. But he was awful proud of that boy, Ms. Patton, I can tell you. Your mother had given him pictures and all—"

"My mother! My mother met Jake? My mother knew about Jake? I can't believe this." I heard my own voice shattering like glass.

"Now calm down, Ms. Patton. She gave her solemn word to Jake not to tell you. I know she must have wanted to, but Jake, he said he pleaded with her. Jake knew he was dying, Ms. Patton. He didn't want to bring that sorrow into your life."

"When did he die?" I said, shaking all over.

"He died right before Thanksgiving. But the cancer didn't kill him. You might better know that. He had been riding his bike out here on the I-45 and he came upon a car accident. A bad one. He was still a licensed doctor, you know. He ran over to try to help. Another car hit him. He died two days later."

"Oh," I said. "Oh no."

"Yes'm, it was awful sad. But it was better than wasting away from the cancer, if you want to know the truth. All in all, it was a damned shame all around from the git-go."

I sat there, holding my face in my hands for a minute before Bentry said, "To make a long story shorter, Ms. Patton. Back in October he had me draw up that will leaving everything he had to his son. And he put together a package. He hoped you'd come looking for him, that it would be your choice. But if you didn't, he asked me to send it on up to you, along with the letter he wrote."

I asked him to send it out FedEx and he said he

would. Then he added, "You mind if I say something else? I'm just an old Texas lawyer but I've seen a thing or two in life."

"Go ahead, Mr. Bentry."

"Jake's parents, they're mighty good folks. They know they have a grandson, and they'd like to see him. But Jake asked them to let it be up to you. So it is. But it was awful hard on them to lose a son. Your little boy, well, they see him like a kind of miracle. They know all about you too. When you're ready, if you can find it in your heart, it would mean a lot."

I didn't know what to say. I wasn't ready to say anything then. I thanked Bray Bentry and hung up. Then I sat at my desk staring at the wall for a long, long time.

You know the old adage: "Never assume. It makes an ass out of u and me." I had made a lot of assumptions about Jake; most of them were wrong. At least the ones I made using reason were wrong. The things my heart had told me were true. There was a lesson in that, and I guess I learn the hard way.

I'm not sure Jake made the best decisions, but I didn't have to walk in his shoes, so I had no right to judge. I suppose he did what he thought was best for me and Brady. Was it? It didn't matter. It was too late to change it now.

When the package arrived via FedEx the next day, it didn't contain anything of monetary value, but its contents were precious nonetheless. A tattered manila envelope contained dozens of pictures of Jake as a baby. His mother had neatly written on the back of each one, captions such as: "Jake's first birthday. February 11, 1979. Aren't the cowboy boots precious?" The envelope also contained a long braid of his hair, the same rich auburn I remembered from that hot August day. The rest of the package consisted of Jake's black leather motorcycle jacket, the title to his

Indian bike, a letter addressed to Brady to be opened on his eighth birthday, and Jake's will.

I didn't open the letter; I did look carefully at the will. Jacob James Allred left everything he had to Brady Nathaniel Patton, which as far as earthly goods went, wasn't much—except for Jake's trust fund, which consisted of stocks and bonds that added up to about half a million dollars. By the time Brady was eighteen, they would be worth considerably more.

His letter to me was short, and yes, it was sweet.

> Dear Ravine,
> Words don't do much at a time like this, but they're all I have. I want to thank you, and that sounds so damned feeble, for having my son. It makes my life worth something after all. It took a lot of courage for you to go ahead and have him on your own, but I knew you had spunk and more the moment I met you. And I thank you for the gift of that day we had together. I can say I love you now, and I loved you then. Doesn't do much good to say it, though. But I am leaving Brady everything I have, and you won't have to worry about saving for his college education.
> I can only say, from the bottom of my heart, that I am so sorry things couldn't have worked out differently for us. If I hadn't gotten sick, we could have made it. I do believe that. But the fates have spoken, and they say no. I'm sorry to die on you, Ravine.
> Don't be too hard on your mother for not telling you I talked to her. I made her swear on a stack of Bibles not to interfere. Also, you'd like my parents. They had to put up with a lot from me, and they never cut me loose or turned me away. They just loved me. They'll love you and

our son. Please give them a chance. Bray can give you their phone number when you want it.

    I'll be watching over you and Brady both. I promise you that.

    Jake

Chapter 19

After I read Jake's letter, I got Brady dressed and drove over to my mother's. I wasn't mad exactly. I didn't know what I felt—hurt, maybe. At the same time, I could see in my mind's eye how she must have reacted when Jake showed up on her doorstep, or whatever he had done. She had invited him in, sat him down with a cup of coffee, and listened, not betraying anything of what she was thinking and feeling. And when she agreed not to tell me, and then when she actually didn't tell me—it was such a Clara thing to do. I don't know how many secrets my mother has kept in her life, but they would fill a bank vault. And she's never told a one of them.

I brought Jake's letter with me to her house. I sat Brady on my lap and told my mother how I had looked for Jake and found Bray Bentry. She asked if I minded if she read what Jake had written. I passed it over to her.

My mother's face was always hard to read unless you knew her very well. As she looked over what Jake had written, she pressed her lips together hard, but nothing else betrayed what was going on inside her. She passed the letter back.

"The boy was dying, Ravine. What else could I do? You were fragile enough back then. It wasn't any of my business, not really. It was between the two of you, and you never once talked about him. As far as I knew, you had cut him out of your life. It seemed you had, as if he never existed at all. At least that young man came looking for you. I credit him for that. And I credit him for putting your feelings before his own. He didn't want to cause you any pain."

"You should have told me, Ma." My voice wavered as I spoke.

"Maybe I should have. I spent many a sleepless night trying to decide what to do. I prayed on it a lot too. But then your Australian Gene showed up, and you were so happy. I figured whatever would be, would be."

I let out a deep sigh. "I know you did what you thought was right. You always do. I can't blame you for my choices when it came to Jake. You're right, I could have looked for him when I found out I was pregnant. I didn't. For all the wrong reasons, it turned out."

My mother reached out and took my hand. "My daughter, what is past is past. You've been through a lot of pain over the last few years. Who can say why Jake got sick. Or why Gene left. I do know both of them loved you. And I believe both of them would have stayed if they had a choice. They didn't."

I guess she saw how upset I was getting. She spoke quickly now. "Listen to me now, you hear? It's not over with Gene. You have to believe that. Trust him, Ravine. I have a feeling about this."

"Ma, I'd like to believe that. I'm sure Gene would come back to me if he could. But you see, I *know* he can't."

My mother looked at me hard, and she held my hand so tightly it hurt. "There's a lot we can't know in life. It's not in our power to know. And you *do not know* what Gene can or cannot do. Do you understand me?"

I nodded yes. I understood what she was saying, but

she didn't know the whole story, and I did. There was no way Gene could come back.

Winter hung on like a snapping turtle attached to a fisherman's thumb all through February. Three times during that bitter month, storms blew in and the snow stayed, piling up on both sides of the driveway until I couldn't see the yard when I left in the Avalanche. Despite the earth like iron, one morning I heard the call of a red-winged blackbird staking out his territory. After that, he was singing each day at dawn.

Eating up a big chunk of Peggy Sue's payment, I continued with the home improvement plans I had made with Gene. By midmonth replacement windows stopped most of the drafts, the house was snuggly warm, new curtains hung at the kitchen windows, and a professional installer came in to lay down a terra-cotta tile floor.

All the while, my little boy seemed to be racing through his first year. At eight months old he was crawling along so fast I couldn't turn my back on him for a second. He had started pulling himself up using the furniture to give himself a boost. He was good at standing as long as he had something to hang on to. If he sat down hard because he let go, he looked surprised and pulled himself back up. I expected he'd stand without holding on any day now. The puppy Cocoa too seemed to grow larger every time I looked at her. Going by the size of her feet, she might turn out as big as a pony; she certainly ate like a horse.

One afternoon I got together all my courage and contacted Bray Bentry. He gave me the Allreds' phone number, and I made the call. The conversation started out awkward and formal but ended up with everybody crying. After that I started e-mailing them Brady's pictures nearly every day, and we all decided I'd bring him down to Houston later in the spring. He babbled to them on the phone too. I knew in my heart of hearts that Brady needed to know where he came from on *both* sides of his family. Even though Brady never met his father, he would know all about Jake. He'd never be left wondering who Jake was and whether he had his father's eyes, talents, or flaws. Besides, no child can be loved too much, and his Grandpa and Grandma Allred let him know he was the apple of their eye.

Some days the hours flew by; other days the time went so slowly I thought the clock had broken. As I said before, life went on.

March came in, if not exactly like a lion, at least like a tomcat strutting his stuff. But after the first week, a change in the jet stream brought a series of above-freezing days. I noticed the pussy willows at the corner of the front yard were covered in furry catkins, and a few days later, a purple crocus popped up in a snow-less patch under the hedges. Even if my heart felt as if it would be cold and lifeless forever, the earth was waking up. Spring's promise whispered in every breeze. And at times when I least expected it, hope, unnamed and unspoken, broke through my pain and emerged like that crocus in the lawn.

On a Monday morning in mid-March, Brady was at Peggy Sue's day care. I was in the kitchen when I heard the doorbell to my office door. Wiping my wet hands on a dish towel, I hurried to answer it and spotted a neatly dressed young man on the other side of the glass. He stood nervously shifting from foot to foot and shivering on the stoop. I assumed he was a salesman for phone book advertising or something like that.

"Yes, can I help you?" I said, opening the door a crack and feeling a bit annoyed at the interruption in my day.

"Are you Ms. Ravine Patton?" he asked, his dark eyes lively in a suntanned face.

I told him yes, and he told me his name was Mo-
hamed Meghaou, the youngest son of Ali Rachid
Meghaou, and the grandson of El-Mohamed Rachid
Meghaou. He also apologized for getting to me late.
He was supposed to arrive on Christmas Day, but his
trip from North Africa was delayed.

When I heard the words "North Africa" my knees
started to wobble, since that's where Gene's plane had
crashed during the war. The first thought that came
into my mind was that the authorities had found his
airplane or even his remains. But why would they be
contacting me? Remembering my manners, I belatedly
asked him to come in.

"You can call me M&M," the young man said as I
motioned for him to sit down on one of the chairs in
front of my desk. Then I asked if I might get him a
cup of coffee or tea.

"No, thank you, Ms. Patton," he replied with great
politeness. "I have only a moment to stay."

"All right, Mr.—er, M&M, won't you please tell me
what this is all about?" I sat on the edge of the chair
next to his, my hands clasped tightly to stop their
shaking.

M&M reached into the inside pocket of his beauti-
fully tailored topcoat and took out a small envelope.
He said that before his grandfather died, in 1974, he
gave this envelope to M&M's father with the instruc-
tions to please get it to me on Christmas Day of the
past year.

I tried to make sense of that and couldn't. I wasn't
even born in 1974, and I couldn't imagine how M&M's
grandfather could possibly know my name. I said as
much to the polite young man.

M&M answered me with great solemnity. He didn't
know, but his grandfather did many things nobody
could explain. He had taken thirty-five wives, and he
was a great practical joker.

Naturally, I asked M&M what was in the envelope. Naturally, he didn't know. He said it had always been sealed.

"Baba, my grandfather, didn't divulge its contents; he just said it would 'put things right.' According to my father, Baba also began to laugh and said, 'I do not have very good luck when I play dice. Maybe I have better when I play God.' "

M&M handed me the envelope. It had my name and address neatly handwritten on the front. The paper felt cool and smooth in my hands, but I could feel the bulge of something hard inside it.

M&M stood up and apologized again for the delay in delivering it. He also apologized for his haste in leaving, but he had to catch a flight to Atlanta from the Wilkes-Barre–Scranton Airport and had a taxi waiting in the driveway. I accompanied M&M down the path outside my office and watched him as he walked to his cab. He turned around and gave me a rakish grin. I swear there was something familiar about it.

Holding the envelope in my trembling hand, I went to my office, sat at my desk, and looked at the three-by-five-inch rectangle again. My name and address, printed on it before I ever existed, looked back at me. I picked up a letter opener and decided to find out what it held.

Inside was a piece of paper and a small red cardboard packet, about two inches across and three inches long. On the outside of the packet it said MINER'S BANK, WILKES-BARRE, PA. Inside the packet was a key. The note said, "This is the key to my heart. Love, Gene"

I recognized that the silver key belonged to a safe deposit box. I also knew that the Miner's Bank no longer existed. I guessed that Gene had found a keepsake or something for me after he returned to the Sahara in 1942 and somehow convinced the caliph to stash it away in the most prominent bank in the Wyoming Valley during those war years. I had no idea what Gene had gotten me, but since it was supposed to have been delivered on Christmas, a few hours after he disappeared, I figured it had to be my Christmas present.

I held the packet tightly in my palm. This key proved that Gene didn't die or vaporize after my third wish. He had survived and made it home. How bittersweet it was to realize he had thought of a way to get the key to me, and how frustrating to know I might not be able to use it. A desperate yearning overcame me to get to that box, wherever it now was.

It was time to pick up Brady, so I put the key in my jacket pocket and drove to Peggy Sue's. Over a new section of her house a colorful sign announced, SUNSHINE AND LOLLIPOPS DAY CARE. I had been impressed by how professionally she set it up, and Brady loved his mornings there.

As I started back to the house, I kept thinking of ways I could trace the safe deposit box. There didn't seem to be any quick way to accomplish it. But I figured it wouldn't hurt to stop at the bank in Bowman's Creek and see what the tellers there thought I should do.

Carrying Brady on my hip, I walked into the bank and went up to Mary Ann's window.

"Hiya, Ravine," she said. "You haven't been in for a while."

"Hi to you too," I answered, smiling. "I don't have a deposit today—wish I did! But I was wondering if you could give me some advice." I slipped the red packet containing the key into the tray under the security grate at her counter. "I received this key as part of—umm, part of an inheritance. Do you think it's possible the safe-deposit box and its contents still exist?"

Mary Ann looked at the key. Two of the other tellers

came over and crowded around her to look. She asked if I had noticed that the safe-deposit box number was written on the little piece of adhesive on the key.

I had seen the adhesive, but I wasn't sure until now that the number was the box number. Mary Ann assured me it was. "But of course Miner's Bank is gone," she said.

"That's what worries me." I sighed.

"The safe-deposit boxes aren't gone though," she added. "As far as I can remember, Miner's Bank was sold to United Penn Bank, which was sold to Mellon Bank, which was sold to Citizens Bank. Isn't that right?" she said to the other women. They nodded in agreement. She explained that nothing had really changed in the bank itself except the management and the name. The building stayed the same and the safe-deposit boxes didn't move. She asked if I thought somebody kept paying for the box.

"I can't be positive," I answered, "but I think it would have been paid either with a big sum up front or regularly throughout the years. At least I hope it was. Had to be, since the person who obtained the box knew I wouldn't be taking possession until Christmas last year, at the earliest."

"Well then, I don't see why you can't go down to Citizens Bank and get whatever it is in there. Of course, it's none of my business—what you inherited, I mean," she said, dying of curiosity.

"I really have no idea what's in the box, Mary Ann. If it's anything interesting, I'll have to come by and show you."

"Another thing to consider," Mary Ann mused as she put the little red packet containing the key into the tray on her side of the grate and pushed it through where I could pick it up. "Do you know what name the box is under? You might have to get power of attorney in order for the bank to open it."

"I don't think that will be needed. I'm guessing the

box is in my name. But thank you so much for your help."

"No thanks needed. It's the most excitement we've had since the bank robber came to the drive-through last year," she said.

Everybody yelled, "Good luck!" when Brady and I went out the door.

I asked my mother to take care of Brady and told her I had to go to Wilkes-Barre, but I didn't tell her why.

"You're nervous as a cat in a roomful of canaries, and you're all dressed up. Carrying your briefcase too. Are you meeting a new client?" she asked as I put Brady into her arms.

I told her I had some business at the bank downtown, the one with the big windows that used to be Miner's Bank. I promised her that I wouldn't be very long. She told me to take my time. She and Brady were going to be baking cookies. Then Cal was coming by and the three of them were going over to look at the building I had wrangled out of the township for the charter school. Since we had agreed to improve the building, the deed was ours for the sum of one dollar.

"We're going to have lots of fun, aren't we, little man?" she said to Brady, picking up a chubby hand and nuzzling his palm.

"I love you," I said and kissed her cheek. Since nearly losing her on Christmas Eve, I made sure I told her I loved her every day.

"Love you too," she said gruffly. "Now you get along. Brady and I have work to do."

My nerves made the half-hour drive to Wilkes-Barre an ordeal. I had to keep reminding myself to focus on the road and not think about Gene or what he put in the box. I would treasure forever whatever I found there, but the note and the key had made my grief at losing him return with a stabbing pain. But then again, he was letting me know he had gotten back, and he had survived—and that gave me comfort, for as much as I needed him in the here and now, I wanted him safe even more.

The old-fashioned grandeur of the Miner's Bank with its marble floors, twenty-foot-high arched windows, and three-story-high ceiling created the awe of a cathedral and reduced all talking to hushed whispers—despite the cheery, green, modern logo of the present owners.

I approached a buxom, middle-aged bank clerk and asked to open "my" safe-deposit box.

"What number?" she asked.

"One nine four two four two," I read from the adhesive on the key, suddenly realizing that I had said "1942 for two." It seemed like it should mean something but I didn't know what.

The teller consulted a file and pulled out a form. "My oh my," she said. "I think this is one of our oldest accounts." Smiling, she pushed the form toward me and pointed at the line where I needed to sign. Then she led me into the vault, found box number 194242, produced her key and turned the lock. Then she took my key and turned the lock again. After that she slid out a long, deep, metal box. The process seemed to go on for hours, although I'm sure it took less than a minute.

"Come right this way," she said, leading me to an adjoining room. She put the box on a table. "Press the buzzer when you're finished, and I'll let you out," she added.

I waited until she had shut the door behind her before I lifted the lid.

I looked in.

A bulbous amber bottle sat in the bottom. I snatched it out.

Even as I lifted it out of the box, I could see a

figure inside. It was Gene, jumping up and down and waving. Something tiny was flashing in his hand. He was pointing to the cork.

I nearly dropped the damned bottle.

But I couldn't let him out. I had walked in here alone; I had to walk out alone or all hell would break loose. I put my finger to my lips and then tried to signal *one minute.* I opened my briefcase and plunged the bottle into its depths, slammed the lid shut on the safe-deposit box, and started pressing the buzzer like a crazy person.

The teller flung the door open. "Is everything all right?" she said, looking concerned.

"I'm claustrophobic," I gasped, hoping I was putting on a convincing act. "I'm about to have an anxiety attack. Can you hurry and get me out of here?"

Reversing the same lengthy process, she did hurry, and I thanked her as I fairly ran out of the bank and jogged all the way to the Park 'n' Lock garage where I had left my red Chevy Avalanche. I threw myself into the driver's seat and tore open the briefcase.

I got the bottle out and popped the cork. A sinuous stream of white smoke trailed up from the mouth of the bottle and slowly took form.

Chapter 20

As soon as the smoke became Gene the genie, I launched myself like a one-hundred-and-ten-pound missile across the console into his arms. Pressing him against me as tight as I could hold him, I was convinced he was solid and real. I couldn't stop touching him, kissing his face, crying and laughing all at once like a wild woman.

"Don't disappear. Don't disappear," I kept saying over and over.

Finally, my sobs subsiding, I became calm enough to ask, "How? How did you get back here? How did you get in the safe-deposit box? Ohmygod, have you been there for sixty years?"

"Sweetheart," he whispered, holding me on his lap, "I'm here. I'm not leaving you. Not ever, as long as there is breath in my body, not ever again. And this ring is not going to disappear again either."

Then he produced my diamond ring and slipped it on my finger. "Will you marry me, Ravine?"

"As soon as we can get the license." I laughed. "Now tell me the story of how you got back."

"I guess you do need to know, now don't you," he teased and kissed the end of my nose. "To answer that first question you asked—I've only been in the box for a couple of months. The plan was for you to come get me on Christmas, you know. And as to how I got here, you should be very thankful I am a gambling man."

"Explain," I said, kissing him on the lips very thoroughly. "But please be quick in explaining, because I'm not sure how long you're going to feel like talking," I murmured, reluctantly pulling away.

Then he gave me what he called "the short version." One minute Gene was in the hospital room; the next he found himself back in the caliph's palace in the Sahara. The crafty old magus was standing right there, shaking his head, demanding to know what Gene had come back there for. He told Gene that most genies figure out how to break the enchantment same as Gene and I did, only no other genie had waited more than sixty years before doing so.

The magus kept muttering and shaking his head, not knowing what to do with Gene. Gene told him he wanted to go back home to Australia. The magus rolled his eyes and said it couldn't be done. Then Gene asked him if he could come back to the twenty-first century, back to where he had just been. The magus rolled his eyes again, mumbling and cursing under his breath. Finally he went and got the caliph. Unfortunately, Gene's return ended up interrupting the caliph in the middle of something he didn't want to interrupt. His mood when he saw that Gene had come back was not a friendly one.

The caliph told the magus to enchant Gene again and throw the bottle in the sea. Gene started talking fast, spinning a tale about love and honor, disappointment and broken hearts. He told a good story and the caliph was entertained. He thought it would be amusing to leave Gene's fate up to chance, as in a game of chance. The caliph proposed a game of dice. If Gene won, the caliph promised to get Gene back to Pennsylvania in time for Christmas. At this point, Gene laughed. If there was one thing he was good at, I was to remember, it was gambling. Gene won, of course.

"Hmm," I said. "As I recall, gambling wasn't the only thing you were good at."

As it so happens, in my new Chevy the back windows are nearly black, tinted so deeply that somebody outside the truck can't see in—not that there was anybody walking around in the parking garage right then anyway. And since Gene really was awfully good at something other than dice, he whisked us with a little genie magic into the backseat, our clothes vanished in a wink, and he used his expertise at pleasing me over and over again.

After a couple of hours, we went to pick up Brady together, and my mother's face shone with happiness when Gene and I walked through the door. She grabbed him in a hug, and afterward made him drink some milk and eat some still-warm cookies. Before we left, she whispered to me, "I told you that you did not know what Gene could or could not do."

But despite the whisper, Gene heard her, and after we headed out the door to go home, he said to me with mischief in his eyes, "I'm an Australian. We have the can-do spirit and we can-do anything. Did you think I was going to spend my life in the caliph's palace, even with its seraglio? Hell no. I was going to get back to you somehow. And lady, I'm an Australian. So I did!"

He also proved his can-do spirit in our bed that night when we did again what we had been doing in the backseat of the Avalanche. And I thought, since the timing was right, that in about nine months, our family would have the perfect Christmas present.

And during that delightful first night, when all my unhappiness vanished like smoke, Gene told me I had three wishes to make all over again. But I took out the paper where I wrote the wish that I had never made, and while Gene held me in his arms, I made just one.

Acknowlegments

It is entirely true that my own ancestors included Native Amcricans, but who they were (and there were at least two) remains lost to history. A gravestone for perhaps one of them is in the Noxen cemetery. But the best evidence for their existence is written on the faces of my forefathers, particularly my grandfather who looked unmistakably Native American. As a child I had gotten into my head somehow that my mysterious ancestors were Lenni Lenape. It turns out that is entirely plausible. One of my cousins who is interested in genealogy says he found out that one Native American ancestor came from Canada. But none of us has any evidence to give credence to our beliefs.

During the course of writing this novel, I researched the Native Americans of Luzerne and Wyoming counties, Pennsylvania, at "first contact." It proved both immensely frustrating—there's not all that much known—and fascinating. My primary source was thc Smithsonian's monumental work, *Handbook of North American Indians,* edited by William C. Sturtevant. I spent my time with volume 15, *Northeast,* edited by Bruce G. Trigger. I also consulted *The Ancient Native Americans of the Wyoming Valley: 10,000 Years of Prehistory,* by John Orlandini, and *Indians in Pennsylvania,* by Paul A. W. Wallace, created under the auspices of the Pennsylvania Historical and Museum Commission. The latter book, on page 176, contains a brief description of Chief Kakowatchiky of Shawnee Flats. Readers might find it an eerie coincidence, as I did, since I did not have this information when I created the novel's plot, that the man who located the ill and dying chief at the end of his life was named John Patton.

When I was very near the completion of this book, by accident I ran across an article by Tom Birdsong in the *Pittsburgh Post-Gazette* from 2003 titled "Rush of Indian Claims for Casino Rights in Pennsylvania Unlikely." Again I was a little shaken that the tale I made up out of my imagination was only a hairsbreadth from reality. The article gave credibility to my premise, although my fictional account comes to a different conclusion about the future of a Shawnee casino in Pennsylvania.

Now as to the matter of Scabby Hoyt. Several specific families with hundreds of living members have occupied this rural, nearly untouched corner of Pennsylvania since before the Revolutionary War. These early inhabitants include Pattons, Crispells, Travers, Sicklers, and Hoyts, to name a few. However, all my characters, even supposed members of those families, are entirely fictional, made up from my imagination . . . except for Scabby. Scabby Hoyt is a neighbor's cat and his name tickled me so much I just had to make him a villain. I meant no disrespect to any of the above-named families, and certainly not to the original Scabby. May he live long and prosper.

A special thanks goes to Beth and Fred Rosencrans and their son Brady, whose name, personality, and babyhood, including the sulfur poop, were the inspiration for the character of Brady Patton. Thanks also go to my cousins and my sister, Corrine, for contributing their memories and funny stories, versions of which have found their way into Ravine's life.

Salutations also go to the wonderful and very caring tellers at the bank in Bowman's Creek.

As for Gene, the genie, I have been asked where such a paragon of virtue can be found. I'm opening a lot of old bottles, but I haven't located him yet.

HIGHLANDER IN HER BED

Allie Mackay

She's fallen in love with an antique bed.
But the ghostly Highlander it comes with is
more than she bargained for...

Tour guide Mara MacDougall stops at a London
antique shop, and spots perhaps the handsomest bed
ever. Then she bumps into the handsomest man ever.
Soon Mara can't forget the irresistible—if haughty—
Highlander. Not even when she learns that she's
inherited a Scottish castle.

Spectral Sir Alexander Douglas has hated the Clan
MacDougall since he was a medieval knight and they
tricked him into a curse...the curse of forever haunting
the bed (the very one that Mara now owns) that was
once intended for his would-be bride. But Mara makes
him feel what no other MacDougall has—a passion that
he never knew he'd missed.

Available wherever books are sold or at
penguin.com